THEIR LIPS TALK OF MISCHIEF

Warner is the author of seven previous novels: *Morvern Callar*, which was made into a film starring Samantha Morton, *These Demented Lands*, *The Sopranos*, *The Man Who Walks*, *The Worms Can Carry Me to Heaven*, *The Stars in the Bright Sky*, which was longlisted for the 2010 Man Booker Prize, and *The Deadman's Pedal*, which won the 2013 James Tait Black Prize.

www.alanwarner.net

Further praise for *Their Lips Talk of Mischief*:

'Glitteringly explosive . . . the perfect summer read.' Melissa Katsoulis, *The Times*

'So very good . . . tremendously funny, poignant and clever . . . Warner's control is uncanny in the final section of the book, which hovers between pathos, humour, deep irony and a genuine uncertainty as to what might follow. Goodness and badness, 'roundness' and 'flatness' of character are convincingly blurred. Life is not vague, but specific and incomplete . . . [Warner is] a writer at the very top of his game.' Brian Morton, *Herald*

'Further evidence of [Warner's] interest in outsiders, his gritty sense of place and period, and his sensitivity towards small details . . . The novel is at its dark best in vignettes of set-piece comedy which satirise the men's attempt at a bohemian lifestyle . . . the ensuing destruction is borne not of evil, as the title seems to suggest, but of apathy, amorality, self-indulgence and ordinary nastiness.' Francesca Wade, *Telegraph*

'One of Scotland's greatest living writers.' *The Skinny*

'The real heart of this ebullient but underlyingly sombre book comes from Doug's largely frustrated love for Aoife, opening up into a brief idyll, and it gains seriousness from the increasing awareness that the undoubtedly warm and extrovert Lou is not quite such a nice guy as he seems . . . it brings a final pathos and gravity to this retrospective tale of old friendships and doomed young promise, even when that promise was probably spurious in the first place.' Phil Baker, *Sunday Times*

'Warner has always been the contemporary Scottish writer most interested in literary style; combining slangy, stylised speech with a baroque phrasing and syntax, he is incapable of writing a dull book.' Richard Strachan, *The List*

---

by the same author

Morvern Callar
These Demented Lands
The Sopranos
The Man Who Walks
The Worms Can Carry Me to Heaven
The Stars in the Bright Sky
The Deadman's Pedal

Their Lips Talk of Mischief

ALAN WARNER

FABER & FABER

First published in 2014
by Faber & Faber Limited
Bloomsbury House, 74–77 Great Russell Street
London WC1B 3DA

This paperback edition published in 2015

Typeset by Faber & Faber Limited
Printed in England by CPI Group (UK) Ltd, Croydon, CR0 4YY

A CIP record for this book
is available from the British Library

ISBN 978-0-571-31128-6

2 4 6 8 10 9 7 5 3 1

For their heart studieth destruction,
And their lips talk of mischief.

Proverbs 24:2 (KJV)

1984

PART ONE

I

A fragile sheath of light lay across the great town, juiced-up pink in benign confusions of cloud at the far end of streets. Beneath this sunset I walked towards a hospital, chosen at random from the *A–Z London* in a newsagent.

The previous night I had sat until dawn in an overheated Accident and Emergency waiting room, amongst that cheerless faction with their lacerated thumbs and temporary eye patches. A teenage girl had leaned forward, vomiting liquid into a cardboard spittoon. The orderlies ignored her. After an hour of punishment, she slid her regurgitations beneath the seat then quietly departed with her whispering pal. I had felt like asking if I could tag along and sleep down on her bedroom floor, among the dolls of her recent girlhood.

I approached the institutional architecture of that evening's hospital: aluminium chimney stacks, yellow night windows in 1930s darkened brick; the familiar, illuminated red and white *Accident & Emergency* light box suspended above automatic sliding doors.

I saw a tall and handsome young man of my own age, standing, leaning against the wall by the doors with one leg canted up, wearing a grey macintosh; he pulled a cigarette down from his mouth and tossed it like a dart so that it burst on the tarmac in orange sparks. Blowing out smoke straight through his lips, he observed me walking towards him and he put his foot down in a scraping motion to pulverise the scattered butt. He turned and strode straight in through the sliding doors of Accident and Emergency.

This waiting area was similar to the previous night's, but busier. There was no sign of the man from outside and it crossed my mind he was a young doctor having a sly, hypocritical puff. About fifteen people were seated in bright blue bucket chairs which were connected by horizontal metal bars, all bolted to the floor so they could not be cast through the fluorescent air by impatient yet sufficiently agile sufferers.

There were no people with axes or knives embedded in blood-matted scalps. Several supplicants leaned into the palms of their hands with despair, as if this would give them priority. A man accompanied by a young child held one arm out before him in salute, precisely supporting it at the horizontal like a spirit level. His kid had assembled an arcane arrangement of health information leaflets and was playfully sliding them around on the floor by the dad's feet.

An extremely fat, seated woman was calmly reading a magazine; she looked as though she'd drifted in for a manicure. Maybe she was waiting on someone undergoing treatment? You could bet she had somewhere to sleep that night.

Up back was an old man with red and watering eyes, white stubble against his black skin, calmly muttering, 'Doctor will give me a little something. Oh. Yes. It's okay, everyone. Doctor will give me a little something.' He didn't seem to have many teeth. I toughed up as I'm a sucker for such figures and soon fall into conversation. I bet even *he* had somewhere to sleep.

I knew the drill. Without checking in I settled, unobtrusively choosing a seat. I had a copy of Richardson's *Ultima Thule* in my jacket but I didn't want to get too comfortable and draw attention

4

to myself. Reading would only come in the small nodding hours before I was noticed and asked to leave.

There was a clear perspex security cage with a colander of speaking holes. Nobody occupied the clear cage at that moment and a member of the public waited there for attention. After several minutes the door at the back opened and a short woman in white trousers and tunic came forth. I looked down at the floor and only glanced up occasionally.

'Yes?'

The waiting man lowered his face to the concentric holes, 'Could I see a doctor, please?'

'Are you registered at a surgery?'

'I'm sorry?'

'Are you currently registered? With a surgery.'

'Yes. In Willesden.'

'Fill this out.'

He seemed frustrated that she had no apparent interest in his ailment. 'I was bitten by a dog.'

A singular bleat of laughter came from far behind me. I turned. The fat woman was rolling her shoulders but, ambiguously, she still stared down at her magazine.

That voice up the back went, 'Doc'll give you a little something for that.'

The dame in the tunic behind the screen raised her plucked black eyebrows and her forehead arched. 'You need to wait,' she told the bitten man.

I live to see her type shaken up. She passed a pen through the small slit; the chewed biro end was anchored back through the perspex by a string, as frantically as if it were a limited-edition Mont Blanc.

'It's okay. I've got my own pen,' he stated.

'Okay. Good.' She smiled: she'd achieved a major breakthrough in community healthcare. 'Fill those out and return them through here.' She knocked her hand on the small gap at the base of the service window as if the geezer was blind and functioned by sound.

There was a swishing movement of air to my left. It was the smoker from outside in his private detective gear – the raincoat – folding himself patiently down. An empty seat remained between us. I glanced at him then quickly back down at the floor.

It was not just his clothes which were faintly anachronistic for a young man; he even had the looks of a handsome fifties English movie idol – the shapely head and neat symmetrical features, small ears close to the skull. He was pale, his slight stubble almost theatrical so you could pass the time counting each embedded hair on the white skin. His fingers moved, touching his fringe or confidently sweeping his rich hair back. He had intrinsic handsomeness – he stepped from his bed looking like that each morning without so much as combing his hair. Suddenly he levelled a finger at me and he frowned, as if ticking off facts; in a low, confidential tone he whispered, 'You don't look so unwell.'

Inwardly I cursed him. 'Neither do you. Pal.'

'Scottish?'

'Guilty.'

'Young Lochinvar is come out of the west.'

'Aye. And he's about to get sent back.'

'Go on.'

I looked around but nobody was interested. I shrugged my shoulders. 'Student last year in Gower Street. University College.'

'Subject?'

6

'English Lit. I've just got booted out for not handing in any work. Or turning up for exams in May. They noticed after all.'

'Go on,' he grinned.

I didn't know if that phrase meant I should continue, or if it implied I was kidding him. 'I got a grant last year so I sat in the pub all day reading books and drinking beer. For a year. Paradise.'

'This *is* the definition of paradise.'

'Yeah. I'd a girl sat on my knee once or twice too. Rosie, but she transferred to Manchester or somewhere. Thought I'd start working properly this term. But I met my Director of Studies day before yesterday.'

'Director of Studies, eh? He sounds like a shit already.'

'She. Told the board in Scotland and now my grant's been withdrawn.'

'Harsh.'

'I asked her out to dinner at this interview.'

'Your Director of Studies?'

'Yes. Thought I might as well go the whole hog while I was at it and I do have seventy quid left, so I could have taken her somewhere nice.'

'Sounds like a deeply premature move.'

'It was. She said no and didn't take the long way round. My poor folks. They are going to go nuts when they find out. All my parents' attempts at social engineering have failed on me. I can't join the middle classes. I just want left alone to read my books. Now I'm booted out the digs and he won't give me any of my books till the back-rent for summer is paid.' I leaned closer and lowered my voice way down. 'A foul rustication. And now, there is the very pressing matter of my adequate quartering in this city. I spent last night in an Accident and Emergency up Harrow or somewhere. Slept on the Circle Line all day. Tomorrow, I reckon to Victoria and the bus back to Scotland?'

'I like the cut of your jib, boyo. Don't worry, young Lochinvar. I'll stand you a pint when I'm done in here.'

I paused a moment and clarified: 'Walter Scott's only honour was simply to be mocked by that scene in *The Portrait* – when the idiot calls him his favourite writer.'

His face changed and he studied me more carefully. 'A Joyce man already?'

'Oh yes.'

'Llewellyn Smith.' He drew back his body very slowly, to suddenly project a hand forward. 'I'm a Londoner, for sure, but really mad Celt too. Never set foot there but I'm Welsh. Like that bastard Dylan T. Now he'd written everything immortal by the same age I'd just found a girl's bra strap at. *The Death of the King's Canary* was the best thing. Fifty-two gin and tonics; it must be a record. Bless his glowing nose.'

Here was my kind of talk at last. I took the hand and I shook it. It was very cold. I said, 'Douglas Cunningham.'

This Llewellyn said, 'No relation to Cunninghame Graham? I guess not. A man once asked Joyce: "May I shake the hand which wrote *Ulysses*?" Joycey replied, "Certainly not. You don't know what else it's done."'

I smiled, deliberately held on to the hand a while longer, then let go.

'Douglas Cunningham.' He nodded, leaning back a touch. His movements were oddly slow and graceful, weirdly cautious. 'Now what was it in *The Portrait*, Stephen says to eh, young Cranly there?

8

I will try to express myself in some mode of life or art using the only arms I allow myself to use: Silence, exile and cunning. That's you. Silence, Exile and Cunning*ham*.'

I laughed.

'Well, well, wait a jiffy.' He began to unbutton his mac.

That bad-tempered dame had appeared back in her glass shack. Llewellyn Smith stood up slowly and he strode forward in his polished brogues. I noted the slacks were ironed with a diligent crease up the middle of the leg. He nodded at the administrator in her den. He said, 'I'd like Doc to attend me, if you please.'

'Are you registered with a surgery?'

'Yes, but I sort of really need to see him, pretty smartish.'

She gave him a compromising look through the perspex. 'Well, what seems to be the trouble?'

'Doc'll know what the trouble is.'

Fury collapsed her face downward in a swift instant. 'You wait your turn with everyone else. Fill out these and I'll issue you with a ticket shortly.'

'But I need to see the doc. Now.'

There was a pause. The woman drew herself up for further conflict. Llewellyn Smith opened the sides of his overcoat toward her, like a flasher.

The woman's hand shot out for a phone.

He slowly turned round to all of us and the coat hung open. He wore no shirt; his pale torso was utterly hairless, slightly muscled – like that of a trained swimmer – but straight down, from six inches beneath his neck to just above his navel, was bright blood, coagulated around the black lip of a huge wound. I noted his belly button was pooled with a little ruby of tacky blood like an

Egyptian dancing girl. I actually drew my head backwards on my shoulders.

'Stabbed,' a voice yelped. The kid sliding around the leaflets stared upwards, his hands frozen.

'Sorry to jump the queue, everyone.' Llewellyn Smith held his forearms high in surrender and I would swear I heard some air bubble in a sickly breath from that laceration between his ribs.

'Doctor will give you a little something,' a quiet voice promised from up back.

'Done in by our old killer sofa once again. Having a little siesta, rolled over and me stitches ripped. Don't hurt or nothing. Had a bit of a heart op a while back there.'

The woman behind the perspex banged on the clear plastic to get his attention, shouting repeatedly for an orderly down the phone. 'Why didn't the ambulance crew present you here, for God's sake?'

'There was no ambulance crew, love. I walked here. I only live up the road, on the estate.'

The waiting room was thrumming with ignited chatter. A nervous attendant rushed in, looked rattled by this broken man, then led him out. As he passed me, Llewellyn winked, 'Hold your horses and stand by your guns. See you in half an hour, boyo.' He motioned with his right hand the act of tipping a necessary pint glass towards one's lips and I now noted a rusted dry bloodstain had been there, along the side of his pinkie.

2

Llewellyn Smith came back into that hospital waiting area and nodded only to me. Others watched and I felt privileged. The mac was on, hanging open, showing muslin or medical lint and some cotton wool sealed under wide white bandages which had been strapped and lashed around his torso to bind him together.

'Silence, Exile and Cunningham.' He sighed and pointed his thumb to his bindings. 'I was starting to feel a draught in my cold heart.'

He secured the large medallion buttons of the raincoat, using one hand as he moved towards the automatic sliding doors with a slight limp. He had a distinctive, purposeful way of walking which over time I grew to know very well; he always seemed just about to arrive somewhere that he had been rushing to, yet he didn't seem frantic or at all hasty.

We moved together out onto the night streets, where he produced a pack of cigarettes with the heavy-looking Zippo and held out a gasper to me. He lit up our Regals in a puff of paraffin scenting.

I said, 'Call me a right bore, but should you be smoking?'

He clicked the Zippo shut and exhaled. 'Smoking's good for me. My heart is very healthy cause the best consultants in London have all queued up to take a good old prod. I had a very rare ventricle-valve problem, so they popped a new component in. I noted it said

Made in Taiwan on the box. Smoking gives the old ticker a bit of a hose down.'

'And beer? Should we be drinking beer after you've just been filleted?'

'Fillet me, smoke me, then sauté me in beer. It's a famous recipe by old Bemelmans and I volunteer. Looks worse than it is, boyo. Hardly bled this time. Last time, cleared out the waiting room. This way, Lochinvar – this is my manor – over the purple heather to my grim local.'

'Where's that?'

'Up in the Sixth Arrondissement. Acton Town. Another night in this paradise where I place my roof over my head.'

'The only roof I'm going to get over my head is on the Glasgow bus.'

'Leaving so early? We'll see about that. There must be a civilised solution.'

'Aye. A thousand quid. Are you okay, you're limping?'

'Its affected, boyo. Always envied a limp and lusted for a collection of ivory-tipped sword sticks. A Penang lawyer with a soft lead ferrule which hits the pavement silently.'

'You're like Frankenstein's monster.'

Was he nuts? God knows I had met enough visionaries on the pavements of London and I had a track record of falling in with such figures. We walked side by side – moving with the traffic, the car interiors so dark and the windscreens so reflective in that late summer night you could not see occupants within.

Curved railings forced a pause at every junction and made us utilise the pelican crossings; the pavement went down into a dip and up again. A high-rise block rose to our left but its edges were not visible and none of its square windows appeared curtained – so bare, clear light bulbs seemed to hang still and very high, way up in the Acton Town sky.

He pointed towards the park. 'Look. Sean MacConnery used to live there, by the Acton Park gates. One of your pantheon. He cleared out the old nunnery to build his bolt hole. Honest. I used to wait outside when I was a nipper for his autograph. Not cause it was him. I thought it would add value to my Ian Flemings. Bond was a linguist, you know. So am I. I only speak the truth. James Bond displaces the Sisters of Seville.'

'Did you get them signed?'

'Nah. Bond gave me the slip.'

When I checked, much later, I learned all this was quite true. We ascended the High Street and over its top until he pointed at a pub on the corner with an ornate display of metal bells over the door, 'Behold. The Five *or* Six Bells. I was brought up by my gran along that road and I live back there now in a penthouse suite. My old dead dad used to drink here. It's The Six Bells. But the bloody Luftwaffe did for it one night in forty-one and the bells got blown clean off – Acton used to get blitzed bad cause of the industries; could only find five bells in the rubble so they strung them back up. Didn't want to concede to Hitler and call it The Five Bells, but metal shortage precluded any replacement. So the name stuck with them hung there. The Five *or* Six Bells pub.'

I counted them and despite the painted sign for The Six Bells there really were only five. 'Hitler only got one bell. The other's in the Albert Hall.'

'Precisely.'

*

13

The Five *or* Six Bells still had both saloon bar and public bar. The public interior was a great dead, hollow triangular space with a polished wooden bar focused and constantly beckoning up at the apex. This interior, in the evenings, had the brightest lights I'd ever seen within a pub, on chandeliers chained up among the high chicken-wire and glass skylights. In the evenings, the pub always reminded me of a Victorian operating theatre where a public autopsy might be about to take place.

The main customer seats were ranged in banquettes along the walls, beneath high windows through which only the very top of the 207 bus or the odd wandering airliner bound for Heathrow was ever glimpsed. Small tables and squat low stools clustered in the central space but I don't think – in all our late mornings, afternoons and nights which we were to spend there – I was ever to see a single low stool and table occupied. The carpet was one of those deep purple and red, swirling, pseudo-Persian affairs you never see in city pubs any more. The clientele were exclusively older men, though I did once see an old dear in a skirt ensemble, circling in the saloon bar with a sherry glass when the connecting door momentarily swung open.

That first night, odd old geezers nodded, curt and silent to Llewellyn – somehow disappointed in us, as if he and I should have had much better things to do. It struck me that The Five *or* Six Bells was pretty much like a more sincere Accident and Emergency waiting room.

Llewellyn bought us beer, sat gently into one of the wall seats, grimaced a little, slid closer an ashtray and arranged his smoking paraphernalia. His tipple was Guinness, which I also turn to as a summer day fades to dusk and summer itself melds into the darker seasons. Llewellyn asked, 'What do you make of this drinkery?'

'I like old pubs still divided into public and saloon bars. In ten years there'll be none left. I hate all these new wine bars.'

'I agree. Only downside: no pretty women come here except jail-bait, tapping Grandad for a fiver on Saturday afternoon. At least one can get on with business. And business, as I'm sure you'll agree, Cunningham – you lunatic – is the acquiring of a certain degree of culture beyond that which our social station requires. Acquiring culture. Acquiring beer. Acquiring women. They do say it's an ac-quisitive society. What kind of women do you go for, then?'

I raised my eyebrows. I thought about this for a good moment but was fairly stumped. 'It's more what kind of women I don't go for.'

'What kind of women don't you go for?'

I thought about this for some time also. 'None.'

He nodded sharply and sympathetically. 'A man of taste.'

'A rich woman would be nice?' I suggested.

'It's all over for me. I'm hitched and she's poor. Old ice knickers. We have issue.' He guzzled his black stout.

'Never. With issue? Really?'

'Sure as fate. Not married. Yet. Have a beautiful, beautiful little six-month daughter. My girlfriend is a bloody lunatic Celt, like us. Irish. Incredible. Look at us: a Welshman, a Scotsman and an Irish-woman went into a pub.' He swallowed a burp.

'What age are you?'

'Twenty-one and hardly a quid to my name.'

'Same age as me but I've seventy quid in my sock.'

'Seventy. You're a lord amongst men.'

'What's she called?'

'The girlfriend or the sprog?'

'Your kid.'

'It was going to be Peril. Not Pearl. I mean "Those in Peril Upon the Deep": P-E-R-I-L. I thought that was very clever till the eleventh hour when I was vetoed. We're both lapsed Caths. You'll be an ungoddy Proddy? Serves you right. Then my gran and my girlfriend wanted Loretta. But Loretta was just too bloody Catholic. Loretta the Bed Wetter, she'd have been known as, once out of nappies. Or out her knickers. So we named her Lily. Little Lil, whom no church will ever christen. Remind me to grab some nappies from the garage.'

I raised my tall Guinness. 'Here's to Lil. Church-free from step one.'

'Yup. You're a godless Scotch Protestant, boyo.'

We both took adequate draws on the beverages. Llewellyn met me with a friendly eye. 'Ah.' He put down his pint and popped another fag in his lips, nodded, calm and knowing, lighting his cigarette. 'And what sort of books do you go for, Cunningham boyo?'

I pulled out Richardson's *Ultima Thule* in Penguin Modern Classics and held it up to him. I was amazed when he accurately stated, 'Ah. The Oz gender-bender. It's a great trilogy.'

I had not read the other novels in the trilogy. 'I like all sorts. Except Henry James and the patience-testing works of Herr Thomas Mann.'

'Quite. Call a cock a cock and get on with it, you pansies. Thank God Bloom took a shit or we'd still all be dancing about gracefully like James's puppets. *Washington Square*. Fuck me, you knew there was going to be no shagging by the end of that mercifully short religious tract.'

'What you were saying there, about acquiring culture. Y'know I've noticed, since arriving in London, that the middle classes only ever talk about houses and food, which is just another way of talking about money. House prices, bloody loft conversions, swank restaurants. It's a sure sign of the utter regression of a civilisation when all a social class with the political power can discuss is food and shelter. The Beaker People must have sat in their caves – if the Beaker People sat in caves – having the identical conversation. Five thousand years ago. "Great cave this. Not too many bats and the green wall slime ain't so bad. It matches the bison painting. Can't wait till tomorrow's boar hunt."'

He laughed. 'Absolutely right, sir. In my armchair with an open can of Carlsberg Special Brew, I do often consider the higher matters. Such as this: how am I going to get a novel published by the book editors of London?'

'We need to write our books first.'

He flipped his pale hand – 'A mere formality.'

I asked, 'You intend to write?'

He drew up and stated grandly, 'I intend to publish. You?' He turned quickly from his cigarette and looked in my face.

'I've never admitted it to anyone. But yes. Of course.' I shrugged.

'Perfect. Do you excel in any sport?'

'Certainly not.'

'Me either. Queens Park Rangers still won't consider me.' He looked down to his hidden bandages. 'Especially not this season. Are you proficient on musical instruments: guitars, drums?'

'Definitely not. I've tried.'

'I'm hopeless too. So what the hell else are we going to do but become great novelists?'

'You've stated a general truth here.'

'Then we will. Why not? And what do you write? Cunningham? You lunatic.'

'Well. I started off with poems.'

He shrugged. 'Those bloody versifiers have the odd image but they're damned slackers at a typewriter keyboard. They ought to look at poor old fucking Trollope. Ten thousand words in one week and holding down his graft at the Post Office. The bastard. Most of these poets are averaging twelve lines a month. Even if they're good lines. Poets are okay for nicking similes off. What else?' He sucked quickly at his cigarette as if we were suddenly pushed for time and he was anxious to bash on with a certain daily quota.

'Short stories?'

He shrugged. 'You can shoot off the names: Delmore Schwartz. He's overrated. In the original French, there's Balzac's *Colonel Chabert*. Flat-down bloody masterpiece,' he burped. 'Welshy Rhys Davies's *Canute*. There's a bloody great short story. He batted for the other side and noised up that twat D. H. Lawrence. Though when Mellors drones on about rigging the men of England up in tight red breeches, it's one of the moments of high comedy in our country's rich literature. *The Death of Ivan Ilyich* is maybe the greatest thing ever written but almost a novel, so forget the bloody short story. It's like a pack of ten fags instead of twenty, or a half pint. No point in them. The novel is the art form for us, Cunningham. It's got to be the novel for the troubled Celtic soul, to tell itself and the world: "Behold. I am a bastard."'

'I plan to do a great novel. When I'm not thinking about beer and girls. How about you?'

'Yes, of course, a great one and nothing less. But it's like Melville said: My body is but the lees of my better being. You need time and money to write a fucking book. Now how is the likes of us going to buy the time and, more important, the tranquillity to write novels? Tranquillity of mind and of circumstances. That's what's needed, boyo.' He suddenly jerked at me, not without serious aggression. I blinked. He said, 'How are you and I going to get the money to buy tranquillity of mind? Joycey boy wasn't immune to ingratiating himself when he smelled a fat chequebook. Where are our fucking patrons, Cunningham?'

'I don't know.'

'None for the likes of us. And look at our writers. A rich person's hobby. Toff Hampstead wives who never had a knee trembler in their lives, scribbling away about the glories of Venice while the cleaner sweeps round their slippers. But you think about it. I'm ill. Now I've the incapacity, dole, housing benefit. It's the only true and Christian way to write. You and I could scratch out a page a day on the dole. You a chapter then me a chapter. Or we could each concoct our own brew. Have a cracking book in a year.'

Suddenly he shifted back in his seat and became noticeably more at ease. I could tell these matters had been on his mind a very great deal. He grimaced and straightened. Impatiently he fired off, 'Right. Best opening sentence in any novel?'

I immediately quoted, '"Take my camel, dear," said my Aunt Dot, as she climbed down from this animal on her return from High Mass."'

'Oh. That is good. Oh, that's terribly good. Who's that?'

'Rose Macaulay. *The Towers of Trebizond*.'

'I'll need to read the damned thing now with a first sentence like that. And obviously a Catholic.'

'I've a copy. Over at the old digs – but I owe the rent so I can't go back there. You?'

'Me what?'

'Best first sentence in a novel?'

'Oh. "The sun shone, having no alternative, on the nothing new." And how do you stand on the Greek and Roman classics?'

'Bit like a lofty *Coronation Street* down there. Give us a Penguin Modern Classic any day. I like *The Satyricon* and— What's his name? Apollious, did he do *The Golden Ass*? A great laugh.'

He chuckled and he shrugged; he didn't agree and was like a plumber commenting on a boiler fitted by some imbecile predecessor. Mildly he told me, 'You pronounce it Apuleius. Lucius Apuleius. Its correct title is really *The Transformations*. Like Ovid. It was about the only book poofy Des Esseintes could bring himself to praise.'

Being on relatively unfamiliar ground, I stated, 'Old Sam Beckett. Personal grooming is not his distraction, unlike Mr Tom Wolfe. Let's have another with my money?' I reached and started removing my worn shoe.

'By all means. We also appreciate the other Irish classics: Murphy's, Beamish and Guinness. But look; lend us ten pence to call the good lady girlfriend. She'll be worried. Need to pop outside to the box so she doesn't rumble I'm in the boozer. I'll tell her I'm just leaving the hospital now and that should give us time for another. Or two.'

I put my hand in my pocket. 'Want twenty pence?'

'No. Just ten. I have to talk to her all day anyway.'

When he returned I had the new beers in. 'I was just talking about *you* to Aoife. Told her I'd found a wonderful lunatic. Another.'

'Ee, Fa?'

'Aoife.'

'Ee. Fa. It sounds African.'

'Steady on. Very Irish. She has a powerful name: Aoife McCrissican.'

'Aoife McCrissican. That's just wonderful.'

'That's nothing. Her older sister's called Attracta.'

'A Tractor?'

'Attracta.'

'God.'

'The sister deserves it. She doesn't look like a tractor but she's so boring. Married a solicitor and treats Aoife as if she ran off with the circus. Which in a way, being with me, I suppose she did. Look, Cunningham. If you don't mind the crying of babes-in-arms, we have a box room, camp bed, spare typewriter.'

Luck had been against me for so long I didn't recognise it when it came right up to my face.

He said, 'Back to our palace of sin with you. Sit out the pogroms. Aoife doesn't mind. We'll keep each other company and start in on our masterpieces at a page a day.'

'That's generous of you, but womankind has her dominion.'

'She'd like someone new around. God knows she's sick enough of me. Come back to Ithaca, whence I must comb Circe's merkin. We'll solve the problem together of how we squeeze ourselves into the bloody novel-writing game. Let's have another from your sock to celebrate.'

3

Standing outside The Five *or* Six Bells, the night was cooler with a clear song of autumn at last. Summer was agony for the idle Scot. It was September, and I had a natural right to some driving sleet, or at least a blessed frost.

Llewellyn reached to his chest. He looked suddenly tricked and stated, 'She'll be able to tell we've been drinking.'

'Could this be a problem?'

'You need to bring votive offerings. If you want to get into her good books and make her think you're the most charming man from the northern lands.' He waved an unsteady hand at me.

'Yes?'

'Chicken dhansak, all the trimmings from Gurkha the Burper, a bottle of sparkling wine. She'll polish your shoes for you then, boyo.'

'No problem,' I said. 'And perhaps a wee drappy of something from the off-licence for us? And nappies too, from the garage. Don't forget.'

'What would I do without you, already? I had bloody forgot. A wee drappy and a nappy,' he said, in a quite-good Scottish accent, and he stumbled a touch, slowly lit two cigarettes in his own mouth, then passed one to me.

We approached The Gurkha in the weighed-down, simian walk of drunken men hauling provisions in carrier bags – bulky disposable nappies, a quarter bottle of vodka, a chilled sparkling wine and the backbone of our strike force: twelve cans of Guinness.

The Gurkha showed two panes of glass to the street, orange-painted wooden window frames, a narrow door and a lit-up sign. The frontage looked as if it would collapse inwardly should you dare place the palms of two hands against it. There were about eight empty tables inside – largely symbolic.

'Hello Loo-Alien!' one of the waiters called, coming forward to us in his white shirt, shaking Llewellyn's hand using both of his – the left one warmly joining, arms lifting up and down as if they were tossing a blanket.

'You don't come in to us from long, long time.'

'No money, Sudama. Sudama. This is my good friend Mr Douglas Cunningham, lately of University College London. He comes from Scotland. A poverty-stricken scholar with ill fortune like myself.'

'Oh, Scotland.' Sudama smiled at me.

'Yes,' I said.

'Rain and cold in Scotland.'

'Yes,' I heartily agreed.

He turned to Llewellyn. 'How is little baby?'

Llewellyn leaned down to this small man and called, 'Bigger.'

Sudama opened his mouth wider, showing many uneven teeth. 'Bigger. This is life,' he nodded with the utmost seriousness. 'Chicken dhansak? The lovely lady like chicken dhansak.'

'Yes, she does. Chicken dhansak for three people. And—' Llewellyn frowned down at the menu and picked his way through it all as if he were reading an out-of-date map. 'And twenty Regal. Something while we wait?'

We sat at the table nearest the door, drinking pints of lager. 'There are about seventeen official languages in India. Isn't that right?' Llewellyn yelled.

'Oh yes,' came a distant reply through the serving hatch. I didn't see how they could have understood or even heard the question.

'In the south you have the Dravidian family of languages and in the rest of India, you know? Indo-Aryan. Sanskrit. Old Thomas Stearns read the Sanskrit when he was at university. You know that? Bloody show-off.' Llewellyn leaned toward me as if finalising a huge project of agreement, and he insisted, 'But Sanskrit's not a spoken language. Hey. You've got to hire a kilt for when we jump the broomstick. Or Aoife'll never forgive you.'

'You're getting married?'

'Sure. I am engaged to be married. And you're invited.'

'You only just met me.'

'Need a witness anyway. Nobody's coming but my gran and damn brother. Ealing Town Hall. I forget the date. Be there.'

Bollo Lane follows alongside the Piccadilly and District lines which run overground into Acton Town station. The trains brake and trundle in, or they accelerate away. According to the random physics of payload and suspension they ignite spectacular contact flashes with the electrified third rail; blue-bordered reports of white light, waspy crackles, bottled lightning. The illuminated interiors of the trains are model-like and often mysteriously devoid of passengers.

Towards the bottom of this lane is a high compound of council flats: the edifice of rough reinforced concrete moulding, badly weathered wood panelling, single glazing. Five storeys in all and no lifts. It was along their frontage in street light that Llewellyn and I approached.

'I take it you're a fan of the suicidal Ukrainian Pole, Korzeniowski? He falls off sharply with *Chance*. Though *Victory* had its moments. Welcome to the West London Centre for Conradian Studies,' he pointed.

There was an enamel sign above the entryway to a stairwell; it was chipped by air-gun pellet shots and in the leaked and parsimonious street light I could read: *Conrad Flats. Almayer House.*

'Well I never.'

'Ironic and very erudite. They were careful enough not to name it correctly, Almayer's Folly.'

'Is there a Heart of Darkness House?'

'Unfortunately, no. They've been careful and censorious. The defeat of Victory House is just round the corner, there's Tide House, where the water tank did burst once. There's Western House – though it's to the east. And Arrow House, where I bet there are a few crossbows. There's no Chance House. No Suspense House, and certainly no Narcissus whatever House. It's prophetic for us, Silence, Exile and Cunningham, because didn't Joe C. and Ford Madox Ford collaborate on a couple of duff potboilers, to keep fat Jessie Conrad in her sweetmeats?'

'They did, that's quite true.'

Lit by square and trembling fluorescent wall lamps, we started to ascend up inside Almayer House; the stairs had been painted oxide red at their edging, as if to mark the outline for an intended but errant carpet. I could immediately smell our carry-out food in the semi-enclosed concrete stairwell. At each floor level, the stairs accessed a long landing lobby and the front doors of apartments.

We briefly crossed this communal area to reach the next stair ascent. These landing lobbies bored right through the building from the south to north; square ends, the size of barn doors, sealed from the sky by a criss-cross frame of thick lattice concrete moulding through which no child could pass, though doubtless they could jettison an array of ordnance down towards the earth below. It was like ascending within some riddled lighthouse.

Llewellyn breathlessly said, 'Cause of these stairs and no lifts, it's mainly single weirdos and younger people with kids here. Oldies on the ground floor. Wonder what the architects actually supposed would heat these landings in winter, eh? The farts of Le Corbusier wafting from the Côte d'Azur, perhaps?' He shook his head wearily.

As we climbed on up and through them, I began to distinguish many, many items placed on the wide landings: unfolded picnic tables and deckchairs, prone for usage on what had been a warm day; bicycles, chained motorbikes which must have been man-handled up the stairs for storage, a live fridge wired to a power cable which trailed into a drilled hole at the side of a front door. I saw an abandoned electric cooker, the enamelled top around the four rings browned with tributaries of spillage which festered on lavishly down the sides. A piled collection of hubcaps. Llewellyn pointed to them. 'They fly off on the tight corner by Victory House; kids collect them to sell for scrap.'

On the third floor were two wooden hutches, one placed atop the other. Some creatures scuffled in their darkness.

'Mr Linton's ferrets. Stink in summer. Get loose sometimes.'

Up on the fourth and topmost floor we came to a windowless front door painted the same ochre red as the stairs: 506. Llewellyn produced a Yale key and turned it in the lock.

I suddenly felt very defensive, threatened by the illustrious presence of the matriarch. I could conceive of no aspect of my arrival the Lady of the House might cherish other than the curry.

The front door opened inward and we advanced: yellowish lamplight, magnolia woodchip wallpaper, warmth and a smell of close-quartered domesticity; the slight and cloying sweetness of nappies, the chalkiness of talc. Coats that hung in the narrow corridor were buffing out. I was surprised to spot another identical macintosh there. I'd assumed Llewellyn had pulled his least valued coat over his bloodied chest, but these garments seemed a characteristic mode of dress for him.

Off the long passage – which had no carpet – were doorways, the first revealing a darkened kitchen with the dull glint of a sink and then night views of street and depot lights way below. Llewellyn quickly turned and stated to my face, 'Reader, if you seek his monument look around you.'

I laughed.

'And that Cyril Connolly bastard. The enemy of promise is the pram in the hallway. Is it now? Our hallway is too narrow to fit the bloody pram in.' He quickly called in softer register, 'Hey, Aoife. The soldiers are back from the war.' He'd moved in through the second doorway. I could see hinge marks where the door had been removed, possibly with some force.

It was very dark within that living room; his plastic bags and the sides of his raincoat brushed against the door frame. A bottle of light – a small enclosed candle – gave out some illumination, deeper into the lumps and shapes of the room.

Then a light – forged only for a precious instant before it shrunk, having defined the perfect edges of two long, rectangular windows. A vista of the railway lay down there and I realised there had been an electrical flash from a train far below, easily reaching up this high. An airy, feminine voice – from where I could not see – spoke out, 'How are you, Lou?', frank and nervous.

I saw two long and bare arms lift over the broad shoulders of his coat to embrace Llewellyn gently.

'Don't squeeze.'

'I won't. I won't,' the voice reed-like and the accent nasal; Nottingham or Derby, I guessed. 'Just like last time, eh?' She was hidden behind the wings of the opened overcoat. The embrace had been brief and now a tinge of outrage was new to her voice. 'Oh, look at you.'

'I'm fine now. Just the stitches opened a little. The rib cage didn't shift. It's fused. They just told me to rest and go back next week. Aoife, this is first-rate lunatic Mr Douglas Cunningham, lately of University College. A scholar. Welcome him to Brideshead Rewallpapered. And look at what he's bought us.'

I could see her now, coming forward from the edges of the light's reach, and she gave Llewellyn a sideways and tolerant smile.

'Sorry to intrude into your home this way.' I actually bowed my head a little and held out my hand, which she took very limply – her fingers felt as thin as a plastic skeleton's – and she let go. To my surprise she laughed, almost just a little escape of air.

She lifted a hand to her lips then asked of me, gentle and sincere, 'Are you okay?'

Before I could answer, a tumble of breathy words continued, perhaps even nervously shy, while she looked at all the booze and all the food. 'Oh. This is a surprise. It's so very generous. We haven't had any treats in a long while now. Lou probably told you how. I'm sorry about this place.' She presented the dark room with a hand held out as if she expected a drip of water to fall into her palm. I almost looked upwards for a leak. 'It's all the council would give us before Lily came. He *has* told you we have our little girl?' Her tone was now oddly vulnerable and anxious.

'Yes. Congratulations.'

In a voice with no hint of humour so I did not know whether to smile or not, she said, 'The only good thing about here is that his gran – The Apple; Granny Smith, who's like a mother-in-law – can't climb up the stairs.'

Llewellyn hoisted the swag bags of our triumph. 'I'll serve,' and he rustled off and up the corridor to the kitchen.

Aoife and I were left there together. I turned my head from side to side looking for the crib, or manger or whatever infants slumber in. 'Is Lily here?'

'She's sleeping in our room.'

'Oh.' And all the while, Aoife's pale face – as if she was being propelled backwards and forwards in a wheelchair. The face came out of the dark towards me and then withdrew into it again.

I thought she wore trousers soaked in black blood. In fact she was wearing leather trousers which were reflecting odd points of light, like starlight upon an oil slick – the hall lamp was smeared on the creases of her narrow thighs as she moved back into darkness. From through the double windows, distant street light had found lodgement in Aoife's legs – then there was another train flash down in the cauldron below and the light pulled and elongated around her lower body – Isis, and her arched torso of stars.

Almost inaudibly she said, 'Sorry it's so dark. I'd a little headache earlier, I was so worried about him. They pass.'

'It's fine. Leave it dark. He's fixed up fine now, so there's no need to worry.' I chuckled, trying not to be flippant but to hit the right tone. I said admiringly, 'I've never seen anything like Llewellyn at the hospital. He was very funny. He was very cool.'

She watched my face, her eyes receptive, her whole body slightly tensed for every bit of information about Llewellyn. She quickly said, 'Oh, Lou's so brave, Douglas. So brave. His illness and the big operation he had on his heart. He must have told you about it?'

'Yes, he did.'

'We've had so much stress in this last year. Stress. The baby and Lou's illness. Please. Sit down.' She leaned over and reached under a lamp to switch it on, which suddenly brought the mainly derelict room into existence around us. She sat down.

All the wallpaper was half-torn from the walls but then the job had seemingly been abandoned. An old-fashioned yellow sofa sat against another stripped wall, so rather than walk the length of the room towards a table and chairs, I had to lower myself, a little awkwardly, seconds after she had. So I sat beside her. Her long leather thigh was very close to my own. My weight drove me deeper into the sofa than she, so our faces were at the same elevation. She stared out across the room – at nothing, or so it seemed – a slight smile on the edge of her lips as if in thought. She told me, 'This is the second time his stitches have gone,' with a tone of awesome amazement. I nodded very slowly – my head aside, staring at her profile. Then I looked down because there was a rumpled-up towel on the sofa which both our bottoms were sitting upon.

'Oh gosh,' she said. 'Sorry. Watch your trousers on that, I'm afraid.'

I frowned, then I realised the towel concealed Llewellyn's blood from when his stitches had torn open, snoozing on this sofa.

But I just looked back up. I felt I had been waiting to deliver this woman a message which had been carried in my throat all of my life. The great moment had come but a dry croak was my voice. Her face, her neck, her eyes and her body actually stopped me, stopped my thoughts, so I found myself just nodding and pretending to be indifferent. I was not listening as I looked at her arms, bared from the pushed-back sleeves of a thin white V-neck pullover.

In the first seconds of entering that dark room, with a bizarre distress, I had seen that Aoife McCrissican was menacingly beautiful.

4

That first night the three of us sat at the table against the far wall of the living room, around that plastic, slidey yellow tablecloth which tended to make objects easily whizz off it; exterior lights beyond the window – the most distant, perhaps towards Brentford – were semaphoring in the clear night atmosphere.

Where I sat, facing her, I was constantly aware of a cautious, trickling necklet of steady lights which crawled along Aoife's slight shoulder, behind her high neck, then re-emerged across the top of her other shoulder. My eyes were drawn to these slightest of stirrings. This slow revolving garland was the lacing of continual airliners, moving toward Heathrow airport as if they were duteously rounding assigned but invisible pylons.

When Llewellyn joined us he had covered his bandages with an old sweatshirt and was transporting plates horizontally with still enwrapped food packages balanced upon them. He sat down very carefully and a twist came in at the corner of his mouth.

She ate without you noticing and not a great amount. In her small cleavage lay a tiny chain and silver crucifix which rested on flatness. She sipped some wine from a glass and whispered, 'Now my headache will most likely come back.'

Llewellyn nodded and ate with a predatory stoop, huddled over his plate, the fork moving quickly, and he talked a lot. She managed to talk too, but consumed her food in a ghostly way. The particular and alarmed energy of her constant grey-green eyes contrasted with her slightly hesitant and soporific movements.

At one point during the meal, Llewellyn called, 'What do you make of the old penthouse suite? Haven't done the papering since I can't afford bloody wallpaper so I was thinking of using the Christmas wrapping paper this year. What do you think? Think you could be happy up here for a bit, working as my valet in the sky?' He looked at me.

'Sure. It's great.'

'Come on, Cunningham. You can do much better than that. Give us a few *bon mots*?'

I said, 'It's *Look Back in Anger* with digital watches.'

He put down the fork and clapped.

After we had eaten, I helped stack and cautiously manoeuvre curry-lashed, naan-bread-smeared plates through to the kitchen. There were no curtains there either. Curtains seemed a mod-con hardly adopted up in the skies of Acton. The window glass was a vertical wall of sepia with the clear sense of the drop outwith. By the cooker I saw a special holder for inverted, sterilised baby bottles with their teats balanced atop.

In an unspoken manner, Aoife had silently vanished so Llewellyn and I took up the masculine prerogative, sipping Guinness cans back at the table, talking books. He smoked, explaining he was permitted to do so but never in the same room as Lily.

Suddenly Aoife put her head around the door and signalled directly at me with one coaxing, commanding finger.

Llewellyn said, 'I'll finish this fag. Go give our miracle child your blessing. You worthless Protestant.'

I rose and respectfully left my can of Guinness on the table, moving out and down the corridor. Their bedroom door was ajar. The shadowy room was lit by a special low-power child lamp, giving it the solemnity of a Nativity grotto. The double bed was to the right and I could not help a brief glance at its pulled-over blankets, the candlewick bedspread and jumbled links of a crocheted bedcover.

Baby Lily lay in an old-fashioned wooden cot, profoundly asleep, surrounded by a barrage of totems: cuddly toys, hanging kinetic mobiles pinned to the low Artex ceiling; devices were clamped to the coulisse of the lift-out side frame. Aoife stood by her daughter, looking down on her with that ever-renewed yet modest astonishment at what she'd brought into the world.

It would be wrong to say I was unmoved by the sight of a beautiful mother and her babe, who was asleep, its bunched fist of minute fingers with perfectly miniaturised nails clenched near its lips. The foundation of my feeling, I now realise, was not for their child – it was, of course, for myself; the deep sentimentality I felt was celebrating my own fortune. Llewellyn and Aoife's was a generosity my tight heart would never understand. I have dispensed indulgence in my life since then but I've never been truly generous.

'She's very beautiful. Is she a sleeper?'

'A log. We can even be quite noisy around her. Lou plays his awful classical music and she doesn't even wake up.'

'Has your eyes,' I said cleanly.

'They're closed.'

I swallowed. 'I mean the shape of you, eh, round your eyes.'

'Mmm.'

34

Of course Aoife and I kept our voices very low and I enjoyed the implied intimacy of us whispering together. I kept smiling and tried to think of what else to say.

'I love their hands.'

'Yes.'

'They're so precise. Like the porcelain dolls' hands in Hamleys.'

'They are.'

'Need to do something.' I stood on my tiptoes, pushed my hand into the pocket of my jeans and quickly withdrew a five-pence piece. 'Scottish custom in the Highlands. When you first see a new-born you touch their palm with silver.'

'Really?'

'For money. Not in a vulgar way; just so they will never go without. Never be hungry. But. Maybe I should go wash the coin?'

'What?' She had been looking down at baby Lily and now she met my eyes in the dim light, that mocking smile on the edge of the mouth.

'Don't want to touch her palm with a dirty coin.'

'I shouldn't fret over that. She crawls up and down that filthy passage, if I don't watch her. We need to get it covered in lino or something.'

'We'll do it,' I rashly promised. 'It would be funny if Llewellyn caught me, wouldn't it?'

She looked puzzled.

'With the coin. A Scotsman a few hours in your home and Llewellyn catches me scrubbing a five-pence piece under the hot-water tap. I know he'd make a brilliant joke about it.'

Her finger shot to her perfect front teeth again. 'If there is any hot water. Both of you are daft together. The way you talk.'

My eyes had helplessly swayed round this private zone once again. Halfway up it, the exterior wall of the bedroom was completely obscured by barricaded clothes racks, heavy hung, leaning and straining under a long and colourful accumulation of garments. More women's clothes were squeezed into plump carrier bags, piled in the space between the top of the wardrobe and the ceiling – one particular arm of a blouse loosely dangled down; tall boots leaned their flanks out and dresses bulged from the wardrobe doors, like some kind of garish wall insulation. I didn't see how a woman of her young age could have accumulated so much to wear. Couldn't they sell the lot and be rich?

Near the end of the bed the exterior wall formed a right angle against the enormous external culvert which ran all the way down the north side of Almayer House. Two windows were placed here forming a corner, each facing the other at a ninety-degree angle. Finally, some thin polyester curtains were drawn across these; then a further windowless wall turned again and followed along the bedside to its head, leaving some access space.

Hung up on that wall to the side of the bed were two very large photographs, unframed but covered by glass. I looked across the bed to them and took a few steps forward. 'Oh, wow.'

In all that chiaroscuro of make-up, I would not have recognised her but for the mouth and the eyes. A cover shoot, theatrically lit. Aoife wore a great deal of sequins on a very, very little amount of dress; one leg in a platform boot seemed insanely long and was placed upon the running board of a cream coloured vintage sports car outside brick stables.

She whispered, 'Oh, I'm a sort of failed model.'

'A model. Wow. Llewellyn never said.'

'That was used. Actual. On a poster. In Scandinavia and Spain.'
She frowned her flawless forehead at the image of herself as if she
was looking at something obscure and modish in an art gallery.

Then there was that other photo in black and white: a horizontal
strip of pale tropical beach, studded with glossy, small black crabs
– the type which scuttle up the surf line then back, on fast tele-
scopic legs. In the precarious midst of them Aoife sat, legs crossed
in the lotus position; both her big toenails on the sand had been
painted with the crab symbol of Cancer. Her face was hidden but
I could already identify that small mole on her lower neck which
always showed above pullovers and low collars, the neck so delicate
it seemed under constant strain, showing pale veins and striations
of ligaments as she turned her slow smile away from you. Her
parted crown was exposed so that long blonde hair fell, obscuring
her torso, to just above her flat belly. The pubic area was submerged
by the camera angle down in the crossed feet, only the tops of her
small breasts showed, semi-concealed by her length of hair. She was
stark naked, imitating the crouched posture of those crabs. It was
gothic, spectacular and erotic.

She lowered her whisper down more and looked cautiously
across to her daughter, leaning slightly in to me. 'Don't tell, but I'm
Virgo. I can't ask anyone else, Douglas. I can't ask my pal Abingdon,
or she would tease me. Why does Lou call this my venereal disease
picture? He won't tell me. I think I look nice.'

'You look very nice. Crabs.'

'Crabs? Why crabs? I don't understand.'

'Never you mind. You look alluring.'

'Alluring?' she pronounced slowly.

'Where is that beach? Seychelles, Caribbean?'

'Noooo.' She did that low chuckle which must have come from her mother; it was too old for her. 'That's Dittisham. In Dorset, I think. The photographer had a nightmare getting all the little tied-up boats out of shot. There's actually one boat hidden behind me. The crabs aren't real. They're plastic. From Pinewood film studios. Oh my God. I couldn't sit on a beach with no clothes on and real crabs running all around me. Oh my God, no. Though I wasn't really without clothes. I'd bikini bottoms on after all. You just can't see them. That was for the signs of the zodiac calendar series. I couldn't be in this year's series cause I was huge, expecting Lily.'

I nodded.

Still we whispered, so we both heard the mighty procession of Llewellyn coming along the hallway. We were helplessly trapped, at the bottom of the bed, before that glamour photograph of Aoife – naked. I suddenly felt the image should – as on the altarpiece of Grünewald's terrifying *Mocking of Christ* – have shutters that we could just snap shut. It would have been madness to lurch aside and examine a gold lamé scarf that hung from the clothes rack, though this is what I felt I should do.

The door swung soundlessly with Llewellyn's heavy clench, his other fist formed around the bottle of vodka. He immediately evaluated our position. 'I am but a pair of ragged claws scuttling up a nurse's hairy arse.' He didn't whisper.

'Lou,' she said. 'Was a pretty nurse bandaging you then?'

'Hyperborean with a moustache.'

I chuckled but glanced at Lily in a presumptuous way – as if I were the responsible male there, concerned for the babe's rest; yet the baby did not stir.

'Stunning photographs,' I continued to whisper.

Llewellyn put his free palm straight out and touched Aoife's leather buttock. 'A fine figure of an innocent, spirited away to Acton in the Sky by the Dark Lord.' He pointed at the shot of her on the beach. 'This is her first communion. Canvey Island in December. With some of the local lads.'

She leaned to him, laughing, one palm gently going against his chest and remaining there. 'You are my Dark Lord.'

'I am.'

I said, a little louder, 'I'm about to conduct a Protestant rite upon your beautiful daughter.'

Llewellyn, standing entwined with Aoife, put on a brilliant expression, eyes popping open wider, the mouth elongating down into a pale, stretched mask.

'On you go. She won't wake,' Aoife said.

I reached carefully in towards Lily, I ever-so-gently touched her minute palm with the cold edge of vulgar coin and I pulled it back.

'What's the meaning of this blasphemy?'

'It's nice, Lou. It's a custom of up in Scotland, so she's never without money to buy food.'

'She can feed us, then. And she's out of here at sixteen. Look here, look here, boyo.' He nodded and stepped away from Aoife, who trailed an arm after him, but as he was excited she allowed him to go. Llewellyn crossed to the bed and I followed him those few steps.

I was now able to identify which side of the bed Llewellyn slept on. Against the inner wall was an assembled, rickety bookcase you could reach out to from the bed. The two supporting pillars to the rough, paint-spattered cross planks were towers of hardcover and paperback books that could presumably never – or only rarely –

be removed for consultation. I soon deduced the demarcation of the books. The supporting pillars were built exclusively of contemporary English fiction. The cross planks shelved accessible volumes of reference books and many, many works in the European languages: grammars, dictionaries, primers and some novels, even folded newspapers in French and Italian. I could make out plain-covered Pleiades editions in French, apostrophe-spattered titles in Italian, black gothic German script and the cracked, fat, wide spine of a Castilian *Don Quixote* published from Barcelona. On the very top shelf was the long duck-egg-green slab of spines to many Penguin Modern Classics. My nosey face confidently gravitated there. I'd spotted Alfred Kubin's *The Other Side*, and was about to sound off about it but Llewellyn lowered himself slowly to sit on the bed and he patted the space next to him. I obediently sat and faced the small wall of books. The bed was very soft.

He shook his head. 'How weary, stale, flat and unprofitable seems all of my library. Especially unprofitable.'

'Know the feeling.'

'Commiserate together.' He passed the vodka bottle.

I knew I couldn't drink vodka straight so I just held it and he didn't seem to notice.

We sat side by side with our knees out in front of us.

I bent my head sideways and read the book-spine titles of one supporting column: Francis King, Burgess's Malayan novels, Robert Nye, Alice Thomas Ellis, all of Richard Hughes, H.D.'s *Bid Me to Live*, Julian Rathbone's *Joseph*, Calder Willingham's *Eternal Fire*, Samuel Selvon's *The Lonely Londoners*, Richard Fariña's *Been Down So Long*, Blair's biography of Beckett with the slim Calder volumes, Jim Phelan's *Wagon-Wheels*, *London Belongs to Me* by

Norman Collins. I touched a spine carefully with a finger. '*A Month in the Country*. Carr is a very interesting guy too.'

'He's quite good,' he snapped grudgingly with a frosty tone.

Lawrence Durrell's *Constance or Solitary Practices* was there. I tapped the spine. 'Did you read Durrell's book about Rhodes? Sort of ravishing. Wish I had a spirit rich enough to respond to the world like that, to write it so fully.'

'You sound like a Christmas Eve with the Salvation Army, Major Barbara.' But after a silence he added, 'The hippies used to read *The Alexandria Quartet* but now us younger folk suddenly don't. He'll come back into fashion. Whatever that amounts to.'

'You have a lot of foreign editions here.'

'I try to read 'em all, boyo. Frankly, reckon I could do much better myself. How are your languages?'

'Terrible. Absolutely terrible; I managed to pass O-grade Gaelic but don't understand a single word any more.'

'You *are* a disgrace,' he told me in a perfectly serious tone and nodded his head.

From over to my right came Aoife's voice. 'Lou speaks French and Italian and Spanish and German and he can read all others.'

'Not all. And my German is very bad. It's horrible.'

'You're a linguist. A sotted polyglot. You should go to University College. You wouldn't screw it up,' I said.

'Ha. I can't afford that, boyo. We've a daughter to provide for. Or the publishers of London do.'

I had slightly shifted to look across at Aoife. I found I had to turn from one of them to the other and then back again, both to give them my attention and to appear polite. I had thought she'd previously left the bedroom but she was folding an orange blanket several times. She walked out and I heard her movements in some next-door room which I hadn't yet seen. A noise began like hollow metal tent rods contacting and being assembled.

Llewellyn lifted down one of a two-volume *Oxford English Dictionary*. It was an old edition. He opened it and turned through the thin, brittle-sounding pages. I noticed, in bright-coloured ink, several words highlighted, almost on every page. I frowned at an indicated word: *patibulary*.

'Look at this.' His eyebrows crept up. 'Look at all the words I've marked.'

'What are they?'

'Great words. The words I'm going to use in my novel.'

'What's your novel going to be about?'

He turned to me. 'I don't have the slightest notion, boyo, but I know what words I'm going to use.' He snapped the dictionary shut. He didn't seem to have noticed I hadn't taken a sip of the vodka and he retrieved the quarter bottle from me, wrenching it away. I started to accept he was very drunk and couldn't hold his liquor. Yet they must have pumped a fair few painkillers into him at the hospital.

'Cunningham.' He placed a chummy hand on my shoulder and we slightly bounced up and down on the bed. 'The fuckers will not resent your work. They will not resent your style, they won't even resent the fact you didn't go to Oxford and rotten Cambridge. Do you know what they will resent? Do you actually know?'

'Who do you mean?'

His head batted forward, almost touching the books. 'These old fuckers.'

'These writers?'

'You know what they will all resent?'

'What?'

'Your youth. It's our fucking youth they hate, boyo. They might be stuck in Hampstead with a bank balance but their youth is all spent.'

'In his defence, I don't think J. L. Carr is at all wealthy,' I tried to point out. 'Jim Phelan certainly not. They don't live in Hampstead.'

'Doesn't matter, boyo. The fact is, the bastards have made it. They've bloody made it and we haven't. They've jumped the wall. For God's sake don't be fooled by fame and reputations, Cunningham; they blind taste and the senses. I am not being told any of these buggers are worth a thing just because they are known names. It's a ticker-tape of bloody names and if you come along, you lengthen the roll call. They'll take it out on us. On you.' He nodded with certainty.

'I see.'

'Simple psychology. It's just psychology.'

'Right.'

'Always remember that. Till you're bloody forty, then you can forget it, cause you've either failed or you'll be one of them old self-satisfied fuckers anyway. You must know what that old biddy says in Mortimer's *Charade*?' He turned round quickly to stare at me.

I mumbled, 'No. I haven't read it.'

He shook his head slowly, like a doctor delivering the worst news. 'You haven't read it?' And he quoted, '"The entertainment world is all a sort of dream. You only wake up when you fail, or when you succeed."'

There was silence. I nodded.

'That novel's here. Somewhere. Brilliant book and you haven't bloody read it.' Llewellyn shook his head again. 'That was his first novel. Only twenty-five bloody years old. Dazzling. He declined immediately.' Llewellyn's head went forward. I shot out my hand and grabbed his shoulder. I thought he'd conked out, but instead, slightly stooped forward, keeping his torso straightened, his arm reached in under the bed and, ignoring my hand – which I quickly whipped back – he retrieved a glossy, red-covered book. He rose again and dropped it into my lap. *The Writers' & Artists' Yearbook 1983*. 'This is your bedtime reading. Every night. Publishers. Agents. Film companies. Contractual blabber. The borderlines where the truth of commerce overtakes and the lies of art are left behind.'

'I'll take a dander at it.'

'Right. I'm shagged out. Off to bed with you. What will we start on tomorrow? Movie script or a novel?'

'Uhm. I'm not sure that I would know how to write a movie script.'

'Oh but we shall, boyo, and make one million dollars. However, just to warm up, we'll bash out a novel each to start with. After a few bloody pints, of course.'

He lay back on the pillows, eyes closed, and he tried to swing his legs up onto the bed but of course they softly impacted against my resting knees and he murmured something derogatory, then, 'You lunatic.'

I suddenly had to slide down the bed towards its end and stand up as his legs – brogues still on – craned over and settled upon the crocheted cover atop the candlewick bedspread. He seemed asleep immediately. I noted the vodka bottle had been dexterously positioned on a shelf in what looked like a previously established niche.

I took a last look at Aoife's photos then smiled at baby Lily. The child seemed able to sleep through any intellectual commotion around her. I left their bedroom carrying *The Writers' & Artists' Yearbook* in one hand.

Aoife sat in the living room upon that sofa, stained with Llewellyn's blood, her unreadable face smiling ahead. Lalique eyes so still, it seemed wrongful to stir them into any action at all.

'Hi.'

'Hi.'

'I think Llewellyn— Lou's fast asleep. He must be exhausted.' I was standing at the doorway, one hand holding that book, proselytising on a threshold. Through the wide windows ahead we both silently looked at the great city spreading to the south; the lights seemed more numerous than ever and all were gently and unstably agitating together in the cool night air.

She stood. 'I've made your bed. I really have made it because it's a camp bed you build up. Afraid you can only have blankets on it to keep warm with. No spare sheets. There's no heater through there either,' she stated in that neutral, slightly nasal tone she had.

'Oh, but that's just fine.'

'I don't think so. You're tall like us; when I used it for a few nights before we got the bed delivered, my toes stuck out the end.' She added with definite clarification, 'Lou was on the sofa.'

I nodded.

'I'll need to borrow sheets off Granny Smith.'

'I'm sorry to be a nuisance.'

She lowered her head briefly and walked past me, off down the corridor. 'But you're not.' Presuming I was expected to, I followed cautiously, fearful she might turn right, into the bathroom.

Above the door at the end of the corridor was a small interior window for light distribution. It had been broken, so there was a ragged glass edge to a missing chunk in the pane.

We were both standing in a small, L-shaped room. The canvas camp bed lay along most of the floor. Near the window – curtainless, of course – were modern weight-lifting barbells with some small, three-kilo discs on the ends. There was an elderly record player and a small accumulation of long-playing records leaning against the skirting board.

'This is a great little den. Does Lou really lift weights?'

'No, he's not allowed. I do. Just for muscle tone. I'm a weakling.'

'You lift them?'

'I have to get back in shape after Lily.'

I nodded slowly. 'This is all dead kind of you, Aoife.'

She put her face quickly to mine, our cheeks just touched and she made one kiss sound with her lips. Her cheek was surprisingly cold before she took it away. 'It'll be lovely with someone else here. It's been hard for Lou with Lily coming and no job. He loves to talk about books and languages. I'm silly for him about that stuff.'

'Not at all. You're both very kind and generous. Lily is beautiful too.'

She smiled.

'Thank you for taking care of Lou and bringing back the lovely food and the wine. Good night.'

'Good night. And good night to Llewellyn. Lou.'

When I pulled my left sock off and sniffed, it smelled so bad it gave me an immediate headache. It was so long since my shirt had been washed it didn't even smell like me any more.

When I lay in darkness on the slightly unstable camp bed, stretched out coffin-straight, I held my breath to listen for sounds through the dwelling but there were none.

Although it was long after the last underground services had ceased, some kind of train movements still went on far below. I saw the silent blitz of incendiaries flash and signify softly upwards.

PART TWO

5

The acoustics always seemed highlighted, localised, when I came out of London underground stations as my constrained senses reached and focused. Rising away from the atmospheres of humid incubation, we three came out of High Street Kensington station. The squeaking wheel of a taxi sounded especially brilliant.

A guy in a leather biker jacket was shuffling a yellow plastic bucket with coins in the bottom and a SUPPORT THE MINERS strip of paper Sellotaped around it. Bold for Kensington. I automatically grabbed from my pocket, sifted the coppers, dropped them in the bucket and trotted away. The guy said, 'Cheers, mate,' behind me.

Lou watched me carefully. 'Yes. This isn't a social call. It's a sociological call.'

On the High Street we'd stepped left, towards the Commonwealth Institute. Aoife walked snugly between Lou and me as we each linked with one of her arms. She moved jauntily in the middle and turned her head towards one or other of us – as we were each addressed or as we each spoke.

I took a foolish pride in walking with Aoife between us. You saw men, late from the office or fresh from the pub, look at her – wearing that dress and those boots and with make-up on. Women also glanced. All Lou had done was put his trilby hat on his head with his usual macintosh, but somehow he looked timeless.

Aoife said, 'You'll still have a good time.' Then, 'I need to phone to put my mind at rest.'

'Cunningham and I are incapable of having a good time at something like this.'

She turned her face to me. Her face with dark lipstick. I found it hard to take my eyes away from her. 'Is that true, Douglas?'

I said, 'Fashion makes me uncomfortable. It can be a tyranny in the other arts so I reckon fashion can be a tyranny in fashion. In theory. Perhaps not in practice.'

'Well said. What does he mean?' Lou put a cigarette in his mouth and lit it with the Zippo – all using his left hand.

'Ooh look. Got ten pence?' Aoife turned her face from one of us to the other.

'I've told you to complain about the phone card and they connect you free.'

'There's no time for all that if you want to meet crazy Abby.'

'Here.' I gave Aoife a ten-pence piece from that shrinking float of small change in my right-hand pocket.

'But Eeef, Gran's known that Mary's family for years.' Lou tipped his head back.

'Just in case Lily's started crying. She might not be able to get her down. She can be hard to get down. You don't think she'll bring a boyfriend round, do you?'

'That Mary? She's fourteen.'

'That means nothing,' Aoife said bawdily and, to our surprise, with a tinge of self-knowledge.

He looked up to the Kensington night sky.

I thought there might be another argument but Aoife went into the illuminated phone box. I watched her thin, naked shoulder blades ruminating mechanically as she dialled.

Lou immediately nudged me and blocked the phone-box view, passing the banged-up silver hip flask. 'Get your tonsils afloat.'

I took it, un-nibbed the flip top and screwed it open. I tipped back my head and took a burning draw of brandy.

'Some conversation juice splashing in our vitals, boyo. That's what we need. I swear we should get that fucking phone taken out the house. She's on it to her mum and her sister and nutso Abby all afternoon.'

'While we are in the pub.' I tried to use a gentle tone.

'Yeah but really. Even when she's meeting Abby an hour later, they talk for half an hour on the phone. I'd get rid of it but soon the offers for our book will be flowing in.' He nudged me.

'If we get out the pub and write something.' I passed the hip flask back.

Aoife came from the phone box towards us. The word from high in the Acton sky was that Lily was asleep and the babysitting girl had complained about the dimensions of the television. 'Don't you have another television? A bigger one?' she had asked. Aoife kept repeating that phrase, giggling to herself as we stepped onward along the pavement.

It took us a long time to get in backstage at the Commonwealth Institute. Everyone was in a state of self-important panic.

'You'd think a nuclear test was about to take place, not a fucking fashion show,' Lou said in front of a hysterical group, mainly women – all liggers. Because he was good-looking and they didn't know who he was, the group snapped into silence after he said this.

We only attained backstage when Abingdon Barbour herself came to the purple curtains to rescue us, stuck her head through, showed the security guy her pass and said, 'Yeah. They're with me, aren't they, you silly sausage,' and she play-smacked the huge bouncer on his shoulder. The unsmiling bouncer smiled at her. Despite the posh name, Abby had the same gorgeous accent as Aoife.

On the other side of the curtain she said, 'So you're Douglas. Aoife's told me all about you.'

Lou added, 'Yes. And we have to pay for it on the phone bill.'

Aoife gave him a bad glare.

'Now let me look at you.' Abby put her hands on my shoulders and sure enough, she looked at me.

'You know I'm not auditioning for anything?'

'Yes you are, cheeky. You're auditioning for *me*.'

I wanted to tell her she shouldn't judge the whole universe by appearance, but when she said, 'You have lovely eyes,' I just kept quiet.

'A Scottish man,' she nodded, zoologically. I tried not to, but immediately coloured as she kept on staring.

'What is it? What is it, silly sausage?'

I became even more red.

'Look at him, he's all embarrassed.'

I immediately hated her. 'Watch out now or I might start hating you.'

I liked her reaction. She turned and over her bare shoulder said, 'Nobody hates Abby.'

Of course, Abingdon was wearily beautiful as well, but her face and eyes were bigger and she was more striding and less delicate than Aoife. It was true they seemed exactly the same size and could share all those clothes, but Abby was peppered about with a constant drama. Her hair up in huge curlers, under her arms a tightened and vast towel which went down to the back of her

54

knees. She led us across the factory floor, hopping and sliding her feet over the tiles in a big, ugly pair of thick blue socks. She said hello to everyone.

'How is Lily? Still adorable?' she suddenly asked as if she'd just recalled the child's existence.

'She's fine; she can hold the spoon a little,' said Aoife.

Abby screamed, her way of acknowledging joy. 'That's a relief.'

All the time we moved through commotions of clothes racks and long tables with garments outspread. Pale-faced, red-lipsticked girls in black sack dresses and gelled hair had their teeth full of common pins. Young gay guys with shaved heads ran crossways in a crouching stance, wearing brothel-creeper shoes. I kept covering my mouth in mock yawns to feign familiar lack of interest.

People looked at us for a moment, probably to discern if we were at all of importance, then – our status being too vague – they quickly looked away.

I had been daft enough to expect a changing room, like in that film *The Dresser* with Albert Finney; bulbs all round a mirror. However, the four of us suddenly squeezed into a fabric-walled area the size of a changing cubicle in Marks and Spencer. The cloth was supported by aluminium tubes; it was like my camp bed gone all vertical. Abby's make-up and accoutrements were on the floor, along with six or seven pairs of high-heel shoes. It was a challenge not to step on anything.

'You've got little changing rooms.' Aoife sounded glum.

'Not when the show starts. Then you stand in the open in your scanties.' Abby looked directly in Lou's face and said, seriously and slightly reprimanding, 'So I hear your stitches tore. Again. Llewellyn?'

'Yeah but they had the technology to rebuild me.'

'You're crazy.'

'Got any markers on you? To show Douglas?'

As Aoife said this, Abby dropped her towel. Apart from small knickers she was – of course – completely naked. Her breasts were small but somehow larger than I'd suspected and each nipple was fixed down severely with surgical tape.

'You've dropped your glove and it's bad luck if a man doesn't pick it up,' Lou said indifferently.

'I'm not bending over,' I said.

Abby screamed with joy.

I didn't know what to do with my eyes but Abby brazenly shoved her index fingers up, pointing to both nipples so I was required to gaze at them.

'You tape down cause we tend not to bother with bras and it's so blimmin cold round back here. If you go out in a thin dress they're like – bazooom. Right out and you've taken the hem up an inch at the front already.'

'Right.' I nodded. Both Lou and Aoife seemed uninterested by Abby's nudity. They all seemed unusually casual about physical openness. To reinforce the point, I suddenly observed Abby frown at Aoife's chest in the gold silk dress, then Abby reached out and took each of Aoife's breasts in the palms of her hands, feeling at them as if testing fruit. 'Girl. I hope you haven't been breastfeeding, have you? Even if you do it once.'

Aoife shook her head. 'Not once. I feel so guilty.'

Lou groaned. 'We're not having all this again.'

Now Aoife put her own finger out and pressed a very thin and faint line drawn on Abby's neck. 'See? Each model has a set amount of garments that go on in a certain tagged order. Except for the model that goes out first, who's well known and gets a fitting, but for the rest of us they have to make adjustments to the clothes so's the helpers make marking lines on your body to show where to tape some dresses. This is for her first dress. It's all very fast and manic during a show, especially London Fashion Week. Sometimes if you go from small dresses to bigger ones they'll leave all their marking lines and not wipe them off. You look a bit like a tiger by the end.'

Lou calmly turned to me, away from Abby's nakedness. 'When I had my operation, before they put me under, I saw the pen marks for the incision up my chest and the last thing I remember was thinking of Aoife's body with these same marks upon it. That was the last thought I had, wasn't it, love? Then the bugger gassed us.' He turned to Aoife. 'Your flesh with this daft calligraphy. A nice last thought.'

Aoife let her head fall against Lou's arm and she embraced his biceps. 'That's nice you thought that, but you're safe now.'

'Poor Llewellyn. Fighting fit now.' Abby whooped.

I blinked and said, 'Degas used to accidentally scratch his models.'

All three of their faces turned to me.

'He scratched their naked bodies with his compass needle, measuring their dimensions for his sketches. Apparently one stood bleeding for hours and he didn't care.'

Abby frowned. 'Not some kind of feminist, are you?'

I smiled at her. 'Time will tell.'

Lou laughed.

There was a small stool and Abby suddenly sat down and began to pull off one sock. She had beautifully painted toenails; we all had to shuffle so her bare, bony, extended legs could stick out through and among us. Then she put her chin in the palm of her hand.

Aoife said, with a sort of nostalgia, 'It's worth seeing backstage. It's more interesting than out front, but the backstage manager won't allow us in, will she?'

'Not for a big show like this. And with poor little you not working in it, darling. Shame for these poor boys. Lots of titties, bare bottoms and long willies round the back here.'

Lou drawled, 'That's all right, Abby. I don't want to see your willy again. Douglas and I are going outside to recite poetry to each other.'

'Oh now,' Abby chuckled.

All of this time, Abby had been making occasional sour faces and curling her top lip. Another model was in the adjacent cubicle and often a hip bone or an elbow shape would bash out its dimensions through the hanging fabric; the other girl's long toes with similarly painted nails would suddenly be visible, thrust in under the space at the base of the dividing fabric.

Abby sighed. 'Give us a fag, Llewellyn.' As Lou fished in his overcoat and pulled out his cigarettes, Abby pointed into the air and said, 'But out front isn't dull, Eeef. Haven't you seen it out there tonight? They're all here. Her that's with thingwey and everyone.'

'Who?'

'Her that's with thingwey. I can't remember the names. The guy in the band. And Chrissie Hynde's always there. She's cool.'

'Any booze?' Lou snapped.

'They don't want us to fall off the walk, Llewellyn. They only let us have champagne afterwards. If it goes well.'

He lit her cigarette, looking down on her. The voice of the girl next door immediately went, 'It's no smoking.'

'Fuck off.'

'Abby?'

'Yes, Llewellyn.'

'Can you get some of your clothes out of our bedroom?'

'I will as soon as I hire a car one day, sausage. I'm so busy.'

'I thought this was the first work you'd had in ages?'

She had on wild false lashes and they trembled upwards angrily. I'd heard that when Abby had no modelling work, she did hours painting decorative candles in some workshop.

'Abby?'

'Yes? What?'

'Since you're leaving all your stuff at our place, can Douglas do supplementary benefit and the housing giro from your flat?'

She pretended not to react but I saw her eyes, which were then looking down and studying her toes, wobble slightly. 'Oh, Llewellyn. Aoife. What if I get a real boyfriend and he wants to come and move in with me?'

Lou said, 'Leave it out. If you get a boyfriend you're trading up. He won't be on the dole.'

'Don't be so cheeky, you sausage.'

I tried not to let myself grit my teeth. All this charity on my behalf.

'As long as there's no trouble from those bloody people at the dole,' she shrugged unwillingly.

'Thanks.'

Abby looked at me and said, 'We did this before for six months with Toninho.' Then she looked at Aoife. 'But Toninho really was living at mine sometimes and he really was gay.'

I looked around, puzzled.

Lou said, 'I'll explain.'

'Right, my silly sausages. Have to start getting out my knickers now.'

'Yeah. You go hawk your mutton, darling,' Lou stated.

We moved from the backstage area into the auditorium to sample how much more alienating it could get. Celebrities of some kind were being ushered or pushing in to the plastic seats – the same type of seat as for our school assemblies – alongside the catwalk. At the top of the catwalk was an area like a chancel with milling authorities dressed in dark polo necks.

Lou surveyed the celebrity quotient and snorted.

I said, 'They look like they're piling into a lifeboat off the *Titanic*.'

'Jumpy tonight. They smell revolution,' he replied, quite seriously.

Aoife pointed to the chancel and called out over the loud electronic music, 'That's Martin. He videos it all. I'm going to see Martin at the mix desk and I'll stand up there.'

'Okay, love. We'll just pop out for a moment.'

'Don't miss Abby.'

'We won't.'

I watched Aoife cross that crowded floor, her dress tapping the back of her thighs well above the knee; she was beautiful and now, among all these human swells, she appeared to me not diminished but returned to the habitat where she belonged.

Lou guided me out of the auditorium and into the corridor with a finger on my shoulder. 'That isn't culture, mate. We've already seen the undraped female form in the shape of Abby,' he pointed out. 'Why would we return to see her wearing ridiculous clothes?'

'That's a very good point,' I agreed.

The corridor was not where the beautiful people wanted to be seen. That hive was navigating itself to the catwalk side, so the corridors were blissfully deserted for us. Lou and I leaned against a wall display, drinking from the hip flask. He lit us cigarettes and we flicked the ash onto the floor.

'Did you observe her bush through her knickers?'

'I tried not to stare.'

'She's trimmed it. As I'd predicted. It's usually much richer. She told me she never trims it unless she wants a man or gets a fashion show. I keep a close eye on it. As I suppose some keep an eye on a neighbour's rose or fruit tree. I keep tabs on the hairiness of Abby's fanny.'

'You three are not having some complex ménage, are you?'

He turned sharply on me. 'Of course not. You don't need to. Abingdon is so open it's like you've already slept with her. I find her really refreshing.'

'She's not shy.'

'She needs a nappy on more than Lily. She's not content unless you get an eyeful. Natural exhibitionist. An existential terror of not receiving attention but she doesn't sleep around. She still goes to Mass. She's terribly choosy. Not much excitement there, but imagine screwing your courage to her sticky place?'

'A mighty prospect.'

He nodded profoundly. 'Meditate on that.'

'I probably will. Look, as my literary agent and sole representative in all territories, could you explain this signing-on-the-dole stuff?'

'Have you never signed on?'

'Never.'

'The way of all flesh. You'll need to get used to signing on, boyo, cause we'll be doing it every time we get writer's block. You'll get the supplementary benefit cause you're unemployed but you can't claim housing benefit at Conrad Flats, cause we're already getting all the rent paid by the council and it would be subletting. Abby has a nice little one-bedroom in North Ealing. You'll use that as your address and we're going to pretend you're sleeping in the front room with her as a flatmate and then you can claim eighty a month; you need to punt, say, fifteen to Abby for the hassle as administration fees, cause your giros will go to her house and you'll need to call round to collect them or she'll have to stick them in the post.'

'What's this gay business?'

'Abby's working, not claiming. When you claim housing benefit, the Social will visit you in her flat to do an interview and inspection. In the spirit of Stalin. If they think you and Abby are a cohabiting boyfriend and girlfriend – rather than just sharing tenants – they won't pay you a penny housing benefit cause she's earning. The nuclear family rules at the DHSS if money's coming in.'

'Very enlightened.'

'When they visit, they'll actually try and suss if you really are sleeping on the front-room sofa or if you're bonking Abby. So don't get caught with your arse – or Abby's – in the air, *flagrante delicto*. They'll check if you've separate instant coffee and cornflakes. I've even heard them ask for separate supermarket receipts. The easiest way to convince them is pretend you're gay. Few *Gay Times* lying round, the right haircut and the girls will get your clothes right.'

'This sounds like potential disaster and calamity, or at the very least personal humiliation.'

He looked thoughtful and changed tack. 'I saw you dropping your coppers in Scargill's bucket.'

'You do support them?'

'Scargill's right. Ten years, there'll be no mining left in Britain. The strike's bigger than fucking coal. This is the free market and MI5 versus human beings, and the market will win, mark my words. They're starving them out.' He lit another cigarette quite aggressively. 'Way I see it, I'm working class. Thatcher has fraudulently refused to pay striking NUM members and it's you and I's duty to fraudulently claim some back and remit it. Not to Arthur Scargill but directly to Arthur Guinness and Company, Dublin. Right?'

'Well said. The Honourable Member for Acton in the Sky.'

Now we could hear the rising noise from the auditorium. I said, 'I tell you this: We're the only bastards discussing the miner's strike at this show. It's *Vogue* meets Caligula in there.'

We ambled back and slid in the door, affecting nonchalance. The lighting had been reconfigured. Behind the dramatically lit catwalk a huge projected backdrop in sharp light read *Death Ship*.

'They've ripped off fucking Traven's novel,' I shouted.

'It's an abomination.' Lou shook his head.

We both stood as if at a funeral. All the model boys looked like extras in Fassbinder's *Querelle*. A skinny Artful Dodger in lime trousers and a yellow vest of leather had electric torches strapped to his skull – facing in different directions; as he crouched through a farting scoosh of blue dry ice, the beams of torchlight went out like huge chopsticks from his hair.

'I don't believe it! The shameful cunts are even ripping Scargill off. Death to fashion. Up the miners!' Lou yelled.

The music was overbearing but one or two people at the back of the crushed crowd turned to look at us.

Now came a bunch of girls done out as Amazons, tits showing through diaphanous blouses, moving slowly ahead; any one of them could have been Abby. Stepping in a group, they suddenly burst free and began to patrol the edges of the catwalk in a laughably threatening manner. People whooped extravagantly, their own sense of vast self-regard confirmed by the wallowing on stage. Lou and I looked at each other, turned our backs and stepped out.

At least there was free booze at the post-show party. Lou and I stood, steadily downing it, ignoring everyone else. Abby did a lot of screaming and said 'You silly sausage' to many people, then she went on to some party which we were excluded from. We hung around a bit too long and Aoife had to phone the babysitter's parents from another call box to apologise.

Despite being so late for the babysitter, we couldn't afford a taxi. We walked up to Notting Hill – Aoife in her high heels – and we waited on the night bus. I was cold and Aoife had the macintosh laid over her shoulders. Lou playfully dropped the trilby hat on my head; he stood there in his shirt, smoking and laughing at me.

The night bus had an empty beer can rolling around on the floor upstairs. Then it was a long walk from Acton High Street down towards Conrad Flats with Aoife in heels, so I gave her a long piggy back while Lou, who was excused for medical reasons, thrashed at her ass with the hat. She felt very light at first on my back – but not for long – and when I put her down I had to lean over and breathe whilst she laughed and laughed.

Slowly we climbed the stairs of the Conrad Flats, Aoife's heels echoing clearly up ahead. We heard voices above but they ceased a long time before we reached them on the third floor. On the landing stage some teenage kids were talking in the open doorway of a flat, even though it was three in the morning.

'All right?' said one of the kids, in that London manner which dares you to contradict. He was a guy with a vague look that I suddenly recognised as a bad squint.

'Hello,' said Lou, who knew them.

I always thought voices sounded strange on those landing levels of Conrad Flats. The elevated outside air, sometimes with birds hanging, right there, drifting in the thermals – all that mass of genuine sky existing up so close seemed to mute the human voice. Exchanging words on these windy landings had the similar temporary, rushed feel to conducting a breathless conversation on a mountain.

All three teenage lads eyed Aoife in high heels. My grim face must have shown that I could feel them storing the image. In a jealous way, I was childishly glad she still had on Lou's coat, mostly covering herself. She nodded at them.

'Lo, Mrs Smith,' the one stood at the doorway in his socks called.

'Hello,' Aoife replied.

Lou let Aoife go on up the stairs first, then he followed. I looked back over at the youths. They were watching me, but expressionless. I groundlessly believed they didn't approve of me. All the same, I nodded at them. I had put my foot on the step when one of them called something to me which I didn't hear. I stopped and looked back. I put on the Scottish accent a bit defensively: 'What was that, pal?'

'Hear about Thatcher, then?'

'Thatcher?'

'They blew her up.'

Lou had stopped on the stairs above and was looking back down.

I called across, 'What?'

'Thatcher was in some hotel down Brighton and my old man says it's Irish IRA have gone and blown her up, but she's still alive.'

'Fuck,' I said out loud.

Lou stepped back down, passing Aoife. 'When?'

'Just a bit back. It's all on the radio and on telly now. Brilliant, eh?'

'I'm so pleased you're taking an interest in contemporary politics,' Lou told him.

The kid smiled maliciously.

Lou strode into the flat and shouted, 'Sorry we're so late, Mary. We phoned your dad.'

'Shush. You'll wake her,' Aoife said.

The younger girl-voice stated, 'Dad's mad at you, Mr Smith. Lily's sleeping.'

The television wasn't even switched on. Young Mary was at the living-room table looking through – or doubtless pretending to have been looking through – Aoife and Abby's archive of *Vogue* back issues. Some were in French and Italian and I'd caught Lou reading them once or twice before.

Lou loomed above the portable television set and switched it on. He and I stood looking at a newsreader talking, with an image of the Grand Hotel in Brighton behind him.

'Christ.'

'She's alive though?' asked Aoife, quietly kicking off her shoes.

I nodded and then strode out of the room and down the hall but glancing back at the television. Aoife was bustling up behind me. For an insane second I thought she was going to kiss me.

She whispered, 'Will you check Lily?'

I nodded. 'I was just going to.'

'Ta. I'm bursting,' and she went into the bathroom and shut the door.

I turned the other way, into their bedroom. It was quite cold in there and I immediately saw Lily's eyes were open and she'd been listening to her mum's voice. The baby wasn't sleeping at all and she hadn't been for some time – I could tell by the alert face and the clarity of her eyes. I turned round and looked back. The bathroom door had an opaque patterned glass window which was usually covered by towels hung on hooks inside the door, but the towels had fallen because Aoife had shut the door so quickly. I could see the seated shape of her directly ahead on the toilet seat, could roughly distinguish the material of her dress pulled up and the whiteness of her bare legs angled down at the knees. I turned away. I heard Lou's voice. He was talking on the phone to the babysitter's guardians. I slid my hand in behind Lily and lifted her up easily. She made a little gurgle of exhilaration.

'Yes. Beautiful lady,' I whispered. 'Both of you.' I slipped my hands round Lily's little Babygro until they were under her fat, short arms, then I lifted her higher, turning her, let her bum move in towards my nose and I took a real hard sniff and screwed up my face. I heard Lou coming down the corridor. I twisted my whole self to Lou and passed Lily to him as he came in. I was shaking my head. I whispered, 'She needs changed. Wonder how long?'

Lou shook his head and made a face at me which criticised the babysitter. He held Lily near to the ceiling, which always made me cringe as the Artex was spiky. 'My little poupee,' he said, looking up at her.

The toilet flush went. As usual, Aoife had peed in some utterly silent way. Now I could hear the sink tap running.

He said, 'They've blew up the whole fucking hotel. She's alive but there could be dead.'

'Wonder how the bomb got in past security?'

'Will you take Mary down and wait with her? Her dad's coming now to get her in the car. Take the smelly nappies down too, will you? Where are we going to buy champagne at this time of night?'

I put on one of Lou's hanging macs; it had the rusty bloodstains on its inside lining. I went down the stairs with that young girl.

'Don't you have a coat?' I asked.

'Nah, I get lifts. We've got two cars. Don't you have a car neither as well as no decent telly?'

'No I don't. You should put that in your pocket before it blows away.' She was holding the ten-pound note payment between her fingers. I thought that was an excessive amount and I didn't want those boys to see it, but the door was closed on the landing beneath and they were gone.

'You speak weird. Mr Smith will give me another if I lose this.' She looked up at me, testing. Little brute. Cone-like tits.

'No he won't.'

68

'My dad's going ga-ga. I might get off school now. It's after four in the morning. It's brill.'

'I'm sorry we're so late.'

'You're drunk.'

I said nothing.

'Is Mrs Thatcher dead, then?'

'No. But her hotel was blown up by a bomb and some people might be.'

'She was a right snotty cow.'

'She's still alive.'

'It could've been them miners of the coal got her.' She smiled with glee at the conspiracy.

'You shouldn't wish physical harm on anyone, Mary. Even a bitch like her. Even though *they* are the ones who deal in violence.'

She laughed loudly, enjoying the volume, and I cringed as the sound rang down the stairs.

'Would we get a day off school cause Mrs Maggie Thatcher was dead?'

'She's not dead. I'm sure you won't get a day off either way.'

'Mrs Smith's right nice, isn't she?'

'Yes.'

'Like she looks real dead lovely.'

'Yes.'

'Let's wait here, not on the street or that.'

We were on the first-floor landing and she stood by the lattice of concrete bars looking out, down onto the street-lamp poles and the road. She put her hands up and gripped the concrete as if she were trapped in a prison. Maybe she was imagining that? I was uneasy about standing there beside her. Probably in case another adult materialised – perhaps from one of the apartment doorways – and found me loitering with a young girl. Both of us were very still in the shadows there, glaring down. The noise of a train could be heard going very slowly but there was no flash.

'Why do you live with Mr and Mrs Smith? Do you sleep on that tiny toy bed thing?'

'That it's any of your business, Mary. I do. Lou and I are working on things.'

'What things?'

'Never you mind. To do with books.'

'Books. Cause he's been in the hospital? My mum said he was dead ill.'

'Yeah. He was. But he's better now.'

'Have you got a girlfriend?'

'No.'

'Why? Are you too scared to ask one out?'

I just gave her a look.

'I would tell you if I had a boyfriend.'

I wasn't falling into any traps. I could hear her saying to her dad: That strange Scotchman guy asked me if I had a boyfriend, etc., etc.

'Lily's nappy needed changed.' I hoisted the carrier bag full of smelly nappies.

'I changed her.'

'Yes. Hours ago.'

'How do you know she needed changing? She's not your baby.'

'Don't you be cheeky, now, or you won't make ten pound again.'

She looked up at me. She had shadows on her face, cast by the street lights outside coming into the landing. Silently, a yellowish car with illuminated headlights drew up Bollo Lane and to a halt.

'Is that your dad?'

'See ya.' She dashed down the last flight. I went after her but by the time I was walking up the path, past the sheds, and had tossed the carrier bag of nappies into one of the big swing bins, the girl was closing the car passenger door. I stopped still and raised a hand in cautious greeting. I was frowning into the car to try to see who was in it. After all, it could be anybody. Jack the Ripper's great-great-great-grandson. I would be blamed.

The driver's door opened and a man stood up, one hand resting on the top of the door as he looked across the roof. 'Bit late, Lou. Oh. You're not Lou. Who are you?' I heard Mary's voice say something about me within the vehicle, using her dismissive tone.

I held both my hands up, as if surrendering to a man with a firearm. 'Douglas. Friend of Lou's. I was just seeing your daughter down safely.'

'She isn't my daughter, mate; I'm her brother.'

'Oh, sorry.'

'Bit late, though.' He shrugged, looking up into the sky. As if all was in some higher power's control and already written in the lavender-tinged night. 'She's got school.'

I shrugged. 'I'm really sorry. The night bus took bloody ages to come.'

He looked at me suspiciously then lowered himself into the car.

I walked slowly back up the stairs so I wasn't out of breath when I got there. In the living room I said, 'Ten quid. That was a bit generous.'

Lily was on the table with her legs in the air as Lou changed her.

'That was the ten you gave us for food.'

'I'll do babysitting from now on then,' I said.

71

He pointed down at Lily. She was turning her round head from side to side and then holding it still, as if trying to listen for the same elusive night spirit in the sky which the car driver down on the street had sought. Now the infant was looking at me. 'See if she calls you Daddy before me, you bloody Protestant. Sit down, open us a Guinness. We're in for a long night in front of the telly.' He smiled.

'Eeef gone to bed?'

'Now the government's blown up she'll sleep soundly.'

'It's not that funny. Could be folk dead? Could even be just hotel workers dead, Lou.'

He smiled. 'Don't be such a fucking Mennonite. Look. Three cans of Guinness left and a little of that vodka you bought on the night you appeared here, beneath your own star of Bethlehem.' He knocked over the talcum-powder drum, made a gurgling noise down at Lily, buttoned her Babygro then lifted her high in the air and trotted, speeding off down the corridor, holding her up. 'Mummy, Mummy, Mummy. Daddy, Daddy, Daddy. Say it, like Chomsky says you should.'

I heard their low voices along in their bedroom, then Lou returned without his daughter, ran up to the black windows and looked over the city with his arms held out in demand. 'Where are the GLC fireworks? Come on!'

We both stood, never sitting, holding our cans of Guinness, looking down on the small telly like two old men in a village high street studying a new model of some low, unfathomable sports car.

The hotel with its prolapsed centre was on the screen, tender, powder-blue light from flashing police cars casting up onto the whitewashed walls.

Lou shook his head and bared his teeth. 'Now we're going to get the plucky survivor theme for a year. Napoleon was right – a nation of shopkeepers and we've got one running the bleeding country. Big sign up: Sorry No Credit Here, her stood behind the scales.' He changed his voice: 'Get out my shop, you malingerer. And go eat with the miners.'

I nodded. 'Eat from the plate that is largely empty.'

'Telling you, mate, it's the sale of the century; they'll bring us to our knees one day, this lot, selling off everything we built up since the war, just so the management class can scoop the top and hide in the shires behind lawns and wisteria. Always money for wars but not for education or welfare, so off to Las Malvinas to boost her popularity and get some Union Jacks waving. Well this a joyous turn of the tables on them for once.' Lou leaned toward me. 'Gotcha.'

6

We were in The Five *or* Six Bells – as we were every day – at our favourite table beneath the windows, pints of Guinness with their yellowish discs afloat, cigarette smoke like a baldachin in the sunbeams above us. I felt immense nostalgia for the pub already, with its early afternoon light guiltily pouring in the windows.

'That's Llewellyn Smith from up by the railway. Myrtle's grandkid. Old man was the Taffy. The sidekick's a Jock.' I heard a pensioner insist on all this to his comrade. These old fellows were mostly pretty deaf, so Lou and I overheard everything: their fluctuating but always poor opinions of us as they sat along the walls in their twos, looking ahead, drinks before them, firing out proclamations. Larger groupings than two seemed to confuse and disgruntle them. They virtually waved away any third man who approached. Yet it was more tranquil than any downmarket city pub of my homeland – certain Scottish pubs, with their windowless, bunker architectures and the imprecation of edgy calamity to the drinking.

Sometimes in The Bells, during my brief enough tenure there, multi-conversations would cease as if they were a stilled roulette ball. A random quietness would suddenly materialise in the centre of that great pub space. One of the old fellows would hulloo across to Lou then speak a few words and we would call back ourselves across the distance: a few words only and no more. Our day's course set at our tables, we were all like passing boaters on some inland waterway, calling through a slight mist from one vessel to another.

Without self-consciousness, Lou was deeply scrutinising an old copy of the *TLS* he'd brought over from Conrad Flats. He looked belligerent. 'The book world is a big digestive system. The review pages are the anus at the bottom of the alimentary canal and the critics, Cunningham, are the haemorrhoids upon that anus.' The publication was violently slapped upon the seat. '*TLS* never reviewed *Ulysses*. You know that? What are these critics and book reviewers? Just the town councillors of literature.'

Before we got much drunker, and with the wedding coming up, Lou took me round for the first time to meet his old gran. His dad's mother. I'd only heard mild hints of it before but now he stated it flat: 'Me and the big brother, Rhys, were brought up by our gran. We're orphans.'

'You're very young to be an orphan.'

'Mum died when I was just tiny. I don't remember her – or only vague shiftings on the edge. The old man was Welsh. Ex RAF. Ground crew. Violent. Wandered back up the Valleys and drank himself to death in the early seventies. I hardly remember the guy, though Rhys does. And what I do remember was scary. All probably explains the way I've turned out.'

Mrs Smith lived in the exact image of the London house I would have imagined Lou to have grown up in. Red brick, two up two down, no bow windows, the North London British Rail line down the embankment at the back. It seemed generously proportioned inside after our flat. Filling the kettle in the kitchen, Lou nodded to the hump of the Anderson shelter and the disused toilets at the bottom of the small back garden. He claimed there was an original Victorian Crapper upstairs as well.

Old Mrs Smith had come slowly to the kitchen door to keep a close eye on us. 'Been at The Bells, then? Well, boys, least you come before my mid-afternoons.'

You could hear the Welsh mixed with the cockney in her accent.

I soon found out that time spent with Mrs Smith was a fairly benign form of goalkeeping. There were quiet patches, then the action came rushing toward you and you had to deal with what was fired. Initially, she didn't really pay my appearance there much attention, but when I sat down in the small front parlour she seemed to register my presence more profoundly and put a suspicious parrot's eye upon me. She glanced once up at the ticking old carriage clock on the mantel. 'Time for my mid-afternoons shortly.'

'Douglas is lodging with us. Helps out, he does.'

'Does he?' she said, her voice heavy with perceptive doubt.

'I try to.'

'Are you one of Aoife's fashion friends?'

This was an accusation.

'I met Llewellyn at the hospital.'

'Are you poorly too? You don't look well. Too skinny.'

'No.' I thought I'd better make up a reason for me being in such a place. 'I was bitten by a dog.'

'Postman, are you?'

'No, Mrs Smith. More like I wait for the postman.'

She made a small movement. 'You'll have to excuse it, my greens

76

are repeating on me. Have you had your elevenses? Lou, make a cup of tea for the poor man.'

'I have, Gran. He's drinking it there.'

'I hope you didn't go give him the good china.'

'Gran! No I didn't.'

She chumped her mouth so her grey moustache shot up and down. 'Sorry we don't have any afternoon dainties. We used to like an afternoon dainty, didn't we, Lou?'

'Not good for your old ticker, Gran.'

'Flo's been round.'

'Good.' Lou turned to me as if excluding his grandmother. 'That's the neighbour. Brilliant neighbour. Good neighbours round here, mostly.'

'Not these new ones coming in. How's little Lady Lily?'

'Touch of the cold, Gran.'

'Oh dear.'

'Gran. Lil'll be staying with you and Flo on the wedding day, in the evening. All right? Then we'll be back to pick her up.'

'That's nice. Wish you'd do it in the church though, Lou. I so wish you'd do it in the church. Your father would have too. You think he wasn't for the church but you didn't see him pray every night. It's not too late.'

'Leave it out, Gran.'

'Is Aoife McCrissican still so thin as well?' She glared at me as if I were responsible.

'Bloody hell. You only saw her last week. Give her a chance.'

She turned slowly and looked up at the clock. 'Time for my mid-afternoons shortly. That's what that young girl's lacking. A good dose of the mid-afternoons.'

Lou and I gave each other an eyeful of legerdemain.

'Yes,' he replied and coughed. He watched his gran and me, rather like a father watching his child's first wobbles upon a bicycle, curious how it will negotiate the challenges.

Eventually she turned to me. 'I don't like the Scotch.'

'Gran! Douglas is a scholar. He loves books, like me. He's a very clever fellow. And a good man.'

'Are you Catholic?'

'I'm afraid not.'

She nodded slowly, taking in the full calamity of this. But then she changed direction. 'Always had his face in a book, did Lou. His father only read the sports news. Till the telly came.'

I sneaked an eye at Lou. 'You know you're quite right, Mrs Smith.' I was holding my china tea cup in my saucer since there was nowhere to place it. 'We're an awful lot, the Scots. We're up there in our caves – most of them licensed – sheltering from the rain and you're all down here in the sun of Merrie England, the spirit of endless sunken lanes, rolling fields, Shakespeare and Dickens, you beat Napoleon and Hitler—'

She turned to Lou. 'What's he on about, Lou?'

Lou laughed.

She said, 'You sound like little Harold Wilson, though you look more like Ted Heath.'

I said out loud, 'You might have got me in one there, Mrs Smith.'

Lou laughed again and even the old bird herself let her straight front dentures slide into view.

'I'll say this. You're very polite for a Protestant.'

Lou laughed even louder.

She turned back on him quick in case he thought he was getting off easy. 'I'll talk to Father Petrie again about getting married in chapel. You'll soon be changing your mind about all this, when you want Lily in the RC School. The father said so himself. Oh yes. The RC School.'

'Did he now?'

On the way out, Mrs Smith suddenly turned her head. 'Call me Myrtle and be done with it, son.' Then she said, 'Time for my mid-afternoons,' and the front door was closed upon us both.

Lou and I faced up to domestic requirements and we visited the supermarket on the journey home. Toilet paper and nappies. The butcher called out to us from behind his glass counter about a special offer on lean mince.

Lou replied, 'No thank you. Concerning our cuisine, we have long ago concluded that porridge and pasta are the staple dishes best suited to our economic and social aspirations.'

There was no denying it. Just before Lou's giro was cashed the week before, for three long days, we'd already been reduced to the Scottish Emergency Plan. A little diced pasta and sauce for Lily but for we adults: watery porridge with honey for breakfast, plain watery porridge for luncheon and then – something to live for – an evening dinner of porridge with a dash of milk, seasoned with dried herbs. The primordial soup, as Lou called it. A sucked orange each for dessert. Then we ran out of milk on the last day and though we fished for coinage deep among the cushions of the bloodied sofa, we couldn't even afford the smallest carton or manage to nick any of the small containers of UHT from McDonald's or KFC. It was black instant coffee from then. The night before the giro came, Aoife had lifted two spoonfuls of the evening porridge, laid down her spoon for good and said, 'Maybe time to cut down on the pub a bit, boys,' before she abruptly left the table.

When we got back to Conrad Flats, Lily was crying. Maybe it was because Lily rarely cried, but baby wails always unreasonably irritated Lou. There was something chaotic about a child's primal appeal – its lack of language – which affronted him. Generally you could feel Lou tensing up after three minutes of Lily crying. In any room where Lily was not crying, he would step back and forth smoking, looking distracted.

Aoife would often sit with Lily in the living room, lifting her from her buggy where she liked to settle, or letting her fall asleep in her arms. Meanwhile I would try to keep Lou distracted and amused, sitting down the corridor in my room with him – the camp bed stacked up on end and leaned against the wall as was daytime custom.

In my room, Lou had some good old singles, long-playing records and his big brother's rejected hi-fi with its one functioning speaker. We played our favourites. We had an abiding passion for Bobby Goldsboro's song 'Summer (The First Time)' and we would play the seven-inch 45 rpm again and again. We spoke along with the dialogue at the top of Iggy Pop's 'Dum Dum Boys'. We liked Atomic Rooster's 'Nobody Else', grinning, nodding our heads violently to the middle section. Or our favourite of Britten's *Nocturnes*. We mockingly held our palms to our sternums and sang along: *What is more gentle than a wind in summer*, until those astonishing, sublime chords of the string orchestra sliced in.

Between songs, when he had overheard Lily's cries through the broken space in the pane of glass up above my door, Lou kept suddenly shooting his fist to his mouth and nibbling at a knuckle, then turning the hand over and going for a fingernail.

Again I asked him – as if I needed his permission – if we really should wait for replies from the fifteen or twenty publishers we'd already written to, touting our so far non-existent wares. Perhaps we really should finally begin our respective novels?

'All right. Let's build some desks.' Lou nodded and blew smoke. It had begun raining outside, compressing drops in an oily way against the glass of the window, sudden mad rushes of it pushing up from the south, bouts of grey squalls passing across the distant gasometers.

We started organising two dining chairs in my room, carrying them from the living room down the corridor.

'What are you doing?' Aoife asked Lou, but he didn't reply.

'Going to do a bit of typing in my room,' I told her.

She nodded temperately as I cradled off a dining chair before me.

Back in my room he said, 'We'll put you in pride of place at the window where you can be inspired as if you were at the forge of Vulcan. By views of the M4 and Brentford.' He went through to their bedroom. I heard various strong oaths and low thudding, the heavy, multi-repeated impacts as many of Aoife and Abby's knee-high boots tumbled out from the bottom of the bedroom wardrobe.

'Lou. What you doing?' Aoife's voice, muffled and weary, was straining quietly from the living room. I knew Lily must be asleep.

That voice was ignored. Lou returned, invisible behind a very large colour television's cardboard box. I could see a bright woollen scarf emerging, casually swung out over the edge from the inside. The box was forced against both sides of the door frame but wouldn't fit through.

'Jesus. Should you be lifting that with your stitches? Give it here. It won't fit through, Lou. Put it down.'

'I'm all right.' His voice came from behind. 'This is your desk. Won't it fit?'

'Nah. Need to sort of squeeze sideways. I'll do it.'

Lou insisted, 'It's light. It's not heavy, Douglas. It's full of fucking knitwear belonging to a certain pussy-flashing, mutton hawker friend of Aoife's.' I was taken by surprise at the volume and vehemence this was snarled with, and a violent shove which buckled in one side of the cardboard and made me step back.

The box was in, though; then he lumbered towards the window and inverted the container. Unfortunately he didn't turn the box over and down quick enough to trap the contents, so with a slump of gravity the knitwear slid out, forming a colourful heap, elevating the box at an awkward angle above the floor.

Lou stood back a moment, looking at the box canted askew with the guts of jumpers spilling through the bottom. He took another step backwards, then he raised his leg and kicked out aggressively at the box with his heel. His foot skated over the surface and slid along the top of the box – he hopped back upon his other leg, but not before the toe of his shoe had just touched the window. There was an immediate crunch and one single chunk of glass fell inward, flopping onto the top of the box accompanied by a theatrical gust of cold air and a splurt of rain which pattered darkened blots upon the cardboard. Some smaller glass shards tinkled, falling delicately down between the box and the outer wall.

'I don't fucking believe it.' Lou looked out into the pure sky. His fringe snapped aggressively and he blinked. It was cold already. He turned his back on me and walked out.

'What was that, Lou?'

'Broke a fucking window, didn't I.'

'You what?'

'I broke a fucking window!' he screamed.

'Where this time?'

'In his room.'

'Oh, Lou.'

'Don't start. How am I meant to work in this fucking place and her screaming there and you sat judging me all day?'

'I'm not judging. Why say I'm judging you? If you want to go round smashing up the place that's not going to help. Hush. You'll wake her. Get the Hoover out. Oh. I forgot. It's broke.'

'It was a fucking accident,' his voice yelled. 'You judge just by your silence, Eeef. Just when you sit there all quiet, I know what you're thinking. That I can't write a great book. You're like a fuck- ing priest sometimes.'

'I was just looking at the telly a bit. I wasn't even thinking about you.'

Suddenly I heard Lily crying.

'Now you've woke her. All over nothing, as usual.'

'There you go. Judging. I'm warning you.'

'Well don't start chucking whole doors and books about again, like the corridor window and this now. Poor Douglas will freeze tonight. He'll need to sleep in here on the sofa.'

So that explained the broken glass pane above my door. And the missing door. I tiptoed along the corridor to the living-room entrance. It was too windy in my room already. This was the third argument Lou and Aoife had had right in front of me.

I knew I should keep out of the way but at the same time I

felt, as a house guest, I had an obligation to function as arbiter.

Lou dropped his voice into a whine. 'Please, Eeef. Shut her up, can't you, eh?'

'I can't stop her. She's a cold. And now the window's got broke. How would you say it? That's not a positive development of the situation. Is it?'

He turned aside and moved past me as if I didn't exist, so I had to shrink in against the passage wall. But then he turned and went back again into the front room and now he started shouting even louder at her. 'And Gran was at me to get married in the church again. Fuck sake. I just wish you'd make some decisions yourself and take some of the flak off me. You're just sat there. Judging. The passive approach. Everything's so bloody passive with you, Aoife. Always has been. If I hadn't got to you first you'd be a right slut by now.'

Her voice just continued, so you could hear above Lily's crying a winded and less confident complaint: 'I'm not judging. You broke the window. It's not a judgement, Llewellyn.' I could hear she was well misted up now.

'Oh shut up, Lily, for fuck sake, darling, please. Aoife, you're sat there day in day out. It's me has to do all the worrying.'

'I worry too.'

'I'm going out.'

'Where?'

'Where do you think?'

'The Bells.'

'There you go. Judging. I'm going to get Jim Faring who I was at school with.'

'Who's that?'

84

'He's a fucking glazier, isn't he? He'll do me a price. Get him round sharpish so Lily doesn't get the fucking pneumonia next.'

'Why don't you telephone?'

'Aoife. When you need to pee, I'm surprised you don't phone down the corridor to see if the fucking bathroom's free.'

He stepped out again and tore his raincoat off the hooks by the front door, but then I saw him look both ways, stride past me once more and up into their bedroom. He returned holding a Penguin Modern Classic and a sealed pack of Regals, and slipped them in the overcoat pocket. I couldn't help twisting my head to try to see the book title. So he *was* dropping off in The Bells. He looked directly at me and winked, then he stuck his face toward mine and whispered, 'Put something on the window. I'll be back with a glazier. Mind Lily on the glass.' And he went out the front door and slammed it very hard. His other mac fell off the coat hooks. I re-hung it and went through to the front room.

Lily and Aoife were on the sofa, crying together. The baby was laying in Aoife's lap. I smiled. 'Happy families.'

'What happened?' The tight skin of her smooth jaw wrinkled up a moment.

'We were trying to build a desk with a big box and he accident-ally broke the window. Looks like book writing might be off the agenda again. Here.' I leaned and lifted Lily from her. I held the baby vertically, her face looking backwards over my shoulder, rock-ing her a little with my hand supporting the back of her head, my left fingers splayed out on the creamy skull and hair. My right hand was against the crunch and bulk of her nappy.

The volume level of the crying by my ear remained just about the same. No worse, no better, and I'd seen Lily's cheeks puffed red.

But then with the novelty of the view behind me and someone new holding her, abruptly, the babe's crying ceased – seemingly to concentrate and reassess the situation. Her head was beautifully warm in my palm, like something just removed from an oven.

'You're so good with the baby.' Aoife was using the back of her fingers to wipe at her eyes and then she looked carefully at each finger. It was because she had once been used to crying only in make-up and though she didn't wear make-up any more, the habit had stuck.

'Nah. She's going to start again in a minute when she susses I'm not you. Freud or the psychologists wrote something about it. How when the baby realises it is other, and not part of its mum, it has its first big crisis.'

'First of many,' she said.

'Yes. A whole menu to come. Especially for girls.'

'Ah. But you'd make a good father, Douglas.'

I looked down at her. She was wiping her eye and looked off to the side. She'd stopped crying. I continued to stand there. I waited for her to say more but she wiped again at her eyes and whispered, 'What was The Apple saying, then? That's what I call her.'

'Yes.' She seemed to think it was tremendously witty.

'It pisses bloody Llewellyn off to say The Apple. Doesn't it, Lily? Bad Daddy.'

'Wants you to get married in the church. Get Lily christened.'

'Oh God.'

'Exactly.' I jiggled Lily a little. I was looking down on Aoife below me, much as Lou and I had looked down on the little television set that night of the Brighton bombing in October.

'Look how happy she is with you, and you were so scared of her when you first came here.'

This was very true. I now understood why many insecure and self-doubting people love to be parents. The baby's utter dependence upon you and your duty to it impart a certain automatic self-righteousness, a simple, humble sense of worth. You are given purpose to love them.

At first I'd just been terrified of physically harming Lily: dropping her or letting her head snap backwards, or choking her on her bottle. Then – I suppose just by dint of the fact Lou and I, when not in The Bells, were always around the flat rather than out working – I'd patiently learned to sterilise and prepare bottles, lift her and feed her with the plastic spoons. Changing nappies was far less traumatic than I'd been led to believe – cat trays are worse – and I'd put her down to sleep some nights when Lou and Aoife were bunched up together on the sofa. As Aoife supervised, I'd even bathed her. I loved the sound of the cupful as I held her head up and allowed the water to gurgle around her ears and over her tiny crown in a corny baptism. What a look of concentration on her face as the water trickled past her ears and tickled in at the back of her neck. She was listening! I loved the dough-soft feel of Lily's pale skin.

'Do I get to be Uncle Douglas now? Eh, Lily?'

'Course you do. Doesn't he, Lil?' Aoife suddenly stood. She sat folded up in that sofa so long, all day, I forgot each time how tall she was just in socks. She was now beside my face and suddenly pecked me on the cheek and I had to hide a flinch.

Her skin, usually without blemish, now looked devastated just by the crying; creased in welts and blotched beneath her coloured irises. Yet her hair was ruffled so she looked passionate and recondite. As she moved towards the hall door I physically hurt with each step she took away from me.

'It was me who said we shouldn't get married in the church but that was— because.'

'Because what?'

'I was nineteen and pregnant and not married. I'd scoffed at the Church since I was teenaged. Seemed hypocritical to go straight back to ask them to marry me.'

'Well, that's honourable, but if you baptise Lily and at least say you'll bring her up Catholic, they'll let you marry there like a shot.'

'Yes. But I'd need to make confession and go to Mass. That's quite a lot to confess. It's a bit embarrassing. All the things I'd have to say to the father.'

'Oh, I think he'll have heard worse. Even if you have doubts, why not just do it? You can have doubt and still do something without wholly endorsing it. You're still a Catholic. The Church has obligations to you as well.'

'Does it? I'm sure it's a one-way thing. It's a covenant and I doubt about getting Lily involved. Even when you don't really believe, like me and Lou, you still sometimes might believe.'

'Do you believe? That sins are absolved; that the tomb was empty on that day?'

'Every Christmas I do.'

I laughed. 'Not at Easter?'

'Both Christmas and Easter would be a lot of believing.'

I laughed again. 'And Lou? What does he want? For the wedding?'

'Haven't you two talked about it in the pub?'

'Eh? No.'

'I thought you would have done.'

'That's kind of private. Between you and Lou.'

She sighed. 'Sometimes I wish Lou wasn't Catholic. Deep down, Caths're all sort of on the same wander back to themselves.'

'Have you never had a relationship with someone who isn't? Wasn't a Catholic?'

Weirdly, she did that thing she did the night we talked in front of the nude photograph of her in the bedroom. She looked at Lily as if the infant could understand. 'I haven't really had many. Relationships. I did with an actor. Ben Torrance. Benji. When I first came to London.'

Benji. I despised him.

'He's getting quite a lot of great work now but really, he nearly killed me.'

'What? Not drugs?'

'Oh God, no. I've never ever tried to take any drugs. Just he was full of beans and up all night at late hours and at parties. Talking. You know?' She lowered her voice and spoke with a ghastly astonishment. 'Goodness me. He ate oysters one after the other. I only lasted two weeks as his girlfriend. He was taken aback. I knew it was finished and he was all upset. I wanted someone a little less enthusiastic about life. Lou was just the ticket.'

I laughed. Lily coughed once on my shoulder and burst out crying. 'Oh no.'

'Oh dear. Give her. Give her.'

'No. You go wash your face,' I said.

She just smiled and went out the door as I jiggled Lily up and down. Then Aoife's long almond head appeared round the door again and above the volume of Lily she called out, 'Don't tell Lou that.'

'What?'

'About the actor who ate oysters. You don't know how mad jealous Lou can be.'

7

'And is Cunningham abroad?' Lou called from the other side of the closed door.

'Nay. He slumbereth yet,' I responded – as usual – horizontal upon the camp bed.

'Air mail.'

The letter flew in.

In the mornings it was the custom at Conrad Flats for Lou to toss the meagre pieces of my mail up through the smashed glass pane above my closed door. Envelopes would flutter down and land upon me in my camp bed. All I'd ever received were my library card, then book reminders from Ealing Central and once, after I'd sent her one, a postcard of Croick Church in my mum's handwriting: *Is This Your New Address? Is it a High Rise? Seeing if this works before I send anything on? Phone. Christmas? Mum & Dad x.*

Shamefully, I had not given them the Conrad Flats phone number, so I wouldn't be forced to talk to my parents in front of Lou and Aoife.

Lou's voice contained some kind of triumph as it claimed, 'Good news. At last. Victory is assured,' and I heard him plod back up the corridor in his socks, to make our first coffee of the day in the metal cafetière.

I sat up directly and looked at the envelope. It had been torn open. It was addressed jointly to Lou and me. Headed notepaper from a huge London publishing house.

Dear Mr Smith & Mr Cunningham,

Thank you for your very amusing letter of the 6th.

Of course I am always happy to consider new and innovative work from young writers. However, it is not just original fiction we handle in Fulham Road. There is often some journeyman work knocking around which clever youngsters may perhaps be interested in? Why don't you both pop round here one day for a quick interview? Belle my assistant's number is above and we can carve out a time which suits us all.

Tobias (Toby) Hanson

'The portals of the Kingdom are yawning,' I yelled. Then I myself yawned. Next door I heard Aoife turn over in bed, groan and sweep the covers up. Or down?

After the coffee, wearing Lou's raincoat, I marched directly on the British Telecom phone box at the bottom of Bollo Lane. Not one of the old red GPO boxes, but one of the new chrome bastards: adhesive logos plastered on huge sheets of glass. Privatisation was due in December, as we all knew from the vast, wearying, limitlessly funded advertising campaign. The first of the postwar family silver was up for sale. I didn't foresee Lou or Aoife, or many in Bollo Lane, profiting much from this new collectivism.

Inside, the phone box smelled of urine as usual. As it still would when it was privatised, but for the moment that stink of urine still belonged to the British taxpayer. I didn't have any money or means of paying for the call.

'Operator? Excuse me, operator, but this is a disgrace. I have a fully charged phonecard right here and it refuses to give me credit. This is the fourth occasion one of your phonecards has utterly failed on me and I have to speak to my mother in Scotland, urgently.'

'Sorry about that, sir. There have been some teething problems with the phonecard.'

'Teething problems? Teething problems. They have a fifty per cent failure rate. I need to phone my mother and because of British Telecom, I'm unable. Might I remind you that you are still a publicly owned utility providing a public service. Telephone calls. And I'm unable to make one because of your reckless, headlong rush to privatisation.'

'Where are you calling from, sir?'

I gave her the box's phone number.

'Have you tried from another box, sir? It could be a fault with the actual box.'

'Listen clearly, operator. I am not obliged to trek around London testing out your phone boxes. I have purchased a phonecard and entered into a contract with you. I either want connected now or I want information on how to obtain a full and immediate refund on this useless card. Don't tell me just to return to the shop where I bought it. I can't even recall where I bought it. Can I speak to your vast superior?'

There was a pause.

'And you're calling to Scotland?'

'I'm trying to. And urgently.'

'Can you give me the number please and on this occasion, sir, we will connect you.'

'Oh. That's really very generous of you. Thank you very much indeed, operator.' I quickly gave her my parents' home number.

'Hiya, Mum. How are you?'

'Howdy, stranger. How are you?'

'Just jim-dandy.'

'Your father's out in the garden already. Will I run and get him?'

'That's okay. Don't bother him. Look, Mum. I'm awful sorry but I'm running that little bit short for next month. You couldn't send me a wee swift cheque. And not tell Dad. Could you? Say for sixty. Or a hundred. Even cash would be better. And my shoes are needing mended in time for Christmas.'

'Shoes. But aren't you coming home for Christmas?'

'I really want to. But there's the huge rail fare and I'd planned on getting down to some extra, extra hard study.'

'And how are things at college?'

'University, Mum. Aye, things are okay. They're working me hard.'

'So how come you aren't staying at your old digs? What's this new place you are in now?'

'It's a lot cheaper, Mum. And better for studying.'

This was met with sceptical silence. 'And you're needing new shoes. Already?'

'Aye, these ones, the front of them got a wee bit squashed. By a London bus. A double decker. I just had my feet too close to the edge of the pavement. You've to watch yourself down here.'

This was met with more sceptical silence. 'You sound a bit all-het-up; are you all right, Dougie?'

'No, no. I've just got a wee bit of a sniffle coming on. Aye. It's coming on really quick. Might need to get something from Boots.'

'I hope you got a good waterproof jacket with that last cheque I sent you?'

'Oh. I got a great one. Yes. A nice sensible one from Marks and Sparks. Or was it C&A's?'

'Oh, that's good. That's very sensible. Yes.'

'Aye. Thanks for that last wee cheque. Look, Mum, I'm sorry, I've been so busy playing catch-up with my studies, but don't you worry.'

This was met with a third sceptical silence, though this time I was sure I could hear the angel voices of a conversation on another line very, very faintly. I looked up at the ceiling of the phone box. The fluorescent lamp was illuminated – in broad daylight. A waste of public money.

'I hope you're not getting carried away with any silly lassies now. You can't afford to be gallivanting around with lassies at a time like this in your life.'

'No. Yes. Well. Wouldn't dream of it. That's the pips just about to be going, Mum.'

'Okay, dear. Thanks for phoning.'

'I love you, Mum. Thanks. Don't sound so weary. Things'll be okay.'

'God bless, Dougie. Take care of yourself down there and work hard at your studies.'

'God bless, Mum. Love to Dad.'

'I'll sort you out for the shoes.'

'That's great, Mum. Thanks. Love you.'

8

In Abby's flat you came in the front door and immediately ascended stairs with banisters and blank walls on either side of you. After her doorbell rang, I went down these stairs alone in my tight, dramatic shirt and drainpipe Levi's.

'Yes.'

He was so young. I had been expecting someone older.

'Housing benefit claim?' He had no briefcase; an active clipboard in his grasp, so he had a car and had driven here. Unless he'd strolled over, taking the air. And from where would such a one be officed?

'Come in.'

Together, with him behind me, we ascended the stairs and he suddenly and cheerily called out, 'This is nice.' He sounded like an optimistic estate agent trying to convince me to rent the place. I turned and smiled nervously at him.

At the top of the stairs he looked down at his clipboard. 'Miss— Abingdon Barbour is here?'

'Barbour. I haven't seen her today but I think she is. I asked her to stay in because I know you have to meet with her and I definitely heard her moving around in her room earlier. She's very busy. Comes and goes a lot. She has the room at the rear and this is mine.'

I gestured to the door of the front room. I turned and looked at him closely for the first time. I'd refused to have my ear pierced but

I'd gone so far as to wear a signet ring on my pinkie. One of Abby's bits of costume jewellery.

I opened the door, walked to the centre of the room and held out my arms. 'In spring it'll be nice with all the trees. Miss Barbour's room is through the back.' I dropped my voice into a hiss. 'I'm not allowed in there. Not sure if you will be, I should say. She's a bit— Well, she's theatrical.'

'Ah.' He nodded quickly.

'And she's a fashion model.'

'Oh.' This appeared to cheer him up. 'Well, I'm afraid it's a real necessity of the inspection that I view the whole of the property.'

'Sure. If I can ask: what is it you're actually checking on? I don't understand.'

'Well, we're just checking that the information you've provided on your application form is all in order. That you're sharing a dual tenancy property at the monthly rent you've stated.' He looked either way around the room. A habitual tic, doubtless picked up from back in the bitchy open-plan office. 'We have to.' He leaned forward confidentially.

I craned toward his neat, small face as if listening for something burrowing in woodwork.

'Sometimes, unemployment being what it is, we get husbands and wives and each are claiming the full rental amount of the same property.'

I frowned and pretended to be puzzled. 'How do you mean?'

'Well. Say the total rent of somewhere is two hundred pounds. The husband comes and claims to be paying two hundred and then the wife comes and claims she's paying two hundred and the government issues four hundred pounds a month. Don't tell anyone but our computer system works on National Insurance numbers, not on home addresses. It's crazy.'

'Oh. That's very deceptive of people.'

'Another problem is that when one partner is working and one isn't, some pretend they aren't even married or living together in a relationship, so one can claim half the rent from us at housing benefit. The government can't subsidise relationships, can it?' He shrugged.

'Oh, I see.' I crammed on the small-town accent as softly as I could. 'That's awfully dishonest, then.'

'Exactly. It's fraud.' He smiled welcomingly.

I said, 'Well, Abingdon and I are definitely not married.'

He chuckled and raised his eyebrows in a cheeky manner. 'Yes. It's a formality, really, Mr Cunningham.'

'Douglas.'

'Douglas. Where is it you're from? That's a Scottish accent, isn't it?'

'A very small wee village in Scotland. So different up there, if you know what I mean? So exciting down here.'

'Yes. It was like that for me.'

'Aren't you from London?'

'Can't you tell by my accent? I'm from Hereford.'

I shrugged, smiling.

He licked his lips and looked around, taking in the elaborately prepared room for the first time. I thought having the Bette Midler album to the front was just too obvious so it was only sticking out behind the Benjamin Britten one. I'd snobbily presumed Lou was overestimating the cultural awareness of the Department of Health and Social Security inspectors. The Christmas lights round the window. Gore Vidal essays with the pink triangle on the cover, the several copies of *Gay News* that Abby had obtained – all scattered in a seemingly random manner by the made-up sofa bed with a colourful silk cover on it.

'Right. So there is just one bedroom?'

'There's two. This is my bedroom.'

'Yes.' He nodded, looking down at his form. 'Can I sit here?'

'Sure.'

He perched himself daintily at the desk. Good old Abby's two or three copies of *Playgirl* were theatrically shelved right there, with the spines facing him. He seemed far more concerned with chalking up the business on his clipboard.

'So you're signing on as available for work in Ealing?'

'Yes.'

'And how long have you been resident here?'

'Twenty-seventh of September.'

'And have you a copy of the lease signed by Miss Barbour?'

'Yes.' I stepped to the desk where the photocopies were and handed them over.

He looked at them and announced in a neutral voice, 'Miss Barbour is free to sublet the property under the conditions of her lease. Okay. Possible to speak with Miss Barbour?'

I stepped into the lobby with the skylight above me and called, 'Abingdon. Sorry to bother you but that's the gentleman from housing benefit's here to see me. Can you have a word, please?'

'And how have you paid your share of rent so far?'

'I haven't. I owe Abingdon for all of it.'

'I see.' He tapped the clipboard on his knee and smiled. 'If a payment from housing benefit to cover your rent was approved, of course you'd receive the back rent owing.'

I nodded. 'Oh yes. I'd really need that.' I said it with a supplicant frown.

Abby appeared from her bedroom at the back. I had been afraid she'd make a grand entrance, swathed in boas and calling the fellow a silly sausage, but she was wearing leggings and in bare feet – an angora sweater and red lipstick were her only concessions to show business. It was just the DHSS, after all. She still looked striking but of course he didn't react, just glanced down at his form and she risked a quick, amazed smirk at me.

'Hello,' she said briskly. 'Is this about Douglas being unemployed? Hopefully he won't be for long. He's a very talented boy.'

The fellow nodded. 'Can I ask? You aren't in receipt of any state benefits?'

'Absolutely not.' She delivered the line with a Thatcherite testiness.

'Could I ask if you'd be willing to provide your National Insurance number on this form?'

'Of course.' She swung into action as if she'd been asked for an autograph and wrote down her number.

Then he asked if he could take a look around.

He queried if I had a separate wardrobe area and the cupboard in the hall was quickly displayed, hung with many garish shirts from a variety of sources – including past fashion shows. He stepped into Abby's very feminine boudoir. He checked the bathroom cupboards where we'd made a clearly distinct male shaving equipment and aftershave area. Then it was off to the kitchen with us following obediently behind.

'Would you call the kitchen a communal area?' he asked.

'Well I suppose so. We hardly ever see each other here,' Abby claimed. 'My hours vary from week to week and day to day and I'm tired when I come home, and then I travel too. So sometimes I don't see him for – what?'

'Four, five days?' I shrugged.

'Longer. Even a week.'

He went across to her tall fridge and opened it. The light came on in there. I was starting to find this ridiculous. In Soviet Russia the state listened in to your telephone calls, and here it was peering into our fridges on official business.

Abby's enormous and carefully prepared fridge interior was like a dolls' house. Those two different cartons of milk were there. Normal for me but soya milk for Abby. A few matching condiments and sauce jars with our names written upon them in little stickers. Two identical Hellmann's mayonnaise jars but prominently labelled with our names – a nice touch – suggested by Lou.

'I'm vegetarian and Douglas isn't, so these are *my* shelves. Down there are all his horrible Scottish meat things. Black pudding. God alone knows what.'

The man from the DHSS closed the fridge door and he chuckled. 'You shop separately, do you?'

'Shop?'

'Do you visit the supermarket together?'

'Never. I wouldn't shop where he does.'

He seemed pleased with how things were going. We had prepared receipts if he asked. Then he tried the cupboards. 'Do you share the same box of cereal?' He asked this casually, in a tone and manner as if a sane existence could be led where one asked such questions of others in an official capacity.

'Certainly not. I have oatmeal sprinkled with wheatgerm and yogurt. I see him eating bloody Rice Krispies.'

'They're cornflakes. I don't eat Rice Krispies.'

'Cornflakes, then. It's processed.'

'Well.' He sighed as if he was fed up with the farce as well. It wasn't so much that he believed us, it was just how did you challenge such elaborate artifice? 'Thanks for your time. That's about everything. If you could just sign here, Mr Cunningham. You can see it's just a confirmation that this visit took place.' Then he pointed his plastic pen, which he chewed the end of, at the telephone. The telephone usually dwelt in Abby's bedroom on a long cord, buried somewhere among the rumplets of her bed, but we'd moved it and run the cord out onto a small table in the lobby below the skylight to make it seem communal. 'This is your correct phone number, yes?' I smiled in admiration at this late attempt to catch me out but I had carefully memorised Abby's number and, just for effect, I said 'Yes' and repeated the digits aloud and quickly while looking him in the eye.

Abby said, 'Toodle-oo, then.'

'Yes. Thank you,' he replied, without looking after her, and he wrote on his clipboard.

She went back into her room, making a point of shutting the door. Then I followed him down the stairs, though I don't suppose I needed to. 'Look, thank you very much for your time,' I said to the back of his head.

'Thanks to both of you for allowing us in your home today.' He skipped ahead down the stairs. He was perfectly able to open the white front door when he got to it but I still followed.

Outside, the trees were fairly stripped across the road and a gaggle of the brown leaves crashed along the pavement in a gust, somehow reminding me of the flapping wings of Llewellyn Smith's macintosh. I realised I was watching the leaves although the boy from the DHSS still stood beside me.

'I have your phone number. If anything came up?'

'Yes.'

'Perhaps I should provide you with mine? If you have other questions about, anything? My own number.'

'Eh. Yes.'

'Here it is, Douglas. John Honeyman is my name. Sweet by name and sweet by nature.' He jotted it on a rip of very unofficial paper and handed it out to me. 'You know. I can only use your number for official reasons.'

'Yes.' I nodded.

The government official said, 'So. You know. You would need to call me. With you down from Scotland. On the scene. If you wanted to come down to Earls Court one night?'

'Earls Court?'

'Yes. Nice places. It's not all the Coleherne, you know.'

'Sure.'

'Okay then, Douglas. See you about, then.'

'Yes. See you.'

'Call.'

'Sure.'

I stepped back in and shut the door. Abby immediately appeared at the top of the stairs, giving both thumbs up and a look of curiosity. I was keeping this to myself for sure.

9

Lou and I couldn't afford return fares on any mode of transport, including motorised public omnibus, so we bloody walked it from Acton to the Fulham Road. It took hours. We were excited and anxious not to be late, so cracked off at ten in the morning. The interview wasn't until three.

I suggested to Lou we hitch it.

'Nobody hitches it in central London, boyo,' Lou pointed out.

'Why not? They do in the countryside, where I'm from. We hitch everywhere and almost every Saturday night.'

'You're not in the Highlands now, boyo.'

'We'll start the trend. You just watch. Next year at London Fashion Week all those models with no bras on will go down the catwalk with their thumbs out. You mark my words. The "Cunningham Walk", it'll be called.'

'Fuck me I could do with a pint.'

'Lou,' I called out, 'there's a pub coming up here on the left!'

'Yeah, but is it open? We started out at such an ungodly hour. Never ever rise before pub opening hours. It's a fatal move.'

The pub was open. Inside it had that miraculous and promising feel of a morning pub: the stale smell of the night before, the worn floorboards still drying from the mop which had been swished across them. The excess of daylight, illuminating corners; sobriety showing things in a clarity that you don't see later on, like coloured beer pipes or an electrical socket in a wall.

We piled our last coins on the bar top and slid them an inch east, accumulating the necessary amount as we were eyed by the older bar lady, who impatiently ticked her fingernail on the beer tap.

The only customers in the joint, we sat with a single half-pint of Guinness to share between us. Dust moved through the bright light, curving round the bankings and shifting fronts of our cigarette smoke. We each took carefully uniform sips from the same glass. Everything, even the beer, gave off a slight redolence of sour eggs.

'Fuck. I wish we were rich,' said Lou flatly.

'Yes. Me too. From the Ali Khan to the alley cat, we can all use the dough.'

'One day we will be, boyo, on bloody royalties. Magnums of French champagne for you and me. Hemingway said you should only ever drink magnums, not bottles. Taste is better. Replace our whole library in hardback only.' He paused. 'The sticky wicket with money is, you immediately forfeit your innocence and there's always an edge of violence and aggression about it.'

'How do you mean?'

'Well, look around you. London today; millionaires' mansions. Keep Out signs, the rich safely locked in Rolls-Royces and these Porsches. There's no escaping it; there is something intrinsically aggressive about wealth. It's the same as adultery. There's always an edge of violence to any infidelity.'

'Mmm.' I nodded and picked up the beer again for a sip of my share.

'You know what this is all about, Cunningham, don't you?' He flicked his head aside so the fringe slid across the pale, concerned forehead, I supposed in the general direction of Fulham Road.

'This interview thing?'

'You know what he's going to do, don't you?'

'I'm not sure.'

'Isn't it obvious?'

'What?'

'He's going to pick our brains, see if we're on the ball and then he's going to get us to be readers of all the tosh manuscripts that get sent in. Isn't he? Pay us a couple of quid for a reader's report on each manuscript.'

'Right now a couple of quid would be okay.'

A look of revulsion came to Lou's face. 'I can't waste my time reading the crap that failures have written in their bedsits. Your housing benefit will come through soon enough and the girls will eat. Hey. Are you thinking of shagging Abby?'

I turned round to look at him. 'What?'

'Are you thinking of giving our strapping Abby a tumble in the autumn leaves?'

'No.'

'You've been over to her place on the sly once or twice, boyo.'

'That's something else.'

'Ah, I get it. Something to do with the wedding? Laying on one of those millionaire's Rolls-Royces for me and Eeef?'

I smiled. 'Maybe. Don't spoil it, Lou.'

'Don't you spoil it. Don't get me wrong, boyo. You and I are beyond any shallow moralising. Fire one into her for me if you're at it, but remember: anything you do with or say to Abby, it all gets back to Aoife. Every bloody word.'

I nodded casually but I felt I was being reprimanded. 'I'm aware of that. I wouldn't worry.'

'I'm not. I'm worried for you.'

I shifted round to look at him as he lit another cigarette. 'Illuminate me.'

'Well. Say you gave Miss Barbour the knowledge of carnal joy – in a windy and cold Scottish way – then she became too much for you. As she soon would. She's too much for any man. Say you ditched her. It could sour the bliss at home for me and you. Aoife loves you, but if you were mean to her best pal—'

'I know what you mean. Abby's beautiful, but I'm not sure I'm attracted to her and I can't imagine in my wildest dreams she is to me.'

'Maybe she likes her canaries with broken wings.'

We killed time in West Brompton Cemetery – laid in its cathedral outline – with leaves scattering stridently through it in sudden, unified lurches. Lou showed me the amazing Burne-Jones grave.

I was starving by three o'clock.

'Then just keep talking to cover up the sound of your stomach squeaking, when you're in his office,' Lou advised. 'We don't want him to suss we are needy by the sound of your complaining guts. Act like a king. That's what they used to say, the rich fellows down from Sheffield and Birmingham when I was working at the hotel: "Tip like a king and you will be treated like a king." And it was true as well.'

It was a disappointing sixties office block near all those hospitals. We had to sign in. I felt as if I was being arrested. Then we took a lift and rode up to the fifth floor. Nobody was there to meet us and we had to ask the way. It was not what either of us imagined a publisher's to be like though, granted, books were piled and shelved everywhere. Our ardent spirits demanded Toby Hanson's office be a wood-panelled extravaganza, hung with framed, handwritten manuscripts.

First came the guardian of his door: Belle. She was our age: tall and thin but somehow outrageously so. Everything about her had been stretched and topped off with bad posture, her legs were in some kind of striped woollen stockings – they looked like coloured marbles assembled in a condom – and she wore a one-piece white dress, like a gigantic christening gown. She had very thick spectacles and buck teeth, circumscribed by lipstick. Yet. Attractive under all that. We both almost ran as she veered towards us like some kind of catastrophe.

'Here to see Toby?' The weak, unsure eyes behind the finger-printed lenses moved too slowly between us both. The expression as she reached for the phone was obvious; as if her job would be gone by five o'clock and the business taken into administration if the like of us had access to Toby Hanson's office. And she got her own way. We didn't enter the office of Tobias Hanson. Toby en-countered us on his way out of his office, wearing suede gloves and pulling on what looked like a cashmere overcoat. 'Chaps, chaps, you came,' he said, as if we'd many other social opportunities we could have been sampling that afternoon. He clapped his hands softly and shook ours. 'Now what one is Llewellyn and what one is Douglas? Excellent, excellent. Fancy a pint?'

'We don't often get the chance to indulge,' Lou called after him, and we pursued him at a fair clip down the corridor.

'Note the calls, Belle,' he yelled without looking back.

The interview itself seemed to be happening before the lift had reached the ground. Toby Hanson shook his head sharply as if he'd been delivered a punch to the head and said, 'Chaps. Ever hear of this new reference book, *Debrett's People of Today*?' Only came out recently. Not the old peerage thing that old what's-his-name pores over on the first page of *Persuasion*. No, no. This is a new thing; significant people of today and all that.' He breathed in.

Lou allowed that first curl of a frown to appear. I assumed we were being offered a job on that publication, and Toby's company was its publisher. I snapped, 'Yes. I know it.'

'Heard just now *I've* been left out next year. Strewth! Can't believe it. I'm dropped. Oh, hush.' The lift had stopped at the second floor. Some colleagues of his came aboard and they looked at Lou and me with a mix of loathing and opportunism, trying to work out the actual value of our unknown quality – they bantered together with Toby Hanson while we remained silent, like smug teacher's pets. No more was breathed about *People of Today*.

In the ground-floor lobby, Toby's colleagues all peeled apart as if controlled by repellent magnets. Feeling pleased to be seen with him, Lou and I followed Toby out into a noisy and windy Fulham Road.

'Yes. Dropped from *Debrett's*. What's the bloody country coming to?'

Hanson began to walk, very fast indeed. Lou and I attempted to follow at the same desperate pace. At first it crossed my mind Hanson was actually attempting to lose us – and might succeed. We quickly passed several perfectly adequate-looking public houses. This behaviour evinced two possibilities. The positive theory was that, over time, Toby Hanson had accrued debts in all the public houses close to his publishing house and now he was forced to forage further afield through Chelsea to seek a clean slate. My other theory was that Toby Hanson wanted to gather Lou and me in a hostelry so far from the Fulham Road there was absolutely no excuse for us to accompany him back to his offices.

Communications were conducted under the greatest difficulty, because as Toby Hanson strode rapidly ahead – our destination unknown – Lou and I swerved and manoeuvred anxiously at the flapping tails of his cashmere overcoat, dodging fellow pedestrians, parking meters, dogs on leads, and those awaiting and alighting from buses. We swerved around shop placards, pram pushers and the mentally insane, then we stepped between parked cars as we crossed roads, looking both ways.

He did talk more of *Debrett's*, and included in what he said was: 'That's it. I'm going to become an agent.' Some of this oath-hurling was made inaudible by the wind and by the distance he drew ahead. The oaths were often conducted with a hand thrown out towards the turbulent Chelsea sky as if he was rehearsing in the street for an amateur theatrical production. When he came to talk of other matters, both Lou and I had to draw up closer to his cashmere shoulders, almost stepping on his heels. 'Never mind *Debrett's* for the moment then. Chaps, do you like rock music?'

'Yes,' I shouted at his back. 'Of course. It's our culture.'

Toby snapped his head in affirmation, the hair of which was speared with filaments of grey and blowing this way then that.

Pausing for timed breaths, Lou spoke to Hanson's other rear flank: 'Our tastes are catholic and eclectic, we like this and that. All styles,' he claimed.

I thought I'd ram it home finally. 'I like the form and craft of song writing, like Dylan, yet I admire experimental free-form work.' I'd called this to his shoulder as we swerved round a fruit stall in front of a delicatessen. I was still very hungry.

'What about the seventies, though? I'm not talking about punk rock or whatever.'

'Even better. We had big brothers. We were brought up listening to their record collections,' I lied.

'I see. Ever heard of a band? Fear Taker?'

Fear Taker. I actually had. Useless knowledge had often proved fortuitous to me. I babbled: 'Course we know them. Huge in the seventies. Deep Purple, Fear Taker, Yes, The Who.'

Toby Hanson strode on ahead. I thought I saw his shoulders react in a hunch. Perhaps I'd revealed an attention to detail that concerned him and he anticipated missed deadlines already?

He spoke not to us but to the faces of those on the pavement moving towards him. 'Well. We have this little subsidiary imprint doing a series of books on big seventies British rock bands.' He looked aside and counted off on the gloved hand. 'Bad Company. The Fear Taker. Peter Frampton. Cockney Rebel. Now I wouldn't want to disappoint you, chaps. Low print run, straight into pocket-book paperback, some black and white photos in the middle. They always come loose after a year with the cheap gum. But would you fancy taking one on? For Fear Taker?'

I feared we were bound as far as The World's End pub – one-time haunt of Sam Beckett, while he was undergoing psychiatric treatment, and also the lair of many, many, many others down the years. Suddenly, though, we came upon The Gertrude on the Kings Road. Hanson stepped sideways and pushed the door with such force it would surely have killed anyone behind, and he didn't slow his walking pace then either. He continued his rush across the carpet, beneath the low-beamed ceiling, and only at the very bar itself did he stop abruptly and fall calm.

'Ul-how, Tobe.'

'Hello there, Charley. Large Bloody, and for the chaps?'

'Large Bloody would be very nice,' I breathed.

'Yes. A great idea. Me too, please.' Lou fumbled for his cigs and coughed. He'd been unable to light up in that maelstrom outside.

I expected Hanson's morale to take a blow at this demand on his hospitality but he just nodded to Charley, the landlord.

The Bloody Marys were no-nonsense affairs: short glasses, double measures, oily vodka sitting in the base among three small ice cubes, the unshaken bottle of clotted tomato juice a quarter tipped in. You could see they had hardly mixed together. We stood at the bar.

The change from cold to the heat of the pub made my face flush up. The tomato juice would set off nicely against my red ears and nose, but I was very excited by this possible commission and I carried on hustling. 'Yeah. I'm quite a fan of Fear Taker. Mark Morrell was the guitarist. Brilliant. And the drummer was called Styx, as in the river. On the first album he had that long drum solo, "ConunDRUM". Brilliant stuff,' I lied. 'You don't get drum solos any more. We'd be happy to write that. How would it work out, deadline wise?'

Hanson tipped in a fraction more tomato juice to his, flipped the whole thing back and cracked the drained glass onto the bar top. 'Well, the other books in the series are all assigned. Easy work, chaps. They're just newspaper-cutting research, basically. You get hold of our press-cuttings contact and Xerox the lot, then build your thirty thousand words out of newspaper and magazine articles. A month or so's work. Two at the most.'

I was nodding repeatedly, but there was something familiar about the nod. I realised it was identical to the obedient nod I had used on John Honeyman from housing benefit. Capitalism – while consistently unable to satisfy our deepest needs – was very good at constantly demanding what its needs were.

'We're not talking cultural analysis here, chaps. Don't worry too much about all this accuracy business.' Then he urgently added, 'Watch for libel, though. Just a narrative with some insinuations of sex and drugs and dull details for the fans. Our legals will take a glance. But I was thinking. Ah.'

Now he held out his gloved hand and cashmere sleeve. He pointed intently. Lou and I turned our heads to look, as if an apparition of Hanson's own dead and vengeful father had just manifested against a far wall. Instead, next to a small round table, two seats and a stool were free. Hanson, Lou and I crossed, holding our glasses and the small red mixer bottles. With despair I saw Toby Hanson had abandoned his almost-full tomato juice bottle and emptied glass back on the bar and was now without refreshment; the impossible onus had suddenly fallen upon Lou and me to provide him with a fresh beverage. I sensed this interview couldn't extend for much longer. We gathered at the little round table while Lou and I carefully poured all the tomato juice from our little bottles into our vodkas.

Yet, sitting on the stool above us, Hanson didn't seem bothered by his lack of a drink. 'However, I should say now. Our people have been in touch with this guitar chappie's people. I've actually put it to his people that it's time for a book of his own, if he really wanted to go for it.' He paused and looked from one of us to the other. 'An autobiography. Of course, it'd need to be done in close collaboration with him. Anonymously. These guys might be okay on guitar; doesn't mean they can string a sentence together.'

I stared at him. 'You mean, we might be able to actually work. With Mark Morrell?'

'If this came off.'

'That would be something else.' I turned to Lou. 'He's a multi-millionaire, man. Sports cars and the whole thing. He actually has a house in Scotland, the way all the rock stars have. Or he did have one there, cause my mates drove up to see it and get their albums signed, but apparently he was never in residence.'

The publisher nodded. 'Yes. That's right, I'm sure. They were a huge band in the seventies when I was younger. In fact he has a bloody massive house right here as well, round the corner in the Vale, off the Kings Road. Oh, actually maybe that's someone else and it's on Gloucester Road at Hereford Square, James Barrie's old house. Barrie was Scotch.' He raised his eyebrows at me in surprise. 'But anyway, he mainly lives down in Kent or East Sussex in some moated mansion and all that sort of palaver.' Caustically, Hanson added, 'He's probably in *Debrett's*.'

Lou wasn't happy about this turn of events. Like Aoife, I'd learned to read the frown. I could sense this form of writing wasn't good enough for him. He'd been looking forward to tearing apart other people's manuscripts. For all my own vanities, I had a realist bent. If writing crap was going to bring beer money into Conrad Flats, that was fine.

'How would all this work out' – Lou added the word, like a gourmet pronouncing a favoured dish – 'contractually?' He sipped the top off his vodka.

'You mean the small Fear Taker book or working on the auto-biography?'

'Let's just start off with the small Fear Taker book. For now.'

'Well, you could work on it.'

'But there would be an amount advanced against possible royalties to allow us to begin work?'

'Of course, Llewellyn. If you want me to, I'll have a contract drawn up. For that kind of quick, easily researched book, I think we could pay you about three or four hundred nicker.'

'Altogether? Not each?'

'Three or four hundred flat would be a fair rate.'

'That would be four hundred, then.'

'All righty.'

Lou mused, 'Would a small deduction from that advance be available, today? In the form of a cash disbursement. Having trouble raising capital.'

'For what?'

'A pint and the bus home. What was it Hemingway wrote? Hunger was good discipline? There's an example of wisdom about an empty stomach being dispensed by a fat one.'

'Yes. Tough times. Left my wallet at the office but I've got a little tab behind the bar charged to the company. Why don't you stick a few beers on it. Say six. Not each. Six in total.'

Lou's face changed completely, converting into smiles and animating more.

It occurred to me this still wouldn't provide the bus fare back to Acton. Suddenly I said, 'Llewellyn's getting married.'

Toby looked astonished. 'Really. My God. You look so young. That's wonderful.'

'And what's more, she's completely beautiful.'

'That always helps. Well, congratulations, Llewellyn. Wish you the best. I'll get contracts to work on this small book. Still drilling and blasting at your own material, are you?'

'We certainly are,' said Lou.

'Well. I'll leave you in peace, chaps. Off to try to talk to someone at *Debrett's* and see if we can't sort this out. Reputation and being distinguished is all that matters in this business,' he claimed. 'I'm so pleased with how it's gone between us all. Congrats on the wedding. Make it eight beers in all. Not each. Eight in total.' He crossed to the landlord to etch that in stone.

10

'But I want a stag night,' said Lou.

Aoife told him, 'You can't have one, you'll be sick hungover for tomorrow and you're not both going anywhere near the West End. Or bloody Soho.'

Without further connection to John Honeyman my housing benefit cheque had in fact arrived. Abby hadn't even asked for a cut – but she was round visiting and she smiled: 'The bride and bridesmaid will do a better striptease for ten quid than some poxy tart in Soho, sausage. Won't we, Eeef?'

'Will you now? That'll be nothing I haven't seen before. We were only going to the bloody Bells.'

'Tomorrow's our wedding day, Lou. I've to go over to Abby's later, so it'll have to be a stag *afternoon*.'

'Why?'

'Cause you two boys need to look after Lily tonight.'

'Why?'

'We're going out tonight. I can't take Lily to stay over at Abby's with me.'

'Why not?'

'I can't get Aoife ready in the morning with Lily there.'

'What do you mean, get her ready? It's just a wedding dress. It's not a fashion show.'

'You know what we're like.'

'Yes. I do know what you're like. Both of you. I told you we should have taken her to Gran's.'

Pascal's Moon, the fourth album by Fear Taker, which I'd withdrawn on cassette from Ealing Central Library, was playing in the kitchen. Aoife said, 'Stop shouting, Lou. You'll go and wake Lily yet again. She isn't safe overnight at your gran's. Your gran could even forget she's there, without Flo about. Leave her sitting out in the buggy above the railway with the rain on, like last time. Remember? Please. You and me shouldn't spend tonight together. Douglas'll bring you to the Town Hall tomorrow.'

'So this is it? Cunningham and I, the breadwinners.'

'Breadwinners. Ha.'

'Have to drink this afternoon so you two can go out on patrol tonight in your fanny-freezer skirts. You'll probably go into the West End yourselves, to meet *your* fashion troll friends.'

'They're her friends too.'

'Who're you going to the pub with then, Lou?'

'Him.'

'Who else?'

'Nobody.'

'What about your brother?'

'Rhys is coming tomorrow with his camera. It'd be a bit too much to expect him to come tonight as well. He is kept busy. As a fully qualified moron. I told you before, Eeef. Apart from Douglas, I got no friends.'

'What about the porter guys from your old work at the hotel?' she suggested quietly.

'They're all sixty. I never see them any more. At very best I could invite Jim Faring.'

'Who's Jim Faring?'

'Came here; fixed the broke window.'

'Oh yes.'

'Still owe him for that,' I pointed out.

'Oh yeah. Forget him, then.' Lou raised his arms up from his sides and let them limply slap down again. 'There you go. You – my friends and loved ones – are all I've got left in the world.'

'Go to the pub, then, but be back here by eight.'

'Seven,' Abby snapped.

Lou turned fast on Abby. 'Without conjugal favours I'm not taking conjugal orders from you.'

'She's going out tonight, and that's that.' Abby stabbed a pointed finger at Aoife. 'She hasn't been out for a single night in a year.'

'So, we're sat here with Lily, while you two are out on the tiles.'

'Yes. Remember, Lou. That's what happens most afternoons the other way round. Aoife's here, you two are in the pub. When there's money.'

He shook his head and turned to me. 'Come on, boyo. They'll be sorry when we're working on the book with a rock legend.'

In our favourite seat in The Bells, Lou's declamations raged on as usual. *Silas Marner* got a kicking and dismissal before his first cigarette was smoked – the Silas sections were acceptable but the rest was *Reader's Digest*.

Lou dismissed books with a deep, nakedly personal resentment towards their authors, simply pressing home the point that so many hours, days or even weeks of his own precious life had been wasted reading their wanting creations. He expended much more bitterness upon the dead pantheon than he did on the living. At first, I had foolishly taken this as a mark of grudging respect for living authors, even though they too did not meet expectations. As I listened to him over time, though, I realised that he was most bitter towards dead authors only because they were now out of his venomous range. With living writers, he was only holding back because he anticipated some specific and concrete personal revenge he could enact upon them for their failings – doubtless through the publication of his own masterpiece, though sometimes it seemed Lou would happily settle for a punch on the nose if he encountered them.

John Harrison's *The Reactionaries* – one of our favourite books – veered into Lou's gunsights once again. The whole book was prodded for narrowness of scope. But I remember he also said, 'The paragraphs are too long. Maybe cause I'd had a few Guinnesses, but it was hard to know if Harrison was still summarising the reactionary views or had moved on to his own.'

He took a long drain of his pint. 'Telling you, boyo. All those lads needed was a good shag with a modern woman to stop them scheming fascist revolt on their pillows. Especially David Herbert Lawrence. They needed to get it on with a *Vogue* model. Or even a Littlewoods model, like Eeef. That's all that was bothering them. For God's sake, Cunningham. Promise me now you'll marry rich, my son. To hell with love.'

'No.'

'No?'

'I'd only marry for looks. I'm that shallow.'

'God help you. Looks! Look at me.'

'Well it's easy for you to take it for granted. Tomorrow you're marrying one of the most beautiful-looking girls I've ever seen.'

'Shucks.'

'I mean it. See a woman the way Aoife looks? I'd find it impossible to be angry with her, since I'm so shallow. Just to look at her each day would be enough. I don't know how you can ever be angry at Aoife. She's very beautiful.'

'Oh God. Just cause you're not squelching away, refilling Abby's fanny, you don't need to go and take her side on everything.' He shot his voice down to a whisper and he rolled slightly on his buttocks towards me. His latest cigarette was smoking and it was cradled preciously, like a fragile bird within both hands, very close to his lips. His thoughtful eyes closed a second. 'Cunningham, my liege, you have to face up to the fact that Aoife is that ever-so-slightly-bit dim.'

'*Lou!*'

'*God* you're smitten. I was too. When I met her.'

'She isn't dim at all. Just cause she's not a slave to books, like me and you, doesn't mean she's dim. I think she's perceptive.'

'Yes she is perceptive. About me and how I get to and from this pub without her sussing. It doesn't mean I can discuss Faulkner with her.'

'There's more to life than talking about Faulkner. My God, Lou. Sex comes before Faulkner. Even Faulkner would have agreed.'

'Oh really? Sex with Aoife comes before Faulkner. And how would you know?'

'Sorry. I didn't mean to be personal. Faulkner was the subject, not Aoife.'

'You haven't offended me. It's just I'm not so sure. As time goes by I genuinely don't understand people who will not apprehend reality through art. And Aoife doesn't apprehend reality through art. It's like she lost religion and replaced it with nothing. Honestly,

Douglas. As time passes, I find everything else more and more meaningless and art becomes everything to me.'

'Yes. I feel the same. It's the recipe for an unhappy life for both of us. But listen, you're not that indifferent to everything; you're marrying a beautiful woman. Tomorrow. And I'm glad for you. So let's drink. How with this rage, shall beauty hold a plea, whose action is no stronger than a flower?'

'I'm marrying a mother.'

'There is that.'

'I'm marrying for Lily, not for Aoife.'

'That's harsh.'

'It's true. Do you know how often I slept with Eeef, before she got pregnant?'

'Umm no, of course I don't.'

'Twice. Two weekends, then she went away for a month up to the East Midlands – that hellhole she hails from – till she phoned in tears about the missed period.'

'Ooo ya.'

'Yup. Aoife's Irish womb: fecund as the Nile Delta. She started wailing about how abortion was unthinkable and she'd regret it for ever and that we're both Catholic for a reason. I didn't even know her and in one month she was pregnant with my child. Jesus, Cunningham, I might as well have entered into an arranged marriage.' He hoisted his Guinness. 'Give me the Mouths of the Ganges and keep your Nile Delta.' He'd had a good bit, and muttered something I couldn't catch.

Two of the old boys across the pub thought Lou was toasting, so they both nodded politely and raised their half pints in agreement.

He suddenly leaned close in again. 'Cunningham. I don't mind you fucking Abby, or even fancying Aoife, that would be normal, but please, please do yourself the dignity and have the intellectual honesty not to romanticise them.'

I physically straightened up. I'd never been haughty to him before and my accent thickened in its Scottishness. 'Just you remember I'm your best man tomorrow before you start talking like that.'

I could see he was impressed but also that he thrived on it. He rose, crossing to get us both two more pints, sneering over his shoulder, 'Let's drink to beauty, then.'

I knew Lou would be home provocatively late and it was twenty to nine before we began to ascend the innards of Almayer House. Up at the third floor, as usual, a confabulation of teenagers was going on, one lad standing within the doorway and one outside.

'Hello there, young man.'

'All right?'

'What's that?' Lou asked.

The guy with the weird squint from that night of the Brighton bomb was thrusting something helplessly far out before him with both hands, as if he were afraid of it.

Ten minutes later I unlocked the front door of the flat with Lou behind me. Ominously, two small packed suitcases rested at the ready in the hall.

Lou stepped ahead, turning boldly into the living room, and I followed behind. Aoife and Abby were both on the sofa, their heads moved round in synchronism, like perched birds, to scrutinise us.

'We're not going to have much of a night out with you back at this time,' Abby started.

But she was subtly betrayed. Aoife was already grinning up at us. She was able to detect Lou's mischievous expression and then the alarming way he had his overcoat tented out by something concealed beneath. Abby raised her razor-thin eyebrows.

Lou said to Aoife, doubtless blowing out beer fumes across them both, 'Hey, you. What's your name? Let's get married in the morning.'

'Okay then,' Aoife giggled.

'I've got you a wedding present,' Lou teased.

Both the young women now gave his ballooned overcoat their full attention and from beneath it Lou withdrew Lamborghini the tortoise, his prehistoric legs thrown out in distress, his scaly neck stretched, the bagged skin like an old man's penis. Around his segmented shell, Llewellyn had sloppily painted:

LOU LOVES AOIFE

'Awww.' Aoife face's filled up. She reached and took Lamborghini in two hands. The tortoise's mechanical-looking jaw opened and closed slightly.

There was a powerful smell of nail varnish arising from that tortoise.

Abby, with a cruel smile, said, 'It's disgusting, Lou. Did you get it off some street tart? I can smell her nail varnish from here.'

'Stop it. He's beautiful.' Aoife moved Lamborghini's extended neck towards her face. 'Where did you *get* it?'

'Watch the writing. It's still tacky.'

'That Viv's kid downstairs found it lost outside,' I said. 'It's looking for a place to hibernate. It needs to hibernate.'

Lou nodded patiently toward me. 'He knows all about tortoises.' He laughed. 'Christ. If we let the thing loose here, he'll have plenty of places to hibernate amongst all your bloody clothes, Abby.'

'Oh. How completely revolting.'

I said, 'I'll need to check his weight and then put him in two boxes, one inside the other. They eat fruit and dandelions and some decent lettuce.'

Aoife said, 'Gosh. Douglas knows all about them.'

'That's cause he looks like one,' Abby screamed.

Aoife stared at the tortoise. 'We'll need to put him in the store room in the cellar.'

I glanced from side to side. 'There's a cellar here?'

'Each flat has a store room down in the basement. Where all your bloody clothes should be.'

'They'll get damp in that dungeon.'

'I'm going to show him to Lil.'

'She's sleeping.'

'Don't. It's dirty,' Abby said.

'It isn't dirty.'

'Where'd you get the nail varnish, then?'

'The guy downstairs' big sister. He nicked a bit for us.'

Lou looked at me, ignoring the girls. 'Des Esseintes has nothing on me. Of course Huysmans stole the jewelled tortoise from Montesquiou, Fitzgerald stole it from Huysmans for Gatsby, and Waugh stole it from Fitzgerald for *Brideshead*, and now I have improved on all of them.'

I nodded in brisk confirmation. I checked a long time after – and he was quite right on these facts.

Abby exhaled in disgust, 'Come on, Eeef. We got to go. Leave them with their bloody reptile.'

Aoife tried to hand the tortoise to Abby but she screamed, so it was put down upon the floor. Lou and Aoife embraced and kissed.

'I'll see you tomorrow.'

'Don't stand me up.'

'I won't.'

I looked at Abby. 'Do you have the ring?'

'Of course. Do you have yours?'

'Yes.'

After the girls had gone, we checked on Lil, who was fast asleep, and I prepared her night bottle rather than leave it till later.

Then there was Lou's bottle to prepare. A quarter of whisky we'd had stashed away. When we'd drunk that, diluted with the cold London tap water, he crashed about the house and procured a quarter bottle of rum with an inch in the bottom, then a quarter bottle of vodka, half empty and hidden on top of the kitchen unit, its glass tacky, like wood sap, with accumulated grease and dust. We drank and talked in the front room late into the hours. I recall once, he looked casually at his watch, an old-fashioned wind-up which I understood once belonged to his father. 'Just think, Cunningham. They'll be in bed together. Aoife will be lying drunk and half naked, in crabby Abby's arms. And we're at home with a damn tortoise.'

'Please. I have to try to sleep.'

He laughed, harshly and enthusiastically.

We heard the small, persistent bumps of Lamborghini against the skirting board in the corridor as he ventured around the place.

PART THREE

With my hired kilt, I had itching, knee-high wool socks and my brogues leaked cold water in the wet grass. I pushed Lily in her buggy across Ealing Common with Lou by my side. He was already drunk.

On Hanger Lane, worker vans and a car had already blared the horn at me – in my skirt. I was in charge of pushing the pram because Lou had a bad habit, which was worsening, of having a fag in his lips and allowing little broken cylinders of ash to twiddle down, landing inside the hood of Lily's red anorak, whilst he lectured on vital topics.

Lou's second hip flask fitted superbly into my sporran and we stopped several times in the middle of the common, clear of society's judgement, to each take long swallows of replenishment. Lily's bag hung from the pram handle: nappies, wipes, talc, baby bottles – all the necessary accoutrements for Lily when she moved abroad in the outer world, when Lou or I – or both of us – took her in the pram to Gunnersbury Park to give Aoife a break. Lily's anorak hood was up – just in case – but when I halted and stepped forward of the buggy to lean down, her eyes were brightly open, surveying obstacles before us with interest.

I patted my kilt. 'If this is my culture, there ought to be some fucking medical law against it. My knackers are so cold, watch out I don't leave one bollock behind me on the ground like a golden dog turd. And how is the groom?'

'Hungover. Terrified. Drunk. Thirsty. We've almost scooshed this and we're only halfway there.' He had screwed the cap on the hip flask and he shook it hard.

He looked good though. He had on a black vintage, double-breasted linen suit – almost a zoot suit – pressed by himself, with a white carnation, cream silk shirt and a black and silver, seventies Charvet silk tie which had come into the household via Abby and Camden Lock market. He'd shaved close and careful, so even the roots of his energetic stubble seemed under a milky sealant.

On the steps of Ealing Town Hall stood Lou's gran in a hat, all done out to meet the Queen – with her neighbour, Flo: a plump and middle-aged lady in a floral dress. I'd never met her but she chuckled at my kilt and barked down, 'Lily's got Llewellyn's hair but she's got *your* eyes, Mr Lodger.' She sent up a loud rattling laugh and looked around as if people busily ascending and descending the stairs or along the pavement should appreciate this. I noted Lou's gran, chuckling irreligiously at the quip.

'The girls is hiding. You two come through now and I'll take Lily.'

A very young, corpulent male assistant ushered Lou and me into the Town Hall as if we'd come to identify a dead and mutilated family member. We were shown to a narrow, long function room full of plastic chairs with a lectern at the far end and white plastic flowers in urns on either side. We were left there together. We sat in the first row, facing the front. There were narrow, high windows like those in The Five *or* Six Bells, but an inch open to an interior corridor and you could hear people passing up and down outside, or even greeting one other.

I looked at Lou and tried an encouraging grin. He had the expression of a confident, brave gambler, but one who had just been served a doomed, eleventh-hour hand. And he was Catholic. Though he'd never admit it, I knew then that the bareness and lack of decoration in that functional, municipal room appalled him. He needed something sacred. Quick.

I said to him quietly, 'Aoife is going to look very beautiful and you are very lucky.' But I had made it sound as if I was aroused.

He chewed his mint violently, expression unchanged. I reached into my sporran, retrieving the hip flask, and this seemed to shake him into action. After a substantial withdrawal he handed it back and I issued a new mint, which he immediately placed in his mouth. He nodded absently, staring dead ahead, concentrating as if I was his co-pilot and he was the captain, putting us down on a tricky runway in a crosswind with two engines on fire.

There was a crash behind us and I jumped. Flo had used the buggy to ram through the swing doors and she let out her bullock's laugh. 'There's a bleeding bottle of plonk hid here with the nappies. Noyce.' So much for that expensive surprise.

The doors opened again. Lou's gran entered with who could only be Rhys, the elusive older brother who seemed pleased to be carrying one of those huge ghetto blaster radio-cassette players. He had Lou's forehead, the eyebrows and even the complexion of clotted cream, but he was flat-footed and much heavier, bulked out in one of his functional Civil Service suits. Rhys swung down to the front and nodded to me, then lifted a camera and blasted off a flash at both of us, like a press photographer.

In a deadpan voice Lou managed, 'Rhys, this is my mucker Douglas, resplendent in the traditional dress of his people. He's my big brother. Rhys.'

'All right,' Rhys groaned, but he'd noticed a plaque of some kind over on the far wall and he plodded to it, leaned close, then, with bifocal spectacles hung on his nose – the specs were attached to a conventional bit of white string – he studied that plaque. He jumped back, clicked a photo of the plaque then suddenly sat down at the far end of the other front row. I thought he was being stand-offish but when you analysed it, that was the best seat to take photographs from.

The doors opened again. I wearily turned but it was the functionary herself, in a trouser suit. She planted herself at the lectern and there was official babble spoken in a theatrically inflated way, to rise above the fucking din Lily's healthy lungs were achieving. And the noise out in the corridor.

Even I had now been massaged into a high nervousness and things seemed to happen horribly quick, like a toboggan run – all tacky anticipation then acceleration and terror. People were nodding, agreeing with everything the functionary was saying. And the doors at the top opened, Lou's throat jumped with a swallow and Rhys, sitting casually with his legs crossed in his front seat, began taking photo after photo so the shutter noise, like a tropical insect against window glass, ticked constantly along with Lily's cries.

Aoife had entered the room arm in arm with a woman I'd never seen before. Her sister, Attracta – giving her away, and the only member of her family who would agree to attend, the mum and dad being sunk deep in Irish Catholicism up near Derby and having nothing to do with this carry-on. I felt a pang of sadness.

I hardly studied Attracta because, in my lizardy way, one look at Aoife was enough. I'd never seen her hair done up in that way before. It had been made into a bower, entwined with minute little white flowers and the fringe an airy meringue – such constructions are mysteries to men. The bare arms were holding up a small bouquet. A simple, off-white, low-cut dress with silver hems a bit far above her knees, showing a lot of cream-stockinged legs and silk, silver-buckled pale shoes. I had been led to understand it was all authentic twenties and thirties clobber.

Abby walked directly behind Aoife, holding a large bouquet, even now with that childish smirk, though she couldn't escape looking stunning as well. She had on one of those twenties felt hats. It was a statement, but maybe a statement too far for Ealing Town Hall on a Saturday afternoon. Abby had not dared wear white, so only the bride matched the groom's doomed complexion.

Aoife alone looked weirdly happy amidst all this ruin. People shuffled for position close up to one another in the seats. Jokes were made. Two, straight away, about what Scotsmen wore beneath kilts. Even across the unfettered wails of Lily, Rhys's camera shutter tapped and then came incongruous voices from the corridor, like the rogue noises you sometimes overhear from an adjacent cinema showing a different film, sounding disgracefully mundane among all our excitements.

When the ceremony business began, Lily fell silent in her buggy, which everyone took as a cute and appropriate good omen. Aoife, Lou and I all let our eyes momentarily and cautiously meet as we observed the look of intense concentration drift onto Lily's

133

forehead; her complexion blushed briefly crimson and she delivered a bulletin deep into her nappy. She took up crying again immediately after. If the others weren't familiar with what had happened they soon understood. Aoife and Llewellyn were betrothed as they lived, in the scent of nappy shit.

I shakily took Lou's wedding ring from the breast pocket of my shirt, where it was safely buttoned in a small crush of jeweller's tissue. Abby had been entrusted with Aoife's ring. Words were said. Abby and I had to sign as witnesses; other papers were signed and rings were exchanged, and the betrothed couple both undertook a surprisingly passionate and lengthy kiss.

I jumped as there came a screech from the other side of the room, then Stevie Wonder began to sing 'I Believe When I Fall in Love (It Will Be Forever)'. Rhys had successfully thumbed on the ghetto blaster and smiled, pleased with himself.

The cautious, fragile song is so beautiful that it was hard not to be moved, but through it all there was an awkward peck between Lou's gran and Aoife. The functionary was shaking hands with as many of us as quickly as she could and making her escape before the next wedding. I quickly unstrapped and lifted Lily from her buggy; as I squeezed her fat anorak she expelled a cloud of nappy smell. She stopped crying immediately, then I put her back down and kneeled – which one always does cautiously in the kilt. I slowly unzipped the front of Lily's anorak, which always fascinated her if you did it very slowly. Sure enough, her eyes fell down intently to watch the toggle and her claw-like fingers tried to intercept it. She remained silent.

Flo yelled, 'Had a little accident, the dear. I'll go change her, love,' and she started barging in so that I was forced away.

Someone stuck their head through the door and shouted. 'Sorry. But can you turn that music off? There are council offices here?'

'I Believe When I Fall in Love (It Will Be Forever)' snapped off before the end.

'You look very fine in your kilt,' Aoife declared to my face in a high and excited voice I hadn't heard before, then she reached down just to let her hand pat Lily's scalp as if she were not her own child. Flo rudely wheeled the buggy off toward the Ladies.

'Congratulations and you look very beautiful, Mrs Smith.' I kissed her on the cheek but I put my arms around her cautiously and felt those bared shoulders.

'Thank you for getting Lou here on time.'

When I drew back from her I saw that we were alone; no one was actually talking to the bride as she awkwardly stood there. Lou was gabbing rapidly, holding court with Attracta; Abby was laughing, so her erect bouquet vibrated in her hands. I had another attack of pathetic grief and realised I was speechless, looking hard into Aoife's face. Yes. She deserved better.

What was it I saw there? She was awaiting something from me and it was only then I realised it was approval she sought. I repeated, quietly and because it was so sincere it came with an over-whelmed tone, 'You just look so beautiful.'

She suddenly blinked. 'This is Atty, my sister Atty.' But she had to turn and call across the floor. 'Atty, Atty here. This is Douglas,' and when she added just, 'Lou's pal,' the pain was in my side and I felt horribly dismissed.

'Hello. I see you have your kilt on.'

I even kissed Attracta upon her cheek. I hadn't studied her yet, other than to shallowly acknowledge she wasn't as beautiful as her younger sister. Her face was squarer, she had a residual and perceptive suspicion about all this – so her smile was fragile. I nodded at what she said, though I wasn't sure what it was.

I could see Rhys, staunchly stood next to his gran, and he had a perfect puckered mouth-shape of Aoife's lipstick upon his pale cheek. Then he had the camera, which looked like a gigantic fly on his face and it flashed towards me again. I thought I was going to be sick and simultaneously Lou threw an arm around me, rocking me from side to side, and he growled warmly in my ear, 'That's it, boyo, time to get a drink in,' and the next thing he was lighting up a fag and I was on the Town Hall steps, posing for photos then digging deep handfuls of confetti out old Mrs Smith's crocodile-skin handbag, which contained nothing else but confetti, throwing it at Aoife's naked white shoulders and then helping carry the front end of the buggy down the stairs.

Our odd party was out and walking the pavements, a surreal procession in front of the ghastly Waterglade Shopping Centre, which already had Christmas lights up. First in our parade went Aoife and Lou, arm in arm with Abby following, fingers anxiously picking like a monkey to get all the confetti off the bride's dress and out Aoife's hair. Rhys, swinging the ghetto blaster like an empty briefcase, had taken up beside me and scuffed the soles of his shoes, talking about the features and capabilities of his camera. I nodded while Flo, pushing Lily in her buggy, and old Mrs Smith slowly followed behind. Aoife's sister tried to get a single moment to kneel down close to Lily but Flo kept moving the buggy ahead. Pedestrians smiled, nodded or remarked towards the happy couple and because it was a Saturday, quite a lot of kids of school age stared in that shameless and critical way they do.

Rhys turned to me as we walked. He might have been having problems with my accent because he enunciated as if to a complete non-English speaker, 'Do, you, like, The Stones?'

I nodded, 'Yeah. Some of their stuff. 'Playing with Fire', 'Citadel', *Beggar's Banquet*.'

He jabbed out the camera toward the junction. 'Just round there's where The Stones started out in the early sixties, when it was Ealing Blues Club.'

'Right.' I was genuinely interested but it came out sounding rude.

'Lou was saying you're doing a book with Marko Morrell of Fear Taker? I was a big fan.'

'Yeah, maybe. Looks like it. We're both doing it.'

He nodded very seriously and thoughtful. 'Maybe you can get my albums signed?' I thought he was going to ask more, but instead he squinted up at the sky suspiciously and suddenly put the ghetto blaster down on the pavement and he was left behind as he adjusted a switch on his camera.

Then something happened I liked very much indeed. Everyone crossed at the traffic lights and we all went into a pub. I thought it was tremendous and wonderfully English. There we all were, including three generations of the Smiths and shouting Flo. Rhys, Lou's gran and Flo sat in against the wall, guarding the baby at the top of the table – still in her buggy – while Aoife, her sister and Abby sat across.

Lou and I loomed in a proprietary manner at the bar end, smoking, and money was passed up to us very pleasingly as the guests fought to pay for a round. Mrs Smith won out and all deferred to her, so Lou was ordering drinks from the landlord, who knew his gran anyway and turned a blind eye to Lily's presence.

Lou and I passed these drinks down very efficiently. Myrtle Smith drank gin and ginger, Abby and Aoife, gin and limes, Rhys drank London Pride and though his bulk in its tight suit was pressed in against his gran – in a childlike and protected way – there was nothing infantile about the way he downed his pint. To this day, I've a real suspicion Aoife's sister took something non-alcoholic. Another round was ordered up, this time paid for by Rhys, waving around a twenty, still with the bride's lipstick upon his cheek and somehow easily looking as if he was having a better time than anybody. He'd offered to buy the round the split second he finished his own first beer. At that rate I thought there was going to be a jolly old cockney knees-up and sing-along, but suddenly, in a very un-Scottish way, they were all up again and that was it. We were flowing out the pub underneath hanging flower baskets of withered cusps back into excessive light.

Flo, with Lily in her buggy, Rhys carrying his ghetto blaster and Lou's gran actually went to wait for a bus in the shelter. Aoife and Lou kneeled to kiss Lily goodbye. There was great hullabaloo made by Flo as I liberated the champagne from the nappy bag. As I removed it I also managed to drag out Llewellyn's other emptied hip flask, which jangled down nervily onto the concrete pavement. Lou raised his eyes to heaven and I thrust it back in the bag.

'Dutch courage. Not surprised,' Lou's gran said and let her painted eyes drift swiftly across kneeling Aoife's body, moving freely in the silk dress while she stroked her daughter's hair. The old lady craned to see if an approaching bus served her needs, then she told us all, 'I'll make it back for my mid-afternoons.'

Aoife's sister was escaping us too. I hoisted the champagne bottle and indicated Haven Green, opposite Ealing Broadway station, but she didn't respond, so we said our farewells.

Abby, Lou and I stood at a small distance from the two sisters as they hugged and muttered in their Midland accents, talking about internal matters, their parents and the fractious politics of the whole marriage. The talk went on and on as if they were cramming into a few moments matters unsaid for two years, so Lou and I – politely followed by Abby – drifted across the road.

Lou nodded glumly, then his bride came smiling across the zebra crossing and all four of us stood shivering in the small grass parkland of Haven Green with the bottle of champagne.

Abby had unfolded a grey overcoat with huge rounded lapels and gave it over to Lou, who draped it protectively upon Aoife's shoulders.

'Bloody hell.' Lou shook his head, gazing in Aoife's face. She nodded knowingly.

'That's it, then. Mr and Mrs,' Abby declared.

Using my skean-dhu, I peeled the foil, put the knife back in my sock and unscrewed the wire on the champagne. I used my thumbs and groaned to make the fat-ended cork pop, fly and smack down invisibly in the brown leaves nearby. As the bottle frothed over, Lou took it and stepped backward, holding it out before him to let it settle and avoid the creeping spillage on its flanks slavering down upon his polished shoes.

The girls had let out high brittle calls into that iced air.

'Ladies and wives first.' Lou handed the bottle of champagne to his wife. She passed the bottle on to me from her own lips and I put the sliding glass into my mouth which filled with the jumping, crackling liquid.

Lou said, 'Let's not start bitching about all the others, including your parents' – and he nodded to Aoife – 'until we're sat down with a hot meal in front of us.'

I said, 'What are our intentions?'

'Well. I can tell you what my intentions are, boyo. To inspect under here if these are real stockings.' Aoife screeched as he tugged a little at the hem of her short dress.

'Course they are, sausage,' Abby screamed.

I turned to Abby and made a face. 'Should we?'

'Now. D'you think?'

'Tell them. Cause I feel I'm messing them around.'

Lou and Aoife were looking upon us.

'Tell us what? What? What is it?'

Lou sneered between Abby and me and said, 'Are you both about to announce your engagement?'

Abby put down her shoulder bag on the metalled pathway and kneeled, her dress came way up over her knee so you could see her lovely but goose-bumped leg. I noticed both their little bouquets had been stowed in the bag. She stood and handed across a fancy envelope. 'This is from Douglas and me to both of you.'

The married couple stood side by side as they opened the envelope.

'Victoria Station Hotel. Tonight,' Lou said in a forensic tone. Then he seemed to wake up. 'Bloody hell. Victoria Station Hotel. Thank you. Good stuff. So this is what you and Abby were scheming at her place, Cunningham, rather than the how's-your-father.'

'Lou. It's our wedding day and you're making it sound like every other day.'

'We know it's not Browns Hotel.' Abby's voice rose encouragingly, 'But it's a nice room. Not the biggest but nice, the man said. We explained it was your wedding night.'

'Bet they don't get many of those,' Lou said, a bit cruelly. 'And what's this?'

Aoife said, 'They're return train tickets to Brighton for tomorrow. Goodness.'

She seemed genuinely thrilled. The English have an oddly persistent and over-reliant belief in the seaside; from the Prince Regent to kiss-me-quick, a day in Eastbourne or Clacton-on-Sea with a pier is the cure for everything.

'We'll come back later, get Lily off your gran,' I volunteered. 'Flo knows about it and Abby can always stay over at Bollo Lane if Lily's difficult with me. You two go to the hotel and then off for a day in Brighton tomorrow.'

Lou actually looked touched. 'Hey, you two lunatics, this is really good of you.'

'You'll have to wear your wedding dress tomorrow. Like an elopement. Just wear your hair down,' Abby said.

I encouraged them. 'You'll be like the Serge Gainsbourg and Jane Birkin of Acton. You already are.'

'Or Richard and Mimi Fariña?' Lou suggested to me, more excited by this.

Abby predicted, 'Now we'll have a boozy grill-up for you carnivores, or one of Eeef's curries somewhere awful.' She looked very sour.

Aoife was concerned. 'Are you sure you two will be okay with Lily, though?'

Abby had turned to me. 'You're absolutely brilliant with Lily, Aoife tells me.'

'We'll be fine. I've never been alone with her overnight but I'll manage.'

Lou paused in swigging from the bottle. 'You mean with Lily or with Abby?' and he chuckled, passing the champagne on.

Aoife nodded. 'I'll phone, or you could always ring this hotel tonight if you're worried.' She looked down at the document.

Lou said, 'What! And interrupt a genius at work?'

'Lou. You're embarrassing me.'

Abby said, 'We'll be fine. You stay at the hotel. A bride can't return on her wedding night to a grotty Acton flat, getting her garter took off with a Scotsman next door, listening through the wall.'

Lou yelled out in joy and clapped his hands.

'I don't listen.'

Aoife had gone bright red too.

Lou said, 'Well, if you two are all alone and Lily's sleeping, no shagging on the kitchen table. I have to chop the vegetables up there. Use our bed.'

I replied with a dirty frown.

Aoife snapped, 'Lou. When do you ever chop the veg?'

I remember when I tossed the empty champagne bottle into the public wastepaper basket of that small park, it looked wrong – a kind of pillage – the thick round base of green glass jammed in there with sandwich wrappers. This expensive luxury item binned, in a city where old tramps were starting to vanish and young homeless appear on the streets – where the newspapers showed miners' families being made Dickensian, where famine was first being reported out in Ethiopia. Then I thought of the big houses I'd gazed up at in Holland Park. I surmised that both guilt and charity should be exclusive to Holland Park residents.

They say London's an unfriendly place, but different people talked to Aoife and Lou as we four rode up to the West End on the Tube that afternoon. My jacket sleeve was pushed flatly up next to Abby's bare arm. A man in a business suit asked if they'd just been married and he reached out and shook Lou's hand. And two separate West Indian ladies – who were always the friendliest folk in London – chatted away to them, asking detailed questions.

We got off somewhere at the back of Piccadilly and into a small pub with lattice windows, answering many of the specifics Lou had demanded as he stumbled through the streets in clouds of his own cigarette smoke, hand in hand with his bride, dismissing one hostelry after another. He described many of these pubs as establishments that 'would sell champagne in a can'.

Aoife was drinking vodka with different mixers. I'd never seen her drink so much. She even smoked a cigarette. When we rose and departed from the pub, I remember how shocked I was that it was night outside in the high narrow street where passing taxis sounded so loud. It was even colder as well. Then we crammed into a cab, laughing inside as I tried to hold down my kilt on the flip seat whilst the girls pretended to cover their eyes.

We stepped out alongside a huge restaurant called Mowgli & Kim's. Its frontage was sleek black with one strip of lime-green neon.

'Did Kipling eat here?' I asked Lou, though I was having trouble getting my words out.

'No. But Baloo did. They think it sounds very grand. Fortnum & Mason, Derry & Toms, Mowgli & Kim's. It's quite ridiculous.' He claimed this loudly inside. 'It's popular for lunches so I thought it'd be quiet for dinner.'

It was. We stood by two tills which formed a sort of entrance to a two-acre gated community of brazenly unoccupied tables. Everything was low lighting and black with polished fake marble. Several smallish woven carpets were under our feet, on the dark tiles. I was drunk and my head had drooped down, so I was staring at my leaky brogues – hating them – on the soft oriental carpet. The place was so large that at first I thought I was looking into mirrors but then I perceived the long front windows did stretch far away to a second set of identical main doors – with two more tills.

Abby immediately told the waiter it was the couple's wedding day. The waiter had been nodding and I felt he'd looked at my kilt with great admiration. He became quite animated and led us across the vast floor, past huge decorative urns, empty tables and unoccupied booths, to a corner table for six with very, very low lighting.

The restaurant was extremely dark and the nearest occupied table was very far away which came as a relief since Lou was loud and objectionable in most of his comments by then. You didn't see that other table with its diners, you just heard them raise the odd, cautious word somewhere in the moody distance, and you had to move position to glimpse them through the screens, fake creepers and the odd fountain here and there which babbled like peeing dwarfs.

Aoife and Lou sat next to each other and actually held hands for a while, just on the edge of the cloth, where Abby and I faced them across that big round table with a set place between us – so it looked like some kind of interview was taking place in a police station or immigration authority, with Abby and me as the interrogators.

Lou kicked off controversy straight away, looking down at the menu and asking the waiter if they sold champagne by the magnum. 'It tastes better that way,' he told the girls. 'Doesn't it, Cunningham?' he raised his eyebrows, implicating me.

I had jumped in alarm. The restaurant was close enough to the so-called Square Mile financial district for them to indulge in just such vanities. But the waiter walked away to check with the manager.

'Don't be so silly,' Aoife slurred. 'Enough champagne; don't go spoil it now.'

Lou shook his head and patted his jacket. 'Only the best for you, my love. And you, my good friends. You don't know what Gran gave me,' he said. 'In cash.'

'Then we should save it.'

'I'll pay,' Abby volunteered.

'Not. At. All.' Lou shook his head several times, decisively, like Oliver Hardy.

The waiter returned to explain there was only French pink champagne by magnum. This was immediately ordered. Then Lou pointed violently at me. 'And a bottle of Tiger beer for my Scottish batman; fine wine is wasted on such a pursing and scurvy lip.'

Rapidly a team of small waiters appeared from nowhere, slashing tall glass flutes down before us and pouring out this maidens' blush in a desperate hurry to encourage us on to the next bottle. Lou eyed the waiters angrily, moving his pupils from side to side. To distract him I called out across the table, 'Rhys seems like an interesting guy.'

'He's a chump,' Lou blurted; he dropped Aoife's hand and placed both of his flat on the table in defence. 'He's a weed with the dreary necessity to tolerate him.'

'He's a genius. Like you,' said Aoife, looking slightly up at his profile admiringly.

'I'm not a genius and he is certainly not. Just because he scored highest in the London Civil Service exam, doesn't make him a genius. The standard was piss poor back then. Hell, I did that exam too and almost beat him, just to annoy him.'

This went on for some time until I asked exactly what Rhys did in the Civil Service.

'He says it's all secret,' said Aoife cautiously.

'Bollocks!' Llewellyn shouted.

I heard the conversation at the distant table switch off. In the quality of their anxious silence, I somehow formed an impression that the far table was listening out not to overhear the specifics of domestic quarrels but instead to discern if Lou was yelling a general warning about the cuisine. When their conversation slowly resumed – across there – it was hesitant and filled with listening gaps.

'He's just a damn number cruncher. A woozy statistician. Though I'll say one thing in his defence.'

'And what's that?'

'Wise man. Never had a girlfriend.'

'Oh, Lou.'

I grabbed my enpinkened glass and lifted it. 'To the bride and groom.'

'The bride and groom,' Abby called.

Lou looked very drunk by now. He lifted his glass. 'Pavese wrote in his diaries, that the only women worth marrying are the ones that can't be trusted.'

I was grinding my teeth but then Lou turned to his beautiful wife and added, 'And you have proved him wrong.'

'Awwww,' went Abby.

I didn't know who poor Pavese was in those days, but I still silently placed a pointless oath against him.

'And what about men?' Abby called out, trying to get a lively debate going.

But thankfully Tuscan soil and gnarled olive trees had now entered Lou's mind and taken root; he launched into a long panegyric about his projected Italian holidays over coming years in which sometimes I or sometimes Abby were to be included – depending what way he faced across the table. He was crossing and re-crossing his legs furiously – a symptom I recognised.

'You need the toilet,' I warned.

'I beg your pardon.'

'You need the toilet.'

'So I do. Mr Silence, Exile and Cunningham, my trusty bladder squeezer.' But he wasn't shifting till he'd lorded it over ordering our food. And he ordered tracts of it, veering madly from the conventional and tested curry routes to other things; he demanded monkfish in batter, clay oven something, lime lassis.

With an amazed relief I saw him curl his nose at the wine list and say, 'Perhaps we're all right for conversation juice right at this precise moment,' and he softly closed the menu then made off to the toilets.

My relief was short-lived. When Lou returned with a burning fag in the corner of his mouth, I was badly mauled to see him intricately cradling two large wobbling tumblers of whisky.

'Where did you get those?' Aoife whispered.

'There's a bloody full working bar somewhere way over there in Andhra Pradesh.'

'Lou. Whisky is so expensive in Indian restaurants. Everyone knows that.'

'Shut up,' he snarled at Abby. 'I've only got a few years left and you grudge me everything.'

That was the first time I'd heard him lay out his Doomed excuse, and I knew it wasn't true. I'd talked for a long time with Aoife about Lou's health and learned the specifics. He was only at serious risk before his operation, but when he got drunk, he often seemed to get the linearity confused and he genuinely thought himself back in that year when he was in danger of losing his young life.

Bored with me, Abby had moved round to sit up against Aoife and she had taken the bride's fingers in her own. She was glaring down upon the wedding ring.

Lou tried to drag over a chair next to me but dropped it onto its side. He simply kneeled down on the carpeted floor close to me.

I snapped, 'Get up. You look like you're proposing to me and you're already married.'

The girls laughed as he rounded the table on his knees the other way and I had to right the chair.

We toasted with the whisky. He jammed his thumb back over his shoulder and looked genuinely concerned. 'Think there are elephants or tigers somewhere out there?'

When food came Lou had two cigarettes going in two different ashtrays. And he ordered two bottles of expensive white wine. I soon had four glasses: pink champagne, whisky, beer and wine, all active and demanding before me. He hardly touched his many plates. I struggled after a plate of prawns. I did observe Lou, quietly shifting some food into the jacket pockets of his beautiful suit, but

I said nothing. Let him suffer in Brighton tomorrow with crushed monkfish pieces in his empty wallet.

The girls were ordered desserts but I was not. A bowl of smelling cognac was placed before me, sloshing greasily. Lou and I sat staring at each other, fumigating across the wide table, long pauses in our disconnected utterances. Sometimes I got the feeling he'd physically lost sight of me in the gloom and I made deliberate movements to help him navigate to my location. Tobias Hanson now came in for a sudden and late barrage of flak for walking too quickly; Lou waved his pointed finger at me – or in my general direction. 'Doesn't he respect that I'm bloody ill? I could be dead soon.' He lit another cigarette – achieving a hat-trick. There was some talk of Malayan dialects, the rubber industry, Tagalog: the language of the Philippines, then speculative and uncomplimentary talk on the Prince and Princess of Wales' sex life.

The waiter came to ask if all was well. Lou informed him that it wasn't in the Prince and Princess of Wales' sex life, but it was at this table. The posse of earlier waiters now rushed the table edges once more. A complimentary bottle of bad Spanish cava had been presented to us. With foresight, the waiter asked if it might be opened now or perhaps later. Even Lou submitted, nodded that later would be best and he rudely grabbed the black bottle round the neck and held it to him, implying it might be taken back.

As soon as the waiters were gone, Lou turned to the girls and said, 'Take off your shoes.'

I thought things had just got more interesting.

'Pardon me?'

'Take off your shoes, we're all doing a runner.'

'Lou. Lou. No. Please. That's stupid. Besides, the girls can't ruin their good stockings.'

'Take off your stockings as well, then. We can't pay for all this.'

'But what about the money your gran gave you?'

'She didn't give me a bloody penny, boyo. It's hundreds here by now. I've cased the dump. Perfect. Two exits and we'll take them by surprise. Split into two teams, meet up at the Victoria Station Hotel. Farewell, my lovely.'

Though he had absolutely no need to, with startling litheness drunken Llewellyn Smith leaped upon the table like a novice surfer. Glass and cutlery protested. Aoife seriously screamed. Sure enough, that re-established stream of talk at the far table snapped off into silence again.

Lou crossed our table in two crashing steps with bottles tipping; my unfinished drinks rolled on their sides then the whole table dipped as he launched himself off the edge, hit the ground on his feet and began running through the dark like a rugby player, with the cheap cava bottle cradled into his bulk like a ball.

A waiter had appeared in the nocturnal ambience. I was about to try to explain; we would be forced to leave some deposit. The police could be called. I thought I'd have to beg my parents for money and pay it off somehow.

I turned to appeal to the girls for rationality. But as if they were about to indulge in a bout of skinny dipping, Aoife and Abby were bent over, their long arms reaching for their shoes, and they were rapidly unbuckling or twisting them off.

'Eh?'

'What goes on here?' A suited man I hadn't seen before was striding across towards us. The manager. The restaurant was so enormous, though, he was a long time coming. The girls screamed, loud, delighted giggles, and Aoife ran one way and Abby another.

A tiny waiter walked towards me very uncertainly. Without a second's hesitation I turned and ran.

I remember Aoife playful, circling a huge planted urn and taunting the pursuing waiter by quickly parting the reeds which came between them, making a rude face through the space while she laughed.

Far across the huge floor I saw Abby, chased between the pink discs of empty tables by two waiters, and I even glimpsed the distant table of diners whom I'd heard talking: hypnotised and in silence, their heads swung this way and then that in unison, following the girl in her wedding dress, carrying her silver high heels as she danced between the ivy screens then pulled free of the shy waiter when he tried to grab her bare arm.

I trotted half-heartedly to the door. I now realised the majority of the waiters had actually gone out through the far main entrance, chasing Lou up the street, which is why so few men remained. I stood at the unguarded door where through the glass I witnessed Aoife – the buckles of both shoes flapping in one hand, her silver clutch bag in the other, feet smacking down the pavement. She was pursued by no one. I heard her soles slap the cold pavement and she turned her head with a querulous look as to why I was standing there unguarded.

She was gone. She was fit. I recalled she once told me she had excelled at swimming underwater in secondary school. I looked down and thought: a wedding present. I kneeled and began rolling up one of the small, bright carpets at my feet, until it formed a tube of about five feet in length. With the carpet roll under my arm, I ran out through the front doors and up the pavement after Lou's wife.

That long street was quiet behind me and I could see the assembled white shirts of a group of waiters morosely ambling back up both pavements, arms dropped, shouting across the street to each other. They spotted me and suddenly gave chase.

Running carrying a roll of carpet while in a kilt wasn't easy. I turned a corner and jousted the end of the tube along the sides of various cars, but I gained speed. At one point I almost jettisoned the carpet but even without it I was so recognisable in a kilt there would be no sure escape. I passed the end of a quiet, shorter cross street. Squinting down it, I could distinguish mainly sixties office blocks and concrete steps. It was darker as well, with no pedestrians. I ran there. Though my brogues needed re-heeling they were making frightful clicking patterns on the pavement. Suddenly as a ghost crosses the line of vision in a movie, Aoife in her white dress floated shoeless across the opposite mouth of the street.

'Hoi.'

She recognised my kilted figure and waved a pale arm busily towards me.

To my left was a wide concrete stairway which turned round on itself and seemed to lead to a first-floor terrace and the entrance to some glass-fronted office block. Everything appeared locked up and was in darkness. The concrete stairs had moulded balustrades marbled in tiny pebbles, polished smooth by wearied human palms through the sixties and seventies.

Aoife Smith was running straight toward me – utterly silent – her hair still up, vibrating lightly like a framework, both high heels held in one hand. I saw a joy in her eyes never there before and I thought that it was Lou's madness alone that could put it there, yet her amazed look had settled on the pipe of carpet under my arm.

'Another little wedding present. Told you we'd lay some carpet in the corridor.' I grabbed her hand with my free one and led her up the stairway.

She laughed loud and completely. 'Did you just?'

'Rolled it up and ran. I think it's called looting.'

I would have testified that she had put on fresh lipstick in the short time since we did the runner. 'We got away together, you and me. We're lost,' she declared in a worryingly dreamy manner, looking about us. 'Let's run for it and find Abby.'

'No. Aoife, listen. I think they might have telephoned the police. A guy in a kilt with a carpet under his arm and a tall girl in a wedding dress. We're not hard to spot on the pavements. The rozzers will lift us on your wedding night.'

'Oh. What should we do, then?'

'Hide up here in this place, let things die down for a bit. No way are the police going to spend long looking for folk doing a runner from a restaurant.'

I led her on up the stairs; the way turned left. It was a type of concrete mezzanine to the main reception on weekdays, but that night it was shut up and dark through the glass doors. Yet both of us tiptoed cautiously, as if we expected humankind to be somewhere. I leaned the carpet against the wall, held my hands to the glass and examined the interior lobby through the doors, looking for the telltale low light, where a security guard might slumber with his feet up behind a reception desk. Nothing. The stone balustrade let you look down onto the street, one storey below. I cautiously peeked up and then down the pavement. The only way to find us would have been if our searchers ascended all the way up and round the stairs themselves.

With a dramatic flick of my arms, I rolled out the carpet along the cold concrete floor. She placed her shoes on the ground and we both sat down upon the fabric with folded legs. I had to carefully adjust my kilt, folding the material down on my crossed calves for warmth.

'Oh God. It's so, so cold. We won't die here, will we? On my wedding night?'

I stood up and I took off the black dress jacket.

'No, Douglas. You'll freeze. You've only a shirt.' I ignored her, bent down and draped the jacket around her bare shoulders. 'I'm Scottish. I'm used to it,' but I tried to suppress the shivers immediately.

Aoife's face looked along the carpet and she shot her hand to her mouth to stifle a giggle. Her wedding ring signalled once. She whispered, 'I just can't believe you stole this. That's so *cool*.'

I smiled and nodded, then I moved my face slightly closer to her small ear, unusually revealed by that construct of pinned-up hair. 'We must whisper really quiet, cause those waiters are still out and about. I saw them. I think they chased Lou all the way down the street but they didn't get him. Lou went really crazy in there.'

She nodded quick and whispered back, her breath touching my ear, which was stinging now, 'I know. I was shocked, but once we started doing it – the running away – I got the most terrible giggles. I was surprised I could run.'

'I saw you fairly moving.'

'I won swimming at school once.'

I nodded. 'You told me.'

She paused and seemed to think about her past. 'Oh. It's awful cold, isn't it?' Her teeth chattered and she quite violently pulled her stockinged knees right up tight, against her breasts. She dropped her face into the depth created by her knees, so her crown of white flowers almost touched my eyes. I could smell her perfume. I heard her breathing out warm exhalation down into that space.

'Where's that great big grey coat you had?'

'It's Abby's. Abby took it off in her big bag. I saw her swinging it at a waiter to shoo him away.'

She lifted her head to look at me and, smiling, we both had to cover our mouths. After a while, when it was clear we wouldn't laugh out loud, she sighed. I whispered, 'If we lay down flat, I could fold the carpet back on top of us. Like a makeshift tent, when you're a kid.'

She looked along the carpet again and frowned. 'Do you think it would make it warmer?'

'We could try. And it would cover up your white dress and my white shirt. We're very white, for folk trying to hide in the dark here.'

She lay on her back then giggled again. She folded her arms over her heart. I stood, got the end edges of the carpet and walking backwards, folded it down on top, then covered her to the neck. She vibrated with suppressed laughter. As if we were in a bed together, I squeezed in next to her. The carpet was narrow so I had to have my shirt sleeve pushed against her arm. We both began to chuckle.

'This is Horrid Horace. That's what I sing to Lily.' And she sang softly, 'Horrid Horace, pudding and pie. Kissed the girls and— Oh, I'm so drunk. Think of all the people who've been walking on this carpet with dirty feet. We'll need to get it shampooed for Lily to crawl on it. Wonder where Lou and Abby are, eh?'

'They'll be okay. They'll make it to the hotel all right. Another ten or fifteen minutes then we'll follow.'

In that very dreamy voice, she repeated, 'Ten or fifteen minutes,' and up so close next to her, I felt the communicated tremor of coldness travel down her body.

'You're freezing, huh?'

'Yes. I am a bit.'

We lay under the carpet beneath the silent office block, under a dark London in this weird and frozen privacy.

'It's my wedding night,' she whispered.

'Yeah.'

'Douglas?'

'What?'

'Can I ask you something? A couple of things?'

I turned myself on my side and leaned on an elbow, the carpet scraping against my skull, and I looked down at her face as one would do at a partner in bed.

She asked, 'What do men like?'

A feeling of blood filling my mouth came and I croaked. 'You're twenty-one; a mother. You know fine.'

'I don't think I'm very good at any of it. Has Lou said?'

'No. He certainly has not. Don't think such things.'

'It's my wedding night.'

My mouth had gone dry and I could feel my pulse – heavily – in my tongue.

'He thinks I'm an idiot and I'm dull in bed and he's only with me cause of Lily.'

'No.'

'I got pregnant the second time I slept with him.'

'He did tell me that.'

'Did he?' she chuckled, throatily but self-deprecating. 'But he didn't say I was boring in bed?'

'No. I think he's very into you, Eeef. Who wouldn't be? Mmm?'

She moved one foot. 'My stockings are all black dirt, ruined on the soles now. I suppose you won't see it in Brighton tomorrow with my shoes on.'

'No.'

She said, 'What do men like?'

'I can't believe you don't talk about this with Lou. You talk about everything else.'

'We just don't. What?'

'What?'

'Do men like?'

'Positions.'

'Positions?'

'Positions. You. To be in positions in bed.'

'What positions?'

'Aoife. You know.'

'What are their names?'

'Spoon.'

'Oh, I've done that. Like this. Lou and me done that for months, when I was huge, expecting Lily.'

'Yes. Well there you go, then.'

'And? Douglas. It's my wedding night.'

'Missionary.'

The three lines on her forehead again.

I whispered, 'That's normal, just you – the girl – on her back.'

'Oh right. I've heard of that. What others?'

'Sometimes men like you on the top.'

'Oh. Right.'

'Facing the other way.'

'What on earth do you mean?'

'Well you on top but twirled around with your back to the man.'

'Oh I see. *Really*? Is that possible? What else?'

'Doggy.'

'What's that? Is it sore?'

'Aoife.'

'What?'

'Hands and knees.'

'Oh. With Lou behind?'

'Yes.'

'And me crawling.'

'Well, or sort of with your arms down.'

'Down?'

'Your rear end is high, and your face is resting on the carpet. Bed.'

But the carpet began to move as she suddenly rolled over. The jacket I'd given her fell aside and with a suction of cold air she lifted the carpet on her rump by rising up on all fours. I nodded mournfully in the affirmative and patiently stated, 'Yes. Like that. But with your arms down. Down so you face is here.' I patted the carpet.

'This?' She rested her cheek on the carpet.

'Yes.'

She was so blithe; her thighs like two identical, erect pillars of slim white. The stocking material was pulled taut in the cup behind her knees – an inch height of lifted gauze.

'This?'

'Yes. That's the way.'

'Is it?'

I let her see my eyes move over her but when I let my eyes go back to her face she seemed asleep.

'Thanks,' her voice said quietly, almost bored. She still didn't shift position, then her teeth chattered and the eyes opened. 'I'm so very cold.'

I took a long breath; my soul was swinging in the night. 'Put the jacket back on, then.' There was a sliver of impatience to my voice but I still watched.

She idly lowered her backside and twisted round on it, sitting up straight, the skirt of her wedding dress now angled and bunched, showing more legs thrown out in front of her but she just didn't seem interested. 'It's my wedding night and I'm sozzled.'

I'd softened my bare voice. 'Yes. And you sound scared.' I reached out and put my hand onto the naked shoulder where I let it remain on her skin. I had to take a breath at the stupid joy this touch brought. The skin was so smooth but cold as a corpse.

'No no. I'm not scared, just surprised that I'm really married and I want to make Lou happy.'

I nodded, incredibly slowly. I didn't take away my hand and I said, 'Hope it's all okay tonight.'

She nodded so that the skin moved and thus my lightly placed fingertips slid and caressed upon her bony shoulder. Then she stated in a voice devoid of eroticism, 'I'll tell you.'

I took a strange and unsavoury hope in this promise.

She suddenly added, 'Shall we get a taxi together to this hotel, then? It's so sweet of you and Abby to get us that.'

I felt something celebratory sink away down inside me and wither. 'Suppose so.'

She looked thoughtful, then stated, 'I am so drunk.'

'Me too.'

'I'll go get the taxi,' she volunteered.

'That might be smarter than me in my kilt. Put on the jacket. It'll keep you warm and make you harder to recognise. This is number thirty-five. See it written up there? You need to get the name of this street.'

'I'll hail one at the end of the street and come right back.' She was buckling her shoes so when she stood up with the jacket round her shoulders she seemed enormous and intimidating as I remained helpless below, sat on the carpet.

After she'd gone, I repeatedly punched one fist into the palm of my other hand as hard as I could.

The taxi driver decided Aoife and I were married. That didn't cheer me up much. She did the talking to him on the way over to Victoria, her voice climbing back into that excited pitch the closer we got. They talked about carpets. I tried my best to chip in the odd word and keep face as the upbeat Scot.

In the wood-panelled bar of the Victoria Station Hotel, Abby sat. Alone. The free, still unopened bottle of cheap cava and some drinks placed on the table before her. She was carefully watched by businessmen in suits at the bar.

In a bright, breathing voice, Aoife said, 'Where's Lou? That man is a loon.'

'He went up to see the room about twenty minutes ago and

bloody well hasn't come back down.' Abby shrugged, pointing to the half-drained pint of Guinness and the ashtray with two butts in it. I looked at Aoife out the corner of my eye. Did I see fear or disappointment?

Aoife dropped her shoulders and in a cowed and quiet voice she said, 'If he's passed out, how will I get into the room?' All three of us now envisaged a much less amorous wedding night.

Abby stayed in hotels a lot and she told us, 'Because you're a couple, they should give you a second key.'

I tried to change the subject. 'That was all very mad at the restaurant.'

Aoife brightened. 'You won't believe what Douglas did. He was so brave and wild.'

'What?'

'You'll see on the way home. He had to get the hall porters at the front door to keep it in with all the suitcases. Lou used to be a hall porter y'know?'

I nodded politely.

Abby glared. 'You didn't roll one of them huge urns out that place and off down the bloody street, did you? One of them'd look good in my front room. Or your front room, according to the dole.'

'Come'n sit with me.' Abby patted the chairs. 'Those guys keep trying to buy me a drink even though they saw me here with Lou.'

'I'll ask about another key,' Aoife said and she crossed over to the swing doors and round to reception.

'He's crashed out upstairs,' I said.

'Probably.' Abby shrugged.

'Not very nice on the wedding night.'

'No. But that's lush Llewellyn.'

'They could both have ended up in separate police cells on their wedding night with that carry-on.'

'Memorable, at least.'

'Yeah, but. A bit unfair on Aoife.'

Abby gave me a wry look. 'What's needling you, Macbeth? I thought you were enjoying yourself?'

'I just think that was all a bit selfish. Involving people in a crime without their consent.'

'Oh hark at you, Lord Hailsham. It was an overpriced dump anyway.'

I said nothing more.

Now she frowned. 'Hey. How did you and Eeef hook up?'

'We saw each other in the street and we hid up outside this office for twenty minutes.'

'Oh,' she plainly stated. 'That was a good idea.'

Aoife came back with a room key. 'He's not answering the phone.'

'We'd better leave you.'

I pointed to Abby. 'I think you should go upstairs with Eeef just to make sure he's in the room. Christ knows, he could be wrecking the room or crawling across the glass roof of Victoria Station making invocations to the moon.'

They looked at each other; the image unlodged something responsive.

Aoife turned to me but said, 'All Lily's bottles in the usual place and the sauce is in the fridge for tomorrow.'

'I know. I know.'

'Don't bathe her. I trust you. I do, Douglas. It's just that bloody hot water is so scalding. I'll worry just a little if you're bathing her.'

'I'll clean her with the flannel but I won't bathe her, I promise.' I stood up and embraced her and kissed her on the cheek.

'Good night,' she said.

'Congratulations,' I replied, taking her hands and gripping them both, then letting them go. I handed her the large dark bottle of cava from the restaurant then she and Abby both headed off upstairs.

I sat alone, shivering. The businessmen up at the bar laughed. I dared not look over at them. Abby came back down about three minutes later and raised her eyes to the ceiling. 'He was awake, watching television. Just left me here like I didn't exist. Something that interested him,' she said. Then she muttered, 'It was a colour telly was his excuse.'

Cautiously, I looked down at Lou's half-consumed Guinness on the table. 'Is this paid for?'

Abby laughed.

I reached for the beer.

12

The next morning at Conrad Flats I didn't even fully comprehend it was a Sunday until Abby said, 'Right. I'm going to church. Coming?' She sat in the front room, wearing a new dress of her own from among the many she'd disturbed in Aoife's wardrobe. She'd done her hair different, wore the same high shoes as for the wedding, the same off-white stockings, because she had one long calf across her knee and was carefully prying a minute black disc of dirt off the silk with her fingernail.

'You're going to church?'

'To Mass.'

'Are you crazy? Aren't you hungover?'

'A little bit. Bring Lily – all the breeding mamas bring their brats to show Father Petrie.'

'Lily's settled and I don't have a suit.'

'Wear your lovely kilt.'

'You liked the kilt?'

'Of course. It's great. You don't need a suit. It's not Protestant. People take Mass in T-shirts because it's a holy sacrament.'

'You look like something out of bloody *Vogue*. *Vogue* isn't known for its overall obsession with spiritual matters.'

'Leave *Vogue* out of this. We're talking about God.'

There was a line I must use, I thought. The phone rang and Abby rushed to it. Aoife and Lou once more. They were using pub payphones almost hourly and I was starting to wonder if we were monitoring their day in Brighton or they were checking up on Abby and me. 'Yes. Lil's fine. Douglas is a fantastic wet nurse. Never.' Abby turned to me with a miraculous look. 'You're both going to Mass? I was just asking Douglas to come along with me. Isn't that remarkable? Okay.'

Abby and I walked to the Catholic church together – me pushing the pram – like two established parents. I'd drawn the line at the kilt. I wore a shirt and jacket from the night before with a pair of jeans. I was still trying to think up objections and I did. 'I can't come in the church.'

'What is it now?'

'Well, The Apple will be there. Granny Smith.'

'Don't be a silly sausage.'

'But she will.'

'She won't. She always goes to the very early Mass.'

Closer to the church, I suddenly asked, 'Do you think Lou and Eeef had sex last night?'

She didn't blink. 'Yes, I think I can hear it in Aoife's voice.'

'Good.' I nodded. Abby nodded too – both of us quite aggressively.

Inside the church – in case Lily started crying – I insisted we take the pew right at the back.

She hissed, 'You shrinking Protestant. That's all the further for me to walk up the aisle to the altar in these heels, making this noise.' Then she added in a real whisper, 'They already think I'm enough of a whore here.' She crossed herself.

I'd watched Abby dip holy water from the font when we entered, with her high heels clicking on the lime flagstones, and I'd seen her curtsey – no, genuflect – in the aisle. I noticed how she never turned her back on the big Jesus Christ, crucified high up above the altar, without genuflecting to him first. Even when she slid out the row to leave that morning, she genuflected first before retreating a few paces backwards. Rather graceful in its way.

I hadn't been able to follow the leaping order of the Mass card, bits were skipped and overlooked and I didn't listen to Father Petrie. I kept an eye on Lily and when they all went up to receive the Host, I watched Abby's tight ass, its slow but responsive symmetry – sure enough her heels clicked on the way up and back. Old ladies glared at both of us from beneath their bushy eyebrows.

When it had come time to make that sign of peace thing, I'd winced as usual; it's like that moment at rock concerts: wave your hands in the air, everyone. We were so far from the next set of worshippers, Abby and I had to nod when they turned round. We shook hands only with each other and had a sly smile together.

Throughout the whole Mass, I had generally thought about the previous night.

It had been instructive, after we had left Victoria Station Hotel, to witness the increasing disillusion of the taxi driver who took Abby and me back to Acton. First he'd witnessed Abingdon descend the stairs in her vintage finery, with her Gatsby hat back on, but immediately after I followed in my kilt, stumbling with a rolled-up carpet which the driver probably suspected I'd torn from the floor of the hotel.

Then the wait outside Granny Smith's as we wrestled Lily free from Flo. Flo was obstructive, and I actually had to threaten to phone Aoife back at the Victoria Station Hotel – in the midst of her wedding night unspeakables – before Abby and I got to take Lily away with us.

Then we had to load screaming Lily and her buggy into the back of the taxi, alongside that carpet, calling out the Bollo Lane council flat address. I caught the driver's disillusioned look when Abby paid him. His entire fare had slowly metamorphosed from *The Magnificent Ambersons* into *Steptoe and Son*.

Getting Lily, her buggy, drunk Abby in high heels and that carpet up the interior stairway of Almayer House took me two trips. I was surprised the carpet was still on the ground floor when I returned down to collect it.

Back up in the flat I leaned the tube of fabric against the wall while Lily was screaming. Lamborghini the tortoise was nowhere to be seen and there were billows of steam in the corridor. Abby had run a bath. 'Abby. I'd shut the tortoise in the kitchen and you've already let him out.'

'I last saw it in the living room. It's monstrous. It touched my toe when I wasn't looking.' I could not believe she had just left Lily strapped in her buggy, still in her anorak. It was way beyond the child's bedtime. She'd been awakened and she was in a poor mood, with corrugated, angry skin round her eyes. I hoisted her high but the nappy smelled okay. I walked up and down, holding the crying baby.

The phone rang and Abby had rushed through in just a smallish towel to answer; I knew immediately from Abby's tone it was Lou and Aoife at that bloody hotel where they should have been concerned with other matters. I was given the handset whilst I rocked

Lil in one arm. Into my ear, Lou's voice sang, '*I Just Called to Say I Love You,*' then he quoted something quite long. In Latin. Was it an invocation or spell? When he was finished, I said, 'Congratulations, mad bastard. Thank you for a lovely dinner. Very relaxing.'

'Very cheap. I hear you have enriched our home with an Axminster and I am wholly proud of you.'

'Go forth. But don't multiply,' I shouted over Lily's cries.

Aoife's voice suddenly came upon the line. Its tones and accent were intensified in my ear without her still and patient face before me. 'Lil okay?'

In a practical voice I replied, 'She got woken up so she's in a bad mood. Flo had let her sleep far too early. She'll soon be fine.'

'Okay,' said Aoife. There was a fractional pause and I snapped, 'Don't worry. Have fun in Brighton tomorrow,' then handed the phone back to Abby.

I put Lily back in her buggy, which did convert the cries into snuffles, snorts, aggressive turnings of the head, then I pushed her up and down the hallway – a regime which would often calm her. But late at night it also made Mr and Mrs Langham from downstairs bang on their ceiling with – it turned out – the ends of their second-hand golf clubs, which, Mr Langham had explained to us once on the stairs, he kept not for sporting reasons but for self-defence.

Abby was still mumbling secretly down the phone to Aoife. More last-minute sexual positions perhaps? I got changed.

'You've got out of your kilt. Why do that?' Abby tutted when I went back to the living room with Lily.

'Hush. She's settling.'

'Is she? Oh goody. I'm going for a bath.'

I needed to piss but I said nothing. I'd pee in a bottle if I had to.

Later, when I rolled the carpet out along the corridor, I noted that the bathroom door wasn't even locked, in fact it was three inches open. She wasn't in the bath, Abby was moving around in there naked.

'Are you laying your carpet, Douglas?' I could see her slim white body turning through the opaque glass.

'Watch you don't trip coming out. It's not a perfect fit.' The carpet was too wide so it sloped up the skirting on each side and it didn't stretch half the way down. I'd need to go back and steal another.

Lily was restless in her buggy so I took her out of it. I cleaned her and changed her nappy, dressed her into a fresh Babygro; then we played with the plastic bricks and the old Fisher Price station on the living-room floor. I loved watching her eyes and sometimes I'd lie on my back very still, hold her on my chest and let her sit there looking around. After a while she forgot me and was concentrating across the room, wondering where I'd gone.

I opened a can of Guinness from the fridge and in the living room touched it occasionally to my lips. It was instructive hearing Abby trying to summon me to the bath side, beginning, 'Sausage,' continuing softly, 'Douglas,' then a mystified, 'Macbeth?' and finally, aggressively, 'Cunningham!' The entire span of a relationship with her, demonstrated in moments.

I completely ignored her.

Lily's eyes followed a movement with fascination. Lamborghini, slowly moving down the hallway on some kind of mission. I grabbed the tortoise, crawled down the carpet quietly and by turning him on his side in an undignified manner I managed to silently insert the tortoise through the gap in the door onto the bathroom linoleum. I could see the painted toenails of Abby's foot resting up by the tap. I quietly retreated and the screams came a few minutes later.

She came up the corridor with an even smaller towel around her waist and another wound up high in her hair but absolutely nothing else, so her perfect breasts were not just free but still shining wetly. Her stomach was flat – almost muscled – with one of those twirly, filled-in belly buttons which hardly exist. Her face was flushed from the hot water. Even half naked, she looked extraordinarily fresh and very English. Her cheeks like a Cox's orange pippin.

'That savage reptile *forced* its way into the bathroom. Can't you lock it up?'

'I need to get a book from the library to put it into hibernation.'

'Book from the library. Book from the library. That's your life. Do you need to get a book from the library for everything?'

'Stop shouting; Lily's almost asleep.'

She went back down the hall. There were bangs and thumps from the bedroom. Abby was invading the wardrobes. I went to the toilet to pee and locked the door behind me. I soon realised the danger I was in. When I opened the toilet lid, the porcelain slopes were adhered with the squiggles, filings and curled scatterings of her black pubic hair snippings. I pissed them into the water at the bottom then flushed.

Lily was asleep when I went back into the living room, so I just sat drinking Guinness until curiosity brought Abby up the corridor. She was wearing a pair of pyjamas which I had seen Aoife wearing. Owner undefined.

'She's sleeping.'

'Awww. So adorable.'

'They are when they sleep. Abby, if you wanted to go home you didn't need to spend the night here.'

'But I'm already in my jammies, sausage. It's just— you never know. If something went *wrong* with Lily, at least you've got me here. It wouldn't be all your *fault*.'

'Yes. C'mon then. You put her in the cot and get her down.'

'No. No. You do it. I'll wake her.'

When Lily was laid in the cot she stirred minutely but remained asleep in that steadfast manner.

Inevitably, Abby and I were caught sitting together on the end of Aoife and Lou's bed, staring at the cot. Abby was leaning forward, rubbing her hair madly with a towel; then, holding Aoife's hairbrush, she yanked handfuls of the other woman's hair out of the bristles, assembling a disturbing and growing clump of it upon the bed.

'You know, it's cold in here, for a baby.'

'It's late, we've been out all day and we need to keep the electric bills down.'

'You're all going to get ill. It's going to age Eeef's beautiful skin.' She used the semi-cleared brush to sweep and tug through her own hair.

I said, 'Aoife was asking me about sex.'

'I beg your pardon?'

'Tonight. We were hiding from the waiters in this sort of door-way place and she asked me outright about what men like. Sexually. As if she had no real idea. Or no experience. She was anxious.'

'Putting on a show for Lou tonight, you mean?'

'I suppose.'

'Well. It is their wedding night.'

'Yes, but they've been living together for so long.'

'Maybe you're ruining their sex life, living next door.' She yelped delighted laughter and pulled a snag in her hair.

'You say some cruel shit, Abby.'

'Oh sausage, darling. I'm only joking. We're Catholic girls. The wedding night is meant to be a big deal and we haven't fucked around as much as all the rest of you.'

'I will say that was a brilliant touch of yours, to think to put them in that hotel. It made it really nice.'

'Yes it did. And I was pleased the big bear with the dicky ticker was still vaguely conscious at the end of it.'

'Yes. Not in a police cell.'

She chuckled. 'I'd just love to have heard your priceless advice to her. I'll ask her just what you said.'

'I'm going to bed.'

'You can sleep here,' she said quickly, and patted the bedspread.

'I'll sleep in my own bed.'

'That bloody thing? It's like a dirty stretcher from the world wars. Looks like someone might have died in it. And that reptile might crawl under it at any time in the night. You don't need to *do* anything in bed with me, Douglas. It's not *Scotland*, where you obviously just lift one another's kilts when you fancy a *wee* bit. You can sleep in a bed with another person and not *do* anything. With boys and girls. I won't *eat* you up.'

'Don't talk to Aoife about what she asked. She's shy enough and that was a private thing.' I lay back on the bed and leaned on an elbow, studying Abby.

She lay back herself, in Aoife's pyjamas, so that she was facing me.

She tapped a finger on the bedspread. 'What did you tell her? To do. With Lou?'

Since she'd lain backwards with her breasts shifting inside the pyjama top, the black and white photograph of Aoife was on the wall just behind Abby's arm. I let my eyes move fractionally so I could see the naked shoulders on that Dorset beach, Aoife's face bent strictly forward as if continuing to fellate the metallically tinged semen from her oyster-eating boyfriend of those times.

I saw it all now and it was useless to resist, as if Abby and I were both fulfilling the word in some ancient book written long before. We would be almost silent, Abby's skin beneath my hands, her expressionless face on the bedspread, me staring over her defined spine at the photograph of her best friend. I wanted to, of course. I wanted to pummel away non-stop at Abby from that moment until at least noon of the following day. But she would tell Aoife and, despite the insanity of it, I knew by sleeping with Abby in the Smiths' bed, under the watch of that photograph, I would de-sex myself for ever for Aoife.

Aoife's daughter cackled twice and began to cry and I tried not to raise myself up too quickly nor show my frustrated relief. I stood over Lily, trembling, then after ten minutes of her fierce crying – all watched unforgivingly by Abby – I lifted the child and carried her away through to the living room without a word. Twenty minutes later the babe was quiet but not asleep. Quarter of an hour after, when I returned Lily to try and put her down, Abby was in the bed under the covers and she had turned out the main light. I doubt she was asleep.

To be as far away from Abby as I could be, I slept restlessly in my clothes against Lou's dried blood on the front-room sofa. Lily slept but of course Lamborghini often scratched around throughout the night and well into the grey sieve of dawn – sometimes showing the word LOU sometimes AOIFE as he traversed hither and thither.

13

Though we couldn't really spare the cash, we'd been borne there upon public transport rather than a two-hour walk. Lou and I arrived at The Gertrude on the Kings Road after a long debate as to buying a round straight off or waiting for Tobias Hanson to get us one.

'We should buy our own drink. You always have to negotiate from a position of strength,' Lou maintained.

Inside the pub, decorations were up. A Christmas tree with flashing lights was doing counterpoint next to the gambling machine, blinking out a frantic contest between the material and spiritual worlds. Foams of old-fashioned paper chains were drooping from the low ceiling so that they touched our scalps and we actually had to turn our heads from side to side to move through them and reach the bar. The landlord did not recognise us.

Toby Hanson, in his diarrhoea-coloured cashmere overcoat, bashed in the door fifteen minutes early. He had a quite large cardboard box in his arms.

Lou and I watched him close in with undisguised terror.

'Chaps. Chaps.' He greeted us like the oldest of friends who'd been through school and many other adventures together, yet he deftly noted both our almost-full Guinnesses. 'Hey! See you're all right there. I'll get myself one.' He put down the box beside us.

As he went up to the bar, Lou murmured, 'Our first mistake.'

I replied, 'I sense the glory days are over.'

Lou grunted at this assessment.

Money had been very tight at Conrad Flats. Again. The way my supplementary benefit and my housing giro fell, the Nativity was going to be a mighty lean one. Pretending I had a faulty phone card, I had continued the campaign on my parents from the call box in Bollo Lane for the still-awaited means to buy new shoes. Yet I didn't see my parents believing they'd benefit from this particular investment. I'd even phoned National Savings Premium Bonds in Blackpool to enquire about cashing in but they had been obstructive. Aoife had already threatened heading north with Lily to her parents in Derbyshire for Christmas – and said she would take Lou with her. Her parents didn't allow drink in their house.

Tobias crossed back to us with a Bloody Mary in his hand and he sat down. 'Yes, chaps. Sorry all that Fear Taker business went so awry. This Morrell guitarist fellow was interested in doing a book but he's just being difficult. Now he wants to work on it with his own collaborator. He won't get the best book that way. Just a yes-man's version of what he wants us all to hear. So that's clobbered the small guide to Fear Taker as well, because if we do his book, my bosses don't want to find us competing with ourselves. Anyway. I've another tasty little project for us here.' He tapped the side of the cardboard box encouragingly.

'Manuscripts,' nodded Lou.

'What's that?' Hanson chugged back most of his drink.

'Manuscripts. You want us to go through some of the novel manuscripts you receive. We'd be happy to take a look at them, evaluate and give you our opinion,' Lou stated.

'Oh. Actually—' He opened the top of the box. Inside were what appeared to be several hundred photographs, some facing upward, some downward.

'Missed the boat for the nineteen eighty-five, but here, we've been having quite a success with this one. What we've got here is the eighty-six. We need you to think up a witty quote to go with each image for each month so, for instance—' Tobias Hanson placed his fingers in the box and lifted a random photograph. Of a cat. It was a massive white puff ball of a Persian, looking out from the picture with a shit-eating yet aggressive expression. Tobias held the cat photo toward our faces as if we were psychic mediums able to guess what was written on the reverse side. He peeked round the edge of this image, 'How about this: "That Blofeld's cat is a right sissy",' and he laughed for some moments. 'You know? Blofeld? The baddy in the James Bond movies with the big white cat?' He repeated for our benefit, 'That Blofeld's cat is a right sissy. There you are. There's one already. It's our Cat Caption Calendar for eighty-six. A real best-seller.'

I did not have the courage to look to my left and see Lou's face. I was sure I could feel the pub bench trembling.

I cleared my throat. 'What would the fee be?'

'Shouldn't take you chappies a day. Say fifty nicker. In total, not each.'

'Eighty total, then it's a deal, or forget it.'

'All righty then. Forty each, eighty in total. Now you write your captions on the rear of the photographs. Actually these're expensive colour Xeroxes of the originals. That's the reference number in the corners. There's about thirty photos here so do them all. We like lots of alternatives. Now you have a pretty free creative rein but obviously about ten words maximum per caption and keep most shorter than that. I stuck in this year's Cat Calender, so you can get an idea. Some inspiration. Now.'

'Yes?'

'You will find a few cats with Santa hats covered in tinsel or climbing the Christmas tree, rolling Easter eggs in the garden. A cat in a summer meadow. That sort of business.'

I nodded slowly but piously, as I was learning to.

'Obviously it's common sense that you might try to place these ones around Christmas or Easter or summer time, and make your captions season-appropriate. So if you write the month on the back of the image as well as your witty caption, our design people will organise it all from there on in. Okay, fellows. Ever onward.' He drained the watery dregs of Bloody Mary from his glass and stood. 'We go on our Christmas hols on, eh, Tuesday. Maybe you could hand the box back to Belle on the Monday.' He left.

I couldn't turn to look at Lou.

There was one saving grace to our work on the Cat Caption Calendar 1986. Caption writing could easily be conducted in the pub. 'Just off to work in The Bells for a few hours, love, on our commission,' Lou was legitimately able to shout from the front door as we both hurried away and down the stairs with the last of our money.

Lou confused the old fellows in The Bells by shouting across to them that we were filling out our betting slips. I had to censor many of his captions, though. His work started fine but after ten cigarettes and a few pints, his style became bellicose. A close-up picture of a cat with an expression was: *Out of camera, I have a thermometer up my anus.* Another read: *I ate all my kittens.*

Then towards the end of drinking and captioning, he just became obscure: *Marcus Aurelius snipped my claws*. Or, *The use of shadow in Japanese art is declining*.

Even working in a leisurely way in The Bells, we were done in two hours. Then on the Monday I made a second mistake. I sent Llewellyn to collect the money from Tobias's assistant in the Fulham Road.

Aoife and I had remained at home with Lily, packing Lamborghini into his hibernation boxes. I'd taken him along to the PDSA office and, free of charge, the ladies there had weighed the tortoise, cleared him for hibernation, given me advice and a bag of straw.

Lily was sleeping, so Aoife showed me down to the cellars of Almayer House. We descended to the main ground-floor lobby. There was an innocuous wooden door which I'd hardly noticed, then four steps down was a locked metal door. McDonald's wrappers and cigarette butts showed the four stairs were another teenage hangout. Aoife unlocked the metal door, put the lights on and I carried the boxes on down.

The store room of the cellar had 506 on the door and Aoife used the key on that. On the floor inside was a small square carpet with dirty tassels, a deckchair and an old-fashioned standard lamp. A skeletal clothes rack with plastic-looking overcoats and jackets which wouldn't mildew was shoved under some shelves. Pipes passed through the upper walls and across the ceiling; you could hear water travelling through them.

'When we first came to live here, Lily was crying a lot more and it drove him so barmy, Lou'd come down here, sit reading and smoking.' She shrugged. 'Or smoking and reading.'

I smiled at the accuracy. I noted two paperbacks on a rusty shelf. One of Arthur Bryant's romantic Tory histories and Isaac Walton's Angler thingummy. 'Not too cold at all here. This'll do.'

'Why do you have Lamborghini in two boxes?'

'Tortoises move around in hibernation, so they can wear through the cardboard of just one box and then the cold gets to them. Cold is the biggest danger.'

'Remember the Blue Peter tortoise?'

'Yeah. But what was his name?'

'Can't remember.'

We both stood there in the cellar looking down at the cardboard box with the tortoise in it. There was a long silence between us. Was her silence caused by trying to recall the name of the tortoise on telly when we were young?

'Look. Know what that is up there?' She pointed to the high shelf beside the books. There was a faded Golden Virginia tin there, but I noted that it had been affixed firmly to the shelf by black electrical tape. Aoife dropped her voice, looked at the door and whispered, 'That is drugs.'

'What?'

'That gay Brazilian friend of Abby's, Toninho, gave them to Lou and me. He was all for trying to get us to take it together but for goodness' sake, I was pregnant.'

'What kind of drugs?'

'Acid stuff.'

'Oh, LSD.'

'Doesn't it burn your stomach if you swallow that?

'No, Aoife. Course not. It makes you hallucinate though.'

'What if Lamborghini eats them?'

'Then he would move fast. He won't if they're safely up there.'

'That was why Lou put them fixed there. He was terrified Lily might find them if they were upstairs inside the house and she might eat them. I told him to flush them down the lav.'

'We could sell them for food.'

'Really?'

'Of course. But I don't want to get involved dealing to kids round here.'

'Some days Lou says he'll put one in Granny Smith's tea.'

'That wouldn't be a good idea.'

'We'd better get back up to Lily,' Aoife said cautiously, oddly unconvinced.

'Of course.'

Aoife called, very soft and sadly, 'Good night, Lamborghini the tortoise; sleep well,' as she locked the door.

Upstairs we sat together watching the television. She'd made a hot-water bottle and it sloshed and stabilised in her lap. Because watching television together was the closest to her I ever physically got, I always studied her cautiously out the side of my eye: she didn't blink much and I was drawn to the very syringe points of her eyelashes; at the side of her forehead you could see submerged freckles that looked as if they were flecks of gold, smeared over with an emulsion of milk. Sunlight – a good holiday on a beach – would lift those freckles out and I painfully wished I had the bread to take her away from Conrad Flats to that beach, scattered with conch shells and large coloured towels.

By eight o' clock at night there had still been no word from Lou. Aoife said, with great insight, 'He'll phone around nine. Nine is the longest he can push an afternoon to, and it's the earliest you can start the night if he gets permission. He always phones at nine though he doesn't know he does and he believes he's wildly unpredictable.'

'Tell him to come back or he'll blow the lot in pubs.'

At five past nine the telephone rang and she and I looked at each other. Aoife reeled him in.

At ten thirty he turned up with chicken dhansak, naan breads, pilau rice, fourteen cans of Guinness and four packets of cigarettes. 'Tell you this, boyo, I think that beanpole Belle disaster has a little thing for you. She was asking all about you.'

Of the eighty quid there was still over fifty left, which was far more than my anxious mind had expected. He gave me forty, counted his remaining share and said, 'Roll on Cat Caption Calendar eighty-seven.'

14

'Is Cunningham abroad?'

I snapped open my eyes on the camp bed and responded, 'Nae, he slumbereth yet.'

'Air mail.'

Two letters popped through the broken glass above the door. I grabbed out for them and missed.

One was a card from the postman: a parcel awaited me at the local Royal Mail sorting office. Parcels were notorious for only being delivered to the ground floors of Conrad Flats. Mine could be collected after eleven that day. The other letter was addressed to Miss Aoife McCrissican – pointedly not Mrs Smith – and it bore a Derbyshire postmark. I raised my eyebrows.

'Lou. This is for Eeef, not me.' I stood, tossing it back out through the broken window.

It was so cold I had to yank my icy jeans on and stand rubbing my thighs. By the time I had shivered, dressed, looked out over the repetitive frost on the sleepers of the railway below then at the angles and bulks of Brentford's great frozen gasometers, I smelled Lou's cardiac-busting coffee. I self-hugged my way up the hallway over that too-brief stretch of carpet.

There was an atmosphere. Lily was lying on her stomach, in the fenced-off play area. She was reaching for a yellow brick just beyond her fingers. I believed there was about to be another domestic quarrel.

'Hullo, Lily,' I quietly said. But she didn't look up at me.

Aoife was on the sofa in her pyjamas with a zipped-up cardigan and Lou was pressed in to her. Then I noticed – like a puzzle – the twenty-pound notes, fanned out on the tiny coffee table: the sharp corners of that table were wadded with torn cloth and parcel tape to pad them, in case of Lily falling. Dust and digestive-biscuit crumbs always clung to the peeled edgings of the tape.

Lou turned and looked up at me. He had an expression on his face that made me believe for a moment he'd somehow learned that his heart problem had recurred and he was in danger of death. He said, with a defeated voice, 'Aoife's parents have sent good money we could have lived on, for bloody expensive train tickets to summon us up there for Christmas.' He stared forward through the window and over the city, shaking his head, as if the solution lay somewhere beyond the West Middlesex Drainage Works in Isleworth – or even as far as Richmond Hill. 'What will I do? What *will* I do?' he turned to Aoife. 'You go with Lily, darling. I'll stay here with poor Cunningham, or he'll have to spend Christmas on his own.'

'I'm not going to Mum and Dad alone. Surely you can do without drink for two or three days?'

I sensed an argument very soon. 'I have to go to the parcel office. Can I get a borrow of your coat please, Lou?'

He snapped, 'Is the other one there or in the wash?'

Asking about the other coat's whereabouts meant he anticipated an argument and his auto-pilgrimage to The Bells. It was as good as arranging to meet me there.

'It's here,' I called from the coat hooks.

In an understandably grudging voice Aoife said, 'I washed it last week.' She changed her tone to a more accommodating one. 'Your shirts are here as well, Douglas, but I haven't ironed them.'

'I've told you not to bother ironing my shirts.'

'I'm doing Lou's ironing anyway. And you only have two shirts, Douglas.'

'Oh. Okay then. Thanks. See yous in a half hour.'

I was wearing the older mac with the brown blood smear on the lining of the inside pocket. My breath showed on the landing lobbies. Halfway up Bollo Lane I was hit by a sleery front of hailstones which stung my face and scampered down the coat's front, then the hail rapidly turned to sleet. The pavements shone with a glossy wetness. I could feel water in my sock, so I sheltered in Acton Town underground station for ten minutes but the sorting office closed at eleven thirty so I had to press on regardless.

When I entered the fluorescent light of the sorting office, I was shivering. There were two service points and a short queue built up behind me. It was an open counter, so surrendered parcels could be easily passed across.

The woman took one look at me, along with my postcard, and asked for identification. I showed her my UB40 card. After she came back with my parcel, I noted how she kept an eye on me as I settled over by the corner. My mum's handwriting marked the parcel. I felt the clot of guilt and I quickly tore open the paper. People turned to look at me: perhaps alerted by my impatience, perhaps nosey as to what was in the parcel. Inside was a pair of size eleven leather brogues. I rooted around further. A note, *From Mum & Dad xxx.* Nothing else; no cheque, no currency.

Not only the counter attendants but the people in the queue watched me as I took off my old shoes, pulled on the new ones over my wet socks then tied up the laces. I stood and tested the feel of the shoes as one does in a shoe shop, then I lifted my old shoes and carried them to the bin. Heads followed me. I dropped the old shoes straight into the rubbish, along with the wrapping, and I stepped outside, making my way briskly toward The Bells.

15

On the morning of the twenty-third of December I helped Aoife down the stairs of Almayer House, carrying the front end of Lily's buggy. I returned upstairs to assist Lou with the two suitcases. He was already swigging from the hip flask in the middle of the living room because Aoife wasn't there.

I'd witnessed Lou pack his case the night before – mainly disposable nappies and some shirts. Both his hip flasks filled to the brim with brandy. He'd also packed the sloshing amount which remained in the big brandy bottle which he had decanted from. There was another small bottle of Martell and three cans of Guinness; single packs of cigarettes in their cellophane were uncovered and they slid into appearance each time he touched any garment. 'I should be able to get at least six cans of Stella drunk on the train,' he confided, nodding as if he was stating the time it would take him to walk a specific distance.

I carried Aoife's case to Acton Town underground station, where they would begin their journey to St Pancras. Lou wanted to take the bus north and pocket the difference but Aoife wasn't travelling with Lily on a bus. I kissed first Lily then Aoife at the ticket barrier. I shook Lou's hand. 'Merry Christmas when it comes.'

He nodded, glum and condemned. 'You too, boyo.'

'I hope you won't have a sad Christmas, all alone. I feel very guilty. You should have gone home,' Aoife said.

'I'll have a sadder one,' murmured Lou.

'Make yourself at home,' Aoife smiled at me.

Back home, a newspaper gave the television and its trusty staples for Christmas Day: *Ben Hur*, *The Wizard of Oz*, a Morecambe and Wise repeat and the Queen at three, who I never miss – to shout obscenities at. Superb. I surprised myself to find it a luxury, contemplating Christmas up there alone in the sky above West London. A council spire for the curmudgeon. Peace at last from the constant and wearying temptation Aoife presented. However, gradually I was drawn down the carpet to their bedroom. Having the nude photo of Aoife there was like being left alone by some gallery director with a Canaletto, a Carpaccio or a Picasso etching. You were going to put your nose right up to the surface of the image and examine it, scrying for the brush strokes of the immortal presence. I did so with the photo. I noted the dust along the top of the clipped-on glass, but I also discerned the mist of an erect nipple concealed within Aoife's vertical cascade of hair. I wondered if there were piles of negative out-takes somewhere, and looked haplessly around. I got on all fours and peered in under the bed. Only more of Abby's clothes seemed to be compressed there. I was a little afraid to lift the photo down, study it even closer and hold it in my arms – I was wary of making tell-tale fingerprints in the dust. It was a sure giveaway. I studied her legs in the colour photo and scowled at the male model pretending to drive the vintage sports car. To look so great on just two days of your life, and to have photographic evidence, meant your heyday was both established and over with, I thought.

*

There was nothing in the flat to eat except half a dry loaf, fit only for toasting, and a jar of Marmite, which I was counting on to get me through all of Christmas Eve and Christmas Day. There was a whole pint of milk! I boiled up spaghetti, the black kitchen windows host to innumerable jewels of condensation; the lights and flashing blue sparked far outside, as if I were within a fly's giant eye. There was no sauce for pasta – we were so broke we didn't even have tinned tomatoes – so when I'd drained it, I melted a tablespoonful of old Marmite in and ate the browned spaghetti from the saucepan.

I peeled and sucked the juice from an orange while staring into space. Then I carried the typewriter through to the big table in the front room. Until two in the morning I slowly typed a long story. We could not afford Tippex so when I made a mistake, I used two coats of Lou's Milk of Magnesia – for his whisky drinking – and this did just as well.

The story was this: A young man in London cannot get his novel published or taken seriously, so he resorts to using the last of his money at a seedy vanity publisher on Commercial Road. He has exactly twenty copies of his novel printed up and bound in a richly embossed leather. He then distributes these twenty books by his own hands, smuggling them in under his jacket and placing one copy each in the Fiction sections of twenty bookshops around Charing Cross Road – including Foyle's. Although he is thrown out of his bedsit and made homeless, he finds himself happy each day of that summer, wandering these twenty bookshops in central London, letting his eye fall upon *his* book lodged upon those shelves. He feels fulfilled. The books can never be purchased as they are not listed stock, so they should remain there, making him happy.

Then, one afternoon in August, inside one of the bookshops, he witnesses a beautiful girl (I saw Aoife in my imagination, dressed as in the vintage-car photo) actually standing and, with great absorption, reading a copy of his book beside the shelves. To his amazement he witnesses this girl conceal the copy of his novel in her clothing and steal it from the bookshop. He follows her through the streets of Soho but he loses her. Then – one by one – copies of his book also begin to disappear from the shelves of all the other bookshops, as he patrols frantically between them. Sometimes he witnesses the beautiful girl's figure turning street corners in the distance, but he can never catch her. The day comes when there is only a single book left. He takes to sleeping outside the bookshop door at nights, trying to guard the book during the day. Just another homeless figure. It isn't the books that concern him any more. He considers them expendable bait. It is the young woman. He must meet her and talk to her. Eventually the bookshop owners call the police, who move him away, and when he forces his way back into the shop for a final time, the last copy of his novel has vanished. He never sees the beautiful girl again and the tale ends with him sleeping on the streets, shivering as winter arrives.

I slept upon their bed that night. On Aoife's side. I could smell nothing in her pillow, though. Sleeping *in* the bed seemed a sacrilege too far, so I slept on top of it, between the crocheted cover and the candlewick bedspread with extra blankets from my camp bed.

On the morning of Christmas Eve I lay in late, then I reread the previous day's writing and I was satisfied – making some small emendations in pen.

I brewed repeated mugs of coffee, ate Marmite and toast, listened to 'Summer (The First Time)', walked from room to room and paid homage to the photographs of Aoife again. And again.

I can remember clearly the feel of me, reading those pages but excited by them, in the cold alert air of that room high above Bollo Lane, taking frequent pulls on the latest mug of coffee. Then the daylight stuttering and drearily dying in a slow, almost thoughtful and testing progression as night came on. Ultimately, I was content. The day escaped under a metal sky and the night grew late. I wiped the condensation clear and could see lights in the distance, like the atmospheric colours seen spangling upon stars – but these weak globules of light, pleading in the dark, were in fact scores of Christmas trees receding in the windows of the south, down through Brentford to the Thames.

Close to midnight I jumped at a knock on the door. Abby? But she too had gone north and had talked of meeting with Lou and Aoife there. The North Will Rise Again. Well, Derbyshire. It might have been a neighbour with a last-minute Christmas card for Lou and Aoife: the Langhams with a remorseful gift, or to complain about the noise I'd been making, clomping about?

'Got some rancid tart from the telephone boxes in there with you?' Lou pushed through with his suitcase. 'I saw a light high in the sky and was drawn here. Hey. All the bloody pubs were closed at St Pancras and I was propositioned by a whore outside King's Cross. A wee Scotty, of course. Perhaps a relative?'

'No doubt.'

I recall a split second of being despondent: despite occupying his home and coveting his wife, I felt the mildest twinge of resentment at Lou just for returning to his own flat and terminating my lonesome Christmas.

He stood in the front room. 'What an unmitigated nightmare. I got the last train out of Derby, thank Christ. The last train out. And I tell you I wasn't the only one fleeing. It was like the fucking American embassy in Saigon. It was like the pier at Smyrna – no, was it Austerlitz? Russians or Prussians trying to escape Bonaparte across the iced lakes and falling through. Anything was better than ending up in Derby for Christmas. It was like VE day on the happy train south. People embracing, crying with joy. I made sure I got next to the buffet car too, for some grog.' He tapped his flat stomach.

'Aoife's staying, then?'

He was drunk and went on for some time: 'Course. I'm in the shit but I couldn't take another minute of it. From the moment we left here. Bloody train up from St Pancras was packed. Lily crying all the way with snot pouring down her face. Every bastard had a cold, coughing up their lungs like they all smoke more than I do and we couldn't get a seat nowhere but *in* bloody no-smoking with this coughing clan. I'd to stand in the aisle. So solid I couldn't get up to the buffet for those beers. And I nearly got in a fight with fucking knuckle-headed Sheffield squaddies who were chatting Eeef up. I told them: "Stop trying to shag the wife and get a mission going lads. Your co-ordinates are the buffet car. Cup of tea for her, six beers for me." They disobeyed those direct orders from a superior officer, boyo, I can tell you.'

I kept listening as I walked through to the fridge, retrieved the single can of Guinness from the back and returned, handing it to him. He took it and cracked the top without pause.

'Fucking king's shilling fascists, restless since the Falklands I should guess. Itching to poke their Armalites into another country's business. The English are never happy unless they are. Arrived at the in-laws' bunker stone cold sober, which is never the way to approach it. They started planning out how many Masses they could cram me into over the following days. You have to say grace before you have a cuppa there. Then Old Minky, their priest, was coming round for a glass of sherry to talk theology with me. Test my Spanish. I speak it better than him but for a shortage of vocab. I'll discuss theology with him okay. Personally, I take the bishop's position. I'm a stickler for it: with a fourteen-year-old blond boy underneath me. Anyway, I lasted one night, I think it was?'

'Yes. You left here yesterday.'

'Oh yeah. Then I had a stand-up row with Aoife's dad, the self-righteous dandiprat. Never trust a Catholic who doesn't drink, Cunningham. They're either converted, poxed or pure psychotic. Like him. Doesn't allow a drop in the house, covers it up with a daily matinee of pious fakery. Only a family like that could produce a woman with Aoife's looks and indolence – it's a cruel joke. Right?' He looked around, as if he were unfamiliar with his surroundings already. 'Is this all the booze?'

I felt a little possessive over my only bottle of wine. 'There's a bottle of Co-op wine left over from something. I was going to have it tomorrow.'

'The hell with that, you lunatic. Reach for the corkscrew.'

'But then we'll have nothing to drink tomorrow. It's Christmas Day, Lou.'

'Nonsense. Course we will.'

'How? We're profoundly broke.'

'Don't you worry about the details.'

When Lou took a sip from the wine bottle, he smacked his lips and said, 'Old Man McCrissican can't moan, I'm partaking of the communion after all.'

I showed him my typed story and he became ominously quiet, reaching out and touching the pages suspiciously as if they were a court summons. 'Christ sake, you're inspired.'

'It's not much good.'

He nodded, 'I'll read it tomorrow, if you don't mind so very, very much.'

That was that. The wine didn't last long so we both turned in.

On Christmas morning Lou and I drank coffee, standing side by side, looking way south: the sky a ceiling of great sagging clouds like droops in wet ceiling plaster, carols playing in the background on television. The Heathrow planes must have been up above the cloud – if they flew on the Day of the Saviour. After a few moments you noticed the underground station's uneasy stillness below.

'The grub's all out. There's nothing.'

'The hell with food, what about grog?'

'Nothing left.'

'Jesus. Why hast thou forsaken me?' But he nodded decisively. 'Pastures new. Capitalism always provides.'

I wore one of Lou's cardigans and a scarf under the other raincoat and we sauntered through Christmas Day Acton in our identical macintoshes. No pedestrians moved but us. Roads were quiet, family cars crammed and shuttling from house to house, but no buses or lorries. Up past Woolies we paused by the windows of that rival to Harrods: Fine Fare. We gazed in at the yellow-label budget range so favoured by us. When Lou couldn't afford Embassy Regal, he often made do with Fine Fare's own: a yellow pack with *Cigarettes* proudly emblazoned upon the front.

Some of the Asian corner shops were open for business, which was frustrating as we glimpsed their rows of licensed liquor bottles, the curved glass glowing in fluorescent light. We moved north, toward the mainline railway, which was stilled.

Lou and I arrived at a low, flat-roofed red brick structure with a high wire fence round it, but the gate was open. The sign read: North Acton Railway Club. There was a Guinness sign up above the door and it was warmly illuminated.

'This is licensed, but they'll be picking over my cheque.'

'Cheque?'

Inside was completely empty of customers; cheap, bright, reflective Christmas decorations were hung around the bar area. A gambling machine quietly signalled its lights with the same morose presence as the village idiot. I walked with Lou up to the bar. For a few moments nobody appeared, then a middle-aged guy stuck his head out from round back.

'Merry Christmas,' said Lou.

'Oh. Hello.'

'Our womenfolk have us running very late on that bloody turkey.'

'Oh. Like that is it?' the barman nodded.

'Knew I shouldn't have bought such a whopper. It's going to take hours in that oven so *we* thought we'd nip round to *you*, slake our thirsts and spend a bit of our old hard-earned on a few quick ones,'

Lou continued without pause but turned to me for effect. 'My old man used to take me here when I was younger. Right. Two pints of your Guinness, please, but I don't have much cash on Christmas Day. Can I write a swift cheque for fifty pounds? We're just going to spend the lot here anyway so, got a pen?'

'Strictly speaking this is a members' club, lads, but— You know?'

'It's Christmas?'

'Yeah. It's Christmas, isn't it, and if your old man was once a member—' He shrugged, passed the pen and he began to pour the first pint.

Lou had produced a chequebook of Midland Bank from inside his coat. I raised my eyebrow because I'd never seen such a totem before. He opened it and began writing a cheque for fifty quid.

'Make it out to North Acton Railway Club?'

'Yeah, please.'

'Did you know Dad? Over at Old Oak Common depot? Jim McCrissican.' He repeated, 'McCrissican?'

I frowned at the lie.

The barman was concentrating on the slow-pouring drink. He blinked and said, 'Oh. Your dad was at Old Oak, was he? Ah, yeah. Yeah. Retired now, is he?'

'Oh yeah. Years back. Got his feet up now, hasn't he?'

'Wise man.'

Lou signed the cheque *A McCrissican*, adding an elaborate re-peating rococo squiggle beneath the signature, which he used to obscure and blot out the 'Miss' printed there. He placed the written cheque upon the counter, facing into the bar, and he positioned the cheque guarantee card above it, while the pen lay vertical, across the plastic, again obscuring the 'Miss'. The barman put down the second pint beside us and was about to pick up the cheque when Lou suddenly added, 'Oh yeah, sorry, mate, and two whiskeys. What Irish do you have now?' he scanned the bottles. 'I only drink the Irish. Ah, Powers. Two Powers whiskeys it'll be as well.'

The barman nodded tolerantly, filled a water jug from the tap and placed it on the counter; he held up the glasses to the whiskey measuring spigots.

'Make 'em doubles, and why don't you have something for yourself as well, since it's Christmas Day.'

'Well, thanks very much.'

'I'm surprised you're so quiet.'

'Most folk come in the evening today; y'know, escape the kids and the toys broke already and all that.'

'Oh yeah. Absolutely.'

The barman put down both the whiskeys.

I now realised that, psychologically, Lou had fixed the surname McCrissican in the barman's mind. That was what the barman was concentrating on when he looked down on the cheque and didn't even pick up the guarantee card to examine it, he just lifted the torn-off cheque, carried it and rung the till while speaking aloud, 'Right. Two Guinness and we'll make that three please, cause I'll keep one in the till for myself later, thanks; and Powers times four and the total. Okay.'

Lou had whipped the guarantee card away as the bell jingled and the till drawer came open. There were actually several other cheques in a compartment with a spring-loaded metal clip holding them together at the vertical. The barman placed this latest cheque amongst them and he removed the change – including four real, undeniably beautiful tenners – conjured from the ether.

Lou and I sat against the far wall. Near the door. 'Drink up quick,' he murmured.

'Feeding of the five thousand,' I stated. We clinked glasses and downed the whiskey in one. Smooth as it was, we made sour faces at its punch. I lifted my Guinness and said, 'And a Merry Christmas to you. God bless us all.'

'Peace on earth.'

I doused the oily burning in my throat with the bitter, yeasty stout and then took pleasure in letting the masculine fumes of it all batter round my front teeth.

'Spare a gasper?'

'Sure.' He peeled me off a cigarette.

'Match me, Sidney,' I quoted.

He slowly took out a household-sized box of matches and we both laughed.

'My Zippo is in the garage for a service. One million ignitions. Actually, I can't afford to refill it.' He lit me off the match that he then used for his own cig.

'You know that? Match me, Sidney?' he asked.

'Sure. *Sweet Smell of Success.* Made by a Scotsman.' I nodded to the bar, 'Well this isn't exactly the 21 Club, but good show.'

He lowered his voice strategically, 'If you think a woman is going to leave you, Cunningham, always steal her chequebook and eat into her overdraft. I knew that these Anglo-Saxons wouldn't know if Aoife was a boy or girl's name, I just had to squiggle out the "Miss".'

'Aoife isn't going to leave you.'

'I'm pushing it near to the line now.'

'Fiddlesticks. She's only just married you and she adores you.'

'She needs someone steadier.'

'You just need to watch yourself on the sauce for a bit.'

'You're starting to sound like her, boyo.'

'We all love our beer, but you're pounding down the hard stuff like your legs were hollow: spirits, brandy, all that shit's like drugs and gets you in the end. Beer just makes us fat and you can quit when you want.' I nodded and slobbered down another few delicious gulpfuls.

He looked at his feet. 'I don't know, Cunningham. That illness fairly shook me up. You don't want heart problems; trouble down in the main engine room. I thought I was on my way out and all my life would have amounted to was me banging up Aoife. Making a widow with a fatherless daughter. What an achievement. I know I should be up, but when you sail that close to the wind some of your glitter gets shaken off. Not that I ever had much.'

I nodded, nuzzled into my pint, then replied, 'I can believe that. You know, some people who have survived an air crash feel all their material aspirations and possessions have become worthless; they report feelings of rebirth.'

'Well that's what it's like. Of course I have a child to provide for, but to me material things have melted into air and I just feel so bloody great, so alive. When I drink. If I want money it's only for my girls. C'mon.'

The barman had taken a step round the back, so Lou and I walked to the club door, let it swing quietly behind us then moved out into the cold grey of Christmas Day. Lou took the change from his pocket and fanned out the four tenners in his hand for us to look at – as if to confirm they were in our possession.

'These are mere tokens of transformation,' Lou pledged.

'Yes,' I said. But on the way back to the corner shop to purchase a great deal of booze, we passed the Catholic church I had been into with Abby after the wedding. People were crowded on the pavement, entering it for Christmas Mass. At first, Lou had merely glanced aside as he talked busily about our choice in grog; he was walking onward but then he abruptly stopped.

'I might go to Mass.'

'You're joking? Won't your granny be in there?'

'Nah. She always goes at crack of dawn if her pegs are in good shape. She's first in. You can gossip with Father Petrie longer at the early Mass. Come, there are cheap seats for Prods.'

'Will there be carols?'

'I'll request them for you.'

So I stood beside Lou, once again inside that Catholic church and its smell of incense. The church I supposed he would have been married in, had they all agreed. He nudged me, winked, sang along with false gusto and forced me to do so also. He rolled his eyes at the prettiest girls, dressed up in their best. I noticed he dispensed quick, ducking genuflections and rapid crossings. He slouched provocatively and met the priest with a challenging eye, as if he might leap to his feet and contend the oration at any juncture. At the sign of peace, he shook hands joyously with those around him, as did I. When Lou went up to take the Host, he positioned himself behind a pretty teenage girl, smirked back at me once and stooped with one hand in his pocket – but he still got down on his knees and did the business with the rest. As we went to leave, several folk – older men who knew his gran – stepped up and wished him a Merry Christmas.

Outside, he borrowed ten pence off me and went directly to the telephone boxes by The Bells to phone his gran. 'Twenty minutes, she'll know I'm back in Acton anyway. Word travels fast in the chapel circles. I'll be a few moments, though. Takes her two or three goes to get to the phone now, the poor old girl.'

When he came out of the phone box he said, 'Couldn't get her; must be round Flo's, she'll go there for the Christmas feed-up for sure, but it's a bit early.' He looked at his watch. 'Hope she's okay. Sorry, Cunningham, we best just pop round. You never know. There might be some grub. I hope you don't mind.'

'Of course I don't mind. It's Christmas.'

After knocking for some time, a hall light came on, changing the stained glass to deep ruby. Myrtle Smith's voice wheedled out from behind the door, 'Who's there? Is it robbers?'

Lou gave me an exasperated look and shook his head. 'It's Lou, Gran.'

Granny Smith opened the door. 'Well, well, look what the cat dragged in. Merry Christmas indeed.'

'Merry Christmas, Gran. I was phoning.' He hugged her.

'Cat must have knocked it off the hook again.'

'Merry Christmas, Myrtle.'

'Merry Christmas, Douglas.'

I was overwhelmed that she could even remember my name. I had to bend over to kiss her on the cheek. She wore a cardigan which hung down very low at the front she was so stooped over; I could feel her shoulder blades through the thick wool when I put my hands there. Her cheek was as dry and fallen as an old wasps' nest.

'It was ringing fine, Gran. You're Mutt and Jeff these days. What cat?'

'Flo's. Old Buggers. He's near twenty year old now, y'know. Started coming in here from round the back, hasn't he, looking for a spell of peace when it's all a bit hectic round there. When Flo has one of her turns. They put him out today cause he can smell the turkey doing in the oven. Come through the parlour with both of you.'

'Old Buggers, he was here when I was a kid. Douglas and I had a run in with bloody cats recently, didn't we, boyo? Going round there for your nosh-up are you, Gran? Pull a few crackers.'

'Yeah.' She quickly stated, 'Don't think there are any spare places y'know, Lou? I thought you were all away up north with Lil. Watch that wife of yours get fed up good and proper with some dumpling and turkey.'

Lou claimed, 'There was a bit of a travel mix-up to do with British Rail. Aoife and Lily are up there now for a few days, while Douglas and I shall be holding the fort. We're doing a spot of DIY while the lady folk are away.'

'Are you now?' We had followed her into that front parlour and out came a sherry bottle and little glasses from the cabinet. 'Have a sweet sherry, boys.'

'Nothing with a bit more kick, Gran?'

Very quiet, she muttered, 'I'll give you a kick for sure.'

For all her acidity, I very much liked Myrtle Smith.

She frowned. 'You want to watch yourself. Don't you, though? Up north. This time of year.' She poured three glasses from the bottle with a very shaky hand.

'Absolutely. Couldn't agree with you more, Gran.'

She handed me a small glass of sherry in her unsteady fingers. I noted the glass was very dusty but, of course, I said nothing. When she turned to give a glass to Lou, he gave me a look. 'Any grub in the fridge, Gran?'

'Oh Lou? You two boys aren't having some kind of awful bachelors' Christmas, are you? Told you before to eat your greens and go for your mid-afternoons, since you was up in that hospital, but you won't heed. He won't heed at all.' She looked at me. 'Cheers, boys. Merry Christmas and the Blessed Trinity.' She hoisted her own sherry and took a sip and so did I. 'Take a seat,' she pointed.

'Merry Christmas,' I said, sitting in the chair I had sat in last time.

Lou downed his sherry in one, left the glass on the sideboard and stepped from the parlour. I heard a crash in through by the kitchen. Lou shouted, 'Out of here, Margaret Scratcher, damned parasitic rodent!' There was the skidding of rapid paw work on the hallway tiles.

Granny Smith leered across at me, revealing her teeth, said warmly, 'Old Buggers,' and chuckled.

'Some spuds in here, Gran, can I take 'em?' he called through.

She looked at me but she spoke at a volume high enough for Lou to hear. 'For goodness' sake. Have you not a tidgy widgy to eat up there? I bet there's booze galore. I don't know, the two of you young fellows living like the war was still on. Lou, I've remembered the telephone ringing, love.'

'Have you, Gran?'

'Yes. What happened, son, is I had to get my teeth in. I had them cleaning in the Lady Di mug, because that's me away through with Flo for my Christmas dinner, so I need my teeth nice and white. I can't talk on the telephone without my teeth in, Lou. You'd think you were through to the Chinese restaurant. So by the time I'd got my choppers about me, the phone had stopped. I swear, I can get one day mixed up with the next.' She had turned her attention back to me again, shaking her head, frowning momentarily as if she had forgotten I was there – or who I was.

I asked her, genuinely interested, 'Were you in London during the war, Myrtle?'

'Course. Where else? We wasn't evacuated. Just the nippers got 'vacuated. Lou's dad was grown by then; he was RAF y'know. Ground crew he was, not a flier. He was down there at Tangmere but that was after the Battle of Britain. I can't claim he was there during it. This was after, when the bombing got worse. Then he was up in Lincoln with the Yank bombers, later on.'

'You were here when the Blitz was on?'

Lou called, 'Leave it out, Gran.'

'Course I was. I'd like to see this bunch of pansies today, when a five-hundred-pounder or whatever they were comes down. Mind you, there was lots of men like that. They march round now, telling you how brave they was, but there was plenty worried faces that I saw. And worse. I saw tears. And all you men thought your end had come, so you were about twelve times more randied up than normal.'

Lou let out a whoop from the kitchen.

She suddenly looked at me as if I was a right queer ticket. 'What? Wasn't your folks in the war, then, up in Scotland?'

'Nah, my mum and dad are too young.'

'Too young. Ah, I see. We thought Hitler was going to be marching up The Mall any day.'

From the kitchen – where I suspected he was leaning against the sink, calmly smoking a fag – Lou shouted, 'He has done. Blonde wig and lipstick. Called Margaret.'

'Tom Daniel and his brothers was talking about how to block up Acton High Street themselves. You know that, Llewellyn? That's a fact.'

Lou came back through with a carrier bag and I could see it was hanging heavily with a jumble of large potatoes pushing against the white plastic at the bottom. 'I was going to say the Nazis were bloody welcome to Acton. But everything everyone fought for is getting pissed on now, by that sell-out shopkeeper from Grantham and her second-rate cast of blethering toffs.'

Granny Smith frowned at Lou. I asked her, 'Did you actually see the German bombers, up in the sky?'

'Course I did. In daylight raids. We was down by Chaucer Road then and you could stand out by the shelter and see them go over or turn back for France. There were two kinds of Jerry bombers, both with two engines, but the long thin ones, like pencils, was Dorniers, one come down right on Victoria station this one time. The hunched-back things, like a raven, with big thick wings, were Heinkel bombers.'

'God's truth, Gran, he doesn't want to hear Commando-book stuff.'

'Shut it, Lou. He's interested. Being Scotch.' I was surprised how raspy her anger was. 'They didn't have the Blitz up in Scotland; it's all hills.'

'Ah, with all due respect, we did. Clydebank got flattened. All down the hill from the Singer works to the river. Six or seven hundred dead in two nights. We had the shipyards up there, you see.'

Myrtle frowned. 'Crikey. Now you mention it, I do remember that. There you go. See, Llewellyn, I was right.'

Lou frowned.

She went on, 'Yeah, old Hitler made war be everywhere. There was no bloody escape. That's what I remember of it, all clear as day. It's a terrible thing, boys, war. Keep well shot of it. It gets up in the air all round you. The Nazis made the wind and the weather all become war.'

Lou gave me a look, raised his eyebrows.

'True, wasn't it? Suddenly it was all war. You woke up to it and slept in it; the weather, the clouds. The chance of where your house was happened to be built, if it got hit or not. In old wars, civilians weren't up for the chop then suddenly we were. But listen here, the most fancy thing I ever saw then was down in Kent, in among the hop frames. Wasn't so much hopping for Londoners during the war but still a good bit was done and we were down there sometimes with the others, the Acton Lane Petersons with old Tom Daniel and his brothers, all the way down to Kent in the back of an open lorry, singing songs. I was into my forties during the war but I was still nippy enough.'

Lou began laughing. 'You never told me any of this.'

'You never ask, Llewellyn. Rhys used to. You always had your mug in a book, then a drink. I was an old lady already when I had my hands full with you two, so I didn't go on. But for all the beer you boys drink, I bet you don't know much about growing hops; hops grow up, on frames. Hard work and we was down there in fortytwo or three when this pencil Dornier goes over, so right down by the ground we can see everything; getting chased back to the south coast by a fighter boy, right behind in a Hurricane or a Spitfire, and the Jerry'd been hit too, you could see the black holes in the sides, that horrible dirty green they was painted, and those crosses; frightening to see it so close up and his engines didn't sound too fancy either. They must have come right down from much higher up in the sky when they could have parachuted out, cause, would you believe your eyes, in the bottom of the bomber was this square hatch opened up and sticking out clear as day was just two legs, two legs kicking away back and forth in the air, like they was running to Dungeness; that Jerry had skipped his greens, ate too many of his sausages and couldn't fit out. Who knows how long he'd been stuck like that, maybe his chums inside were trying to tug him back up and in, so they could get out, and just as he went above us, over them Kent hops lands, didn't one of his boots come sailing off, floating down and I always remember, he was so low we could all see that the fat devil had no bloody socks on – dirty Jerry bugger. Not on that foot, anyways. Imagine. No socks. Both planes went on south in a moment and they say the Hurricane boy brought it down near Romney Marsh. He was just waiting to be clear of the towns before he shot it down, so they said. And didn't all of us start arguing, did the bloody Jerry get in the plane that morning with no socks on or was the sock still inside the boot that came off? So two of the Daniel brothers went out across the fields to search for it – the damn Jerry's boot fallen from the sky into the English trees – but they never did find it that year though they looked and looked. The next year too.'

Lou burst out laughing again.

'And there's a war story for you,' Myrtle told us.

Lou shook his head. There was quite a long pause and in that silence I felt the war and all that it meant. I also had the strange, unwholesome feeling that Lou felt slightly upstaged by his grandmother's story. He bluntly stated, 'We have a tortoise now, Gran.' He went on to tell the story of Lamborghini's arrival and the painting of the slogan upon its shell.

When Lou told his grandmother he'd been to Mass, she appeared more delighted to hear it than she was about he and Aoife getting married.

We departed, leaving his gran to go next door as we scarpered up the road. He looked at me and he twirled his fingertip next to his temple. 'She's going barmy, the old girl. The myth of the missing Luftwaffe sock.'

I said, 'I thought it was a great story.'

His eyes flared at me and then he went quiet for a while. After a bit at my side, as we walked, he used both hands and widened the top of the plastic bag, for me to peer down at the large potatoes, studded with small buds. 'Mark that, boyo; half a dozen big fellas and a slab of cheddar. I couldn't nab all her butter but I took a good dollop wrapped in greaseproof paper. Now we needn't waste any good drink money on bloody food.'

I nodded. 'Yes, oven potatoes. I'll do them. You scoop them out then butter and salt them after an hour in the oven. Food of the Gods.'

At one of the corner shops we bought a full-sized Ballantine's whisky with its slightly rectangular-shaped bottle, twenty cans of Guinness, a carton of Embassy Regal and a box of Christmas crackers.

Back in Conrad Flats, Lou started in on the whisky with water immediately – to spite me mentioning his excessive spirit drinking earlier, I believed.

I cleaned the tatties under the icy tap water, corked the buds out, then got them in the oven. Yet Lou soon complained that the whisky hurt his stomach so I suggested that old classic of mixing it with milk. He tried this but rapidly changed over to Guinness without comment. Then he sat in the light from the living-room windows, legs crossed, smoking as he read my story. It was probably just his position by the wide window and that broad skyline view which gave me the illusion he was having a dramatic experience.

I was nervous of his judgement and every five minutes which went by marked by his utter silence turned me to gloom. I grated cheese, then, when the potatoes were three-quarters done, I halved and gutted them, burning my fingers nervously. I mashed the potato using cheddar, salt and butter then re-stuffed the skins with the mix and put them back in the oven.

When I went through to the living room, holding a dishcloth, I was surprised to see he had – apparently quite some time before – finished reading my work. The typed pages were placed neatly on the floor and he was smoking, looking out over the view with his feet up on the windowsill.

'Well, well, Cunningham.' His voice had an odd edge to it.

'What?'

'I'm disappointed.'

'Oh, well. Thanks. Merry Christmas to you too.'

'Oh now. Come on. Sit and have a Guinness and we'll pull a Christmas cracker together. There's nothing wrong with it as a story. Frisson of mystery. Just a slight matter of surface style.'

'Surface style?'

'Touch of pompous diction, weird use of commas. I like the story. A sort of greasy cafe, egg and chips of Huysmans and Borges. You have that almost in your pocket. You need to be sure you have a piece of writing, not a piece of publishing, and there's a very clear

209

difference between the two. Most of what we have around us today is just publishing, not writing. The manuscripts of Kafka, *Elegy for the Madonna Fiammetta. Adolphe.* Those are pieces of *writing*, Cunningham. Not of publishing. I'll tell you what I would want to express in any writing I did.'

'Go on, then.'

'I want to express nothing other than the perpetual motion of the book's own style.'

'What does that mean?'

'From the first word to the last, the book must be inevitable.'

'Novels where you can't imagine a word changed?'

'It's almost more to do with conception, style meeting subject, so each sentence is its own inevitability. Then you move on to another, until you have a chain of inevitabilities.'

I said, 'Yes. But life isn't like that. Life is awkward, full of eddies and baggy bits, and irrelevancies.'

Lou said, 'How do you get that into a novel? Half of art is trying to crowbar in the vagueness of this life. None of us are good enough.'

'Who is good enough, then? Could we not just study them, and learn from them?'

'If it was that easy everyone would be doing it, wouldn't they? It's what's inside you that makes what's on the page, boyo. That's the spiritual snag. As well as style, when we write, we're searching for virtue inside each of us and sometimes we don't find it. Every great writer is a great sensibility.' His voice became soft as if all the cigarettes had strained it. 'I don't want to just write a bloody novel, Cunningham. You've got to influence the form.'

'Influence the form?'

'Change the way novels in the English language can be written and change what they can do. If you don't change the form, what are you but a bloody Sunday painter? Is that all you want to be in the end, Cunningham? A Sunday painter, like Sartre says. What was it old Poundy told us all us writers are: we're all either inventors, masters or diluters. Is that what you want to be, boyo: a diluter?'

From the telephone in the living room I phoned my parents to wish them a happy Christmas and thank them for the shoes. It was a rather stiff conversation since they weren't happy I'd remained in London, and also Lou was sitting smugly on the sofa listening to everything.

At three in the afternoon we both heckled and shouted at Her Majesty Queen Elizabeth II with great gusto while we ate our potatoes. The Langhams battered their ceiling with their golf clubs. 'And Merry Christmas to you too. Cunts,' Lou bellowed downwards. With his stomach lined he was able to recommence his work on the whisky and I took some with water as well.

'See. We're both diluters,' I mentioned.

Eventually he faltered and vanished to the bathroom. I thought he was being sick but he returned with the large bottle of Milk of Magnesia I had used as correcting fluid and he simply alternated between a large swig from this blue bottle then a drag of whisky.

We'd disposed of the whisky and it was onward with the Guinness, 'Summer (The First Time)' blasting out up the corridor at steady intervals. Each time one of us went to the toilet, the floor jumped again with golf-club thumps below.

'Our failures,' I told partly Lou and partly the ceiling. 'Nearly all our failures are usually failures of imagination.'

'Yes, that is true.' White flakes were caked all around his lips.

'Wars. Like your gran was saying. Wars are failures of imagination. Like Ethiopia. "Do They Know It's Christmas?" That's a failure of the imagination already. They do *not* know it's fucking Christmas.'

'That's true.'

'So. A sacrifice to imagination.'

Lou said, 'You're not going to flash the whole of Brentford now, are you? They'd settle for a good moon of a pale Scottish arse. Hopefully you'll bring down Santa's sledge if he's running late. Bloody hell. Crikey. Steady on, you lunatic.'

I'd picked up the pages of my story and I grabbed one of the rickety-backed dining chairs, dragging it over, scattering a few of Lily's play bricks. I jumped up on the chair. At Conrad Flats only the two narrow panes along the top of the wooden window frames opened. They were the originals from the sixties. The top gap had been taped closed with clear Sellotape. 'It's taped.'

'Oh yeah; I did, to keep the draughts out. Tear it away, boyo. Never mind the draughts; get the first *draft* out.'

I turned the handle and tugged, so with a suck the dampened tape ripped away and the window opened. The frozen air hit my face and then I began to feed the carefully typed pages of my story out the open window, high above Bollo Lane.

Lou leaped up and yelled, 'Yes! Cunningham, the sky's the limit, when it comes to your abilities.'

Sheet after sheet writhed in the lift of air sliding up the frontage of Almayer House, but the pages were suddenly grabbed and rushed southward, jerking stupidly from side to side as I fed out paper after paper. With slight intervals a pattern to their descent materialised.

'I thought your work was in its decline, boyo, but it's really soaring with a second wind now.' His face right against the window, he watched with a delighted intent.

At first, as the pages turned you could distinguish which sides had typed text, but eventually they just became curved papers, fluttering away towards Gunnersbury Park while one squadron descended in among the works by Acton Lane junction.

16

Aoife and me. Together in the corner of a pub which I'd never been in before, up beyond Acton Town station. Just the two of us, drinking strong draught Löwenbräu, which was then a new and fashionable drink in Britain. Pints for me, half pints for her, which she lifted daintily in fingers with coloured nails.

Aoife had come back with Lily on New Year's Eve and I'd found it hard to conceal my happiness. Then, after a week or so, Lou had taken me aside with an air of seriousness and for a moment I believed I was in trouble.

'Listen.'

I clenched my teeth. 'Yes?'

'You need to take Aoife out to a local one night.'

'Pardon?'

'You need to take Aoife out one night for a few drinks.'

'Why can't we all go out one afternoon and take Lily?'

'Nah. I'll stay here, look after Lil and you go out with the wife, have a few drinks and a laugh – you know. The bright lights of Acton put a sparkle in any girl's eye. Cheer her up, Cunningham, and that's an order.'

'I'll try. I am Scottish.'

'Have a laugh. Just the two of you,' and he playfully punched my shoulder.

So one Monday afternoon when the giros had been cashed, he'd suddenly sprung it on Aoife that she and I should go out to the pub that evening. She had looked surprised and hesitant.

'You need a break. Go,' he'd ordered.

She finally shrugged and agreed, I got the feeling, mainly not to insult me. When she went to get ready, Lou became restless after fifteen minutes. 'Bloody hell. She's having a bath! Aren't you the golden boy?' He seemed to think it was funny but after an hour he became furious about how long women took to get ready, then he just as suddenly calmed down again.

Aoife appeared in the front room where we were watching the news, her head tilted over to one side, putting in earrings. 'Blimey, Cunningham. Changed my mind; I'll go out with her instead,' and he reached a privileged hand that touched the back of her burgundy tights.

She smiled down at him through her ghosting of make-up.

'Okay; look after my beautiful wife.'

'I will.'

Aoife asked, 'Will we bring anything back, from the Burper?'

'No. Get drunk and don't dare return till the back of eleven.'

'I can't drink for that long.'

'Cunningham will teach you.'

So there we were in a pub, other than The Five *or* Six Bells, which she didn't want to go to for good reason – we would ignite a forest fire of gossip had the two of us sat in the saloon bar there.

'He's drinking too much.'

'Yes, I think he is. I told him to stick to beer.'

'Good. He listens to you. He won't listen to me.' She frowned. 'He doesn't seem to want to get a job, though.'

'Nope. He talks about us writing books all the time but when I suggest we do it, he just ends up in the pub and takes me with him. I know what's going on. He has, eh, quite strong opinions about books. He's terrified that if he writes something it won't live up to his own high standards. Do you see what I mean?'

'Yes.'

'You can understand how he feels?'

'But it's a fear he has to get over by writing something.'

'I agree. I wrote something when you were away.'

'Oh goodness. That's wonderful.'

'Lou sort of made me throw it out the window.'

'What? Why?'

'I did it to encourage him. I can more or less remember it word for word. I could rewrite it at any time.'

'Oh well.' She looked down at the table and then shook her head.

'What?'

'Watch him, Douglas. Sometimes I've noticed – with myself – that he likes to keep you on a leash. He was very jealous about me modelling, even in that short time before we knew I was pregnant. I could have modelled for months after and brought in good money but he wouldn't let me. Even when he got very ill.'

'What do you mean, jealous?'

'Not jealous. That makes it sound as if what I did was important or I have some kind of talent. I don't. Partly it was cause I earned more than him when he was hall portering. Mainly it was because I was out all day with men around me, sometimes shooting for catalogues and with a lot of my clothes coming off and on. I couldn't win with Lou and work. He was unhappy if I was doing catalogues and magazines, cause of the male photographers, but he thought the catwalk was stuck up, and then when I had a chance to do a television furniture advert, lounging on a sofa and getting on Anglia telly for hundreds of pounds, he told me it was too downmarket. Have you ever thought— Oh, nothing.'

'What?'

'I've thought that when I was modelling a bit— How to say it? Lou's life is about words, and reading books. A model is the opposite of words. I become just part of an image – a world without words, it's all about seeing. You can be part of a crappy image, but you could be part of a great image which is a model's job. I think some modelling can make you part of art. You know, some very good *Vogue* stuff. Herbert List and Walde Huth?'

'I don't know anything about fashion designers.'

'No. Walde Huth was a photographer. A lady. They were great photographers.'

'Oh.'

'Sounds very grand, coming from me, who did Debenhams and Littlewoods catalogues, but you dream of getting to work with great photographers.'

I shook my head. 'Sorry.'

'I'll show you some of them. In books.' She tisked her lips. 'But my books are up folks' house at home.' She'd dropped the definite article in the way that Northerners do. She humped her shoulders and because she was drunk, tutted to herself.

'I know nothing about photography. I read too much.'

'But it's a whole world. I have to go to the toilet; this stuff makes me pee and I shouldn't have wore this skirt.'

217

When she came back, she'd redone her lipstick but looked pensive. She sat forward and put both her arms straight, hands resting on her knees so the big metallic wrist bangles suddenly clunked down, and she leaned toward me as if about to lecture a child. 'I'm thinking of going back to work. Doing some modelling again.'

I nodded. 'Good. Great. So you should.'

'Need to go see the agencies cause they took me off the books. I told them to when I was pregnant.'

'Well, you should work again.'

'Don't think Lou wants me to, though. He said once, when I was pregnant, that he was happy, cause it trapped me with him, otherwise I'd never stay with him. Isn't that not a horrid thing to say?'

The question wasn't rhetorical, it required an answer and she scrunched up her nose so it made a Japanese house of wrinkles in the midst of her forehead.

'Aoife, I think someone with your looks needs to understand it makes men react. You could be with any man.'

'Oh, don't be so silly.'

'I mean it. And Lou is very handsome, but he's just like us all. Insecure.' Suddenly I said, 'What were you like when you were younger, back home?'

'Me? Insecure too. Shy, lanky, ugly duckling. I didn't know what life was so I didn't know how to go about planning for it or even enjoying it. My parents were very religious, so me and Attracta were always brought up with the church. Talking about Ireland like we were Irish but we weren't. Our parents are Irish, but we grew up English. That's what happens. Like Lou thinks he's Welsh but he's a right Londoner. Do you know where we went every year for our holidays with our folks?'

'Where?'

'Leeds. There's a big Irish community in Leeds and we'd go there. Who goes to Leeds on holiday every year?' She nodded firmly. '*We* bloody did.'

I laughed. 'Were you and Abby mates from young? Were you both so pretty?'

'We were actually awful little fat chubs cause our parents shovelled three meals a day in us. And we were the only Catholic girls of that age in the village, the three of us. My sister, Abby and me went to the Catholic school in town, so our parents took turns driving us. It was sad for my sister cause people thought me and Abby were the sisters. Abby had braces and big curly hair; then, in nineteen eighty-one, we decided we were New Romantics or something and cut it all off. My dad went potty.'

'Were your parents strict?'

'Very. I remember once when I was little, the Monsignor came to our house for dinner because my parents did so much volunteer work for the church, and my father said to me, "Now, Aoife, you tell the Monsignor what we always say before dinner" – meaning the prayer, with grace – but I said to the Monsignor what my father really always did say, "Go easy on the butter, everyone."'

I burst out laughing.

'I could tell the Monsignor was trying not to laugh but Dad was furious and he smacked me on my knickers afterwards, he was so sure I was being deliberate.' She shrugged, then lifted and sipped from her drink. 'I'm not that witty.'

She got drunker as well. Each time she returned from the toilet I noted her lipstick had been re-formed. I didn't want to leave the pub that night, with the corner seats all to ourselves. I knew fine what I was plucking up courage to ask her: how it went on her wedding night. And I was aroused by it too.

Then a man with a beard appeared. He meandered towards us – the same way a sudden, loosed bead of water on a steamed-up window darts, quick and hapless. Drunk already, he banged his pint down on a table and spilled some, muttering as he sat, directly across. Aoife and I abruptly stopped talking. I was furious at his intrusion; the rear of the pub was empty and yet he'd sat there.

For something to say, I stated to her, 'You'll need to show me those books, then?'

Aoife turned her face to me. 'What books?'

'The photography books.'

'What's that?' the male voice went.

I couldn't believe it. He'd not wasted any time barging in to our company. Aoife and I turned to look at this man.

'What's that?' he repeated.

I looked at him and said in a hostile, warning voice, 'Pardon?'

The man's arm was stretched out and he seemed to be pointing directly at Aoife's breasts. But then I saw the CND symbol badge that she always had, pinned to the lapel of that corduroy jacket with the flared cuffs.

Aoife looked at him and she made me angry because she smiled amiably. 'This?'

'Ya.'

'That's the sign of the Campaign for Nuclear Disarmament.'

He leaned forward, rolling a cigarette. He was small, stocky, with a clipped beard, and he was wearing some sort of expensive-looking complex ski jacket, with zips and toggles. He had an accent, German maybe.

'So you think. We. We here in England should have no nukes so fucking Russkis can walk in?'

I turned my face to Aoife, hidden from him, and I raised my eyes to the ceiling, signalling not to get in an argument.

'I am Czech; Russkis walk in. Same as Hungary. Same as they'll walk in here you don't have the bomb. You can store one in my back garden. It's big enough.' He shrugged so his jacket rustled and hissed and the bobbles and zip-pulls on it shook. 'What the fuck. Better than under the Russki fuckin' commies.'

Aoife went to speak but I'd had a few beers and I interrupted, 'The CND symbol isn't a pro-communist Russia symbol; it's saying that nuclear weapons are insane and inhuman. Nuclear weapons everywhere.'

'You think, guy, at fucking Agincourt an axe go into the side of a man's face – you think that's nice? Always there was these machine for slaughter; since man began.'

'You can't destroy the world and everything that lives on it with an axe.'

I could see he was ignoring me now and his eyes had settled firmly on Aoife. He kept looking at her then he dropped his eyes to lick the paper for his rolled cigarette. 'Your husband talk always for you?'

I flicked my head at him.

Aoife didn't correct him but said, 'I'm a mother with a child. A nuclear bomb could go off in another country and still kill my baby. It's disgusting. I don't want any wars, but most of all not that one.'

The guy looked at me. 'You the father?'

I gave him a final, warning look but the truth is I was charmed to be mistaken for her husband.

221

'Hey relax, big boy, I just joke with you. I'm Czech.'

Staring dead at him, I tried to mellow out. 'I read some of your writers.'

'What you say, writers?' He chuckled. 'Fucking writers, what is writers?'

'Klima, Hašek, Hrabal, Kundera. Kafka is Czech.'

'You pronounce names shit. Prague is not just fucking writers and Czech is not just Prague. Writers. They all fuck off out like me. Out Prague, so they can lay some decent women.' He chuckled.

'Have you been here long?' Aoife said, her helplessly sweet and childish voice sounding musical.

'What you think, baby? Since sixty-eight, beautiful. Since I been here. Now I'm fucking rich, and I worked hard for it.' He quickly looked at us, as if daring me to challenge this.

I clapped my hands together in a slow, cynical applause.

This wasn't good enough for him so he had to prove it.

'Yah want me buy you guys a drink, then? Good whisky for both, eh? Expensive?'

I turned to Aoife in despair but she lifted her shoulders just a fraction in foolish assent.

'What you drinking, darling? I'm just joking with you kids, just joking, what you wanna drink, eh?'

'We're just drinking beer.'

'I'll have whisky,' Aoife said. I pursed my lip and shrugged in agreement.

'Come back to my place and we drink some real champagne. I just live next door.'

I said, 'I think we need to be getting back.'

'You don't wanna come to my house and drink some champagne after?'

I turned round to Aoife, furious, but she lifted the shoulders an inch again.

At least he wasn't lying about the house. Half an hour later we really were just a few doors along from the pub, walking up his garden path. Some kind of metal sculpture was in the front garden with lots of pampas grass.

'This is my place. You'll see inside. Buy the next-door house and make them together. See? See how there's no door that side?'

'Oh yeah.'

'These were two houses now I make them together one house. I'm rich as shit.'

'Yes. You told us.'

I looked at Aoife and she made a tittering motion to her face. She had a long scarf wrapped round her high neck.

He bent over and meticulously undid about three locks. Then he opened the front door and we stepped in, onto some dark, carpeted mezzanine area, and he switched on the lights.

I had to admit, it was impressive. The whole place was like a very large hotel's lobby area. He'd somehow knocked out the partition walls between the houses, and the floors – Christ knows what was holding it all up. The ground floor was a wide carpeted space with white shelves of books, ornaments and mechanical devices. Above us, a minstrels' gallery with balustrades on a deep balcony. At the bottom end, a curved, carpeted staircase now swept up on two sides to that first-floor balcony.

'Gosh. You have a wonderful home.'

'Thought you'd like it, baby.'

He led the way down off the mezzanine and began crossing the huge carpeted floor, moving around the obstacles of chairs and tables.

'You live here alone?'

'All alone, buddy. I had wife and kids but they gone. Thank fuck.'

Aoife asked, 'May I use the toilet, please?'

'Sure. I show you where.'

They went up the right side of the stairs together but he struggled a bit and had to hold on to the banisters. I stood, head tipped slightly back watching for any monkey business, but after pointing Aoife down a corridor to the rear of the house he immediately came back down slowly. He glanced up at me and chuckled. 'Fuck me, I pissed pissed pissed. Hey, I get some champagne, but we sit.' He indicated an oasis of chairs.

On the way there he placed himself before a hi-fi music centre, reached into a large glass jar, absolutely full of loose music cassettes with no plastic covers – maybe a hundred of them – and he lifted one at random into the tape machine, then jammed it on. Music came from all round the bloody place – ironic-sounding waltz music with fiddles and accordions.

'Yah like it?'

'What?'

'Good. No?'

He sat in a black leather and chrome swivel chair, clearly an original sixties piece, and I sat opposite, facing him.

'You bring that chair with you from Prague?'

'What?'

The awful fiddle music was so fucking loud, the old prick couldn't hear a thing. It was exactly the chair I would have imagined him sitting in, wearing a nasty bathrobe, flicking through back issues of *Playboy*.

He leaned forward. I noticed he still had the ski jacket on. I'd got used to the noise it made but now that noise had vanished into the polka music. At least he couldn't sneak up on Aoife easily.

'I see what goes on.'

I looked at him.

'She's wedding ring, you not.' He tapped the side of his nose. 'You guys wanna get out the pub, man, where there too many people. It's okay with me; I understand affairs. Spend the night here. I got plenty berths on this ship, baby.'

I leaned in to him a bit and waggled my finger. 'You're dead wrong about me and her.'

He shrugged and chuckled. 'Oh yeah? I don't think so. I see her too. Long Tall Sally.' He leaned back and he said, 'Don't be sucker.'

'What?' It made me furious that he was dead right and that I wasn't cool.

'Don't be sucker.' He leaned forward again and tapped my leg. I half thought I might kick out hard at his crotch and see what way he spun round on the chair.

'Yes?'

'What you want people say about you when you're gone? That you was a nice guy? The nicest guy in fucking cemetery.' He shrugged and looked at me as if this was profound, not ten-cent bar philosophy.

That Löwenbräu and whisky was quite a mix okay. I was feeling a bit spinny. It suddenly struck me that this man might be an actual

225

emissary from the devil. A demon of the lower orders, Balakan or Massapiel himself, invoked from a scum bath of bloody bones, boiled semen and the slippery pelts of skinned children. I frowned at my involuntary thought.

'You wanna know how I make all my money?'

'You sold your soul to the devil?'

'No.'

'You had construction contracts for the Gulag?'

'What? Constructions? I'm in movie business but not the sucker bullshit end. I have movie *equipment* business. Cameras, cable, generators, support trucks: BBC hire me *all* time, some movie that come hire me in the seventies, always. I make a lot of fucking money then, man. I fuck a lot of beautiful women. Stupid actress bitches. I own all stuff in warehouse.'

'Plant hire. Good for you.' I nodded.

'Yeah. Movie plant hire and I got the contacts, man.' He slapped his own thigh. 'I got the fucking contacts; you wanna Panaflex thirty-five mil in one hour, I got you it, you, fucking guy!' He shouted, exhilarated at this state of affairs.

I nodded patiently as if I had a sore throat and muffler on.

'Hello, baby!'

I squinted at his shouting and turned suddenly. Aoife was standing at the very top of the stairway; tall, the skinny legs in burgundy tights, but she was carrying her jacket and scarf: the freshened lipstick smile, erect as a sunflower on a windless day, down the stairs she came. I groaned at how much I was in love with her but I also really wanted to fuck her, and when I looked over at my companion he was thinking *exactly* the same thing. Men of the world unite.

'That's fun music,' she called lightly, trotting down the steps. 'Oops.'

The Czech was up. I creaked round in my chair and yeah, right enough the old bastard was circling quite smoothly, dancing with Aoife, they turned one two three, one two three. And Eeef knew the steps. I couldn't dance. I stood up. 'I'm going to toilet.'

'Yeah, yeah. Guy. Hey. You dance with lady while I get the champagne.'

'I'm just going up to the toilet.'

'You need to have more fun, buddy. What's wrong with you? That's the nice toilet for Lady Hefer up there. That's your name, baby?' He'd let go of her and she was standing before him, her cheeks a touch pink from the whisky and dancing.

'Aoife.'

'Eef-herr. That's her toilet, guy. I show you another less better one for guys.'

I followed him deeper and deeper to the back of his huge barn. If I'd been carrying a saucepan I might have hit him hard on the back of his fat neck, returned and kissed Aoife on her lipsticked mouth – but I didn't have the balls. There was a huge kitchen and black windows out into a rear garden, I suppose. He showed me to a small modern bathroom.

'There you go, guy. I take her back the champagne and we have little party.'

I pissed with trembling hands, quite happy that I squirted some on the black tiled floor, and then I stared at myself in the mirror. I washed my hands and splashed my face with water then dried around my ears, making sure no tell-tale water was left dampening my fringe, taking care I had not soaked my shirt. I took a big breath.

I walked back towards that ridiculous, macabre vaudeville music. Aoife was standing beside him and the Czech was bent over something: a metallic champagne bucket on a permanent stand, and he was opening the bottle in the shuffling ice. There was a sorrowful pop, killed by the huge acoustics of space. Aoife had her head a bit more forward and a hand up to her lip, nibbling at her thumb. I recognised the stance. Imitating Lou. It meant she was upset. I shouldn't have left them alone.

'He's back. He come back when he smell the wine, Hefer,' the Czech laughed.

She was looking at me with eyes that seemed to vibrate.

I said to her, 'Okay?'

Still nibbling her thumbnail she nodded quickly and uncertain. 'Need to pee again,' she said, looking right at me. And she raised her eyes.

'You pee again, beautiful, but you just did? You like my toilets? You not sniffing the jizz in there?'

'I drank too much beer.' She strode ahead but she grabbed my hand as she passed and quite spun me around, so I was tugged forward with her on the end of her arm. Hand in hand we went up the curved stairway together.

'Okay, you guys both go to sniff the jizz and give me none. I got good stuff, kids. Better than you. Maybe ya don't like the music. I sit. I sit and we have a little champagne now. Eh?'

She kept pulling me up the stairs then at the top, down the corridor we entered a large bathroom together and she shut the door behind us. The bathroom was very luxurious with a huge bath tub.

'He's a horrible man.'

228

'I tried to tell you in the pub not to come back here. Did he touch you?'

'No. I wouldn't let a man touch me, but he's disgusting. What he said. He offered me money to do things.'

I tried not to smile. I was absolutely delighted the Czech had discredited himself so utterly and so quickly. I could almost have gone downstairs and hugged him. I said to her, 'Don't worry about it. Don't let it upset you. We'll just go.'

'Okay.' She glared in my face. I would reach out and I would kiss her. That is what I would do, among all this white stone and mirrors. I smiled. 'You're not going to cry, are you?'

'No. No. I'm more angry than anything.'

'Want me to go down there and smash his face in?'

She looked shocked. 'No!'

'C'mon, let's go home.'

'Suppose so,' she groaned.

She took my hand to go down the stairs as well. It felt a bit like making an entrance in a musical show, descending the carpeted steps, hand in hand, to the fiddle and accordion. I was ready to confront him but he was sat back in the leather swivel chair, his head to one side, big stomach pushed out. He was fast asleep in his ski jacket.

Aoife and I both stood before him, still holding hands.

'He's not dead, is he?' she whispered in an aggressive hiss, over the music.

'Sadly not. Look at his big belly going. C'mon. Let's nick the champagne and go.'

'Maybe he's pretending?'

'Hey. Dickhead? Czech fucker. Your house is a shithole.'

229

'He's completely asleep,' she said, sort of fascinated.

I leaned forward and I quietly slid the champagne bottle out of the ice bucket. It wasn't French champagne. It was sparkling wine. Czech wine. Drops of water blotted noisily on the top of my new shoes.

'A cheapskate at heart. It's sparkling wine.' I held out the bottle for her examination.

'Thirty pounds to show him a glimpse of my boobs, he said.' She whispered this looking down on him.

'A definite cheapskate. I'd pay more than that.'

'You're sweet.'

Still we stood, looking down on the man, unconscious in his own house. I craned my lips in towards Aoife's small ear, almost touching the lobe, and whispered, 'Shall we do something awful?'

She turned and looked at me, 'What?'

'I don't know. Turn on every water tap in the house with the sink plugs in and the overflows blocked with bog paper?'

She delightedly opened her eyes and her mouth, wide. For the first time, despite her perfection, I noted she had a silver filling on one of her top molars, toward the back. I imagined trying to feel it with the tip of my tongue whilst kissing her.

Suddenly she said, 'Let's nose around.' She dropped my hand smartly.

I was surprised. I took a swig from the sparkling wine bottle – it tasted bad – and I followed her back up the stairs.

She made a circuit round the minstrels' gallery of the first floor and all the time looking down at him, asleep in the swivel chair.

There was recessed shelving right round the minstrels' gallery, then the original windows were above the front door, giving a view out over the street. She walked round the other side. I followed her like some uninspired hanger-on and I said, 'This dickhead doesn't have enough books for so many shelves. What a waste. If I owned this pile, I'd fill the shelves with books.'

'Would you?'

'Sure. I could go into every secondhand bookshop in London, and come out with treasures each time.'

'What else would you do? If you were rich?'

'I dunno.' I looked at her. 'Have fun and buy you diamonds.'

She smiled.

'I guess in reality, just lie in bed looking up at the shadows and not actually do a thing. Daydream. Same as now. So it'd be wasted on me. That's the problem getting rich. You use up your whole life doing it. Just to sit up the front of the aeroplane. What would you do?'

'Make sure Lily got everything she needed.' She leaned on the balustrade and looked down. 'Save it for Lily. Go on a holiday.'

'Not Leeds.'

'No. Not Leeds.' She smiled at me, then walked on.

I decided I would make money somehow and I would take Aoife to New York and Venice. We were back where the luxury toilet was. We'd left the lights on in there. She moved down the corridor and pushed open a door, reached out her hand and insolently slapped a light switch. It was a huge bedroom, very neatly kept, done in white and red with large red drapes over the windows. I could see a distant bathroom – another – through a door, in dark blue and white tiles.

'This bastard has too much money.'

We could still hear the polka music away downstairs – but only faintly, his home was so large.

She said, 'He's rich but he's lonely. You can tell.'

I jerked my head at the large bed. 'I'm surprised to see no mirrors above the bed.'

She looked to me. 'That means dirty, doesn't it? So you can watch yourselves?'

'That's it.'

'That's what he likes.'

'Pardon?' I stared at Aoife.

'Know what he said?' She lowered her voice. 'He said you and me were having an affair, so thirty to see my boobs or two hundred if you and me did it while he watched.'

I looked at her and repeated blankly, 'Two hundred.'

She said, 'Imagine, with him watching.'

There was an ambiguity which puzzled me. But then she looked sickly – and I didn't know what part of the equation made her look like that.

I swallowed. 'Want to get out of here?'

She nodded rapidly, still looking at the bed. I found myself passing the sparkling wine bottle to her. Why? She drank a very large-seeming gulp for her and handed it back, then she turned round.

I followed her down into the gathering polka music. He was still asleep. I was walking to the right, so I was between the wall and him in his chair. She moved straight up the wide lobby, heading for the front door, but as I passed behind him I signalled with my face to Aoife. She stopped, and so did I.

Between the padded leather cross-bar and the cushion, his jacket was ruffed up. His wallet was half birthed from the back pocket of his jeans. That would be just the kind of reckless place he'd keep a wallet. I never could figure out why men kept their wallets in their back pockets. Asking for liberation.

Kneeling behind him, I touched the leather with my finger to figure how loose it was. The wallet almost came away free. Using two fingers I plucked it out and I stood up.

Aoife watched: daunted, curious. The wallet was very fat, split, and it was stuffed with credit cards. In those days we were ignorant of their workings but there were also the purple and brown folds of cash. I tipped the wallet over to display to her. Aoife held out her hand and summoned with her fingers. I tossed the wallet and she caught it. She pulled out cash between her fingers then leaned and dropped the wallet into the mashed ice and water of the champagne bucket. With a fistful of notes she grabbed the hem and yanked up her blouse, revealing her bared breasts to me and to the sleeping Czech. She wore no brassiere, her tits were on the smaller side, nipples pink, sunk and restful, both breasts jumped once in rubbery obedience from the shirt fabric being suddenly drawn up across them. Her stomach was flat like Abby's. She tugged the fabric back down and marched to the door, clutching the money. It had seemed as if I wasn't there – or as if I was her eunuch servant. The polka music came out onto the street with us, then I pulled the front door softly behind me.

On the pavement, she put her jacket and scarf back on, took my arm and we walked forward together between the front gardens and the wing mirrors of parked cars. 'I took sixty pounds cause I've two boobs and showed both.'

I chuckled, and passed the sparkling wine bottle to her. We stopped and she used both hands to gently manoeuvre and tip the bottle backwards beneath the street light. She suckled at that great chunk of green glass, the bubbles within it like some furious nest of disturbed insects. She smacked her lips, passing the bottle back.

'We can tell Lou he was a pain in the ass but maybe we better not tell him all that.'

I said, 'Yeah,' wishing it was some other intimacy we had to lie to Lou about.

For a while we didn't talk, just walked side by side. In her boots, her steps seemed quite fast and aggressive. She said, out of her thoughtfulness, 'That was sinful what I did, but I was angry, wasn't I?'

'It was funny and justified.'

'Was it? The sixty goes into the housekeeping, not the till at that Bells.'

'I won't say a thing.'

On the top of Bollo Lane, she looked at me and suddenly dropped my looped arm so that if Lou was watching us from the high windows above, he wouldn't see us like that. We walked on side by side, but she moved slower as if she wanted the night to last longer. I swigged at the bottle, held it to the street light and said, 'I should save some of this for Lou.'

She held up her nose and stared high, toward the top floor of Almayer House, as if the night hands of some gigantic, illuminated clock face threw forth the hour up there. The bone structure of her face was so perfect, her skin was completely horizontal under her chin. If she stood on her head you could have placed a glass securely on the tight, delicately inverted jaw. She took a long couple of swigs from the wine, which popped and swished when she moved the bottle away from her lips then handed it back to me.

As we went into the lobby of the Almayer House stairwell, Aoife said suddenly, 'I've got the keys. Will we check on poor little Lamborghini?'

'Lamborghini?'

'Will we both go down and check him; that he's all right?'

'He'll be fine.'

She stood still. 'Oh. We could just check quick. Five minutes.'

I frowned. 'I'll check on him tomorrow.'

'Okay.'

I suddenly changed my mind. 'Oh, okay then, let's go and check.'

She nodded and she put her hand down to mine but she took the bottle from me again and drank from it. Then she said, 'Nope. C'mon. I need the loo.' She turned. We both began to climb the stairs slowly – her ahead of me – without speaking. I studied the weave of her wine-red tights just above the knees. I could almost feel the heat wafting back from her living body. On the second floor, she passed the bottle back to me so she wouldn't be associated with it in front of Lou.

Lou was impressed by the quarter-full bottle of sparkling wine and he alternately held it away from his face to study the trophy, then drank from it as he listened carefully to my sketches, analysis and descriptions of the fat Czech, his big house, both of us sneaking out whilst the beast slumbered. 'The licence payer's reactionary', Lou rather brilliantly christened the Czech.

Aoife and I said nothing about the money.

Lou looked at his watch. 'Christ sake, you lunatics. Do you think the Slavic loon's woken up yet? Let's get a hand cart and take Lily's buggy, go back and strip his bloody house out. When he wakes, he won't have a light bulb left and Acton will divide the spoils amongst its citizenry.'

Aoife stood above Lily's buggy, looking down on her child as if she did not remember giving birth, then she bent quickly at her waist to peck with a kiss. Both Lou and I turned to amiably witness Aoife's ass as she did this. Then she swayed toward both of us, 'Hoi. You. Smithy,' and she snatched the wine bottle off Lou. She stood above us. Still with her boots on, which, by custom, she normally zipped off at the front door. Her waist was inches in front of both our noses, the bottle tipped back and earrings hung down. We both looked up at her from the sofa as if we were to sail between the legs of the Rhodes Colossus.

'So, did Cunningham keep you entertained, my darling?' he leaned forward, freely taking both her slim thighs in his grip, and I wanted to do the same. I watched how his fingers moved a little into the soft, burgundy-coloured material.

'Yes-he-did. Charming and a gentleman, as always. He protected me from that creepy guy.'

'You two nymphs *have* been talking about me, haven't you? How can you pass so many hours together without talking about the great Svengali?' His head shot toward me. 'Do you know Her Majesty's Theatre was built only on the proceeds of the play adaptation of *Trilby*?'

'We talked about you okay, mister.' Aoife laughed above him, 'You're a holy terror, Lou Smith.'

'I've retired from the class struggle for a period of theoretical reflection. Nice to know you two have been out, following in my footsteps, creating bloody havoc.'

'I. Am going. To bed.' She turned her bum to us and, still carrying the wine bottle, stepped away and off down the corridor.

Lou clicked his tongue and leaned privately towards me; he whispered, 'Good show, boyo. She's blotto! Sloshed.' Then he talked about what had been on the telly and the political news, to which I nodded, not listening to a word he said. I heard only the taps and hot-water tank going in the bathroom. I heard her come out there and cross into their bedroom. After a spell I said, 'Got to take a leak.'

I slouched down the corridor. Their bedroom door was open and Aoife must have been in bed, with the light switched off. I stepped into the bathroom and could feel humidity from her washings at the sink and with a lumpiness underfoot I looked down and saw that I was standing on her discarded blouse – the actual one she had lifted thoughtlessly in front of me. Her skirt and the crumpled red tights were kicked in against the skirting board. Halfway through my peeing, I twisted my head round and saw there were no towels blocking the window on the bathroom door behind me. I flushed the toilet and washed my hands. Then, fingers still wet, I bent to pick up her blouse. I tried to resist and I held it as if it were an injured animal, then suddenly I buried my face in the cloth and breathed as deeply as I could: both that perfume and what else? Fabric that had moved against the skin of her body. I breathed in again, then I held the garment with my hands and looked down upon it. Pathetic. I hung the blouse on the hook, unlocked the door, but as I did so there was a shadowy movement to the right within their bedroom.

From the corridor I saw the weak night light fixed to the side of Lily's cot had been illuminated and its angle corrected. Aoife had crossed the bedroom to do that. I gritted my teeth.

Over two hours later I was still awake on my camp bed. I'd heard the sounds of Lou carrying sleeping Lily to the bedroom cot in his arms, placing her in there while he muttered. Later he washed himself then moved to the bedroom. The exhalation not of human breath but of the soft mattress as a new pressure was put upon it.

A sound I had never heard before in all my nights of listening and pretending to myself I wasn't listening. Unconfirmed then definite came the rhythmic movement, then a reaction and a sudden whipping of sheets. Then silence. Long silence. Lou grunted once and the rhythm began again. The creak of a floorboard from a foot. A faster rhythm and the rapid but almost silent breaths of the mattress. Then Aoife's voice, new-sounding and thick with determined intent, said, 'On my— bit.' (Or possibly even 'butt'?) She began to groan almost immediately. Then, maybe through the shield of her own fingers, I heard the tight gasp.

I woke, illuminated my digital watch, and it was an hour and a half later. There was no sound next door. Then out of perfected silence my relief vanished in the slowly pained cry of her once again, calling out as she ranged forth in the dark.

17

There was tension I could feel in the flat. It was nothing specific and difficult to tell if it emanated from one or all of us. It was an ambient change – as if a huge new building had been built next to an old one and the atmosphere, the light and sense of enclosure within specific rooms, had permanently shifted.

There were the furtive and snatched phone calls going on – by both of them; when Aoife was down at the Co-op for nappies, or Lou popped over to visit his gran. Sometimes Lou would bring back a large frying pan of chops or a pot of soup from Myrtle, covered in tin foil, which he'd openly carried for a mile through the streets. Then we'd re-heat it. He'd often return smelling of beer, so he'd also entered The Five *or* Six Bells with the actual pot or frying pan and openly sat with it placed on the pub table in front of him, enduring ridicule from the old fellows for a sly pint.

Neither Aoife nor Lou wanted the other to know about their phone calls, yet both privately kept me abreast of their purpose. Aoife was arranging interviews at modelling agencies and while Lou was in the toilet she muttered to me in the gloom, both our faces lit by the television, that she had secured an interview with LTM – the biggest agency.

To my amazement I learned that – despite his drunkenness – Lou had been in touch with a language school somewhere near Worcester. He'd been asking about the possibility of a teaching job and the wage there. Things seemed to be stirring just beyond the reaches of my subtle influence and perhaps I was a little uneasy on account of it.

We were summoned by the belle Belle and, once settled in The Gertrude, Lou and I were impressed to hear Toby Hanson say, 'Ah, Yeats. Last time I read old Yeats was sat with a paperback in a strip bar on Isla de Margarita off the coast of Venezuela. Don't think poorly of me chaps. *Every* bar on the Isla de Margarita is a strip bar. Now. I've brought the chariot today. Parked round the corner; so give us a hand one of you.'

I accompanied Toby out to his car. It could only have been his. It was a shit brown – once grand – 1976 Mercedes Benz 350SL. I noted the distinctive Mercedes Benz gunsight above the radiator had been broken off; a wooden cocktail stick with wind-ravaged tinsel from some country-house soirée was now lodged there instead. Through the windscreen, his leather driving gloves were on top of the dashboard amongst an archive of ignored parking tickets. I don't know why, but at that moment I looked up the Kings Road and felt like just walking east to Euston and Scotland and away from everything. And I should have. Instead I lifted the box out of the boot and carried it back into the pub.

'Tobias,' asked Lou, 'how are we meant to get all this bollocks home? We'll need a taxi fare,' he quickly added.

'Carrier bags from the grocer's across the road and split them among four plastic bags? Yes. That should do the trick.'

'What do we do after we've read them?'

'Dump 'em.' Toby brutally shrugged.

Lou had leaned forward and stared down on one of the white

volumes bound together with staples, and he drew it from the opened top of the box. The cover read: *Roland C. Matterhorn. The Vampires of Smithfield.* Lou looked up at Toby as if he'd betrayed his own family to the Gestapo. 'Do you actually publish this?'

'No, no. An *imprint* of ours does. Sells like hot cakes. Horror, erotic stuff, true crime, all to shifty fellows in garages, railway stations, airports and all these sorts of places; you can forget about bookshops for the hard stuff. This is all horror.'

'You can say that again.' Lou was leaning over the box, flicking the top pages as if he were positioned on a toilet pan, with a pained expression. His tone had an outraged, metaphysical objection engrained in it. 'This is about cockney vampires, working in the meat market in Smithfield.' He looked up at me, agonised.

I picked a volume myself. Another of Mr Matterhorn's works, *The Werewolves of Wandsworth*.

Toby let his eyes flicker down, 'Oh *he's* just completely ridiculous,' he said, revealing he knew more about this material than he was letting on.

Underneath was *Brothel of the Vampire* by Vanessa Lather. I pointed it out. 'Bags me this one.'

Lou flapped the volume in his hand. 'What are these, proofs?'

'Printers' galleys stapled together. We don't bother with bound proofs for work of this nature. No one to send it to. So you chaps dream up the back-cover copy. Hundred words max. Make them seem irresistible. Art department will concoct some gruesome front covers.' He clapped his hands together. I could tell by his sudden jauntiness we had just freed up his weekend. I had an intuition he was banging beanpole Belle. 'Good work; I'll get you eighty nicker.

Those beers are on me,' and he was out the door with a raised arm of farewell.

Lou dropped the stapled block of paper back in the box.

'Eighty quid,' I said. 'C'mon, get some plastic bags from across the road.'

He nodded. Literature was fading away and beer was triumphing – and surely this had long been the true golden balance?

There were seventeen of Toby Hanson's horror novels to read and to write the back-cover copy for. As with most endeavours in this life we set out with some sincerity. I sat in my room at 506 Almayer House, looking down on Brentford, during my grateful pauses from *Brothel of the Vampire*. Lou sat in the living room, dealing with the blood-sucking at Smithfield. Lily cried and then Lou became peripatetic, shifting between the kitchen stool and their bedroom, fleeing Lily's noise in balloons of cigarette smoke. Lou was reading slower than me, because I soon noticed that – using a sharpened pencil – he was making outraged grammatical and anachronistic corrections in the margins of the text: *WHAT is the subject in this sentence??!! This is a MIXED simile. There were no MACHINE GUNS in the eighteenth century.* I had to tell him to stop doing it or he'd never get through.

After another hour of vampires, Lou came to the door of my room. 'How much money do you have?'

'Three pound seventy-two pence.'

'I've almost a fiver in coppers. Know where I found two pounds?'
'Where?'

'I went through every pair of jeans and trousers bloody Abby has stored in this joint.'

'Where *is* Abby this weather?'

Lou said, 'I'll need to ask her round. From what Eeef tells, candle painting has taken precedence over *La Moda*.' He called out loudly, 'Aoife, darling. We have to go to the pub. It's just impossible to read this stuff sober.'

We arrived in The Bells with the stapled proofs in Co-op bags which Lou occasionally shook as if there were something living in there. We settled in our usual spot beneath the windows with our pints. Lou sighed and wrenched open the middle pages of a new work: *A Virgin Grows Sharp Teeth*, by Tamara Cleo.

'Tamara Cleo. You know fine it's some greasy, bearded bloke up in Barnet.'

'Yeah. High Barnet,' I said.

Lou slapped the pages. 'Look, boyo. Here's how we'll do it for easy money and to preserve sanity. For each book, one of us reads the first ten pages, one of us reads the middle ten pages then we both read the last ten pages. Do we really need to know any more? Then we'll rustle up fifty bloody words of some blabber, or whatever it's called.' He frowned at my copy. 'And how is it at the Vampire Brothel? You don't see the same customers twice?'

'*Brothel of the Vampire*. Hero is a dozy copper, outraged by a dropped crisp packet or a vampire chewing a toddler's neck. Actually seems to be some real anti-vice sentiment; you can't have a book where the whores triumph, so both vampires and whores look doomed to go down together.'

'These books *are* terrifying, but not in the way intended. Let's get some lovely Guinness down us for a bit of Montezuma's revenge. It'll go nicely with the reading.'

So that's how we did it for horror book after book, suffering through the beginnings, the middles and the ends.

This time it was I who went to collect the cash from Toby's secretary on Fulham Road.

The belle Belle was behind her desk in a dress that looked more like a sequence of small stoat's or weasel's footprints which had been run over by a tractor on a big white sheet.

'Toby's in the country,' she made clear before I'd even reached the desk. 'With his wife,' she smiled vacantly.

I handed over the A4 envelope of our copy and she slid across a smaller one. I checked it was eighty quid, right in front of her.

'Where's your friend today? Loo-Ell-En?'

'He's otherwise engaged.'

'So you'll be taking me for a drink this lunchtime, then?'

'I can't, Belle. I'd love to, but I've had to give up alcohol. I'm on antibiotics.'

She nodded. 'I won't ask,' she said, but she leaned back in her seat, quite relaxed. With a knowing voice, she went on, 'So, you two aren't writing a book on that man, from that awful band?' Now she leaned forward and twisted a pencil round and round on her desk. 'I prefer Scritti Politti. Something soulful.'

'That all fell through.'

She nodded thoughtfully. 'Really? It fell through, did it? Funny, that. The same thing happened with the last fellow Toby was getting to do all his little bits and bobs. A small man; can't remember his name now, though it wasn't so long ago. He wanted to be a novel writer too. Some people would say that Toby was just using you, wouldn't they?' She moved her long fingers and peppered little repeating rhythms onto the A4 envelope. 'Yes, funny, that.'

I moved my head at her and smiled in both acknowledgement and admiration. I walked away. 'We needed the money. See you later, then.'

18

It had happened. Aoife had an interview coming up at LTM, the big model agency, and Lou got me alone in my room. 'You need to go with Eeef tomorrow.'

'Abby can go. She's coming over in the morning anyway, to help with all the make-up stuff.'

'I know that, but I need you to pal her up to this agency joint. Needs to be a bloke goes with her.'

'Why?'

'We can't afford taxis, Cunningham. She needs to go there and back on the Tube. Wait till you see how she has to dress. You can't turn up looking like a nun at blessed Easter. Have to show you're confident about your body and you need to show it off. None of them admit it, but they're showing how skinny they all are, so they wear short skirts, smoky sunglasses during a London winter; all that kind of shit. I need you to go with her. Keep men off her.'

'It's London in broad daylight. Not a football club in Donegal.'

'Please, Cunningham.'

'If it makes you happy, of course I will.'

'Ta. Keep an eye on her at this agency. Stupid gorillas and damn sleazers up there.' He winked.

Abby materialised at eight thirty in the morning – an hour not agreeable to those crafting in literature – and she began creating

Aoife, who'd got up and bathed at seven. Aoife and Abby seemed more preoccupied with appearances than they had in preparation for Lou and Aoife's wedding – perhaps they were even more excited.

Lily was crying and I had to hold her and feed her in the front room while Lou lunged about with a fag in his mouth, to no purpose, like the expectant father he once was.

Aoife came out of the bedroom much more subtle than I had feared. Hair down naturally, powdered, louche face, an extraordinarily short skirt, black tights and tan leather boots.

'Her legs are too thin for those boots,' Abby maintained.

Aoife looked directly at me and shrugged apologetically. 'I love them.'

It was like looking at someone you knew well, transformed by a uniform of duty for a strange and distant war. She'd been replaced by an idea which had been thought up somewhere else, by another sensibility. A male one, of course. Aoife as cosmopolitan beauty was a first-class disguise and she confessed to me, 'You have to dress like this. Every girl walking round in there is really beautiful and all done up and they know I've had a baby so they'll be all *watching*—' Her voice trailed off and she looked out the window, squinting at the harsh natural light.

I nodded. 'But that's okay. You look super sexy.'

'Steady on, the bloody Scotch lodger,' Lou muttered.

Aoife turned back to me, her eyes hard into mine. It was a strange look – as if I were the only one untainted by this perilous game and she sought consent.

Lou clapped his hands much like Toby Hanson. 'Right, great. Cunningham's going to tag along with you, love.'

247

Aoife had obviously been firmly briefed on this matter and she stubbed her head once, but Abby was amazed.

'Why is Douglas going with her?'

'To keep an eye on her on the Tube and up the West End.'

'What's going to happen to her on the Tube?'

'Look at her, Abby. She looks— Some weirdo could follow her.'

Abby frowned at me but spoke to Aoife. 'He's not going into the actual agency with you, is he? Oh for God sake, Lou. It's not some porn agency. That's Susie Bic's agency. It's upmarket; respectable.'

Lou stood still. 'Why shouldn't Cunningham go inside the agency?'

'For one thing, he might be taken for a moody, possessive husband or boyfriend.' Abby stared at Lou. 'That's why you aren't going. Agencies don't want the slightest hint of that. They want independent gals. And in those unspeakable shoes that are as bad as his old ones; jeans, tartan work shirts and that dead Scottish otter jacket, or whatever it is. He'll cramp her natural style.'

Aoife said, 'Don't be so cruel. Douglas is very handsome. And he has beautiful eyes.'

'Okay, Cunningham. She's convinced me. Wait outside the agency, and wear my coat at all times.'

She was so tall in those boots, Aoife had to step sideways, descending the stairs of Almayer House with her arms held up, hands supporting her on the walls all the way down. I walked ahead to catch her if she fell and Abby snapped orders from behind us. We headed along Bollo Lane, waving upwards at Lou, who watched us from the living room, holding Lily to the window. What did he make of us from up there? Abby carried her make-up bag, which folded out like a field medic's amputation set. I was wearing the macintosh with the small bloodstain on the inside lining and Aoife had a dark woollen coat over her short skirt.

Before she left us, Abby fired out quite a lot of information at Aoife about other girls to name-drop, but I couldn't help myself thinking that, for all her bluster, Abby wasn't getting that much modelling work herself. She kissed Aoife on both cheeks, then Abby moved up the road back towards Ealing.

Inside Acton Town Tube station, I tried to ponder if we should buy full day passes and go somewhere in town together, after her interview.

She asked, 'Where? We've no money.'

I tried to encourage her. 'There are things you can do for nothing in London.'

'What?'

'Go up the Monument.'

'Where's that?'

'Monument.'

'Where is it?'

'At Monument. That's what it's called. Where the Great Fire of London started. You can climb up the stairs inside looking three hundred feet down the middle of it.'

'Oh great. For three hundred feet below me, people will be able to look right up this bloody skirt.' She slapped at the flank of her wool overcoat, whipping out a glimpse of long thigh.

'Leave your coat on,' I said.

She stared directly back at me. I'd never seen her in such a bad and snappy mood. I went morose.

We got onto a Piccadilly Line train for Aoife's intended stop at Green Park. She swiftly told me that Green Park was once Lou's stop, *when* he was hall portering. She spoke as if it were some lost golden age, and with a hint of a reprimand to me.

On the train we sat on the seat row which faces the one opposite, Aoife taking her place first. I had hesitated then stepped beyond her, one seat further and I sat down against her left side. Someone had jettisoned most of a *Guardian* on the seat across, so I reached over, drew it to me and looked at it for a few moments with disinterest. Cluelessly, like a dribbling liberal, the *Guardian* was still straddling the fence over the miners, as if there actually were two valid arguments. You could feel dark, undemocratic forces were at work, smearing and fearing and being supported by middle-class cluelessness. The Secret Service, doubtless in action as usual, justifying their huge cost, protecting the national interest and other millionaires' assets. In the future, people would ask where you stood and what you did at this historical moment during the miners' strike. What was I doing? I'd dropped a few coins in a bucket and I was looking at a female model's leg.

Piccadilly Line trains ran fast and non-stop after Turnham Green, through Ravenscourt Park until Hammersmith, so we battered along at quite a velocity on the elevated track. Aoife's upper left arm rocked, pushed and actually bumped a few times, against my right arm.

I turned towards her. 'Not nervous?'

'Course I am. It's not like a normal job where who you are actually counts for something. With this job, who you are doesn't matter one little bit, it's only what you look like. Imagine how that would feel to you? It's like you have no soul.'

I nodded. I saw her left hand resting there, the coat hanging open. Her skirt so short – she was just all legs in black-patterned tights and the hand with the wedding ring rested uselessly on the thigh of her left leg. I reached with my right hand, gave her fingers a silly little squeeze then withdrew my hand straight back into my lap. She turned with a very weak smile.

'You look great. Very beautiful. You'll be fine and they'll put you back on the books.'

She nodded. Just maybe two smart bumps of her head. I could feel I was smiling, the same forced, muscular grimace as when I pull back my lips to brush my teeth. I looked down. My right hand had reached out and rested upon Aoife's hand again. I looked at my hand there. Was that why I had sat on her left, so I could use my right hand? Her hand didn't react, it just lay there as my own rested on top, like two trilobites, one mounting another. I could feel her wedding ring so I took my hand off and moved it slightly forward, beyond her fingers. I put my palm down softly on that uncrossed left leg, a bit above the knee. The train's movement cautiously shook my hand while it lay limply – as if trying to dislodge it. I widened out my fingers, shaping them to the contours of her leg; the heat through the black tights was of her living flesh which I speculated so much upon.

I couldn't look at her face. I looked at her leg with my hand spread out on it like something that had fallen from a height, as if it were justified being there. The train lurching from side to side was very noisy and I wasn't sure I was taking in breaths.

I was looking ahead across the slatted floor to the varnished wood of the far windows. My hand was resting on Aoife's leg as we rocketed along and she hadn't even told me to drop dead yet. I dared to shift my eyes toward her. She was looking directly ahead. Suddenly her red lipstick turned to my ear and my body violently stiffened. Her voice seemed to have dropped into a lower timbre. 'Douglas, I have an interview.'

I nodded slowly and I turned to look and her. I frowned at her flecked, damaged irises.

'Douglas?'

'Yes?'

'I have an interview ahead here.'

'Yes.'

The bloody cursed train was slowing down. I just wanted it to keep moving through London and onward, up to Theydon Bois or wherever-the-hell; some technical emergency so they could never stop, for two hours. Two days. Circling the Circle Line. We'd sleep on the floor together.

I realised how dry my throat had become. 'Yes, I know.'

'I need to think right now. About that.'

'What else *could* you think about?' I replied, full of dread. The train was really slow by then and not moving in open air but submerged down in some sequence of black brick walls with the sky a bright roof, rammed up somewhere above us.

'I don't want to be upset or distracted.'

'No.'

'I don't want—'

There was a jerk and we both nudged into each other a bit. The train had stopped in the Hammersmith station. The doors hissed and opened soberly.

'—you to be upset.'

'Aoife?'

'What?'

'How could I be upset, how could I?' With a huge effort – because I saw a man stepping on to the train and coming our way – I lifted my hand from her leg and swung it back toward me.

This person sat diagonally across from us, glanced at Aoife's legs, as any normal man would, then he looked down. He appeared sad, I thought.

Nothing was said. The doors closed and the train began moving again.

'You look so beautiful.'

'Douglas.'

'What?'

'I—'

I interrupted. 'I wish there was somewhere we could go. There's no bloody escape.'

I moved my hand back towards the leg but now she slowly shook her head with an aware certainty. 'Somewhere to go?' she suddenly queried.

I took heart. 'Maybe you should come away with me somewhere? For the day. A day out. Today.'

She looked round.

'Can I put my hand back?'

'No.'

'Okay.' I took a deep breath. 'Okay. I can deal with that.'

She frowned. 'Have you and Lou been drinking this early?'

'No. I'm telling you what I feel.'

In a blank, very low voice to try to conceal it from the other passenger, she turned her face toward me, 'What you were *feeling* was my leg.'

I smiled at her.

'How many more stops?' she said in a clear, casual voice.

Then I closed my eyes and opened them. We jerked to a halt and our faces had moved closer. The doors hissed. We'd arrived in some damned shadowy grotto, a chlorophyll light – actual ferns were growing down here – I could see them, just out of my peripheral vision through the window glass and behind her small shoulder. I could see ferns because I'd turned my head far aside to try and kiss her on the mouth but she saw it coming and jerked her head away as if a fly had settled on her lips – as she must have done at thirty school dances, in the shadows of disco light. A similar mausoleum gloom.

'Watch my make-up.'

I whispered, 'You're a Catholic but don't you ever think we're already living in Hell? We might not be, but some are.' I knew there wasn't much time so I stood up and quickly walked out the open doors onto the platform of Earls Court station and the train doors closed behind me.

I leaned slightly over and looked back into the train, through the window glass; Aoife and her legs, alone on that bank of seating. It was as if I were peering into a miniaturised, petrified doll's house interior, lit by small bulbs, considering a scale model of a preserved past where I'd once existed.

Aoife was staring straight ahead, seemingly with relief, as if I did not exist and never had in her entire life. The train moved off, rattling with an hysterical excitement.

I slid my Yale key into the lock of 506 and turned it. I'd taken two steps into the hallway when I knew something was badly wrong with Lily because Lou said a word with an aged and inevitable weariness and he'd phoned up Abby, who spoke back to him in fear, but with no attempt to talk quietly – for Lily's sake – as if Lily were not present or worse: unconscious.

'What is it?' I called and ran quickly down the corridor, over the patch of carpet – yet the bedroom was darkened by the curtains as I saw Lily asleep in the cot and then Lou and Abby in the bed together. Him next to the bookshelves, his shoulders white and bare, surprisingly narrow – Abby on Aoife's side, looking right at me.

'Okay, then,' I said in the manner of a statement.

'Why are you back so soon? Are you alone?' Lou asked in a reasonable voice.

The air was cool in there, so the bedspread mostly covered them – which was human enough. Soon they both sat up, only slightly on their elbows, each with a certain impatient, querulous expression as they watched me in the half-light as I looked at them. They listened beyond me into the stillness of house space behind.

'She's at that agency. I came back alone.' I made a huge mistake then; I took a step to the cot and held out my hands as if to lift the sleeping baby.

Lou did not raise his voice, which made his tone more chilling, and he also moved out of the bed with huge speed in a frantic, feminine bustle – but nonetheless he stood beside me in an instant.

'Don't you even *dare* wake her,' he said.

My hands fell back uselessly as if my arms had been broken by his words.

'You are not my wife's conscience so leave the child alone.' He held up a pointed and trembling finger to my face. 'And don't forget that.'

I frowned at him the way you did to scolding parents and teachers when you were young; your frown both as a submission and a sceptical criticism, blinking slightly in case you are struck.

'Me or Aoife have a right to pick Lily up at this moment. To walk out. Not you.' He repeated with violent emphasis, 'Not you, Douglas. I won't be judged that far by you.'

I was going to bother to say that I wasn't judging him at all, but I found myself looking at Lou's naked body. I'd never seen him completely naked before. His slim, girlish body was pale and hairless; he was minutely nippled and he had no belly at all, despite the constant drinking; he was tenderly toned – not muscled. A dark-haired young man with five o'clock shadow, yet utterly hairless all over his body apart from a neat, vibrant pubic gathering; the paleness seemed to make him actively glow in the dark, into which his eyes vanished like a vampire's – or an angel's. I found him as physically beautiful as any woman – his body full of erotic variation and novel possibility which I hadn't even considered in life before. But for the one blemish. My eye was overwhelmed by that scar, from below his neck to above his stomach. Now it was narrower and string-like; it was such a mesmerising destruction upon his perfect beauty. I thought, the scar looked like this angel had grown a mutant third wing which had since been amputated.

'You must have Japanese blood.'

'Japanese?'

'You don't have any body hair, hardly.'

'Oh, my old father was quite like that, I'm told. Went bloody bald then the drink killed him. Bet I go bald.'

Perhaps for the sake of speaking but implying some sort of

helpless compulsion which excused her, Abby told me, 'His skin is unbelievably smooth.'

I nodded and I held out my finger and touched the scar at its very summit, then I slowly drew my finger down and frowned.

Silently Abby watched from the bed and then blurted out, 'Are you going to tell Aoife, sausage?'

'Shut up,' said Lou.

My finger was halfway down his scar and my finger had vibrated from his diaphragm when he'd spoken.

I took my hand away and looked him in his face. 'You're okay now, aren't you?'

'This?' he dipped his chin. 'This can't open again. It's healed. I was a broken man and now I'm whole again.' He smiled. 'I'm not meant to be drinking, though; was drinking a week after the op.' He chuckled.

'But your heart is okay? You're not going to die? You never really tell me or even talk about it. As if I don't care, Lou, and I do care. Of course I do.'

He nodded. 'I was very afraid for a year before the op, when I was ill. I was scared of going to Hell. But look at me. I don't even have fear of death as an excuse any more.' He nodded over to Abby in his bed.

'Lou,' said Abby. 'Why are you always demeaning women? Well, actually not women. You're always demeaning me. Or Eeef.'

'Oh fuck off. It's not the moment for you to get protective about her.' He turned to Abby as if explaining a movie plot. 'That's what I'm saying to him. Before my operation, I'd have slept with you because I was sure I was going to die. Fair enough. Now I know I'll live but I've still gone and done it. It's bloody inexcusable.'

Abby shrugged her shoulders. 'Well, I'm very sorry about that.'
She tutted.

I said, 'Have you done it before?'

They didn't look at me. She stared at him so it was a giveaway.

Lou said hollowly, 'That time you and Eeef sent me to Fulham
Road to get that money from fucking Hanson. I was round at hers
all day.' He was cold so, reasonably enough, he climbed back into
the bed with his knees drawn up and he tugged the covers to his
chin. He reached out for his pack and went to remove a cigarette,
remembered Lily was in the room then tossed the pack back down
by the books again.

I nodded.

Abby called to me, 'Douglas. If you and me'd done it the night
of the wedding, sausage, then I wouldn't have done it with Lou.
Would I? You're not very good at the signals.'

'Oh, I see. My fault, is it, Abby?'

'Frankly? Yes. I'm Catholic. I'm only going to do it so many
times before I marry.'

I shrugged, and spoke in a softer voice. 'Don't think I'm judging
you both or that I believe for a moment I'm any better than you
two. I certainly don't.' Academically I asked, 'You don't happen to
have any booze, do you?'

Lou nodded encouragingly, and as he did, his arm went down
to the floor at the bedside and up it came again with a half-empty
bottle of white wine. 'Good stuff from the off-licence by The Bells.
She brought it back with her.' He flicked his head at Abby. I felt a
bit sorry for her.

'Huh,' she went.

I had to cross to the bed to take it from his hand, so I loomed above them both as I guess doctors and nurses must have stood over Lou when he was helpless in a hospital bed.

Lou said, 'Are you going to tell Aoife?'

'Of course I'm not.'

'Why did you come back, boyo?'

For a moment I wondered if I should tell him I was in love with his wife. 'She was uncomfortable with me there. She was very nervous about the interview so I just came back.'

'Bloody hell. And left her in town, dressed like that?'

I gave him a reprimanding look. 'What was that about this not being the moment to be protective about her? Christ sake.' My voice rose in volume and anger. 'The three of us aren't worthy of her. Look at us. She's better off out on the streets of London.' I swung round and ridiculously gestured at the photo of Aoife, semi-naked on the beach at Dittisham. We all turned to look at the portrait. 'The harm is being done here.' Then my voice trailed off. But Lily woke up and immediately began screaming.

'Oh for fuck sake. You and your sermons,' Lou groaned.

'I'd better get out of here.' Abby suddenly hurled back the bed-covers, showing me her breasts, then turned and sat on the edge of the bed with her spine visible down the long bare back as she retrieved and put her knickers on. She came off the bed and kneeled, picking amongst her bundled clothing. I walked through to the front room so I wouldn't have to watch her dressing. I looked out over the view.

Lou had put on his tracksuit and he carried Lily up the corridor into the room and handed her to me without a word. I took her gently and without the slightest hesitation or objection. She stopped crying in moments as I shoogled her. He soon came back through from the kitchen with a made-up bottle for Lily and she filled her gob with it immediately as I helped her hold it.

When Abby came up the corridor I called, 'It's deemed in the national interest that you give me and Lou a tenner to get drunk on.'

Without resistance she said, 'Okay, then.'

I announced, 'I'm going to the Co-op.'

'Good.' He nodded sincerely.

'What will I get us?'

'Demolition juice.'

I handed the baby back.

Abby and I descended the stairs of Almayer House again that day. The sound of a screeching, clanking Tube train came through the top lobby and we moved down the steps to the third floor. Mr Linton's ferrets scrabbled in their hutches. As spring approached you could smell them more.

We were in the stairway between the second and third floor lobbies when Abby said, 'I'll give you your pocket money, sausage.' We stopped on the stairs between the blank walls and the long-worn brass banister. She was still carrying the make-up folio and she had thrown on some kind of wool-and-mohair poncho with innumerable holes, gaps and flaps on the patterned fabric. She reached into her leather bag, took out her purse and peeled a tenner, which she passed to me with a cynical, bitter expression.

'Fuck you, Abby,' I said to her face, forcing the money into the pocket of my jeans. She was standing there, each tan boot of Cordovan leather placed on a different step. She backed herself against the concrete wall first. The make-up pack landed on one step with a dramatic slap. I put both my hands in under her poncho and placed them on her shoulders; she was so slim it was like holding two billiard balls in each hand. I put pressure against her body so she flattened and I kissed her on the lips, turning my head to the side and forcing my tongue far into her mouth. She put both her hands down and rubbed my cock through the annoyingly thick denim of my jeans.

I knew what my tongue was searching for in Abby's mouth: the tobacco taste of Llewellyn. I was weary of being taken by surprise by my own self.

I moved my hands down and round her breasts in a manner that seemed obvious and conventional but then at the front of her jeans I pulled the zip down. It was almost impossible to get my hand in far as the jeans were so tight on her and we were standing, suspended there on a ridiculous stairway high above the earth, writhing at each other, precarious on precast concrete, all imprisoned in tight denim, cool airs blowing upwards around us with hostility.

I took a step back and drew her forward off the wall by the waistband of her jeans. She let her hands drop to her sides, away from my crotch. I bit my lip in concentration and used both hands to snap open the top button and fold the waistband of her jeans apart. I put my hand in behind her purple underwear and straight on down between her legs. She stood there baring her teeth like she was leaning back on a water ski, eyeing me with resentment but clucking at the back of her throat two or three times as she tipped her lovely freckled chin up. We both stood very still, the only movement was my hand. This went on for long minutes until a door closed down on the first floor with an echoing bang. I pulled my hand out, leaving her there. I said, 'Eeef could come back.'

She nodded, still looking at me.

Then I added, 'Lou is watching from the window, waiting for us to come out together.'

'I know,' she hissed.

'He can time how long it takes to get down these steps.'

'I know. So what? Make me go to my orgasm thing.'

I licked my two main fingers while looking her in the eye, then I walked on down the stairs ahead.

I waited at the bottom by the bin huts until she sauntered out too. We walked side by side on the pavement, up Bollo Lane.

'Thanks for the money.'

'Thanks for not making me come. You oaf.'

'Aoife could be back any minute.'

'We'd have heard her boots coming up the stairs, you Scotch chicken. Anyway, so what? God. You boys.'

'How'd we explain you being back at the flat?'

'Silly sausage, we'll tell her the truth. You're just crazy about me and you were taking me back there.'

'Did she tell you about our night at that drunk man's house?'

'*No?*' she said, quick and genuinely curious.

'Another time. Have to go this way to the Co-op.'

'I know.'

'See you.'

'Douglas? Don't tell her. Please.'

'I won't.'

'You promise, sausage?'

I nodded.

'Say it.'

'I promise, Abby. People act on their passions, do daft things.

That's okay. That can be forgiven. But passions are different from trying to fuck someone up deliberately.'

'I'm not trying to hurt her. I just got curious and put my toe in the water a bit. Have you never done that?'

A key went in the lock as Aoife came home before two o'clock that afternoon. Me and Lou had been drinking two bottles of Blue Nun, and a bottle of Black Tower in the front room. We were so drunk I had changed Lily's nappy when it was clean and then Lou had also, twenty minutes after.

Aoife wasn't fully in the door when Lou nervily started yelling, 'How was it?'

In a voice soaked in normality, she replied, 'It was good. They were nice.'

'They took you on?'

'Yes,' she said, putting her head in the door. She had the wool coat draped over her arm.

'Course they did.' Lou nodded.

I was sat defensively inside Lily's penned-off play area, my back against the wall on a dining chair. I was looking at her but Aoife moved the benediction of an equal smile over us all, then stepped to Lily, leaned in, lifted her and kissed her, using the same smile.

And which of us deserves that smile, I thought.

'You'll bollix your back one day doing that, love,' Lou grumbled.

'Where'd you get the money for that?' she said softly and nodded at the empty bottle of Blue Nun on its side.

'Cunningham found a bloody tenner. Never mind, dear one, you'll be bringing the bacon home soon enough, from la-la land.'

She tutted and handed Lily to Lou. 'Don't drop her.'

Aoife went through to the bedroom. Lou and I looked at each other, plunged in misunderstanding. Aoife came back in just a few minutes, her make-up and hair the same but in a tracksuit. She sat down and watched the television. Sometimes she stood to go and play with Lily. I couldn't detect any change in her and I found it erotic that she'd let me touch her leg. I was fearful I would make the mistake of thinking it granted me some huge future permission.

When she phoned Abby, Aoife spoke in front of Lou and me as we watched the telly with the sound considerably turned down a bit. Aoife described the whole interview to her best friend in detail and both Lou and I could distinguish Abby's tinny, normal voice far in, through the earpiece.

That night I lay straight out on my camp bed; unknown to each other they both performed a theatre for my benefit – the mattress sighed and even the bed head thumped repeatedly before a fist suddenly grasped and secured it, or maybe Aoife folded both of her hands up against it, elbows sharply pointed forward. I imagined Llewellyn's glabrous being, palely repositioning itself around her in symphonic variations of one grander ecstasy, the little silver crucifix wetted between her breasts, his fringe touching on the mole of her neck as she bent forward.

19

Lily was sleeping down in their bedroom and there was nothing to drink except tea. Aoife was on the sofa next to Lou, swinging those legs about as I watched them cross and then re-cross like purposeful weaponry. She was talking about *Nineteen Eighty-Four* and *Brave New World* and how they had to read these books in school.

I claimed, 'They teach dystopias at school so you refuse to imagine a better society.'

'It's true,' Lou nodded. '*Animal Farm* too. We had to do that.'

Aoife said, 'I remembered being frightened by the drug in *Brave New World*: Soma.' She sighed and suspended her foot way up in the air and left it there, surveying her left leg, then it was lowered. Aoife said, 'See the drug things down in the basement. Do you think we should try them? There's no way they are going to be Soma, are they?' She humped up a swampy, singular giggle, like a hiccup, and she covered her mouth with straightened fingers. She looked excitedly at Lou as if he gave final permission on all things.

I said, 'I don't think you should do that.'

'How come?' Lou turned to me, touchy to be refused anything.

I shrugged, 'Different personalities react in different ways to LSD. For some it's benign, for others, no. A baptism of fire. Till you've taken it, you don't know how you'll react and by then there's no going back.'

'And you've taken it, you fiend. I suppose you had a Presbyterian revelation?' Lou chuckled.

'Yes, but it's deeply unpredictable. Depends on personality.'

Aoife suddenly demanded. 'How do you think *my* personality would react?'

'Can't predict. There's no set rules. You're sweet and a calm personality so you should have a benign experience.'

'What is benign?'

'Good,' Lou snapped at her.

Aoife twisted her lips. 'Is it like when you swallow the worm in that tequila drink thing? Cause that didn't affect me. That was just disgusting.' She turned to look at my eyes. 'He made me do that on our second date in a Mexican bar in Covent Garden. How did you find such a place, Lou? And he was talking with them all in Mexican.'

'Spanish.'

'And he made me drink it. Didn't know it was a *worm*. They said it would make you hallucinate but all it made me feel was so repugnant. I sobered up in a minute. I thought it was clung on inside of me.'

Lou changed voice to an intimate register he would only use on her when I wasn't present. I recognised that tone from sudden murmurs through walls, from beyond doors which stood fractionally ajar. 'Come on. We're bored stiff. Me and you do it, Cunningham will keep an eye on us and Lily. There's no booze to drink so I shall turn to drugs in that grand tradition.'

I looked at Lou as if something had changed in him; as if he was already restlessly tugging at all the ropes which held him together.

He went off down to the cellar. I told him to check on Lamborghini while he was there. When he came back up it was two tabs

266

of Superman LSD – like I had bought at Glastonbury that time.

'But it has a little man on it,' said Aoife.

'Yes.'

'Oh, how cute.'

'Will we go for it?' Lou looked at her.

As I placed a tab of LSD in each of their palms I felt a guilty relish at the psychic turbulence it would bestow on them both. I imagined it as an electrical force shooting to the ends of their limbs. I said to them, 'You won't feel a thing for maybe an hour. Just try to remember this drug can in no way harm you physically; you cannot overdose; everything you'll experience is psychological. If you both stay around me you can come to no harm.'

They placed the small squares of card on their tongues.

I said, 'The body and blood of Christ.'

Both of their eyes only flickered, their voices briefly and helplessly muted. They swallowed the drug down, sharing from the same sloshing glass of milk.

'Amen.'

'Amen. Bloody hell, boyo.'

Lou slapped his lips and looked at the glass of milk.

For close to an hour we sat talking in a desultory manner, huge expectant gaps between their sentences as each waited for something to change in their perception of this world. Although Lou sat close to me, his informal voice strangely projected the impression that he was physically distant; as on occasion shifted furniture, screeching two syllables in some distant room of another apartment, had tried to speak out my Christian name: Doug-lass.

It was a pleasant day out the window, and across the view white clouds were moving west with stately hesitation. Smoke – more like steam, generated by temperature differential – was blubbering at the top of a silver chimney stack in the works down by Boston Manor. Lou and Aoife were both sat on the sofa, holding hands as if awaiting a doctor's confirmation on a long-sought-after pregnancy. Close to an hour had gone by since I'd looked at my digital watch.

Aoife said, 'The lamp shade is laughing at me.'

'Yes,' said Lou. 'I mean. Is it? Gosh. This is— All the buildings down in that place are climbing on each other and reassembling into something more agreeable. It's like Braque and Picasso. They must have taken this.'

I smiled. As if I were the author of all this and thus, in some way, in control.

'Remarkable, Cunningham.'

'Just keep cool, folks, and relax. You'll experience unusual things but nothing bad. Only good. I'll make some of those mint teas that Aoife always has.'

So for another hour they sat. They were both very different from what I'd expected; calmer than my reactions had ever been and I was not without a childish jealousy. I couldn't help considering a leap into the room dressed in a wolf's costume with ketchup dripping from my fangs, screaming at them about werewolves from Wandsworth. Not that we had any ketchup in the house, of course.

An odd moment came when Aoife suddenly said, 'I need to pee now.'

Lou jumped and called out, 'Cunningham. The lady requires the throne of contentment in our *salon de nécessité*,' and he took Aoife's

268

hand. I supervised their walk down the corridor. He sat on the edge of the bath to watch over her and I retreated to the kitchen door. Eventually, they both came back up the corridor again, holding hands. Aoife said, 'That made a brilliant sound.'

Another ten minutes on the sofa and Lou stated in an exasperated voice, 'It's just too fucking high up here. We must be inconsiderate to live this high up. The birds have to go *round* us, or *over* us, and it must be exhausting and inconvenient for them. Why would we live so high up? We don't belong here. Are we trying to escape something that I've forgotten about, Cunningham?'

'No. Everything's quite fine. Everything's at rest and peaceful.'

He nodded, unconvinced, wiped the back of his hand across his brow then studied it for sweat. 'No. There's fucking too much going on out there for me to analyse. I need to speak to Saint Francis of Assisi about this. It's not stacking up, even the way the buildings coalesce in the east and the other bloody way too.'

I announced, 'Okay, then. The show's over. We've no curtains here so off to the bedroom we go, to visit lovely Lily.' I went ahead and I drew the bedroom curtains.

As they came down the hallway in single file, Lou placed his hands on Aoife's shoulders as she walked ahead of him, like those linked chains of blinded, gassed soldiers in photographs of the Great War. Aoife asked, 'Lou. You all right?'

'I'm okay, yes. It's a bit tiring. Are you okay, love?'

'It's different than I thought. I can't believe I've had Lily.'

'I was thinking that,' Lou cried out.

'Isn't it so strange? Most of my life has been without Lil and now she's here, I find it really funny she came out from the inside of me and we both made her.'

They gathered round the cot and stared down on the child, then sat gingerly on each side of their bed – with a temporary air to their positioning, as if they didn't know whether to sit up straight or to lie down. Lou stared at his bookshelves, looking blown and shaking his head. 'You could never write anything. The flow and change of information is too rapid and there aren't sentences for the logic of my thinking right now.'

I spoke in clear and scientific tones, slightly emphasising, as if I were dealing with a patient. 'Lou. What you are saying is interesting. Could you talk about it more?'

'Yes. Well. The thing that preoccupies me most is time.'

'Yes.'

'What I'm concentrating on now are, well, three things. Aoife's hand like it's fizzing on the surface and I'm looking at these book covers, cause I thought they were all familiar to me but now I'm seeing new things. I know I'm on your drug stuff but it's changed time. There was a beginning when we took it but when I try to think of an ending, I can't. I can't conceive there is an ending to all of this truth that's unfolding before me. One thing after another. I am back at the beginning of the world. Consciousness is just an intervention in the flow of time. Time was minding its own business until consciousness came along.'

I nodded politely. 'Aoife. What are you feeling?' I was hoping for something less speculative.

'I don't feel things happening quick, I feel them slowing down. I was worried there that the world might stop or even go backward then that means I won't have done all the washing and ironing and I'll have to do it all again. Not just the other days. All I've ever done. Then that interview at the agency. I'm able to go back in my mind and think things over that happened. What I said and what I should've. Not just that. Way back in life. Like before Lily and I'm thinking about them days in a new way. My tongue's a bit numb and I don't feel like talking much. My lovely, lovely boys.'

Lou smiled, fidgeted nervously for a brief second and looked over at me, chuckled, then repeated in a hollow way, 'My lovely, lovely boys.' He turned and patted Aoife on her hand. That hand.

'I'm going to fetch you both glasses of water now cause your mouth can get dry without you knowing.'

When I brought back the two glasses of water, they'd both swung their legs up on the bed in imitation of each other. I handed the glasses of water first to Aoife, then I rounded the bottom of the bed and gave one to Lou.

Later I had carried one of the dining chairs down the corridor and I sat in it, observing them both on their bed, as if I had positioned my seating to witness some meticulous and specific lunar eclipse.

Aoife said, 'I'm not so much thinking things as seeing things in this bedroom, and I wish they would just go back to the way they were.'

'They will. Don't worry.'

She had folded her legs beneath her, in the lotus position, so I glanced up at the black and white photo to see a replication of her, naked in that identical posture. She looked down at the candlewick bedspread and bit her lip concernedly.

Suddenly, Lou demanded, 'Exactly what is Harmondsworth all about?'

'Harmondsworth?'

'Yeah.' He lifted up a Penguin Modern Classic, its artwork on the front framed by black, its spine duck-egg green, its back cover dark; it was opened to the first pages. 'Penguin Books Limited. *Harmondsworth*, Middlesex. It's a village out by Heathrow. But why there? What's going *on* out there? What are Penguin Classics *doing* out there? For Christ's sake. Let's go straight out there, Cunningham, ask to see the boss and tell the guy: "Why don't you just publish me and Cunningham straight into Penguin Modern bloody Classics and the hell with fiddling around with a polite pause for thirty years till you figure out we really are Modern Classics already? Why should we wait? Just put us straight in to Penguin Modern Classics. Now."'

He appeared to have got a little lost in the passion of his scenario, and he squinted at me quite threateningly, as if I were the sole representative of Penguin Books in the room.

'Yes, let's go—' Aoife grappled with the concept, then pronounced: 'Outside.' She pointed.

'Yes.' Lou warmed up to this revelation. 'Let's go out into the outside, out into it.'

'Well. For your first trip that's not such a good idea,' I claimed. 'What about Lily?'

We were standing at the bus stop on Gunnersbury Lane. Lily was all fattened out by her anorak in her buggy, still looking startled. We were The Startled Family and I was trying to explain that a quick circuit round Brentford would be preferable. I had to make clear to Lou that even if we made it to Harmondsworth – which I suspected consisted only of warehouses, whence Penguin publishers shipped their exports – the office would be closed and nobody would be there of sufficient authority to accept our writings immediately. Especially since there were none, though I did not bring this matter up.

Aoife and Lou had nodded obediently. They had become a little daunted since we moved out into the opennesses of the world. On my orders they walked linked arm in arm ahead as I pushed Lily and there was to be no solitary wandering.

I lifted Lily out and folded up the buggy. 'Let's just go onto any old bus.'

'Yes,' said Aoife. 'A bus is safe. I didn't mind when I knew where I was but if we're going somewhere I don't know I was, or is, I want to be sat on a bus and to take a bus back again if a bus comes back again to where I was again when I started out that first time.'

I frowned.

Lou nodded solemnly, understanding her.

A Routemaster bus came along; we boarded, me leading the way up the steep steps, carrying Lily and the folded buggy, trying to get to my seat before the bus started moving. I sat them together, halfway along the top deck, while I put my back against the window of the next seat in front, holding Lily who looked back at them. They smiled at their huge achievement in getting there but they seemed slightly oppressed. The low, moulded ambience of the Routemaster's metallic ceilings and the yellow, sometimes naked light bulbs in the roof gave a strange and crepuscular feel to this tubular world.

When the young bus conductor came upstairs and along the aisle, his arms jabbed out naturally, grabbing at hand holds as he swung forwards. I could tell he had disapproved of me taking the baby and folded buggy upstairs but I wasn't leaving it down there to get nicked when the Smiths couldn't afford another. Lou and Aoife both tensed and said nothing as the machine ratcheted out three Brentford tickets. The conductor briefly glanced down at the passive and rigid crowns of their heads, sensing we were involved in some kind of grand occult activity together but he couldn't pin it down. Out the windows the bus bore us forward through boulevards of gunmetal grey and traversed vast, traffic-lighted crossroads where cyclists hesitated warily with one foot on the ground and pedestrians dashed for the shores of pavements.

We rode on in silence for some time. At one point Lou sneaked a look out the corner of his eyes and Aoife glimpsed back at him simultaneously; they both blew hissing air through their front teeth in a conspiring giggle and they looked around startled, exasperated to communicate what was happening to them. I sensed them moving into some more complex level of intercommunication.

The bus moved through streets where some occasional and premature light bulbs were switched on; eventually we were in a high street looking through the unwashed first-floor windows of disused store rooms above shops. The bus pulled in and the conductor yelled up the stairwell, 'All change.'

I had not counted on that. We had to debus into the busy thoroughfare. I rebuilt the buggy and strapped Lily in. Aoife and Lou shuffled off down a quiet-looking lane towards what I presumed was the direction of the river. After a while, I started to believe we might actually be heading north.

I directed them up a mews which seemed to have a way out at the top end, then, around a corner, the road widened. It was full dusk now. The sound of fast traffic began to increase like the coming of a tense and great catastrophe. We were right up close to the elevated motorway. Accompanying the aggressive air-pocketing of passing vehicles above, a strange and sudden holy light thumped against the walls and pavement around us. Aoife frowned. Even I looked up.

'Cunningham.' Lou shook his head slowly. 'You brought me to the Alhambra Palace at its cultural peak.'

Above us was the enormous side of a building, completely dedicated to a vintage neon advertisement, which spelled out:

LUCOZADE

And a leviathan, orangey-yellow bottle slowly tipped over and poured its frothing contents into an expectant glass which filled, draining out the bottle.

REPLACES LOST ENERGY

The sign faded like the culmination of a great and dramatic narrative, then with infinite and generous energy, all this was soon repeated as the bottle slowly drained and the glass filled up in sequence again.

'We must drink Lucozade,' whispered Aoife.

'Yes. It's an incredible drink. What a colour. It replaces lost energy,' Lou told us in a mystified voice.

Across the road a small bald man came around a corner and, as he approached, Lou called out, 'Good evening. So this is Harmondsworth at last, is it? What a place. Have you worked at Penguin Books for long?'

'Sorry?' He tried to be friendly.

'Why are you based in Harmondsworth? And so close to Granada?' Lou's hand helpfully pointed out the neon sign and the man glanced up. 'Handy for holidays, is it?'

The man rightly kept walking.

Lou yelled after him, his voice rising, 'Oh yeah, you can walk away now, like Toby Hanson did, but me and him are going straight into Penguin Modern Classics and there's nothing *you* can do about it. I'm not accepting anything else.'

The man stepped up his pace and hurried into the night.

Aoife and Lou must have stood twenty minutes watching the neon sign drain and replenish itself. At first they talked together, monitoring minute variations in the neon's regular pattern, but then their dialogue staggered into silence and the light flooded onto our faces successively without any commentary, just a mute, doctrinaire acceptance.

I turned to Aoife, her beautiful reflecting brow colouring as if she were watching a firework display high above us, her head held back, yellow light moving across her cheeks like a cloud of tea diluting through clear water.

Quietly, Lou now compared the neon to Bernini's sculpture of Saint Teresa. He turned to me several times to tell me this. Then he became silent and physically agitated.

I managed to retrace our steps back around the dark street corners to Brentford and there to lead us on to the more sensible bottom deck of another Routemaster bound for Gunnersbury Lane. Aoife seemed to be coming down a little because she was more talkative but Lou was silent and unpredictable.

*

I pushed Lily ahead in her buggy and they both followed me along the pavements to Bollo Lane, arm in arm. I kept turning my head to monitor them.

Back up in his bedroom, lucidity of sorts was coming Lou's way.

'Are you okay, Lou?'

'Yeah, I'm great, love. It's just— Well, it's all true after all, isn't it? After all the doubt and the suffering.'

'What's true?'

'What the Church says.'

Aoife turned to me. I shrugged and said, 'He'll be okay, when he comes down. It's normal.'

'All absolutely true.'

I didn't want him raving. Ecclesiastes meets *Sergeant Pepper*. I said, quite harshly, 'Come on, Lou. Get a grip. Don't let yourself get convinced by dogma.'

'Everything the Church says is concrete actuality; from transubstantiation to Saint Peter himself.'

'No it isn't,' I said.

He looked at me. 'You're Protestant. You can't protest people's inclination to be good. Who else are you going to get down on your knees to and give thanks to every day for the good things?'

'Go tell the starving Ethiopians that. Or the parents who just lost their children.'

Aoife frowned. 'Hush, Douglas.'

Lou said, 'We can't trust the converts to be our conscience, Cunningham. All bloody converts; your Greene and Waugh and Spark and all the rest of that shower. They'll never be the real thing. They treat Catholicism like it was a Mediterranean cruise and they demand to see all the sights. They're just bloody aesthetes, they'll never have the faith of an old woman in an Italian village. They'll never find the peace and love of Christ that she has, with all their vanities. There are still good things. Even you can't deny there are good things. You're an atheist, Cunningham. I accept that, but I ask you this. Who do you thank for the good things that come your way? When something is given to you that you wanted so bad – how does it feel for you? You have no one, nothing to thank. A thankless universe where you just take. Is that it? You have to be thankful.' And his arm went up.

She sat on with him while I was along in the front room watching television and playing with Lily and the Fisher Price blocks.

Aoife came once then twice from the corridor and she sat at my side, gently complaining that he wouldn't sleep. He would just babble about the Bible. I had to take over from her for a while and sit in there nodding as he lectured me on different aspects of theology and the concept of sins of omission.

Eventually, Aoife took over and after half an hour there was no cloisterish babble from down the corridor. When I leaned into their bedroom, Lou was slumbering. Aoife curled up flat alongside him, one arm over his shoulders. She was awake and gave her eyes to me, white and startled, and she nodded once, curtly. I thought a good way to avoid them was to have a quick bath so I did, lying in the steam trying to finish *The President* by Miguel Angel Asturias. When I went back through to the bedroom they both seemed to be sleeping.

All was darkness when I awoke. I let out a small exclamation and my eyes tried to adjust. The door to my little room was slightly ajar, so

I could see a line of cast lamplight up the dark carpet, then Aoife's sombre face hanging just above me, head bowed, as she kneeled beside my camp bed.

'Are you awake?' she whispered.

'What is it? Is Lou okay?'

'He's fast asleep.'

I frowned past her arm, mystified and clotted with sleep. I had never lain on the camp bed with the door open so I was strangely fascinated by the long, shadowy perspective, far away down the corridor. There was something terrifying about the rigid dimensions with the streak of milky lamplight – as in that mysterious Velásquez painting of the woman pouring the olive oil and who is that, in the shadows behind her? My eyes were adjusting. Aoife was wearing a pyjama top. It was the same one which Abby had worn the night of the wedding.

I said, 'Are you okay?' My hand was resting on my chest in that coffin-like repose I had adopted for the camp bed and Aoife had dropped both her hands, taken my fingers in a clutch. 'You're a very sweet guy.'

'No, I'm certainly not.'

'You are so.'

'Are you still stoned, Aoife?'

She blew out air. Her two hands were concernedly writhing upon my one hand, but in the manner that you would hold a relative's hand who is in a hospital bed, moaning with illness. I raised my other hand and placed it atop hers.

She put her face down close to mine and whispered, 'You tried to kiss me on the train?'

I nodded. 'Yes.'

Our whispered voices reminded me of that first night we met, six or seven months before, when we had stood and spoken softly together in her bedroom above the baby.

She said, 'Do you want to know when I knew that you were very, very into me?'

'When?'

'When I caught you holding my shirt in the bathroom. You put it to your face in the bathroom and I saw through the glass. I realised in a moment you were very, very into me.'

'I am into you. Very.'

'I didn't realise. So you wanted to kiss me?'

'Yes. I'm sorry.'

'And everything else too?'

I nodded, though I was still lying flat. 'Of course.'

'That's bad, cause I'm getting a bit fed up with things. What are we going to do?'

I said nothing.

She whispered, 'Get up.' Her arm swept aside the wool blanket and she walked off in her baggy pyjamas, up the corridor, and as I still lay watching her she turned her head and used her hand to beckon me to follow. I creaked up off the camp bed and crept along the carpet in bare feet. She'd already closed their bedroom door.

In the living room was darkness and she was standing by the windows. Of the silver and white lights which showed so far down below, some were occasionally shuttered by shunting tree branches in the night breeze. I walked up and stood by her side, looking out as well, as if we'd both been summoned there by an ancient prophecy to witness a special star.

She still whispered, 'Lou might hear us talking in your room.'

'Yes.' I nodded. 'What do you want to talk about?'

Aoife said, 'I wanted to kiss you.'

I smiled. 'When?'

'When we were going to go down into the cellar that night after that horrid man, to see Lamborghini. I was going to try to kiss you. I don't know why. Sorry.'

'I wish I had known. Maybe I did and was scared.'

'It's so awful of me. I'm married. But you're a lovely boy. Come on, then.'

'What?'

She turned, leaned in and kissed me on the mouth. When she broke away she said, 'It's this pill you've gave us that's made me not care. I feel like I'm just skating over silver ice.' She kissed me again, harder, and I took her glass-like jaw in my fingers and moved my face upon her. She broke off from my mouth and said, 'You're a boy and you need to every two weeks. At least. Lou once said all men need to,' and she nodded seriously.

Her own fingers peeled off the pyjama top from her shoulders and let it fall, my fingertips stroked up her breasts to hard cones, as if I were repeatedly attempting to get dry sand to form into a stable pile. She breathed heavier.

The light around us which lit that dark room and faintly illuminated these things we did was waste light – the unintentional and meagre leakages from that calm city below.

'You smell of the bath.' She had drawn back her lips from my mouth and she kneeled. I felt her rubbery nipples stutter down over my bared pelvis because she'd swiftly hauled down my pyjama bottoms as she descended – the same ones she'd often washed, even ironed and neatly folded. Using just two fingers of her right hand, held up like a casual salute, she was keeping her loose hair from swinging across her cheek and getting caught up around her mouth while the left-hand finger, with the wedding ring, was politely suspended as if holding a tea-cup handle.

She only stopped a brief moment. 'And you taste of the bath.'

Yes. The light that was there was from those meagre leakages below and I thought of the sewers which flow beneath that great city, how at that early hour only low waters must seep there, through the slimed tunnels. This hour that suited Aoife and me and all conspirators and assassins.

I whispered, 'Look up, into my eyes, then' – and she obeyed; her head remained rigidly in the same position but both eyes turned up and she looked into mine, quite continuously, communicating nothing until my hips jerked distinctly forward, just once and she swung her head knowingly aside with a dark and opened mouth. More was ejaculated onto her collar bone and yet more again all over her bare, ivory shoulder. She lowered her face, using her right hand to wipe a heap of semen from her extended tongue and she flicked the majority of the globule downwards, onto the tightened thigh of her own pyjama trousers. She slowly but repeatedly wiped her hand – some on the right thigh then some over on the left, almost playfully. She closed her mouth. There she quietly kneeled. Then she touched her pyjamas again and told me in a matter-of-fact whisper, 'I'd better put these in the wash straight away.'

20

In the morning, no mail came sailing through the broken window but when I looked at my watch it was way too early. Lou tapped on my door and I feared the worst. He looked in. 'Bloody hell, boyo, that was thunder powder we took last night. I'm off to Mass and to meet Gran. Coffee?'

I sat with him at the kitchen bench, staring. 'Why are you going to the early Mass?' I asked.

'I don't rightly know.' He passed a cigarette and I took it. 'I feel sort of— Well, I need to rearrange my synapses.'

Aoife padded up the corridor, stood in the door and yawned at both of us. I noted her different pyjama bottoms. 'Why are you two all up so early?'

'I'll go over to Gran's for the day. Get a fried breakfast, back this afternoon. Want to tag along, boyo?'

'Ah, no thanks. I'll stay.'

He turned to Aoife. 'Will you come? I'm going to Mass.'

'I want a lie-in, Lou.'

He nodded – 'Oh. Okay' – and he blew out smoke. The loneliness of the pious was on him already.

When Aoife kissed him goodbye and shut the door, she stood there beside the coats with her head down. She came into the kitchen and looked at me and I watched her. After a minute she strolled across to the living room. I stood at the kitchen door while she watched down through the window until she must have witnessed Lou, wearing his mac and trilby, striding quickly up Bollo Lane.

She turned and walked past me back to the front door. My eyes followed her. From her hanging corduroy jacket, Aoife took out her house keys, put the mortice lock key in the door then turned it. I pondered why Lou and Abby had never thought to do that.

She pulled me into her and I pressed Aoife back into the fat, hanging cushion of coats, her hair scraping against Lou's other overcoat, her arms stretched out. As I kissed her, she pushed her lips down hard over my teeth and whispered, 'I'm safe for getting pregnant just now but you might give me this Aids if you do all those different positions on me?'

I said, 'You won't get Aids from me, Aoife.'

I knew what I was feeling. Just awe of her body and its erotic potential. Each morning now, Lou put on a tie and left to attend eight o'clock Mass. Every time he absented himself from the flat, Aoife or I waited, watching out of the window until he had been confirmed on his route up Bollo Lane, then one of us mortice-locked the door and we took each other in our arms – but never in the same room as Lily. The baby's cries often brought lovemaking to a wanton and speedy conclusion on her part, but Aoife's domestic parameters were quite clear: Lou couldn't smoke cigarettes in the same room as Lily and she and I couldn't fuck in the same room as Lily.

Several nights, I lay in the camp bed and listened to Lou and Aoife make their own, married love. I was by then familiar with some of her preferred physical stratagems and so fancied I could define from the sound patterns what their specific activity was.

There were those following mornings after Lou had left for church and Lily slept on in the bedroom cot. Aoife's body still warm from her marriage bed, she opened her mouth on the sofa cover, beside the burgundy stain of Lou's dried blood. Birds soared up next to the window glass – in that documentary-light of the front room, Aoife would utter a single cry, as if she had cut her finger with a knife in the kitchen.

That swish LTM agency had telephoned her – wanted to do a

series of test shots with a slightly famous and fashionable photographer, Ross someone, who would shoot only with a small stable of models he knew. If he chose you, it was steady work for years, she told Lou and me.

Yet it was immediately after that phone call that Lou stopped attending Mass quite so regularly. For a spell he was in the house every day and all day. On the fifth day of this, when he'd briefly left the living room, Aoife had impatiently leaned across and kissed my mouth, then moved violently away. Moments afterwards, Lou had re-entered the room with a cigarette and continued talking about books. He was rereading the Catholic novelist Mauriac, which I had the nerve to smirk at. After kissing his wife seconds before, I realised that, rather than a friend, I was a viper who resented his very presence in his own house at his daughter's side.

On the Saturday after I started sleeping with Aoife, our giros came, so me and Lou hit The Bells together. But our usual seat under the strip window was now taken by two of the old fellows. When I witnessed the brief, exchanged looks between us and them, I realised what they meant. The looks from the old guys were warnings, signifying a shift in the power structure. Lou and I had been away from the pub too much and thus had abdicated the right to our usual seat. The old fellows' look was stubborn and committed: Standards aren't being maintained; don't count on this being your seat unless you take this seriously; report for duty each day here and win our respect.

So Lou and I stood at the bar, where we began to sip at our pints then sauntered with fake insouciance to seats closer to the bar, which meant all the old fellows passed on their way to the toilet and they often stopped for a word with us. Sometimes the old men paused on their return journey as well – to continue or complete an anecdote or opinion engendered on their first passing.

With a Guinness before him and a smoke cloud up above, Lou talked like back in the old days for a while. He shouted out about the translated title of a Mauriac novel. I was told the title had been changed for the English translation to make it more appealing to the mundane Anglo-Saxon mind. It had been cheapened and in fact rendered nonsensical in relation to the original title. Lou yelled about this for a whole pint's worth and also declared that translation perhaps interested him more than authorship. Then, 'Listen, boyo. Been talking to Gran and the priest about me and Eeef tying the knot proper. In the church.'

My Guinness stopped its ascent and wobbled from side to side. 'Really?'

'In fact, I was wondering if you'd tenderise Aoife up a touch, before I pop her on the frying pan.'

'I beg your pardon?'

'Wondering if you'd drop a couple of hints. See where she stood with jumping the broomstick on consecrated ground.'

I nodded and frowned. 'I think you know she'd not be that keen. She'd have to go to confession. And confess.'

'Yes, she would.'

'She wouldn't want to do that.'

He turned to me. 'No, she wouldn't, but why is that? A few impure thoughts and actions with me hardly makes her the Scarlet Woman. But in Derbyshire they think it does. I don't see that she has much *to* confess apart from being at the receiving end of The Piston of Acton. She must have had to give two or three hand jobs at high school. Mary Anne with the Shaky Hand. The Who are Acton, you know?'

I nodded.

'Anyway, the Church doesn't recognise our marriage. It as good as doesn't exist.'

'A civil marriage is perfectly legal, Lou. And perfectly significant in a divorce settlement under British law.'

He gave me an odd, smug look. 'We need to get Lily baptised, too. Gran was right about getting her into a school that has a good languages department though. I needed to make some changes anyway in my rotten life.'

'Abby?'

He grimaced and looked around. 'Everything, boyo. Everything; even the sauce, need to lay off on it for a spell. Like you said that day about Eeef. We don't deserve her.'

I nodded sharply.

'So I want you to have a word with her. Butter her up good. She listens to you; doesn't listen to me. You'd be best man, of course. Do it proper this time. The church and a small hall or hotel. Hey, maybe the North Acton Railway Club of the Christmas Day cheque.'

'It put her empty account into overdraft.'

'Sometime next year we'll do it. What's the matter?'

I must have been nodding glumly without even disguising it. 'Nothing.'

'Look here, boyo. I'm feeling guilty too. I don't mean about the bloody cheque. About—' He leaned towards me and dropped his voice. 'About Abby.' He showed his teeth. 'Poor Aoife. I'm so guilty.'

It didn't sound very convincing. 'Lou. Just cause you decide to, sometimes those around you aren't ready to clean up yet. They still want to be sinners.'

He nodded. 'Well, Madam's all yours if you want her.'

'I'm sorry?'

'Abby. I'm not passing on seconds or anything, but I tell you, she's worth a roll. Leaves her leather boots and gloves on. And what a racket when she gets up a head of steam. Like a fox getting into the chicken coop.' He took a gulp of Guinness.

'Simone de Beauvoir will not be proud of us.'

'She was worth a roll. When she was young. The Castor. And great pillow talk afterwards, I'd wager. Jean-Paul was no winner in the looks department, but he did well there. Cunningham—' He wiped the condensation on the side of his Guinness so it looked like a window onto night time. 'I need to ask something of you. Take care of Aoife and Lily for a bit. I'm popping up to this place in Worcester for a chunk of teaching. Get off the booze, attend the chapel.'

Now my Guinness slopped. 'You serious?'

'Too right. Clear five hundred a month. A *month*. We'll be bloody rich. They treat you like a slave; you're teaching Italian teenagers from half eight in the morning till eight at night, but there's digs and free grub. I'll have to sign off but with the odd pint, even after cigs, tax and having to pay rent on Bollo Lane, I'll make a bob or two. If I do Easter till June, I can get in on the summer schools they run there too.'

'When are you doing this?'

'Now. Have to go up now for the Easter induction course.'

'You're going now? To Worcester. Now?'

'What's wrong with that? Aoife and Lily'll be safe with you. I trust you more than Gran or Rhys or fat Flo, boyo. I'd trust you with their lives. I'll be quitting the dole, but you just keep signing on and claiming at Abby's. I'll be at a different address. Doesn't affect you. I'll be sending the hundreds back to Eeef soon enough. Beer galore this summer, boyo. And there's another thing.'

'Have you told Aoife?'

'Just about to. By me doing this, the money I'll make will put a sock in her doing the modelling caper. She'll have Lil to think about. Now we love you, Cunningham, but you're not the wife's au pair. You have your own life, so don't let her treat you like a flunkey while I'm away up there. What I'm saying is, I don't want my wife out modelling. So don't let her go there with those whores. I need you to assure me that.'

'But I think she wants to model, Lou. It's a big deal for her.'

'The hell with a big deal. I'll get the money. She's going to get well poked one of these days by a damned fashion victim.' He leaned towards me. 'I tell you the thing about getting cuckolded, boyo.'

I looked straight at him, trying to empty my eyes.

'It's not so bad if you can choose who she does it with. I know Aids has come along to enrich the soup of despair, but it's not the sex that makes you so mad, is it? It's the feeling of being laughed at by a bunch of gossiping, cultureless fashion fuckers.'

I continued to look at him. 'Aoife isn't going to go with someone like that. When are you leaving?'

'Monday.'

'What about Lil? Jesus, she's nearly walking. You saw her yester-day. You're going to miss it. She'll be talking soon, too. You can see her trying to. She's her father's kid, the way you rabbit at her. It'll be fascinating what bloody language she's going to talk in first and I'm expecting a fully formed sentence too.'

He laughed but then frowned at me. 'Bloody hell. Leaving my gorgeous wife and conversational daughter alone with you for weeks up in a luxurious penthouse, posting you back beer money; Aoife'll be scrubbing your back with the Body Shop loofah in no time. Most men would be gagging for it and you're complaining in that Caledonian Cunningham way. I can't accuse you of trying to muscle in on my old lady, that's for sure.'

'No, it's just all— a bit sudden.'

I looked out over the bar. I squinted across the carpet and up at the hanging chandeliers with a fixed smile. Six months before I had loved that pub dearly and looked out across it as the future seemed drenched with possibility.

On the Saturday night, Lou had taken her into their bedroom. In the corridor she turned her thin neck and looked back wildly at me and there was something far too needy about the speed she twisted round at. I saw Lou note it. She thought he was taking her in there because I had confessed everything in the pub, so she had to hide a certain flightiness when she came back up the corridor and tried to conceal it further on into the evening. We had no opportunity to whisper together, though sometimes we touched hands in the corridor and glared into each other's faces.

They had an awful lot of sex that night.

On the Sunday morning, Aoife had gone with Lou to Mass and then to the Co-op whilst I remained at the flat taking care of Lily, holding her hands and letting her stand unsteadily in her romper suit, trying to get her to move towards me, grabbing her when the little legs suddenly folded beneath and she sat down.

By afternoon, with his packed suitcase laid out at the bottom of their bed, Lou's send-off party began. A red cotton tablecloth – slightly stained – was draped on the dining table. Three places were set: knives and forks which did not match, some silver plated and engraved with *Browns Hotel* upon their handles. Glass tumblers which were once free gifts from BP garages, and two bottles of sparkling white wine.

Aoife cooked a whole roast chicken. I lifted it in and out the oven and basted, in case she burned her hand – which, she kept repeating, she could not afford to do because of the photo shoot on Tuesday. Lou had tolerated this and stood next to me, peeling potatoes and veg, entertaining her with projections of his future existence among the fields between Worcester and Stratford-upon-Avon. Spiritual cradle of Shakespeare and Lea and Perrins sauce.

'How do you get there?'

'God knows. Via Birmingham? I suppose Victoria bus station will handle it tomorrow.'

'Birmingham. City of Transformation,' Aoife said. She was in a great mood.

'How come?'

'M6 turns into the M1 near there.'

Lou and I laughed.

Aoife said, 'Listen. Worcester's not *that* close to Birmingham.'

When we sat at the dining table, lobster bisque soup was served. Baxter's tinned variety. Lou stated, 'Up there, I'll be like a Roman governor at my desk, surrounded by pure savagery, longing to be recalled to Rome. Acton on the Tiber. *Buon appetito.*'

Aoife said, 'This is the height of refinement, cause I notice Lou's not going to serve the wine with the soup.'

'Wine shouldn't be drunk with soup. I'm sure of it.'

'They'll know in Stead's Language School.'

Lily was up in her high chair with the little tray which swung down over her head. She didn't want to eat but sat with us at the table and shoved her small, white stuffed rabbit around in circles, lifted it over her head, smiled and dropped it on her skull so it bounced and I kept having to kneel and retrieve it.

Slurping soup, Lou said, 'So, Aoife. This photo-modelling lark. I think you should jack it in. I'm not joking. You'll have Lil to look after while I'm away.'

'It'll only be a few hours each time. Douglas will look after her.'

'Douglas isn't here to be your au pair.' He turned to me. 'Is that not so, Cunningham?'

'Well, ah.'

She looked at me. It was a cold, ironically betrayed look. 'So you two've been talking about this? I'll leave Lily with Flo, then. Or with Abby.'

'*We* don't think you need to do the modelling right just now.' He quickly looked at me. 'I mean, you're not even making money. Haven't earned a penny of late and you won't make much at these stripteases.'

She put down her spoon. 'They are not stripteases, Lou. And I could be making far more than you if this photographer, Ross, takes me on.'

'Ross. Really, Eeef, don't fall for that. He must have fucked more models than he has changed film. He just wants to get your clothes off and when he's visually exhausted your body – like he soon will – he'll see you as a worn-out piece of wasteland and he'll move on to a new,' – Lou leaned forward – 'younger, seventeen-year-old to run his lenses over.'

Patient and firm, she replied, 'Ross is married to Cally Pearson. She's stunningly beautiful.'

I shifted my elbow.

Lou drove straight over that statement. 'You are married too. And not only will he try to fuck you; when he succeeds, he'll give you this Aids or an exotic pox. And all those little tossers will be laughing about us.'

Aoife turned, looked at me with pity and she held up her finger. 'I took him to one party a year and a half ago, and he's had a big chip on his shoulder ever since. I can't believe I'm hearing this from a man about to lock himself up in a huge country house with teenaged Italian and French schoolgirls.'

Lou straightened and, though it sounded weak, actually said, 'I'll have you know I took this job on the understanding there was a Catholic church nearby. That I would have access to on a daily basis.'

'Christ!' Aoife shouted. 'His new local is the confessional.'

'It would do you no harm.'

'I have to be a saint already to be married to you, Lou.'

Lily dropped her small rabbit. I slid off my chair and put it back up in front of her, on the folding table of her chair.

Lou leaned across the table towards Aoife. 'This is an exact example of why you and I need to get properly married. For Lily's sake.'

'We are. Married.'

'Proper married.'

'What's an example of that? I'm not obeying and honouring everything you say, Lou. Any more than you obey me.'

'What was there ever for me to obey?'

'Jesus, Lou. You got me pregnant too. It wasn't all my own nasty work.'

'That wasn't my fault. If you weren't this stuttering, novice nun when we met, you'd have mastered the rhythm method.'

'Don't be disgusting.'

Lou spat out a hard laugh and turned to me. 'She thinks the rhythm method's some type of sodomy, which I'm pleased to recall isn't unknown to her – though she's a saint.'

I moved my head quick and looked out the window at a crawling airliner, afar.

'Know another fact, Cunningham? In these photos, you would notice, it's not just her knickers she slowly peels off. Look at her hand in them. The wedding ring comes off as well, in case it spoils the feeling of possession for the men hamming off over them.'

'Oh for goodness' sake. You're such a child sometimes. I've told you before. It's standard that models take off their wedding rings. You do it on catwalk too. You have to wear jewellery. You see the girls backstage, putting fake tan on where their wedding rings normally are.'

'What faithful lambs. There's a nice image of her chosen profession, Cunningham.'

'It's not *me* in a photo, Lou. You're always too strung up in your own ego. You think its me, but it's not. I'm just a servant of the image.'

He sneered. '"Servant of the image." Were you bending over at the time when you heard that one, love?'

'You're meant to know all about language and stuff. Think about what the word model actually means. You are a subject. It's not me, I just represent something. A form.'

He turned back to her. 'More like a whore. Then I got ill. You got pregnant and I nearly died, all in six months, and you've come out the other end with a beautiful, healthy daughter, yet resenting me for both those events. You think there is nothing to be grateful for and the best way to deal with motherhood is to rake out your perfect mons pubis for the first pornographer who comes along.'

More quietly she said, 'I do fashion photography.'

'You do nudie arty porn stuff.'

'Once. You were quick enough to put that photo up in the bloody bedroom and to blow off about it to folk. It was embarrassing for me that night you went on and on about it to Rhys. And in front of my bloody parents too. Now you've right changed your tune.'

'Take it fucking down, then,' Lou shouted. 'Now you're a mother.'

'You want to make a slave of me in that bloody church. I'm not going to confession.'

Lily dropped her rabbit again. I got out my seat, bent down to put the toy back up on her little table.

Lou turned down to me as I kneeled. 'Stop that. Can't you see the child's taking advantage of you?'

I had still to rise from my knees, but I did and before I sat back down at the table, I dropped the rabbit on Lily's high chair in front of her.

There was an odd pause. Lou suddenly banged the table with both fists and I jumped. Lily stopped looking around the room and stared at her daddy.

'Did you fuck a photographer?'

'No.'

'Did you *ever* fuck a photographer?'

'It doesn't happen like that, Lou. There's no time for all that. You're trying to make photos.'

'You fucked that guy on the beach.' He jammed his thumb in the direction of their bedroom.

Aoife looked at him. 'You're a woman-hating bully. You're taking on the character of the father that you never knew: a bigoted Catholic bully, just like your gran told me he was.'

'If trying to provoke me is the best way you have of debating matters, it's a poor show. So did you? Do the beach guy? Like that ponce actor you went out with.'

Aoife looked down and shook her head with weariness. 'Poor Llewellyn Smith. Obsessed about getting dumped with second-hand goods. You mock me being naive but at the same time you're furious I wasn't a virgin when we met. Now the soup's gone cold.'

Her soup bowl was almost full. So was Lou's. Only mine was guiltily empty, the spoon resting in a shallow pink puddle, the thick, treacle spoor of rocky sea-life rising to my nostrils. I felt a bit sick. Aoife stood and lifted her plate, then Lou stood also and lifted his own plate and mine.

'Thank you,' I said.

Lou carefully placed both the plates back down on the table-cloth.

I was reminded of Lily, the way she concertinaed down when she failed to stand unsupported. Aoife slid up the wall behind her then came back down limp. Her pelvis hit the edge of the table and her whole upper body swung forward at great speed so the side of her face smashed the wooden table top and her hair shot up in a pale rush. The table tipped on its side and she rolled once on the floor, then the edge of that heavy table cracked down beside her – soup, glasses, plates and cutlery rolling around her.

Lily began to cry as her high chair rocked, the air striated with fear.

It happened so quick I'd had no time to move and my denim legs just stuck out before me, unveiled from beneath the toppled table, soup all over them. I could feel the lukewarm liquid seeping through to my thighs.

Lou moved towards Aoife but I was out of my seat and stood in front of him, waiting to be hit myself. I croaked in a weirdly reverential and frightened voice, 'No, Lou. No,' and I looked in his eye. The thing I sought in there was the same madness I saw amongst the luminous flecks of her blinking iris when Aoife had kissed me in the vague light of the dawn.

I was hardly there for Lou, I was just some resistant ectoplasm; he leaned first this way then that to get his arms around me, to reach at his fallen wife and hurt her more. I shifted to keep him away, glanced at the floor to get my footing and saw that my ugly shoe rested upon a stream of her golden hair.

I pushed him back and he recovered some shocked sense but he still had to unburden himself, so he crossed away, at a perverse angle from Aoife, raised his shoe flatly and brought it down with a definitive crunch upon the small coffee table in front of the couch – the one he'd padded the corners of to protect his child. The table splintered and imploded beneath him. He had to shake a wood shard free as it clung to his foot. Lily screamed louder in her high chair.

I thought Aoife was dead or unconscious, then she sat up and rose to her feet and I put my fingers out and took her elbow. Something was wrong in her face.

The golf clubs from the Langhams' below began to bang on the floor by our feet, joining the unnerving din caused by Lily's screams. Lou looked across the room at Aoife.

I could not believe my ears as she started to speak.

'I deserve it, Lou; don't feel bad. I deserve it. You don't know how awful I am.' Her voice seemed different. Aoife had to raise it across the howling of Lily and as she spoke she spat ends of red blood outward which stuck on her white teeth and settled like crimson leeches around her mouth.

'Oh God,' Lou said. 'I'm so sorry. I completely lost it.'

Quietly, I commanded, 'Go to the bedroom, Lou.'

'Let me look at her.' He moved toward us.

'No.' I turned on him for the first time, ready to physically fight. 'Just fuck off to the bedroom a minute.'

Strangely, he obeyed me. I sat Aoife down on my dining chair. In the kitchen I opened the drawer with the two clean dish towels and soaked one under the cold tap. I filled the fabric with the ice cubes, dropping the emptied ice-cube tray to the lino, then I felt heat on my thighs. I turned and switched off the oven with the chicken still in it.

Aoife held the ice pack to her jaw while I stood over her with my hand limply round her shoulder. In cowardly shock I noted how I suddenly did not want to touch her and claim my part of this. I hoisted Lily out of her seat and rocked her in my arms until she stopped crying. Each time Aoife took the cloth away to show me, I saw that the jaw was more swollen until it was bloated out a full three inches. I started to panic. 'Put on your coat. I'm taking you to the hospital.'

I picked up Lily and took her down to the bedroom. Lou was

sitting on the end of the bed, prophetically, beside his packed suitcase. 'I'm taking her to hospital. You must look after Lily, or I'll need to take her with us. Then next thing fucking Social Services will be calling round here and Lily will be taken away. For fuck sake, man.'

'Yes.' He nodded without the least resistance and said, 'Yes. Yes. That makes sense.'

'Lou. Lou.'

'What?'

'Are you rational? Is Lily safe with you?'

Now he spoke with a candid admission, the voice full of horrified concern. 'She might need an X-ray.'

'Yes. She will.'

He waved his hand dismissively. 'I'll take care of Lily.'

I used both hands to swing the baby over to him and we looked at each other. I said, 'I've switched the oven off. I have to change my jeans.'

'Silence, Exile and Cunningham. Always calm in a crisis,' he whispered, but more to himself than anything else.

I had changed out of the soup-soaked jeans. Aoife with her busted, swollen face walked up Bollo Lane beside me, ice pack held to her jaw and soaking the sleeve of her white overcoat into a grey blue. People coming out of Acton Town station stared at her – and at me – then they looked away immediately.

I said, 'What are you going to tell them?'

'Who?'

'Hospital people. If they think there's been an assault and hear there's a child in the house they might call police or Social Services.'

'Might they?' she said naively. 'I'm not blaming Lou. Next thing they'll be taking Lily off me.'

'Exactly. He hit you. It's against the law. He might do it again.'

'I deserved it.'

'Stop saying that, Aoife. Nobody ever deserves that.'

'I'm more upset about Tuesday. I can't go to a photo shoot like this and he probably knew it. Look at me, for God's sake.'

She'd taken the ice pack off her jaw to speak; with surprising harshness I said, 'Keep the ice on it.' Then I added, more caringly, 'How's it feel?'

'My tooth seems loose. Might be my imagination.' She poked her forefinger deep into her mouth. 'It's cut in there on the cheek as well.'

'I think your jaw could be broken.'

She looked at me and nodded. 'It's really sore to talk. What will I tell them?'

'I'll stand by you whatever you decide.'

She stopped walking. 'I don't know what to do, Douglas. What should I do?'

It was my chance to win her for myself and I knew it. 'He could have killed you. There were glasses on the table so your face could have come down on one and you'd be blinded or scarred for life.'

She said, 'We shouldn't be doing what we're doing.'

She had a lisp. Appallingly, I found it sexy. 'He didn't hit you because of what we're doing. That's the problem. He doesn't even know a thing and he's done this.'

'So now does he deserve what we're doing to him, then?' She frowned at me the way I knew she would ask a question of her priest.

'He's probably going to kill us both when he finds out.'

She smiled, an eerie and crooked grin, her two top teeth invisible, like comic missing teeth; blood had stained them dark, as if by rich, red wine. 'Are you scared?'

'I'm worried about you. Look at your face.'

'What will I tell them?'

I clenched my fists. 'Say you were changing a light fitting and you fell off the chair right onto the table. But if Lou hits you ever again, I won't lie.'

We entered through that same sliding door of Accident and Emergency as the night I'd first set eyes on Llewellyn. I pondered if I might be in some cyclical penance and here meet another family to enter their world and destroy it.

It was a Sunday afternoon, though, and the Sabbath held: there were very few other victims in A&E. That old Medusa was not guarding access behind the perspex but some younger woman, who listened to Aoife explaining that she had a photography session on Tuesday and needed advice about getting a swelling to go down after a small fall. Aoife was surprisingly calm and convincing.

'I think that needs some looking at,' the lady said with caution.

I was glanced at suspiciously. I was convinced the woman behind the perspex could smell lobster bisque off me and was trying to figure this into the equation. A doctor immediately appeared and Aoife was taken into that mysterious behind-the-scenes area which I had never quite graduated to. Until Lou found out about me and his wife, no doubt.

They took an hour, then Aoife just walked straight out with a plastic electric-blue ice pack held up snug to her jaw. When she came close up to me her face was so pale I detected freckles that I'd never seen before. Outside she looked around and said, 'It isn't broke but there might be little cracks, and my tooth isn't loose. I want a cigarette.'

'Were they suspicious?'

'They kept saying it was odd I'd hit the table twice, once to knock the jaw and a bit on the side of the forehead here that's going to bruise. I said I'd hit a shelf on the way down then hit the table but I don't think they believed.' Suddenly she started to cry. She glanced back nervously at the hospital. 'I *so* wanted to do the photo shoot on Tuesday.'

'I know you did. I know.'

'That bastard. He's such a bastard sometimes.'

Back in the flat, Lou was playing it up, mucking around on the floor with Lily. He had righted the table, cleaned most of the destruction, and I could smell he'd put the oven back on again. The shattered coffee table was neatly stacked in pieces against the wall in a mockery of domesticity.

I went to my room, lowered the camp bed from where it leaned against the wall and lay out on it for half an hour, listening for a fresh outbreak of hostilities but giving them private space to talk, until Aoife called me. I walked up to the front room.

The illusion of the happy family disgusted me. The tablecloth had been pathetically restored, complete with wet soup stains; torn pages of *Vogue* layered beneath, so bottles of perfume and the lithe torsos of Parisian models showed through the wet cotton. Lily was back up in her high chair but seemed anxious – quietly turning her face from one of us to the other. Even she wasn't fooled.

At least Lou made no pretence when he uncorked the wine, swigged, then just passed the bottle round. Aoife smiled wanly and tried to pretend chewing wasn't hurting her, but she only picked at some lean white chicken and cold broccoli. I made a point of being silent so there were huge gaps in their rags of conversation, interspersed with the sound of the television and Aoife delivering one liners, like, 'I have to go back in a few days to the outpatients.'

Then, ten minutes later, 'I have to go back if I get bad headaches.' She smiled at Lou as she said these things and I realised that, despite it all, she was pleased to now have a connection with the same local hospital that he did.

Lou nodded compliantly. I had an urge to lean over and begin caressing Aoife's breast, right in front of him. I knew what I was up to, with my broody silence, forcing his eyelashes to flicker away from me when he tried to meet my gaze. If I emphasised the degree of my outrage, it was only so that one day it might temper his fury and make him feel he deserved it, when he found out about Aoife and me.

Towards the end of eating, the first bottle of wine was emptied and Lou sat at the table and uncorked the other. He passed the bottle round but Aoife shrugged again and said, 'I was given painkillers.' He nodded and immediately passed the bottle to me. I took it from his hand then drank from it.

Aoife said, through her slightly puffy lip, which had altered her voice. 'It was so mild out there today.'

I said, 'Yeah. Let's talk about the weather; another lovely day at A&E, the Smiths' second home.'

The rest of the meal was conducted in silence.

22

Not a sound leaked from their bedroom that last night before Lou left us and when we rose to urge him off, before dawn, the side of Aoife's face was a cautious blue. A black semicircle was manifest underneath her eye.

The four of us were all crushed up together in the tight space of the hallway, against the coats by the front door. I was in bare feet, tugged-up jeans and T-shirt, and I nodded only a serious 'Ciao' to Lou. He didn't put down his suitcase.

Aoife was in those pyjamas again, holding up Lily in her left arm, but the baby was sleeping because it was so early, head flopping aside as Lou leaned in towards the child and kissed.

He moved out his fingers and touched Aoife's bruised face. 'I'm sorry.'

Immediately after the front door shut, Aoife carried Lily to the front-room window, 'There goes Daddy, there goes bad Daddy,' but the infant was asleep and refused to see her departing father, far below in the dark, lit by the lush then pale finery of a single train flash.

I said softly, 'Will I put the mortice lock on?' Aoife carried Lily back down the corridor to her cot and called back a sharp 'Yes.'

I stepped into their bedroom. She was looking down at Lily, placed back asleep in the cot, then Aoife crossed to their bed beneath her photographs and she swept aside the sheets, the blankets and covers, and waved me to join her even though the child was there. I imagined I could feel the heat of the male body still in the sheets.

'I don't want you to have to look at my face,' she muttered, as if to herself.

Later she unambiguously said, 'A bit harder.'

'He's a bastard,' I said between my teeth.

'No. He isn't.'

'Look what he did.'

'I deserve it. For the loveliness of this.' Aoife giggled strangely then she gasped air in a long calamitous groan.

The phone went in the evening after Lily had been fed and fallen asleep in her buggy by the dining table. Aoife walked up the corridor, stepping into her tracksuit bottoms and draping the top round her shoulders. She answered the telephone in that cautious, scared voice she always used when she picked it up. I could tell by her tone it was Lou as I bunkered down in their bed, but in moments I was surprised by Aoife at the door, whispering across the darkness: 'He needs to speak to you. Lily's still fast asleep. That early start knackered her.'

'Cunningham, boyo. How are my charges?'

'Black and blue. And Worcestershire?'

'A web of rural intrigue and cow dung. Bit of resistance at this end. A problem.'

While I spoke to him, Aoife came in the front room and kneeled down to Lily, sleeping in her buggy, but then Aoife rose, crossed and pushed in hard against me. I played idly at her hair in the confidence of ownership as I listened to her husband's voice down the phone. She let the tracksuit top fall, and she led my free hand to a breast. It only struck me just then: Aoife liked having two lovers, and why not?

'A problem? What's that? Have you gone twelve rounds with the governess?'

There was a silence, then, to explain how much that silence had cost him, he clarified, 'Got to make it quick. I'm in the call box down in the village – for want of a better noun. The people bloody stare at you from the houses – all three of them – when you use the phone box. An old dear in her cheese-making apron came out her hovel just now to tell me the number seven sometimes didn't work on this phone.'

I toyed with Aoife's nipple like it was an insect.

Lou's voice in my ear was saying, 'They're probably still listening in at the local exchange round these parts so watch what you say. Look, I was told I was being paid eight hundred a month. And I am, but I'm not being paid till the end of next month and I can sit that out. The grub's no great shakes but I'll last, and the buggers are renovating the staff quarters so we're bloody dossing in the empty student dorms just now. It's like the Boy Scouts with verb conjugation.'

'What's the problem?'

'I'm on this induction but they're trying to screw a fee out of me right now for the course.'

'You have to pay for a teaching course in order to teach the course there?'

'Exacta-bloody-mundo. A rip-off, but a fly move and I have to hand it to them. There's a future in language schools, Cunningham.'

'How much?'

'Three hundred up front in cash. All the other bozos here have it. Now I've eighty here but I need two-twenty, pronto, and am I not correct in saying you have your canny Scot savings still in your old sock, from bloody Hanson and some of your giro scrapings?' There was a pause down the line. 'Don't you?'

'What's the alternative?'

'There isn't one. If I can't pay, I'm gone. I'll need to sneak out here at six in the morning and elope to London, then at least you and me'll be back in The Bells by tomorrow night.'

'Two hundred and twenty.'

'I know, boyo.' He sighed. 'I'm really sorry but we'll have five hundred cash, end of this month and five at the end of next as well.'

'Hold on.' I laid down the receiver and signalled Aoife to accompany me back to their bedroom. I grabbed her in my arms and whispered in her ear, 'He needs two hundred and twenty quid, to pay for the teaching course. I *knew* the place would be a rip-off.'

'Two hundred. Where from?'

'I have it saved.'

She quickly thought about this. 'What if you don't give it him?' She still whispered and she coughed to clear her throat.

'He'll come back. Tomorrow.' We looked at each other. 'What'll I do?'

She looked at me. 'Send him the money. Keep him away from us.'

I nodded and returned to the telephone in the front room, 'Okay, then.'

Coldly, Lou stated, 'Meeting of the Board of Governors, was that?'

'I was checking what cash I had.'

'It'll need to be cash you send in the envelope, Cunningham. Disguise it well or the yokels here will tear it to pieces for pig trading and scrumpy. I already heard the postman took a shotgun to his wife, but she didn't press charges.'

'Sounds your kind of place. I'll post it first class tomorrow, so should be with you the next day. Eeef's got the school address. Here she is.' I tried to take a respectful step back as I handed her the phone but Aoife startled me, taking the receiver yet grabbing my other arm and leaning in against me. Aoife's hand slid down over my thigh, where it remained. I held my breath, fearful Lou would hear it.

In her quiet voice, she tested, 'Is that okay?' She nodded at what it was Lou said next. 'She's sleeping in the buggy right next to me.' She looked silently straight into my eyes and tightened her hand on my leg. I thought to myself right then that she was going to leave Lou and come away with me and there was going to be years of conflict over Lily. Aoife said, 'She's fine. Douglas took her to the park on his own this afternoon and the fresh air wears her out. I couldn't go. Obviously.' There was a pause as she listened to a question. 'Still a little sore, Lou,' she whispered.

I heard his voice down the phone with a sudden edge of despair to it and my heart twisted for him. Did he secretly know I was extracting penance on his wife's body, almost hourly? Each time I touched her skin with my fingers it would have scalded him.

She took her eyes away from me and looked at her feet. She put her forehead down. 'I love you too.' Very slowly she replaced the phone and dropped her head on my shoulder. I couldn't help squinting at the receiver, to make sure it had been correctly returned. I could see him, lifting the collar of his mac, glancing up at the night sky, shuffling like Tam o' Shanter through the dark country miles.

Then I put my lips to her collar bone and took her little silver crucifix upon my tongue. I tried to lift it onto the tip of her tongue and it did reach there but then I dropped to my knees and kissed around her belly so the muscles went into a block of tension while I slid my arms far round her tracksuit bottoms on the glassy skin of her ass. I looked up and I saw her push the crucifix out her mouth with her tongue and allow it to fall with a string of bright saliva, lit by the street light, and it stuck to her collar bone.

I got her on the couch.

She whispered, 'Don't wake Lily.'

With her tracky bottoms gone, I kneeled where the shattered table once used to sit, my head between her thighs and her fingers in my hair. Her sound of final satisfaction was like an annoyed, dismissive grunt.

Back in their bedroom, her fingers splayed out on the crochet colours when she was too tender. After an hour and more she said, 'I'm hurting a little bit.' The shining mucus was around both her vagina and her anus. Then we lay on our backs looking up at the Artex ceiling, just breathing, until she said, 'Let's have a bath together now. We never have.'

The enamel was worn off the bottom of that old bath and you had to be cautious never to suddenly slide along it, or you inevitably skinned your ass; but it was large enough for two and for my upper torso to lean back, fitting between the taps.

She said, 'Lou never takes baths with me,' as if this were a grave failing. 'Poor you and Lou. You're both married to the same bride now.'

I nodded, 'But only I know it.'

She looked at me along the rising steam and the thin slick of suds and she took my cock in her hand, making it break surface, so she began moving her fist up and down – eyes intent. 'I'm not so sure. Maybe Lou is sharing me?' she said idly.

I made a noise of dismissal but added, 'So beautiful, you should be shared. But he's destroying you and I want to build you up.'

'We've Lily to bring up. He's going to marry me in the church and he'll get his way.'

'Could we still not?' I made a sound. 'Both be your lovers? On different days or something?'

'Or at the same time would be nice. One night maybe?' she whispered.

I nodded. I didn't think I had any left inside me but a sperm dribble – as tiny and white as an infant's new tooth, lifted out and melded down over her knuckles into the water, where the spineless ampoule of it meandered.

Lily started wailing from her buggy and with a whooshing of water, Aoife stood and stepped carefully out. I could see the bruise on her pelvis now. Most of the left side of her face was full blue with a smoky edging, whilst below her eye looked like black pudding.

The cash was posted, folded in foolscap to Lou, keeping him up there so his wife and I could keep going at each other in bed together. Aoife hid in the apartment all the time, letting her face heal while we made love. I wrote nothing and read nothing. I visited the Co-op for shopping, and took Lily in her buggy through

Gunnersbury Park. I'd acquired a family overnight, by cutting out the middleman.

Lou phoned nightly and she phoned back to his payphone in a hallway. He described – to us both – the school and the course, then the first teaching and his long conversations with the local priest: as if it were a novel, but some nights you could hear he was just too tired to talk for long.

Aoife spoke to him patiently but it made no difference to his case at my end. She was no Penelope, unravelling the day's weaving as she waited for her Odysseus. We moved around the flat naked, making love in rhythm to Lily's sleep, and I could detect a quite precise relation between Aoife's ardour and her degree of daily disaffection with Lou. Like on the day she had to wrap her face in a scarf, wear sunglasses and go to the dentist for a check-up. Those were generous days for me.

One evening on the telephone to him I'd carefully asked when Lily would see him next and he'd revealed, 'Forty days and forty nights, boyo. It's all I deserve.'

I nodded admiringly and also delighted. I suppose I tried to convince myself he knew about Aoife and me. Since that would justify it.

23

Weeks into our sky-set idyll, the telephone rang and I picked up.

'Sausage. I've been ever so busy. At Mass Lou's gran told me he's somewhere up north, teaching, and you and Eeef are all alone. Two poor sausages. Why didn't you tell me?'

'Hi, Abby.'

Aoife looked over at me – alarmed – pointed to her jaw and shook her head.

'Yeah. He found this teaching job that pays well and he's away for a few weeks. We're just lying low. I'm writing.'

There was a silence, slightly paranoid with perhaps the implication I had murdered Aoife and concealed her body. Abby demanded, 'And how is Eeef?'

'She's good, she's good, I'll go get her.'

'Okay. I'll need to come round with a bottle of wine. How about tonight?'

I turned to look at Aoife. 'A bottle tonight?'

Aoife shook her head and buried her face in her hands.

'Well we haven't been out in ages. Maybe we should meet somewhere for a beer. Sometime?'

Bluntly, Abby enquired, 'Me and you?'

'Well, all of us, and we can see if Flo or Granny Smith'll take Lily.'

Aoife shook her head but I waved her down with my hand. 'Here's Aoife.'

She took the phone with a cheery, 'Hi. No. He's been up there a few weeks. No. It's very good money. I'm a bit tired. Why don't you and Douglas go out and I'll tag along another night? Yes.' She giggled. 'Okay, then. Oh yes. He'll remember it from the wedding.'

They gabbed on for ages and after she got off the phone, I said, 'You've set me up. The last thing I want is to go out drinking with Abby.'

'But we can't let her see me with my face like this. It's impossible.'

'I know that.'

'She knows everything about make-up so she'll be able to tell if I try to conceal it.'

'I know. But she's a bit of a man-eater.'

Aoife just laughed. 'You know the pub in Ealing where we were on the wedding day? You've to meet her there at seven.'

'But Eeef. She's—'

'Do you think she's out to eat you?'

'I'm not trying to flatter myself. She's just a lioness. She can't help it.'

Aoife laughed, threw herself down on the sofa and put a thoughtful finger to her lip. 'Do you really think she's after you?'

'Lou was trying to match us up.'

'Lou can't match anything. Even us. I mean me and him, not you and I. You and I are matched.'

'I'm warning you. She's on the prowl.'

She giggled. 'What are you going to do, then?'

'Be afraid. I'm warning you.'

'Well I don't care, Douglas. Do anything to stop her coming here.'

'Anything?'

'Anything to stop her coming over here and seeing my face for another week. I'll hear about it for the rest of my damned life.'

I stepped inside that pub on Ealing Broadway where we had gone on Aoife and Lou's wedding day. Abby had her hair cut short; it was darkened and spiked up. I was shocked and didn't like it. 'Thanks for posting on that last giro. What have you done to your hair?'

'Had it cut.'

'I don't like it.'

'Thanks. You oaf. You just think women should have hippy locks, flowing down their shoulders, you Scotch lumberjack.' Then she pummelled me over the first pint on every single detail about Lou going to teach and if Aoife was okay about it – if there had been any arguments.

I said, 'I thought Aoife told you everything.'

'Well, almost everything.' She looked around the pub and lowered her voice. 'Think Aoife suspects anything about me and Lou? She hasn't called me for ages.'

'No. She's got other things on her mind with Lou away. I think you should just forget about it.'

'Do you think Lou's forgotten about it?'

'Yes.'

She swirled her drink so aggressively her ice flew round and one melting glob shot out and fired across the scratched varnish of the table, silently plonking onto the carpet. We both looked down at it.

Then she probed about how much work Aoife's agents had got her and what had gone wrong at the photo shoot with that guy Ross. I don't know why, but I began to get suspicious Abby might have been to bed with Ross at some point.

I denied everything that needed to be denied; I bored her with detailed descriptions of Lily trying to walk.

Eventually, I sat looking at her and said, 'I'm starting to like your hair the more I drink.'

She observed, 'It's getting busy in here.'

'It's a Saturday.'

She leaned towards me again. 'I've some dope and a pipe; will we get a bottle of wine, take it over to Aoife?'

I said, I had to say, 'Why don't we just go back to your place?'

When she opened her front door I ran up the stairs in a familiar way – as if it really was my residence. My fake bedroom had now been restored to that fantastic long front room with wall hangings and bean bags, so we sat in them, listening to her fashionable music that wasn't good to listen to on dope, but *Ocean Rain* by Echo and the Bunnymen was full of echoes, of depths, of dripping caves; it was fatalistic and romantic.

She made me take my shoes off and sit in my socks because of the carpet. She had a bong so we kneeled around the Indonesian table, burning up small chunks in the brass burner and sucking in the cooled smoke through the bulb, but it still burned the back of my throat.

Everything I said from then on seemed to be thought of after I had already said it. When she disappeared I knew she would be waiting in her bedroom, so I obediently went in there and lay down next to her. Her bed was surrounded on the three sides by clothes on sagging hanger rails, like those withered, flattened corpses of monks that are hung on the walls of monasteries.

'Must think I'm a right old tart,' she said – almost to herself – pulling her shirt over her head. I felt I knew those breasts fairly well by then.

'On the contrary.' I crawled on the soft bed, sank in and rolled over in its marshmallow. 'Lou himself told me, you were very sparing in the distribution of your favours.'

'Is that a good thing?'

'I think you're very virtuous.'

'I don't do anything without a condom any more. Okey doke?'

'That's okay.'

'Anything. Okay?'

'Yes. Okay.'

She looked at me. 'I'm going to the bathroom.'

On my way over to her bed, beneath my cautious-stepping foot, I had felt the glossy slip of plasticity. Her buried telephone, sliding underneath a scarf or a flowered skirt – or even knickers, which were everywhere on the floor. I remembered how she had taken the phone from the bedroom and set it up in the hallway at the top of the stairs, for the DHSS visit. I could hear the hand-held shower head spraying about and slashing the shower curtain next door.

I dangled my arms down and dug out the phone. The entire floor along the side of the bed was filled with a layer of clothing.

Aoife answered and I whispered, 'I warned you.'

'Where are you?'

'In her bed. She's in the bathroom.'

'You are joking. God. That didn't take both of you long. She's a right old tart.'

'Should I leave now and come home to you? Or do you want to listen?'

There was a long silence. Then she said, 'But when I hang up, she'll hear the tone of the phone.'

'Don't hang up, then.'

As I put on and pulled off condoms and was sent to the bathroom to shower myself, I paused frequently to throw out leading questions to Abby and she often answered them. Yes I do like it. No, I don't. Do you want to? Stuff along those lines. For an hour, everything physical was verbalised into some form.

'You really like to talk dirty, don't you?' she pointed out.

I was awaiting disaster; for her to shout out that I wasn't as good as, or better than Llewellyn. It added risk, but she never did refer to him. He was forgotten and it was only immediate sex she devoted her utterances to. And her fantastic cries and shrieks. The phone handset lying hidden beside the bed was the most erotic object I'd known – it was like a huge eye, greedily gathering everything up.

'Go to the bathroom and change your condom, again. And don't make a mess,' she told me each time.

I listened yet again when I returned, expecting the electronic tone of a hung-up phone, me claiming I'd kicked it off the hook on my way out, but each time I returned, the silence hung out there in the near dark, like God himself, monitoring all things.

I got back to Conrad Flats before midnight. The mortice lock had been on and behind me Aoife turned it again. She kissed me in the shadowy corridor. I had only been five hours but I realised it was the longest I had been away from her in a very long time. I squinted at her face.

'She makes so much noise. I can't believe it. Do you want me to make that kind of noise? Do you like it?'

'I like it with you.'

She repeated, 'I can't believe how noisy she is. She's absolutely comical. And sort of sexy.'

'I can't be bothered having a bath.' I climbed into their bed with Aoife.

'No, don't have a bath, I like the thought and the smell of her on you.'

Lily was silent in the cot, so all we said was in whispers as we embraced.

I told Aoife, 'Guilt is amazing. It's like it's ordained. Even though you gave me permission, I feel the guilt now.'

She looked at me and nodded. 'But it doesn't matter. It's nothing. It's funny. It's just sex, not love.'

'Even though you let me and you were right there with me all the time. I feel I've betrayed you.'

'Do you mean because you and I don't always use condoms?'

'I mean emotionally. Yet I don't feel guilty about Lou.'

She quickly whispered, 'I touched myself while I listened.'

'Good.'

'I love you,' Aoife said into my ear, quickly and so quiet I could just distinguish it.

'I love you too.'

'All the girls want Douglas,' she whispered sleepily. There was a long silence and she murmured, 'I want you too.'

You couldn't see any blemishes on her face now. They were not visible at all to anyone but her and me. Her bruising was like a ghost that only she and I saw, locked in that summer apartment, sweating onto each other. I wasn't convinced Abby would have noticed a thing wrong about Aoife's face had they met that night.

I reached into her to find the lust and to keep doing it again and again, until we had to put the pillow down the back of the head-board – she and Lou did that, she told me.

24

On the Thursday afternoon I picked up the ringing phone quick to try not to let it awaken sleeping Lily, in her buggy. I was expecting Lou's voice.

'Who's this, then? Eeefie there? I need Eeefie.'

'Ee-fah.'

'Oh. Scotch fella. We need Llewellyn Smith down here right away. It's his gran and he's gone away someplace.'

'Is that Flo?'

'Yeah.'

'Something wrong?'

'Too right. Old Myrtle Smith from next door, isn't it? Me that found her. Wasn't it?'

'Oh God. No?'

'You can bring Lil to me and I'll take care of her.'

'Is it that's she's— Mrs Smith hasn't passed away, has she?'

'I should say so, my dear. I'm very sorry. Looks like she conked out during her afternoon nap. Sad. But she loved the naps. I was fond of the old thing.'

'Oh my God. Oh my God.'

'Don't you panic now,' Flo told me.

'I'll get Aoife to phone Lou now. Anything we can do?'

'Nah. Rhys, that's the elder brother, he's down here with the undertakers now. Don't you worry now, we'll get something in the *Acton Observer*. Any old how, you get Eeefie to bring poor Llewellyn down south again. Funeral'll be next week.'

Aoife was in the kitchen staring at me. I told her, 'That was Flo. It's bad. The worst. It's Lou's gran.'

She opened her mouth.

I nodded.

She put her hand to her mouth. 'It's our punishment come at last. Yours and mine. Poor Granny Smith. It's our punishment that we deserve.' Aoife repeated this in variations for minute after minute, shaking her head.

'You have to phone Lou.'

She waved her hand at me. 'You get him on the phone. I can't speak to people.' She sat down. Then she looked across at me and this astonished look came over her face. 'Douglas!'

I realised, stunned, that I was weeping. It took me completely by surprise. I shook my head and sniffed, said, 'I realise. I really liked that old woman,' and I sort of choked off on the last word as all the sorrow swelled in me.

She launched herself up and embraced me. 'Douglas. She was well into her eighties, darling.'

'That doesn't matter. Nobody wants to go.'

'That's true, that's true, my darling, but she was ready, she prayed every day and when Lou was really very ill, she asked that God take her and not him.'

'Oh my goodness.' I sniffed again and wiped at my eyes. 'You are all so dramatic in this family.'

She laughed.

'I think we've been under more pressure than we realise,' I said, and I wiped at my nose with the back of my hand. 'I didn't like the way you said it was our punishment. I don't believe in that, Aoife. I don't believe in a punishing God.'

'Oh Douglas. I'm sorry I said it.' We began kissing, and before they dried some of my tears were transferred onto the skin of her face.

Initially I got somebody of an administrative nature at Stead's Language School – and she sounded sceptical about the situation amounting to an emergency, so she sought guidance further up the hierarchy. It was like an avant-garde radio play based on the ascent of the English class system. Nobody seemed ready to accept the death of Lou's gran as official. As seniority rose, the voices got plummier and fatter. The question was passed higher and all the higher ranks seemed to exist at the far end of lengthy lawns, or up right-angled, creaking stairways, or down linoleum corridors where their names were called, in the Worcestershire afternoon: 'Mr Clitherow?' 'Mr Bone?' and this always after the receiver had been rested with such a series of low bumps upon the desk that it was impossible to imagine anything but a heavy, antique phone. Footsteps were heard moving away from it and onward, deeper into the old dwelling, seeking greater seniority yet again. Then footsteps drew near, returning. Eventually, I heard the low chorus voice comment, like a piece of exposition on a stage, 'Here's Mr Stead,' and the voice of the same came on the phone.

'What *seems* to be the problem?'

'Llewellyn Smith's wife needs to talk to him.'

'He's teaching a class. Is it something I can assist with?'

'Mr Smith's wife needs to speak to him absolutely immediately. There's been a sudden death in the family.'

'I see. How terrible. A close family member?'

I felt an incongruous puff of pride for Lou. Had he proved to be a lousy teacher, I couldn't imagine this twit trying to hang on to him so scandalously. 'Yes. His grandmother who brought him up. And we'd appreciate if you'd allow his wife to break that news to him.'

'Of course. I'm most terribly sorry. I shall fetch him up.'

I'd given the phone to Aoife but I heard Lou's deep voice which I recognised as having just exhaled tobacco smoke, with its slight quiver of breathlessness.

Aoife said, as soft as breath, 'It's your gran, Lou. Your gran.' I clung on to her, with my arm over her bony shoulder and spine. As I might have done at this moment even if we were not illicit lovers. Lou didn't seem to have responded, so she added, 'Flo found her this afternoon. Her heart must have finally gave in. Rhys is there now but you've to come back. I'm so sorry, baby.'

Lou spoke in low monosyllables that I couldn't quite make out, but Aoife did say, 'Yes. He's with me now, thank God,' and she looked into my face, nodding. 'Will you arrive tonight or—? Night bus.' She nodded at what else was said and she added, 'I love you too, Lou.' She put the phone down and raised her face with determination. I nodded. She said, 'Poor, poor old lady. She thought I was slutty for getting pregnant so soon and modelling, but if I'd bothered and went to Mass. Just once with her.'

'I understand,' I said.

We were in an embrace again, as if we'd been dancing together for hours – alone in the ballroom of a cruise ship over the Java Trench – and had just paused in a waltz. 'I'd better phone the house. And Rhys.'

324

'Yes,' I said, but neither of us moved.

'She chucked it in our faces – Rhys too – that she was leaving all her savings to Rhys, and I think she had quite a lot. Since she didn't trust Lou with cash – wisely, I must say. Always said she'd be leaving Rhys the savings and Lou the house.'

'Don't think about these things now.' I took the edge of my hand and pushed her golden fringe back off her forehead, over her crown, so it fell away to each side. But I was helplessly thinking about those things.

'Might as well face it.'

'Yes.'

At first she wouldn't. The gas of death had stilled her, but then she forgot it all in our arms and legs, whipping together and locking, turning the flannelette sheets into ropes around us. When it was still dark, before dawn, we both stripped those cotton sheets from the bed and put them in the washing machine. We remade the bed with fresh sheets and then Lily cried for an hour, whilst, naked as Adam and Eve, we passed the child back and forth between us.

At six thirty in the morning, the telephone rang.

'Cunningham. An abysmal hour.'

'Lou. It's terrible. I'm very sorry. Where are you?'

He lowered his voice. 'I need you to get the cot brought over.'

'Shit, are you here?'

Aoife stepped into the corridor and I saw her eyes go to the mortice to confirm it was locked.

'Yeah, over at poor Gran's. Got the night bus from Birmingham. One of the teachers drove me there last night, which was good of him. That bus was full of the most awful specimens. Things are going to be swirling round till the funeral. Best if me and Aoife and Lil are over here.'

'Yes. Of course.'

'Abby's hired a car and she's coming round later with Flo to get the cot and everything. You know, I was thinking. While we're at it, will you get Eeef to pile up as many of Abby's bloody clothes as you can and get them out of there at last in the car. And as well, send that bloody tortoise over here where there's a garden.'

25

The night before the funeral, Aoife and Lou suddenly turned up at Conrad Flats without Lily.

By that time I'd been alone for three days and I hadn't seen Lou since he'd returned to London. Aoife had taken herself out the equation, overtaken by her fears and her warped sense of duty. The loss of her was physical to me. Sometimes I gently punched the walls on either side as I walked up and down the corridor, grimacing at the slight pain, waiting for the golf clubs to begin knocking at my feet. And all that kept her from me was my own cowardice, which excused itself as the lie that I was really doing the correct thing by giving her up. Yet when I tried to imagine having Aoife in any context other than the current one, I frowned in the darkness, where I rarely bothered to switch on the lights any more. The wantonness and the love seemed uniquely cultivated by our absurd circumstances; remove them and it would crumble.

Lou was standing there in the doorway with light streaming in behind him, through the windy concrete lobby – he was thinner in the face and wearing a new, long overcoat, bottle green and very handsome. In each hand he held one of his silver hip flasks, both with the tops off. Somehow, in the coat, he suddenly reminded me of Toby Hanson.

'Silence, Exile and Cunningham.' He nodded as if remembering.

I knew he was seeing me anew, considering something sincerely with genuine puzzlement. 'But what are we going to dress you in tomorrow, boyo?' Then his mind quickly worked and he said, 'My old suit. What else? You'll be able to find it now Abby's got all her shit out. What you wore to that fashion bash of Abby's last winter. Remember? First time you saw Abby's tits and from what I hear from her, not the last.' He laughed and walked deeper in, through to the living room. Aoife shut the front door and followed us through.

He was dismissive of his surroundings – I could already feel Lou had passed beyond Conrad Flats and into another phase of his life. Already he was wandering through memories there. Surprisingly, he threw his arms around me and hugged. I heard the liquids gurgling vividly inside both open-topped hip flasks, somewhere at the middle of my shoulders. I put my arms more cautiously round his back and said, 'Jesus. How the fuck are you?'

He looked me in the face. 'I was in shock. Then the drink finally got through, thank God. Like my coat?' He thrust out one of the hip flasks – the old one – and I grabbed it and held it in my hand. I was trying not to turn and look at Aoife, behind us, though everything inside me made me want to do so.

'The coat's a beauty,' I quietly admitted.

'Isn't she just? Isn't she just a beaut? It was my father's. Gran had it hanging in the wardrobe, shrouded in brown paper and moth-balls. Never would let me near it.' He lowered his face to the lapel and took a sniff. 'Drenched it in Aoife's perfume.' He held out the sleeve and obliged me to inhale. Yes, it smelled like his wife's breasts and her neck. Lou flicked a smile and walked closer to the front-room windows.

Aoife was carrying a tartan-lined holdall – the type of baggage that could only emanate from the house of an old woman. I nodded to her and smiled, then she gave me a look and a gesture I have never forgotten. The head was turned slightly down to the left shoulder and she smiled, but she frowned simultaneously – utterly helpless. I reached out my hand extremely quickly and she shot her hand forward and squeezed my fingertips so hard they hurt, then suddenly she let go and our hands fell apart; we looked at each other and I turned away and heard a groan inside myself.

Lou was standing, surveying the great tumble of the city before him, as if checking it for small changes.

I came up to stand beside him and I tipped the hip flask back into my mouth like the old days. It tasted good. He had his face turned to me in satisfaction. 'That's better, eh? That fucking house. *Our* house, it now appears.' He turned round to include Aoife in this new property-owning class. 'It's full of mad Welsh relatives we've never heard of. Flo's even got them billeted in her house too. Can't wait till after tomorrow and it'll just be us. Eh, love?'

'Yes,' she answered.

He looked around the apartment as if he were considering taking these rooms on a rental basis. 'I should have sent some relatives over here to torture you. I would have, if there had been a single example of young female stock. Or even a more mature, well-preserved woman. But these Taffies are all bloody pensionable and without issue. I guess you have Abingdon on your case anyway. So we thought we'd escape over here chez Cunningham for the night. Got some goodies for you too.'

Aoife was offloading bottles of wine and cans of beer onto the dining table.

'I've got to sort out my clothes for tomorrow,' she declared.

'Okay, love.'

I listened as she moved silently away up the corridor and then through in the bedroom I heard coat hangers able to slide in the emptier wardrobes.

Lou nodded his head. 'Know what's going on over there?'

'Twickenham?'

'Nah. Gran's house.'

'No.'

'A vigil on the coffin.'

'You are joking?'

'Oh no. I can't face it. Sat up there, with the old lady and those ones. All old ex-miners. Great fellas, but not all night, inhaling their farts. They're chowing down the black pudding something awful.'

'A vigil. I never knew that went on still.'

He nodded. 'Ah. Twilight, arbiter 'twixt day and night, or whatever Milton farted out.'

Lou and I stood drinking, watching night come down over the city and the frantic spread of its lights. Every so often, one of us turned and walked to the table in the growing gloom to replenish a can of beer or swig from a bottle. Neither of us moved to switch on a light.

'I quit at the language school.'

'Did you?'

'Yes. Think I'll sign back on from Gran's house for a spell.' He crossed to the fitted shelves and lifted up the dusty binoculars on which only one lens functioned; we had sometimes used them for spotting the Heathrow-bound aeroplanes on clear days, reading the names of the airlines. He put the binocs to his face and scanned out over the night. 'I can't see it,' he announced in a general manner, using a hushed voice.

'What?'

He whispered, 'The glow. From the Lucozade advert' – as if it was a secret between us. He added. 'So you rolled Abby. She told Aoife. She likes you.'

'Aye.'

He turned and listened, we both heard a bump through in the bedroom. He put his lips to my ear and whispered, 'Abby is noisy.'

I smiled and nodded, 'Aye, she was,' then I looked back out the glass. A train sparked below – the light almost purple.

Aoife was coming along the corridor. 'What are you two up to in the pitch dark?' She clicked on the light. I didn't turn round. I kept looking, squinting straight ahead, watching them both in the dark reflection.

'Have you eaten, Douglas?'

'I'm not hungry. Thanks.' I turned and smiled.

She yawned. 'We're stuffed with endless Flo sandwiches.'

'Yeah. Let's turn in early tonight, Eeef.'

From the camp bed, hands resting on my chest – doubtless in exactly the same recline as Myrtle Smith in her coffin – I listened to Aoife and Lou having vigorous, undisguised sex. The pillow was not inserted behind the headboard.

In the morning they had a bath together.

I dressed in Lou's old suit. He wore the fish-scented suit from his wedding day. Aoife had on a black dress and a hat with a long black feather which went up straight. The dress was not especially long and her black heels were not short, and the black stockings were the hold-up type. I was sure of it because we took a cab to the church and I was on the fold-down seat in front of her. Lou and I were drinking from the hip flasks, holding on with our other arms as the cab swung corners. We'd been drinking steady all morning and when we got out of the cab at the church, I felt a surge in my bladder. Lou leaned down and reached in to pay the driver and the cab drove off.

'I really need to pee,' I said.

'Oh I do too, come to mention it. Look, there's Father Petrie, the scourge of Ampleforth.'

The priest, stooped, was striding up the side of the church beside a tall boundary wall, into the strongly contrasted shadows – it was a beautiful day.

'You go in, love, and see who's there.' Lou made off after the priest, up the side of the church building, lighting a cigarette as he strode. I took a step then I stopped, and turned back to Aoife.

She was standing very still in her dark dress and hat, looking at me. I said, 'I don't know what to do.' The moment I said it, I thought she was going to mistake my words for a question about how to make myself useful during the funeral.

She nodded gently. The expression on her face created by our indecision had suddenly found its ideal location at a funeral. 'It's going to be okay,' she suddenly told me, nodding like a convinced Christian.

I turned around and looked up the side of the church. 'You haven't told him, have you?'

'Of course not.'

'Then how will it be okay? What we did was not okay. And it was never okay. I want you, right now, but it's not okay.'

She looked left and right and she began crying, then continued to look at me. I said, 'You are very beautiful all in black. I just want you so much. I'm sorry, I really am bursting,' and I walked away from her.

I caught up with Lou at the back corner of the church. I was suddenly struck by how serene that old graveyard there is. The leaning, ancient limestone walls overhung with late-flowering magnolia trees and it was breezy with a coolness in the air – creamy petals fluttering steadily into the fringes of the graveyard and drifting all around.

'Father,' Lou called out.

The priest was just at the wooden door, which was studded with big nails. 'Llewellyn. Sad day.'

'Yes. Father, this is my friend Douglas Cunningham, who I've told you about.'

'How do you do. Sorry. Sad circumstances.'

'Yes.' I nodded. I wondered if he could detect a full-scale sinner like me.

Lou was standing still, smoking. He said, 'Father Petrie and I often have long talks.'

The priest nodded. 'We do we do, indeed we do. Books. I tend to have read the same ones again and again and Llewellyn many divergent ones. I understand books mean a great deal to both of you?'

I nodded seriously. 'They have probably ruined our lives with ideas,' I said. I was surprised myself to hear it come out.

'Well, lads. It depends what ideas they are and how you act upon them.'

Lou smiled and turned to me proudly. 'Cunningham. Father Petrie has read Sartre's fiction. In French. And *Adolphe*.'

I nodded, impressed but disappointed they hadn't affected the priest with any visible form of spiritual crisis.

Lou nodded. 'Father. A few glasses of wine, a few cans of communion beer were taken this morning.'

He chuckled. He had hairs growing out his nostrils.

'Could we quickly use the toilet?'

'Of course, of course. Well, actually the old sacristy toilet is broken, so you'd need to use mine, so that's up the first set of stairs then past the blue door then up again onto a next set of stairs then take a left and go down that corridor. Oh, lads. Lads. If you don't mind, just go against the wall over there. But between the graves. Between the graves if you please.'

As Father Petrie shouted these instructions, Lou and I walked ahead, out into the blossom fall.

'Yes, over there. Left a bit if you please. Not next to old Ben Barnham, died eighteen thirty-seven. He was a big temperance man, in the friendly unions I read.'

Lou and I stood side by side but with the distance of a grave and a gravestone lying between us, pissing down at the base of the wall, frothing magnolia blossom round and around in the accumulating puddles. Lou called out as we faced the stone. 'Douglas plays centre forward for Glasgow Rangers.'

'I do not, Father,' I called. 'When it comes to the Church, I'm strictly freelance. I'm up for sale to any club.'

Father Petrie chuckled behind us and called, 'Llewellyn and I are QPR bigots.'

I was impressed the way Lou had pissed while still smoking. He walked back towards the priest.

'Poor Myrtle.' Father Petrie nodded.

I noticed they'd both turned to look across at something. I pulled up my zipper and stepped gingerly over the graves towards them and I saw they were in fact staring at a freshly opened gap in the earth, its maw daintily fringed with glistening new green Astroturf.

I looked at Lou. 'Is your gran actually to be buried here as well? I thought it was just the service.'

'Oh yes,' said Lou seriously. 'She's coveted that grave since nineteen fifty-nine.'

The priest smiled. He and Lou seemed to share an overly relaxed relationship, I thought.

It was a very nice spot to be laid to rest in. Right up against the wall at the bottom of the churchyard, a steady curtain of white petals snowing upon it and into it. Father Petrie said, 'And blessed with the blossom today, Llewellyn. We all hope for such a peaceful spot ourselves.'

'That's true, Father.'

'What are you reading from today, Llewellyn?'

'Settled on a short William Morris poem. One of the most beautiful things in the language, Father.'

'A good man. A good man and there's Manley Hopkins himself, who would be my favourite. Of course. He spent some years in Glasgow now. Did he not?' The father turned to me sharply.

'He did.' I nodded obediently.

'Gran had a tiny little Everyman book of Morris poems that was in the house when I was young. Even before I could read I used to leaf through it, looking at the decoration. Looking at the shape of the poems. I caught her once, reading them. Glasses on. Lips moving to the words.'

'Very poignant, Lou. Very poignant. Well, lads.'

'Will you come up to the house afterwards, Father?'

'Of course, of course. Your lovely wife. Coping?'

'She's fine.'

I saw it then, that Father Petrie could have married them both in that beautiful church within a year; but how was I to know that medical science would be proved wrong, and I would soon return to this graveyard once again.

Flo was within the church, guarding Lily. Rhys was standing at the front with Aoife. He'd been crying. Lou walked straight up to his brother and they embraced. Abby walked out, genuflected, then came straight up the aisle to me, she linked arms and led me without any choice down to the front. I glanced over at Aoife.

When she had genuflected her way back in, Abby and I sat together, halfway along the pew, pointedly behind Aoife and Lou.

Lou read from the Bible very beautifully in his smoker's voice. The night before he'd joked with me that he was going to quote the two excerpts of the Bible which feature haemorrhoids: one in Romans and one somewhere else. But he did not. He read from Proverbs. Chapter 24.

I listened carefully to Father Petrie's words but Abby kept leaning in on my shoulder, confident and proprietorial. Yet when I put my hand on her thigh she lifted it off immediately.

Lou went up a second time, and read the Morris poem. The very beautiful one which begins: *Pray but one prayer for me, 'twixt thy closed lips.* It started to break me up – not on account of Myrtle Smith.

Come the Mass and people crowded to the front as if a rock star like Marko Morrell were there, happily giving out autographs. Flo and I were the only non-Catholics.

The closest members of the family – Rhys, Lou and Aoife – held back, and Abby presumptuously joined them. They all stood aside until the Welsh visitors had finished, then each of our group – except me – went up to take the holy sacrament. The four of them almost rushed to kneel before the father. I also realised, strangely, that I wanted to join them there. I too wanted my wild shot at salvation.

As usual I watched the dimensions of both Abby and Aoife's bodies through their dark dresses as they moved and it was hard in that place not to feel self-satisfied that I had explored those potentialities so fully. The church makes you meditative but I was drunk and couldn't help a bad thought. When I saw the back of Aoife's erect neck, I thought she was like all the used-up perfume, risen in the air and now gone for ever.

Abby genuflected her way back to my side and placed her head on my shoulder again, as if we'd been married for years.

The blossom still drifted in the breeze, coming in as shoals which billowed when Myrtle in her coffin was carried by the pall-bearers that short distance out of the church. I saw white petals rested in Aoife and Abby's hair. Lily started crying, of course, but Aoife lifted her from the buggy and it was the blossom falling around the child's head which stopped her cries and caught her attention as the fingers grasped out curiously at the petalled air and the swarms of little multiple shadows which it surely cast.

One of the men sang solo in Welsh, deep, damaged-sounding and noble; then we were all leaving the graveside, heading back to Lou and Aoife's inherited house.

I could see Aoife ahead of me, surrounded by mourners and with Lily hitched in her arms. In an eerie echo of the wedding day when she had picked confetti, Abby now walked behind Aoife and picked blossom petals from Aoife's clothes and hat. The sun made the black feather on the hat glow along its edges. We retraced that path beside the church and people began to walk on along the road towards Myrtle Smith's house, following Flo, who was shouting and gesticulating to the Welshmen in their dark baggy suits and hats. Suddenly Lou seized my arm. 'Christ sake. Bells,' and he guided me in another direction.

Too fast I said, 'But shouldn't we tell Aoife?'

'Then Abby will be on your case. Just a quick pint.'

Lou and I were stepping it the other way, looking backwards guiltily then dashing round the corner where The Bells was up ahead.

I said, 'You read beautifully.'

He only nodded.

The pub was almost empty and our seat under the window was free. As we sat with our pints of Guinness, Lou nodded, then he turned directly to me. 'Yeah. Abby's all over you, squire.' He chuckled. 'Love's tear, let it not dry.' He spoke in a voice like a quote: '"Cunningham retained, until his demise, a pure Pre-Raphaelite taste for dark bags beneath the eyes of pale and slender women." We would make two crazy couples, no?'

I smiled.

Lou chuckled. 'We won't tell Abby you're living at the new place. We'll tell her you're still over at Conrad Flats, so you might get a few days' respite till she kicks the door in.'

'What?'

'When you move over to Gran's house with us. We won't tell Abby.'

I looked at him. 'You want me to? Move over.'

'Of course. Where else are you going to go, boyo? Need to clear out the back room for you cause it's full of bloody junk. Aoife said she'd do it tomorrow, when I'm at the lawyers'.'

Then I said, 'That Morris poem was— The way you read it. Beautiful.' I turned and looked him in the face. 'It nearly broke my heart.'

He smiled. 'Better get back, see if there's any booze left; peel those Welshies off the wall and try to herd them to a bloody Cardiff train. Father Petrie's good fun when he has a drink.'

'You go on ahead. I'll have another.'

'You lucky devil.'

As he made for the door I said after him, 'Lou? Thanks.'

He lit another cigarette and he turned towards me and gave me a silent military salute, straightening and stiffening his whole body to do so. Just as well the old boys were not in or some would have struggled to their feet to return the gesture.

I walked back to Conrad Flats, hung up his suit and changed into my jeans, lumberjack shirt and the antelope-skin jacket, which was my father's.

I left Lou's old hip flask on the dining table. I didn't take a single book. I posted my set of house keys through the letter box.

I walked all the way down through Shepherd's Bush as Lou and I once had to the Fulham Road. At Victoria coach station it was so warm I felt poached. On the paved colonnade I heard

339

the rifle-bolt snaps of young skateboarders practising their artful techniques.

Just down and across the road was the Victoria Station Hotel, where Lou and Aoife had spent their wedding night. I now was certain Abby and Lou had been up to no good that night, before Aoife and I had arrived. Confused and grasped embraces in the wedding chamber between the bridesmaid and the groom as the deluded bride arrived. A groom who himself would soon be deluded. For God Almighty's sake.

The cheapest bus from London to Glasgow was the overnight. I sat down on a seat with people ranged around me. The odd Euro backpacker, a lost-looking Indian gentleman with a leather suitcase tied with string, a circling alcoholic counting change in his palm. The ranked seats resembled those of the Accident and Emergency waiting rooms. People with suitcases moved through the transitory space. If I bought a ticket, this huge city would thin out peacefully at its boundaries in the dark. Around me, I would see few glimpses of old England as I headed back to my encoldened north. I would sense more than see the hedgerows and the sunken lanes lashed with briars, or some ancient tree in the corner of a meadow. I thought of those weeks Aoife and I had in the curtained bedroom – more like a laboratory – where I had seen her hand clench and re-clench in the gloom as we both reached for some other world.

I tapped my shoe and looked at it. I was going to go over to the ticket booth, which resembled the booth at the hospital that night, or I was going to take a bus back up to Acton and claim I had needed some time alone. They would all be in poor Myrtle's house at that moment, Lou drinking, Abby asking where I was, Aoife sometimes smiling but not too much, nodding politely to relatives and holding Lily up so they could pet her. Aoife would be surprised to see me changed out of the suit. I would tell her, oh, accidentally pulled the Yale behind me, could I borrow her keys? Yes, of course. Aoife smiling, the mole just there, maybe I would reach for her arm in that black death dress – Eeef, Eeef; Douglas, Douglas – desperate touches of fingertips outside the bathroom, relatives awkwardly interrupting; Abby snooping.

Under a new roof, it would be Lou who would strip Aoife from her mourning gown that night. Perhaps a single petal of blossom from the graveside had been carried all day, somewhere within the dress, and Lou's fingers would release it? The bus – or them, and thence destruction? From where I sat, I could still hear the hard cracks of the skateboards. I had to make my choice and my right hand trembled. My lips moved silently with the answer.

Acknowledgements

Almost all the locations and of course all the characters in *Their Lips Talk of Mischief* are completely fictional.

The circumstance of a man alarming an entire hospital waiting room with his badly torn but painless sutures is a biographical detail related to me by Robin Robertson many years ago. Robin has used this experience in several of his own exquisite poems.

The image of the Luftwaffe crewmember stuck in the escape hatch of his doomed aircraft is related by Crelin Bodie in *Ten Fighter Boys* (Collins, 1942), edited by A. Forbes and H. Allen.